# KILL SHOT

THE BULARI SAGA

## JESSIE KWAK

First edition September 2020

*Book cover by Robert Kittilson*

*Edited by Kyra Freestar*

*Map by Jessie Kwak*

www.jessiekwak.com

*For everyone who rooted me through to the end.*

N
W E
S
To the Maraka Valley
Geordi Jimenez
Space Terminal
Jet Park
Casinos
Downtown
To Julieta Yang's

BULARI
Dry Creek
Altamira
(Blackheart territory)
Tamarind District
University of Bulari
Carama Town

1

———————

## JAANTZEN

Death has already paid Willem Jaantzen a visit tonight, and she seems content to linger. He can feel her close, fingernails at the nape of his neck: *Julieta's mine now. Who else should come home with me tonight?*

And he's trapped, powerless to do a damned thing even as his spinner races across Bulari.

SECURITY BREACH AT THE TABLE. DO NOT APPROACH UNTIL ADVISED.

Jaantzen refreshes his screen, willing it to say something else, but the message remains stubbornly unchanged. In the nearly ten minutes since Oriol Sina sent those words, Jaantzen's spent every second reining in increasingly darker fears about what's happening outside his control. A police raid. A bomb. An all-out assault on the building.

His closest allies — his *only* allies — are gathered at the Devil's Table tonight. Whatever this security breach is, it means they're all in danger.

Phaera is in danger.

And with each passing moment, it becomes clear this is not simply a security drill.

Manu Juric can't pace while sitting inside the Dulciana JX; his lieutenant's hands are braced on the spinner's controls, fingers drumming a frenetic beat, a furious gleam in his eyes. In the back, Calanthe Yang is silent and still, leaning back against the seat with one hand cradling her belly. She shouldn't be here at all; she should be at her mother's deathbed, mourning with the rest of her family. And she would be, if this meeting wasn't the only way to stop Chief Justice Geum-ja Leone from burning them all to the ground.

The glaring neon wash over his constantly refreshing comm screen tells Jaantzen they've made it to the Casino District. Manu glides the spinner to a halt at the south end of the drag; kilometers away at the north end is the Devil's Table, which Jaantzen can barely make out from here.

Its dark, blocky shape is bathed in a blood-red glow from the enormous twin torches framing its entrance, but there's no smoke. No flashing police lights. No sirens. He knows it's merely optics, but the building now looks like a trap, one he set himself for all his closest allies. For Phaera.

Manu flinches as Jaantzen's comm chimes with an update from Oriol.

"She's safe, they're securing the building," Jaantzen says aloud. "Oriol says stand by."

She's safe — but she hadn't been until now, or Oriol would have reassured him before. Death scrapes a nail along Jaantzen's jaw. He represses a shudder.

If Leone caused Phaera to suffer a single scratch, the woman will die in agony. Jaantzen will see to it himself.

"What the fuck is happening," says Manu. No one answers.

A moment later, another chime.

"All clear. Go to the service entrance," Jaantzen tells Manu, who's jammed the spinner into gear even before Jaantzen finishes speaking. Oriol's written *NOT VALET* in all caps. Oriol and the Table's security team must have found a problem at the valet stand. Meant to kill him? Other guests? He'll worry about that once he finds out if Phaera is all right.

Oriol greets them at the service entrance, opening Jaantzen's door with one hand, wicked-looking pistol in the other.

"Phaera?"

"Inside," Oriol says; it's both an answer and an order. He's scanning, weapon readied, covering Jaantzen and Calanthe across the narrow space from the Dulciana's door to the Devil's Table's service entrance. He's dressed in the usual military black he wears when working — when working for *him*, Jaantzen corrects himself. When Oriol's working for Phaera he wears a nice suit. The man's as lethal either way.

And he was supposed to keep Phaera safe.

The door shuts behind them and Jaantzen grabs Oriol by the collar. Shoves him against the wall, pinning him there with his forearm. "What. Happened."

Oriol's body is loose, relaxed; his expression is not. "I fucked up, sir," he says simply. "Tierren slipped our perimeter and got Phaera alone on the roof. Hiro spotted her. We acted as fast as we could."

"Tierren?"

"Dead."

"And why was she alone?"

"I don't know." There's real pain in Oriol's golden eyes. If Jaantzen threw a punch, Oriol would take it. And maybe if they were younger — maybe if Jaantzen couldn't see Manu in the corner of his eye — this would have come to blows.

Jaantzen lets go. Steps back, adjusting his cuffs and his temper — it's keeping him from Phaera. Oriol straightens against the wall, holsters the pistol that's still in his hand.

"What was wrong with the valet entrance?" Calanthe's voice cuts through the tension. Jaantzen nearly forgot she was here.

The service entrance opens into a storage area, crates of canned goods and bulk sauces, a bank of walk-in coolers. The casino hall, kitchen, and offices are all on the floor above them. Calanthe is sitting on a beer keg, eyes red-rimmed and grief-stricken despite the fresh coat of mascara. From her mother's deathbed to whatever new hell this is.

"The valet was booby-trapped," says Oriol. "Set after everyone else had arrived."

"To kill me," Jaantzen says.

"Or to catch the rest on their way out."

Oriol jerks his chin at them to follow him. From the angle of his shoulders he's no more relaxed now than when they were out in the open. Manu has naturally matched Oriol's vigilance, bringing up the rear. Oriol's checking doorways as they pass, talking at the same time. "Phaera's people are taking care of it now. I think Tierren was working alone, but we can't be certain. She messed with the security feeds."

"And Phaera?"

"In her office now. She's safe." Oriol stops at the foot

of the stairs and gives Jaantzen a searching look. "She asked me to take you directly to the meeting room with the others."

She doesn't want to see him? "Why."

A muscle jumps in Oriol's jaw. "You should know she's in bad shape. In other circumstances I would have taken her to the hospital. She's tough, but you need to give her the space to not fall apart until she's ready."

Jaantzen goes still.

"What do you mean, bad shape?" Manu asks.

"Nothing she can't recover from." Oriol's tone is calm, but fury and self-recrimination are warring on his face. "Doctor's on the way."

Jaantzen wants to push his way past and find her, see for himself what Oriol's not telling him. But he forces himself to follow Oriol, to go slowly up the stairs for Calanthe. Forces himself to respect Phaera's wishes.

He's been inside the Devil's Table only once before, when he and Phaera were beginning their short slide from business associates to lovers. He'd come in part to help her upgrade the Table's security, in part to learn whether or not she'd ordered a hit on Starla. It seems like ages ago he could have suspected her of that.

Tonight the gaming floor is empty, though a few table lamps and chandeliers are lit to create a pleasant lounge ambiance. The felt-topped tables and rich burgundy rugs drink in the light; the polished wood bar at the far end of the floor is dark, the rows of liquor bottles glittering like broken teeth.

One of the meeting rooms at the far end of the floor is flanked by guards. The voices inside are hushed by velvet curtains.

"Copy that," Oriol says to someone in his ear, then

turns to Jaantzen. "The valet bomb is dismantled. Security systems are all back online."

And Victoria Tierren is dead — and depending on how this meeting goes, Leone will soon be, too.

Jaantzen glances across the room to the set of curtains he knows leads to Phaera's office. He forces himself to turn back to the meeting room. Pushes aside the curtain to usher Calanthe in, Manu slipping in after him.

It's a gorgeous private dining room, put together with the same care Phaera takes with everything else in her life. Impeccably. Surrounded by warm red velvet and lit by a pair of antique onyx-and-brass chandeliers, the stately sideboard and twelve-person dining table are real wood. Matching mirrors keep the intimate room from feeling too cramped.

Everyone's here.

Teo Lordeur and Mizal Seti are leaning close to talk, the aging banker in rumpled gray conspiring with the young gentech baron in a dapper sunshine-yellow suit. The casino crowd have congregated together, Wiljo Cavenaugh chatting cordially with the Demosga siblings. And two men Jaantzen hasn't met are sitting together near the far end of the table, both ill at ease in their suits. The lanky one must be Dal Jaxon, the head of the cab drivers union. The stocky older man is Aden Damyati, Thala Coeur's lieutenant.

The room falls silent when he enters.

"Phaera will be joining us in a few minutes," he says. "Thank you all for coming."

"What's going on, Jaantzen," Aiax Demosga asks loudly.

"The security team assures me everything is under control," he says. This room will empty in seconds if he says Leone sent her assassin to plant bombs. "I'll let Phaera explain when she gets here."

Calanthe collapses in a chair beside Teo's wheelchair; when he leans in to ask her something, she shakes her head, lips pressed tight. Mizal pours her a water. Jaantzen wonders how quickly word has traveled. Do they know yet about Julieta Yang's death? That's for Calanthe to share when she's ready. Jaantzen makes quick handshakes around the room, keeping things brief with those he knows and introducing himself formally to Cavenaugh, Jaxon, and Damyati.

Jaantzen will never trust Thala Coeur; he'd sooner rely on the whims of a sandstorm. But she has a long history of choosing reasonable lieutenants who *can* be dealt with, as though she knows her weakness and relies on them to compensate for her capriciousness. Jaantzen had been able to work with Coeur's old lieutenant, Naali Hinoja. From all reports, Aden Damyati is as steady.

"I appreciate you coming," Jaantzen says.

Damyati nods grimly. "We have a common enemy," he says. "We'd also like to share a mutual respect."

"Understood," Jaantzen says.

"Is Fay all right?" asks Dal Jaxon in a low voice. "Because if anybody laid a finger on her . . ."

"Thank you," Jaantzen says. And straightens, because he can hear footsteps in the empty casino beyond the velvet curtain, women's heels and voices.

Phaera's voice.

He excuses himself calmly, but his heartbeat is pounding in his ears when he pushes through the curtains.

Phaera is crossing the casino floor, Vanessa Dosantos

at her side, and when she sees him she freezes, her shoulders stiff, her determined mask cracking.

He's made a mistake. "Give her the space not to fall apart until she's ready," Oriol had told him, but Jaantzen can't force himself back inside that room now. Even in the moody light of the casino floor he can see the pain creasing her brow, the bruise on her cheek, the bandages on her right hand.

Before he can decide, she holds out her unbandaged hand to him, palm up — it's a request, and he crosses to her and takes it, studying her face.

She's wearing the same outfit she'd had on the night she met him at the Jungle, the night they first discussed how to take down Leone. Flattering white trousers and a sapphire silk blouse, tonight under a dove-gray jacket. Black heels, her gold cuff, and a black and white floral scarf that doesn't go. Her eyes are bloodshot, a bandaged cut on her temple is almost hidden by her magenta hair.

"Phaera," he starts, but she shakes her head fiercely.

"Don't." Her voice is badly hoarse, and his gaze drops to the scarf. She reaches her good hand to cup his cheek and bring his attention back to her face, tracing icy fingertips down his jaw. "I'm all right."

She's clearly not, but insisting otherwise would be a disservice, and he's already let fear push him past the one boundary she'd set for him tonight. He lets it go. When he leans in, her chin lifts, so he brushes a kiss over her lips. She tastes like smoke, he breathes in her perfume, spiked with dried sweat and fear. She's almost smiling as he steps back. And he is going to burn the world down until everyone who conspired to hurt her is dead.

Beside Phaera, Vanessa Dosantos's expression says she's thinking the same thing and she's not yet sure whether Jaantzen belongs in the path of her rage. He inclines his head to her. He can respect that.

Phaera takes his arm when he offers it and he leads her through the curtain, studying every single person as they see Phaera's bruised face and bandaged hand, searching for signs of betrayal. He knows Manu is doing the same from his seat in the corner.

Dal Jaxon looks like he's about to murder someone; Wiljo Cavenaugh's not far behind. The others are shocked; Aden Damyati and Calanthe Yang are the only ones who don't seem stunned by Phaera's appearance. Calanthe knew already. Damyati's surely seen worse — probably done worse himself — and must have guessed between the lines at what had happened while they all sat waiting. Strangely, the one thing Jaantzen's certain of tonight is that Damyati's boss, Coeur, didn't have anything to do with the attack on Phaera.

Aiax Demosga shatters the silence. "What the fuck happened? Phaera, are you all right?"

"I'm fine," she says; the rasping of her voice says otherwise. "Shall we?"

Jaantzen pulls out the chair at the head of the table for her. Her lips part in surprise, but she accepts, and whether it's pain or practice, her movements are deliberately slow. Regal.

Jaantzen takes a seat at her left hand, and Phaera D raises her chin like a queen.

"Thank you all for coming," she says.

2

___________

## PHAERA

"Thank you all for coming."

Here's a silver lining of being strangled nearly to death, Phaera thinks. She'd been afraid her voice would betray how nervous she is, but now no one can tell. She's got the hoarse, ragged tones of a lounge singer who's been smoking for the last eight decades. And another silver lining? This meeting — the moment she's been terrified of all week — feels like a walk in the park compared to surviving Tierren. All she has to do is keep herself together for another hour.

By the expressions on everyone's faces, Vanessa's makeup magic didn't hide much of the trauma she went through not even an hour ago. Jaantzen's initial horror was bad enough, and he hasn't seen the half of it.

Best to address that elephant in the room right away.

"Some of you know Leone has been working with a mercenary for the last week or so. Earlier this week, the woman poisoned my mother and sent her to the hospital. She attacked one of Jaantzen's people, and she kidnapped a couple of little girls to intimidate their parents, who were witnesses in a murder investigation." And she broke into Phaera's apartment and tried to rattle her with threatening messages all week. Which barely seems worth mentioning now.

Phaera takes a deep breath, willing herself not to start coughing. "Tonight she tried to kill me." She lets the surprised murmur die down; she can't make herself be heard over even the quietest background noise. "It was meant to be a message to you all. Walk out now, and there's still a chance to stay on Leone's good side. Any takers? I'm sure the offer's still good."

She waits, heart beating in her throat, the band of fire around her neck blazing with every pulse. No one moves.

"No one? Then allow me to make introductions." She turns to her right. The fierce expression on Cavy's face nearly breaks her. "Wiljo Cavenaugh, co-owner of the Aterciopelado, and a mentor of mine." She tries to give him a smile, fails. Moves on. "Teo Lordeur, who's probably loaned most of you money." Laughter around the room; everyone knows Teo. "Calanthe Yang, lawyer, daughter of Julieta Yang. Callie, I'm so sorry."

Oh, gods, she's going to lose it at the raw grief on Calanthe's face. She looks away — Damyati was next and she's not ready for that, plus, she can't keep Calanthe in her view. She clears her throat and turns to her left.

"You all know Willem Jaantzen, of course," she says, hurrying on without letting herself meet the simmering anger in his gaze. "Mizal Seti, who's investing heavily in the Jet Park neighborhood with his gentech businesses. Aiax and Lhasa Demosga. They own an impressive agricultural corporation, as well as a few small up-and-coming casinos in orbit." Prickly Lhasa's mouth sours, but her barrel-chested brother laughs loudly at the joke; the

Demosgas' three orbital casinos draw more traffic than all the businesses in Bulari's Casino District combined. Phaera gives him a grateful smile.

"You may not all know Dal Jaxon," she says. "He's been head of the cab drivers union for more than a decade, and he's been an invaluable friend and ally. He has connections all over this city, high and low." Jaxon inclines his head to her, and she's seen that expression on his face more than once over the years: *Point me in the right direction, Fay, and I'll beat them to a bloody pulp.*

And now everyone's looking at Damyati. Phaera takes a deep breath.

"Finally, we have Aden Damyati. He represents Thala Coeur."

Shocked murmurs around the room; apparently Dal Jaxon was the only one besides herself and Jaantzen who knew the quiet older man was Blackheart's lieutenant.

"Absolutely not," Mizal says, getting to his feet. He turns to Jaantzen with a glare. "I thought I made it clear I wasn't working with her."

"You did, Mizal," Phaera says before Jaantzen can answer. "But things have changed."

She tugs the scarf from around her neck and the room falls silent, but for a vicious curse from Calanthe. Phaera keeps her gaze locked on Mizal, who's staring at her neck in horror. She knows what he sees: the raw rope burn, the bloody scratches left by her own fingernails, the vicious, swollen bruising — still spreading. She can feel Jaantzen's fury radiating like flame beside her.

"Leone wanted you to know she could strangle me to death in my own building," she says calmly to Mizal. "While you all sat downstairs, oblivious. If you're comfortable accepting that price for her patronage, feel free to walk out this door."

Mizal slowly sits back down.

Jaantzen's fingers brush her thigh, she squeezes them and lets go, then wraps the scarf back around her neck. She still can't bear to look at him, so she makes the mistake of turning to her right. Cavy's jaw is set in cold rage; she tears her gaze away, searching for a face that isn't going to crack her composure. Of all the people at the table, Aden Damyati's the only one not watching her like she's a broken doll in need of repairs or vengeance. His faint smile, his encouraging nod: *You're doing fine.*

"Does anyone else have a problem working with Coeur?" Phaera asks, and sits back against her chair, grateful to be yielding the floor. Sometime while she was talking, Vanessa had brought her a cup of tea. She takes a sip. Blood orange, mint, honey soothe her raw throat.

She's shocked Mizal, but he's not conceding. He holds out a hand to Cavy. "You have to agree with me, Cavenaugh. Working with Coeur is dangerous, and delegitimizing."

Cavy leans forward, hands folded over his lips, thinking. Light sparks in the gemstones on every knuckle; the tips of his gray braids brush the table. "I don't know her personally," he says finally. "But I voted for her as mayor. She spoke to business owners in the Fingers. And she made an actual difference before she got sidetracked." He looks at Damyati. "I'm willing to believe people can learn from their mistakes."

"She has." Damyati turns to Mizal. "She sent me with an apology to you, Seti. She wants to find a way to move forward."

Mizal ignores him. "Lhasa," he says with frustration.

Lhasa Demosga holds up her hands. "The Demosgas have never quarreled with Blackheart."

Mizal glares at Jaantzen, but he doesn't bother asking. Jaantzen's choice is clear. "Teo. She's fucking bad for business."

"I agree." But Teo's drumming his fingers on the table, obviously annoyed with this digression. "Tara and I have never lent her money, and we won't start now. She's too unstable. But if she wants to sink her teeth into Leone, she's welcome to."

Mizal's jaw tightens. "Calanthe. I know your mother and Coeur maintained a working relationship, but — "

"My mother is dead," Calanthe says sharply.

The room goes silent once more. Calanthe looks like she's trying to speak but can't. The grief in her eyes could burn a hole through the table.

"This evening," Jaantzen says, and the room's attention shifts to him; it's the first time he's spoken since they came in. "The great Julieta Yang is gone. Leone had her arrested earlier this week, in retaliation for supporting me, and Julieta contracted pneumonia during her night in jail."

Mizal looks stunned. "She and Leone were always so close," he says finally.

"Coeur is a monster," Calanthe says. "But don't fucking tell me Leone is the lesser of two evils when I just came from my mother's deathbed."

Murmurs of assent fill the room. Mizal sinks back into his chair with a resigned sigh.

"Then we're agreed," Phaera says. She turns to Jaantzen. "Go ahead."

She cups her good hand around the tea in front of her, savoring its warmth. She's still so cold, but the painkillers

Oriol gave her are finally starting to take the edge off the ache in her hand, her head, her neck. When Cavy catches her eye to silently ask if she's all right, she nods, then tries not to make eye contact with anyone else. She can't deal with that question over and over.

"Tomorrow morning, two things are going to happen," Jaantzen is saying. "First, Calanthe's office will file an amnesty plea for an Alliance agent who wishes to testify about how she provoked Levi Acheta to attack Cobalt Tower and her role in the murder of several of my employees. She will also testify to being the one who killed Acheta."

Others around the table glance at Aden Damyati, he nods solemnly in confirmation.

"That could put a wrench in the trade agreement talks," says Aiax dubiously. "But it won't be enough."

"Second — and more pertinent to your interests, Aiax — a story will be published with evidence the Alliance has been negotiating with New Sarjun in bad faith. They've been secretly terraforming the deserts around Redrock Prison, and we believe part of the reason is so they can undercut the New Sarjunian agricultural market once they negotiate lower tariffs."

Aiax Demosga laughs. "Terraforming the desert, Willem? Sounds like we need to have a talk."

Jaantzen inclines his head. "I have plenty to discuss with you and Lhasa. But this isn't just about the agriculture industry. One way the Alliance has been keeping this under wraps is by paying New Sarjunian officials to give higher sentences to our citizens who are convicted of petty crimes. Those prisoners are then sent to Redrock, where there is no official trail they've arrived."

"Those bastards," says Jaxon from the far end of the

table. Around the table, other people seem various degrees of confused. "Using our people's labor to make New Sarjun even more reliant on the Alliance for food."

"Chief Justice Geum-ja Leone is one of the officials who has been paid off as part of this scheme," says Jaantzen. "She's also received kickbacks from Alliance corporations in other sectors — not just agriculture — to help get the trade agreement passed."

"You need evidence," says Lhasa. "Rumors won't carry weight for long."

"We've seen the operation firsthand," Jaantzen says, and even Lhasa looks impressed. "Believe me, we're not dealing in rumors."

Phaera checks the time. Jaantzen's goddaughter and the rest of his team were supposed to be returning home tonight, which must be a weight off his shoulders. Both because they'll be home safe from their raid on the Alliance's secret facility, and because the evidence they're bringing with them will finally help them pin these crimes on Leone.

"Nicely done, my boy." Teo Lordeur's grinning.

"Calanthe has been working with me on the Alliance agent," Jaantzen says. "And Coeur has been an invaluable help in tying Leone to the prison labor scandal."

Mizal shifts in his chair but doesn't comment.

"But we all know how easily Leone can sweep this under the rug. The Alliance agent only attacked me, and my name's not worth much since Leone got hold of it. And the terraforming? The program selling New Sarjunian prisoners to the Alliance? The kickbacks from Alliance companies in exchange for getting the trade agreement passed? Leone can spin it all. Unless people with more reputation than I have are outraged."

Lhasa clears her throat. "The Demosga Corporation will certainly have something to say about the Alliance undercutting New Sarjunian food production. As will others in our industry. I can start reaching out as soon as the story drops," she says. "I'll have you a statement with fifty industry signatures by sundown."

"Thank you."

"What other kinds of companies have been giving Leone kickbacks?" asks Mizal.

Jaantzen glances at Manu, and comms chime around the room. "We're sending you a list."

There's a rustle of fabric as those around the table pull out comms or peruse the list on cuffs and lenses. In the conversational lull, Jaantzen lays his hand on Phaera's thigh. She braces herself for another round of *I'm fucking fine*, but for once it's not concern on his face. "Thank you," he murmurs, the faintest smile tugging at the corner of his mouth. She squeezes his fingers and returns the smile. Soon. Very soon all these people will be gone and she will get this man all to herself.

Around them, quiet reading time is punctuated by exclamations and curses. "Have you seen this list?" Cavy says to her, and Phaera shakes her head. He points out a name: Silver Dice Limited. The Arquellian casino corporation who'd tried to edge in on the drag last year.

"Fuck them," Phaera says. "I ran them out of here once before and I'll do it again."

Cavy laughs and shakes his head. "I know it," he says. "And you won't be alone."

"Indiran gentech companies," says Teo to Mizal. "Gaming, agriculture. One of the first things Geum-ja told me when she asked me to start attending her dinner parties was that she was committed to helping the people in her circle grow their businesses. Who wants to bet she's taken everything she learned from us about doing business in Bulari to help her Indiran friends get a foothold in our market?"

"She's been doing it from the beginning," Aden Damyati says, a touch of exasperation in his voice. "Coeur could've told you that if you'd listened back then instead of running her out of town."

Tension squeezes the breath out of the room.

"I might've listened if she hadn't murdered my wife and children," Jaantzen says coldly. Damyati sobers. "I appreciate that she's trying, and I welcome her help now. But my only regret about 'back then' is not putting a bullet in Thala's skull when I had the chance."

Jaantzen glances around the table. "Believe me, she knows. And if I didn't think we could trust her, she'd be dead already."

Dal Jaxon clears his throat in the prickly silence. "That trade agreement has some pretty nasty anti-union concessions," he says. Phaera shoots him a grateful smile for the change of subject. He taps a finger on the list on his comm. "Spearheaded by Blacklode and Hypatia, among others. We bitched about it at the beginning, but their lawyers make more than ours." He scratches the back of his neck. "Course, that was before we knew our own politicians were in on the scheme. You need visibility, I'll get signage on every union cab in the city. And once the other unions find out? Let me know if you need the space terminal shut down. Restaurants closed. We can get this city on its knees if you want."

"You can shut down the space terminal?" Aiax Demosga looks alarmed; he spends most of his time in his orbital casinos, coming planetside for meetings.

Jaxon raises his hands modestly. "Not me. But the good folks over at the space terminal workers' union are very well organized."

"Thank you, Jaxon," Phaera says.

He gives her a tight smile.

"I think the Casino District Business Association will have something to say about Silver Dice," says Cavy, folding gnarled brown hands in front of him. "Keeping them off our drag is probably the one thing we've ever all agreed on. Will this list be made public?"

"It will."

"Then I'll call a meeting once the news hits."

Beside him, Teo Lordeur laughs. "And I'll call in our debts on Leone. Tara and I have been looking for an excuse to do that for a while. Seems like as good a time as any, since she's apparently flush with cash."

"This is a good first step," says Jaantzen. "But she'll fight back hard. Hopefully I'll maintain the brunt of her anger." Phaera had almost forgotten his hand on her thigh until he squeezes so hard it's almost painful. "But the rest of you should take precautions. Make sure your people are safe. Mitigate whatever leverage she has on you — we can all share resources, so don't hesitate to reach out if you think someone else here can help."

"And give you all our dirt, Jaantzen?" Mizal asks.

"That's not what I said. I said look around. If you need help and don't trust me, maybe you trust Calanthe. Maybe you trust Teo. Maybe you have your own lawyers you feel comfortable turning to." Jaantzen pauses, no one challenges him. "I want freedom. I want to know the people I care for are safe. And I want to trust the people I'm doing business with. Trust doesn't come from manipulating you or holding your secrets." When no one speaks, he looks to Phaera. "Did we cover everything?"

"I think we're good," Phaera says. "Thank you all for coming."

Phaera stands, offering others her good left hand, ignoring the glances at her bandaged right. On another night there might have been more lingering goodbyes, but other than a few conversations on the side, a round of condolences for Calanthe, the room clears quickly. Yet it's not a speed born out of fear — people seem focused, determined. Ready to fight. Phaera's taking it as a good sign.

Finally, only Jaantzen and Cavy remain.

As soon as the velvet curtains fall still, Phaera sinks back into her seat and rests her forehead on her good hand, her hair shrouding her face. She still can't allow herself to break down, but at least she doesn't have to pretend she's all right anymore. Not in front of these two.

Cavy's chair creaks as he sits back beside her. He squeezes her shoulder.

"When Vanessa told me what happened, I called a doctor I trust," he says. "She's downstairs. Should I have her come up?"

"Thank you," Phaera murmurs.

Movement beside her, and Jaantzen sits as well. Phaera forces herself back in her chair, not bothering to hide how much pain she's in. The adrenaline that's kept her going through the last hour is wearing off, along with the painkillers. She's freezing; a sudden shiver racks her body.

She catches the look Cavy shares with Jaantzen. "I'll go get her," Cavy says.

And she and Jaantzen are finally alone. Phaera lets her head rest back against the chair, reaches for his hand

and pulls it onto her thigh; it's a comforting pressure, warmth. "Hey," she says.

"Tell me what happened."

She can't tell him what *happened*, she hasn't had time to process it herself yet. But she can recite facts without losing it. "I went up on the roof for some fresh air. Tierren was waiting for me. She sealed the door and hacked the comms. It took Hiro and Oriol a few minutes to get to me. By then she'd — " Phaera swallows; fire burns down her throat. "I fought back, but she . . . I mean, I'm not . . ."

"It's all right."

She watches Jaantzen's face this time as he pulls the scarf from around her neck, brushes back her hair, fingers feathering across her jaw, the back of her neck. She pulls him closer, and finally his expression softens, his touch becomes less tentative. His lips meet hers.

Welcome heat radiates through her, chasing away the icy chill of shock.

"You are incredible," he says when he finally breaks the kiss. "And I am humbled by you."

She frowns; it's not what she was expecting. "I don't feel very incredible at the moment."

"I'm serious, Phaera. You brought together some of the most powerful people in the city and you dazzled them. If anyone had doubts before tonight, they're gone."

"They came here for you." Before Jaantzen can answer, there's Cavy's voice outside the curtain, and a rustle of fabric. Cavy ushers the doctor in; she does a double take at Jaantzen, then settles in Cavy's abandoned chair, her expression grim.

"I hope you're filing for assault charges against the bastard," the doctor says.

Phaera wonders if that pointed tone was meant to be

a barb at Jaantzen, but she's too tired to be angry if it is. And she can't imagine how many defensive wounds the doctor has patched up while everyone in the room pretended the injuries weren't caused by the man sitting next to the victim.

"It was an attempted assassination," Phaera says. "And she got what she deserved."

The doctor doesn't answer, but her movements do become easier.

"Walk me through what happened."

She gives the doctor the short version, aiming for detached, and doesn't realize exactly when her good hand finds Jaantzen's, only that she's gripping it far too tightly as the doctor scans her throat, makes a satisfied sound, then slathers it in salve and bandages.

The doctor turns her scan to Phaera's injured hand. "Nothing's broken, but you're going to have a lot of tissue damage around the dislocated joint. Especially since it was reset in the field. Hold your hand straight?" She leaves the tape Oriol used to immobilize Phaera's finger and covers it with a splint. It warms, then cools as it molds into place around her hand. "I'm setting up automatic icing cycles," the doctor says. "Temperature adjust control is here. Wear it to sleep but turn off the icing cycles." She glances at Jaantzen when she says the last, confirming he heard her, too. He nods.

The doctor runs a scanner over the bandaged cut on Phaera's temple then ignores it, presses a smooth device the size of her thumb over the bruise on Phaera's cheekbone. It's cool to the touch, humming slightly. "I'm not seeing any internal damage, but this will help the bruising," the doctor says, then sits back. "What are we missing?"

Phaera shakes her head. The movement sends knives through her skull. "I think I'm fine."

No one's convinced, but the doctor reaches into her bag and pulls out a vial. "This will help with the pain so you can sleep tonight. It'll make you drowsy, so plan ahead. It would be best if you went to a hospital for overnight observation." Phaera shakes her head, she's not making herself vulnerable tonight. "Then call me — about anything. If anything at all seems out of the ordinary, call me first and think about it later."

The doctor stands. "Is this visit on the record or off?"

"On," says Phaera. Jaantzen's lips thin. "I have a hunch I'll want to press charges."

She barely listens as the doctor gives her final instructions; Jaantzen seems like he's paying attention, and she can't hold anything else in her mind. When the doctor leaves, Phaera pushes herself out of her chair.

Cavy stands, too, seems ready to catch her if she stumbles. "Where are you staying tonight?" he asks.

Phaera blinks at him, suddenly realizing. Tierren is gone, and part of her had been thrilled to go home to her own bed. But she can't. Not if Leone really wants her dead, and not with Jaantzen. She needs to lie low until she knows she'll be safe — and she's definitely not spending another night sleeping at the Table.

Cavy waves a hand before she can answer. "Stay at the 'Tercio, I'll have a suite made up for you." He glances at Jaantzen, back at Phaera. "I won't make any presumptions, but you're both welcome."

"Thank you."

"My pleasure." Cavy gives her a gentle smile and leaves Jaantzen with a fatherly scowl that makes her want to roll her eyes. The curtain falls behind him.

And Jaantzen wraps her in his arms. She savors the warmth, his scent, the rumble in his chest as he murmurs, "I'm sorry, Phaera."

"Stop it." She takes a deep breath, steadying herself. This night isn't quite over yet. "I need to talk to Hiro and figure out how she got in."

"I should have been here."

"Then she would've waited and tried again later," Phaera says impatiently. "She was just using me to hurt you."

"No. She picked you to show she could take the strongest of us and cut her down." He releases her and steps back, meeting her gaze seriously. "But she was wrong." His lips part as though he's about to say something else, but there's a faint knock on the wall behind them. Phaera turns, wincing at the pain in her ribs, her neck, everywhere.

"Crew's coming to take care of the body," Manu says to Jaantzen from the doorway. "I figured you'd want to get up there before they did."

The thought of going back up on that roof sends a wave of nausea through her, and she squeezes Jaantzen's hand. "Come find me in my office when you're done."

3

______________

JAANTZEN

The rooftop of the Devil's Table is at once peaceful and unsettling. The constant chaos of the city is hushed this high up, traffic and sirens distant, the lights and glamour of the casino drag made more vivid and yet somehow softer by the perspective. But he's not admiring the view, because the whole scene is marred by signs of violence. An overturned chair. An ice tub full of melted water, half of it splashed on the ground around it. A dark spray of blood on the wall beside the door, a coil of rope tied into a noose. A pair of women's heels — Phaera's — tossed carelessly aside.

And in the middle of it all, the body of the woman they know only as Victoria Tierren. She's sprawled on her back in a pool of blood, a clean hole in her temple. Oriol hadn't needed a second shot.

Once he finally got on the scene.

"Perimeter's secure, boss," Manu says. His usually bright hair is black these days, his suit black, even his manicure is black. A sober midnight silhouette against the city lights. "How is she?"

"Shaken. Probably in shock." Jaantzen crosses to the body, but he doesn't bend to examine her. He's choosing more carefully these days what's worth aggravating his bad right knee over.

So this is the wolf that's been hunting his people. In death, Tierren's tawny skin is ashen, the predator's spark gone from her eyes. This is the first good look he's gotten; the only other time he saw her in person, she'd been using Manu as a human shield.

"Anything on the body?"

Manu shakes his head. "We'll take another look, but she's a professional. No identity, nothing to trace her to Leone or say where she's been hiding out. Facial scans and fingerprints are worthless."

"Fingerprints erased?" Jaantzen asks.

"No. But every time you run them, they come up with a new identity, each one faker than the last."

"Get her prints to Starla's cousin. She may be able to help."

"Are we leaking rumors she's dead? Or no."

"Keep it under wraps. I want Leone wondering what happened tonight."

"Copy that." Manu cracks his neck. "Don't know if you saw Tosh's message, but Starla and the rest are home safe."

They're back at the Maraka Valley property, Manu means; Jaantzen doubts any of them have a normal sense of what "home" means. But there's one load off his mind tonight, at least.

Jaantzen turns slowly, scanning the rooftop for any further clue to what could have been Phaera's final moments. Lets himself imagine — just long enough to sear it into his memory — what Tierren had wanted him to find. To live through his failure to protect yet another person who'd tied their fate to his.

A subtle thumping bass from one of the clubs in the distance squeezes like a vise around his temples. He bends with a wince to pick up Phaera's discarded heels, then heads for the door.

"Make sure this body stays buried," he says to Manu.

Downstairs, Phaera and Hiro are in her office, watching her wall of security screens. She's propped against the back of one of her couches, arms crossed over her ribcage.

"She got on the roof the same way Oriol did," Hiro is saying to her. "Climbing up the side. Normally our systems would have caught it, but she hacked the AI."

"It's possible," says Jaantzen from the doorway. Phaera and Hiro both turn. "But very difficult to do."

"We installed this new system when we were dealing with Acheta," Phaera points out. "He was hardly a professional headhunter. Could someone have given her access?"

"Of course." Jaantzen turns to Hiro; the big man has gone stone-faced and slightly pale. "Change all the access codes. Here, at the Lorelei, everywhere. I'll have Starla call you tomorrow to walk you through reviewing your black box data to find out how she got in."

"I'll get it done tonight." Hiro clears his throat. "I'm sorry, ma'am. I'll have my resignation for you in the morning."

"Don't be ridiculous," Phaera says. "Anybody else wouldn't have noticed until it was too late. I'm alive because of you."

Hiro's expression says he doesn't agree with her. Jaantzen doesn't either. When he catches Hiro's eye, the other man breaks first, Adam's apple working as he swallows. Phaera is not an easy woman to guard, but Hiro's inattention nearly got her killed tonight. Hiro knows it, and even if Phaera dismissed his apology, he knows that Jaantzen knows it.

And whether out of loyalty to his boss or fear of Jaantzen, Hiro Matapang will never let Phaera walk within a kilometer of danger again in his life.

The security video is still playing in the background. Victoria Tierren scaling the side of the building. Walking to the edge to admire the view before straightening and melting into the shadows. The rooftop door opens, and Phaera steps out of the square of light and into the darkness.

"That's enough," Phaera says. "I saw this already. Front-row seats." She smiles like it's a joke, but she's scraping one fingernail over the cuticle of another on her good hand. Jaantzen didn't notice when she started doing it, but she's already drawn a bright bead of blood.

"Phaera, you need rest. Hiro can finish up here." He tries to make it sound like a request, and it's a sign of how exhausted she truly is that she doesn't argue.

It's a short drive to the Aterciopelado, where the receptionist at the valet simply gives them a suite number and access code without logging them into any systems. Phaera melts into him as soon as the lift door shuts behind them. She's shivering.

Jaantzen wraps his arm around her gently, wary of other injuries she may not have thought worth mentioning to the doctor. "Did you take that painkiller?"

She nods against him. Her hair smells faintly floral, and beneath it is *her*, that warm, heady scent so familiar even after a week apart. "Before we left. I think it's starting to kick in. Either that or I got a whiff of whatever they're smoking in the 'Tercio valets' break room."

Jaantzen laughs into her hair. "It was strong, wasn't it?"

"Remind me to tell the valet in the morning they should stuff something under the door."

The lift opens onto the thirty-seventh floor, into an empty hallway, and Phaera stays pressed to his side as they find the suite. When the door opens, the view is stunning. Rich greens and golds overlying lush, pristine cream carpets and couches in the large sitting room, a gleaming chandelier over the dining table, a hallway leading to the bedroom beyond. The curtains are drawn back, and as the tallest building on the casino drag, the Aterciopelado's hotel tower has an incredible view of the glitter below.

Jaantzen has a few things in an overnight bag, and he's shouldered Phaera's small bag. Given how light it is, it's clear she'd been planning on going back to her apartment after a few long nights sleeping at the Devil's Table. Maybe it would have been fine. But. Oriol and Manu will check out her apartment after they finish at the Devil's Table, and they'll bring by some of her things in the morning. He and Phaera may not be able to stay here long, but they can spend one night recovering in peace. Especially with Tierren dead and the next phase of their plan now in action. He checks the locks on the door. Phaera sinks onto the couch and slips off her shoes, bending with a hiss of pain.

"What can I do?" he asks her.

She gives him a long, glassy look, processing his question.

"Do you need to eat?" he prompts. "Shower?"

"Sleep," she says finally. "I just need to sleep."

He offers her a hand and helps her to her feet, leading the way to the bedroom. The light blooms automatically when they cross the threshold, illuminating a spacious room with a giant bed and another small sitting area, everything cream and gold.

"The bed's enormous," she says, a touch of wonder in her voice. "Cavy really pulled out all the stops."

"I think he's fond of you," Jaantzen says. "And worried."

She's stalled in the doorway as though unsure what to do next. Whatever the doctor gave her for pain must be kicking in, and she obviously self-medicated as well — he can smell the faint smoky sweetness of mezcal on her breath. He tugs on her hand, drawing her into the room. "Let's get you into bed. Do you have something to wear?"

"There's robes," she says. "All the rooms have them."

He opens the closet and finds a pair of robes, mint-green silk embroidered around the cuffs and hem with the 'Tercio's signature snake logo. The deadliest snake on New Sarjun is also one of the most gorgeously patterned.

He picks out the smaller robe and turns to find Phaera sitting on the edge of the bed, watching him.

"I'm going to be all right," she says. He doesn't have an answer.

He lays the robe beside her on the bed. "I'll get you a glass of water."

When he comes back, she's still on the edge of the bed, and still dressed. "I'm sorry," she says. "This is fucking stupid, but I just can't." She waves her splinted hand like a club. "This hand, my ribs."

"Your ribs?" She hasn't mentioned her ribs.

She looks annoyed at the question. "I don't know, Jaantzen. Everything hurts."

"Let me help."

He kneels gingerly beside the bed to help her out of the slim white trousers, trying to keep his mind firmly centered on making Phaera comfortable.

"What is it?" she asks.

Apparently he's failed to keep his mind on track. Jaantzen gives her a faint smile. "When you wore these the other night, at the Jungle? This was all I could think about." He watches her face for a sign he's crossed the line.

She laughs, and he relaxes. "That's why this is my last-minute date outfit. Throw a jacket on and it's a good last-minute secret-cabal meeting outfit, too."

"Very versatile."

"And now you've seen it twice. This doesn't work if I keep going on surprise dates with the same man — women can't just wear the same gray suit over and over."

"I'm not. I don't think."

"Yes, you are."

"In my defense, my attention was entirely on you that night, not what I was wearing." He folds the trousers over a chair and turns to find Phaera with her back to him, struggling with her blouse. "Let me help," he says, slipping it over her head, tugging the sleeve carefully over the splint. He tries not to think about lavender-gray lace, the way the delicate, feathery, scalloped edges feel under his calloused fingertips as he unhooks the latch of her bra, or the heat of her skin under his hands as he smooths straps down her bare shoulders. She shivers as he sets it aside, and he wraps the silk robe around her. She fumbles with the belt but gets it tied, then turns to face him, pulls him down for a kiss; it's brief.

"Thank you."

For nearly getting her killed? He won't say that, he knows what her answer will be.

"I'll let you rest," he says instead, trying to ignore the bruise on her cheek and the bandages circling her neck. "I'll be in the other room if you need anything."

"Don't," she says quickly. Her hand catches his, her grip on his fingers almost painful. "I don't want to be alone."

She doesn't let go until he nods assent; he undresses as she climbs awkwardly into the enormous bed, then turns out the light and slips in beside her. She curls into his side, shivering, her head resting on his shoulder. He breathes in the scent of her hair, then kisses the top of her head. "Phaera?" he murmurs. "I'm so sorry."

She doesn't answer, but she's stopped shivering. Her breathing slows, and for a moment he wonders if the drugs have finally taken over and she's fallen asleep.

But then her breath catches and she shifts lazily — maybe she'd dozed off. "The only thing you did was be there for me when I asked you to," Phaera finally says. "Leone did the rest."

A giant weight is bearing down on his chest, the pressure of things unsaid, of the emotions he's been pushing aside all evening. Maybe here in the dark isn't the place, but he almost missed his chance forever to say this, and he can't let another go by.

"You're incredible," he says. It's a wholly inadequate word for what he's trying to express, but it's the one that's been on his mind all night. "You're one of the strongest people I know, and you are far too good for me. Wait," he says, when she tries to interrupt. "Not being near you this past week was excruciating. Tonight I couldn't stop thinking about what it would be like to never touch you again. Never hear you laugh again, and it destroys me to even think about it. I need you."

Her breathing is coming shallow now, her entire body tense against his. She doesn't answer, but this time it's not because she's sleeping.

"Phaera Dalvinia Harris, I love you."

She breaks against him gently, sniffling turning to tears, to sobs, her good hand clutched in his undershirt. He holds her as she cries against his shoulder. He holds her until she stops shaking, until her breathing evens once more, drawing out long and smooth and finally uninterrupted by hiccoughing sobs. He holds her until she's snoring softly, his arm long gone numb, staring into the dark and cursing himself for an idiot, desperately planning for how he'll fix this when they wake in the morning.

## 4

## TOSHIYO

Starla and the rest of the *Coldfire*'s crew are back. Toshiyo can feel the paralyzing weight of their energy at the top of that flight of stairs, through the door that leads into the hangar.

She hesitates. Hand on the railing, one foot on the bottom step.

She'd been so preoccupied with going through the files Starla stole from the Alliance, she hadn't considered until now that the *Coldfire* isn't just carrying Starla, El, Simca — people she knows. Along with the *Coldfire*'s crew, and the reporter, they also have an unexpected passenger list including nearly two dozen escaped convicts from Redrock Prison.

Murderers, terrorists.

And children, Starla had said — at least six of the *Coldfire*'s passengers are under the age of fifteen, kids who were born in the desert around Redrock Prison and have never known another life. Maybe they didn't know another life existed.

She certainly hadn't. She'd been almost twenty years

old when she saw Bulari for the first time; she still remembers her awe that buildings got so big, remembers being dazzled by the glare of the streetlights, by how many people were on the streets even after dark. More people than she'd ever seen at once, and not a single one of them working for Blacklode Corporation. She'd felt blissfully anonymous as Jaantzen's spinner glided through the crowds. None of them knew her name, none of them gave the spinner a second glance. She could walk right through them and be invisible, she thought — they wouldn't even notice her. It had felt liberating, beyond the knowledge that she never had to go back to the hellhole Jaantzen had pulled her out of.

Will these kids feel liberated by the anonymity of the big city? Or will it crush them?

Toshiyo's not sure how long she's been standing at the foot of the stairs, feeling the draw of the long stairway, and of the hallway behind her leading back down to solitude.

Solitude, but also Lucky.

Toshiyo had let herself get too comfortable with their strange new alien companion. She'd come to think of him as some sort of friendly, overly toothy pet who could actually communicate in words, and she'd been completely caught off guard when he became agitated at her music a few minutes ago and attacked her. Her elbow still aches from where it smacked the floor, but more than anything, she's spooked by how much more damage Lucky could have done.

They need to figure out what to do with him. Quickly.

And Toshiyo needs to stop stalling.

She forces herself up the steps and pushes the door open.

Heads turn.

The *Coldfire* is a little worse for wear, with fresh scrapes and blast marks along its hull gleaming in the bright lights of the hangar. The crowd around it looks worse for wear, too.

The escaped prisoners seem tired more than anything. Their clothes are threadbare and strange, handmade or repaired so many times they're almost entirely patches. Yet some are wearing furs that would cost a fortune in Bulari, skinned from the terrors the Alliance created by injecting alien venom into wild animals, who then started breeding in the desert. Toshiyo's been reading about those tonight, too.

Relief floods through her when she spots Starla standing under the *Coldfire*'s wing. She's having an intense conversation with an older man with a snarling, scarred face; his attention snaps to Toshiyo and Starla follows his gaze, gives Toshiyo a tired grin, and waves her over. Simca Anahoy's interpreting beside her, but El and Gia are nowhere in sight.

"This is Toshiyo Ravi," Starla signs to the scarred-faced man. "Our operations manager. Toshiyo, meet Henri Bassot. He helped us break into the research facility."

"It's a pleasure to meet you," Henri says. A smile twists his face as he holds out a hand.

"Same." Toshiyo nods and shoves her hands in her pockets. The hangar is too crowded, the pressure of people around her a physical force making her skin crawl. After a moment, Henri lets his own hand fall back to his side.

"We were discussing the next steps," Starla signs. Because she's got Simca interpreting, she's going fast and using more complex USL signs than she does when it's just her and Toshiyo. "Coeur has housing set up in Dry Creek, and Beto is going to take them back to the city tonight."

They're leaving soon; the tension in Toshiyo's shoulders eases slightly. But she didn't miss the operative word. "Coeur?" she fingerspells.

Starla nods. "A few of these people worked for her before getting shipped to Redrock, so it's perfect. Jaantzen will work with her to help them reintegrate."

Nothing involving Coeur can be categorized as perfect, but Toshiyo lets that go. Sounds like the decision's already been made. And it's not like the prisoners can stick around here, not with the chance they'd run into Lucky and find out the boss had an alien all his own.

"And then we figure out what to do about the Dawn," says Henri.

Toshiyo frowns at him. Starla's expression becomes serious. "Felipe Zacharia escaped from Redrock," she signs to Toshiyo. "When we broke into the research facility, we accidentally enabled them to escape. They were heading to Bulari, last we heard. They potentially have a living specimen of one of the creatures with them."

A chill traces Toshiyo's spine, one that has nothing to do with how claustrophobic the hangar is. Felipe Zacharia and his sick cult have already caused enough damage, while he was locked up in Redrock. Even after Jaantzen killed his brother and halted the Dawn's progress in the city, they'd still managed to poison the water supplies of several corporate towns — including the mine Toshiyo had spent her youth indentured at — killing everyone who drank it.

She's been reading Zacharia's files from Redrock all evening. They describe a man who's cunning and manipulative, who's able to inspire stunning displays of loyalty to his own personal cult. He'd codified that when he founded the Dawn, but he'd had followers willing to die for him, to kill for him, even before. One guard who'd raised a hand to Zacharia in front of his followers was found hanged in his room, having apparently gouged out his own eyes with a pair of scissors.

The psychologist's reports say Zacharia believes he has psychic powers. Two weeks ago, Toshiyo would have dismissed that outright. But she didn't believe aliens existed then, either, and now she talks to one every day. Maybe Felipe Zacharia *can* control minds.

Because he can, can't he? Maybe it's not psychic power, maybe it's just his magnetic charisma that convinces otherwise sane individuals to do what he tells them.

And now he's free?

In Bulari?

Toshiyo lifts her hands to Starla. "There's a lot of information about Zacharia in the files you sent over," she half signs, half fingerspells; Simca doesn't interpret for Henri, correctly assuming if Toshiyo wanted him to know what she was saying, she would have spoken aloud. "We can talk when everyone's gone."

"Finding Zacharia is our number one priority," Starla signs; Simca's interpreting again. "Henri has offered to help — he and some of the others are familiar with the Dawn."

"He'll be starting fresh, is that right?" Henri asks.

"You said his brother's dead and Coeur wiped out the rest of his followers here. So he doesn't have the foothold he once did."

"Of course he does," Toshiyo says before she can stop herself, and the other three look at her expectantly. Dammit. She doesn't know this man — but Starla trusts him, right? Toshiyo takes a deep breath.

"They're still working. Trying to re-create the serum, testing it out." And now that she says it out loud, the conclusion is so obvious she can't believe she missed it. "Boss killed Bennion Zacharia, but someone's still in charge. They're not just acting randomly."

"Any idea who?" Starla asks.

Toshiyo shakes her head. Adds "Find out who succeeded Bennion Zacharia" to the overflowing mental list of things she needs to figure out.

"I'd like to stay here and help you plan," Henri says.

"No," Starla signs. "Your people need you. I'll be in touch tomorrow."

Henri takes her outstretched hand. "I look forward to it." He claps Simca on the shoulder, gives Toshiyo a scar-twisted smile, then turns and bellows around the room, louder than he needs to be. "Everybody on board, we're heading home!"

People slowly start milling towards the ship once more, and Toshiyo presses out of the way.

"Hey," says a familiar voice from behind her.

Toshiyo spins with a smile. "Hey."

El Anahoy tucks a strand of electric-blue hair behind one ear and gives her a lopsided grin, the ring in his nose glinting. He looks as exhausted and filthy as the rest of them, the healthy warmth of his brown skin washed out in the bad lights of the hangar. He was injured in the crash,

Starla told her that much, but Toshiyo can't see it. She throws her arms around him.

She's nearly forgotten the crushing discomfort of the busy hangar. Strange how some people's presence is a blanket over the chaos of the world, dampening the constant buzzing electric panic. The boss is like that. When she walked into her manager's office at Blacklode twenty years ago and saw Jaantzen, she'd felt like she could breathe for the first time in months. She hadn't known why he was there, just that his presence somehow disrupted the waves of predatory threat emanating from the other men in the room. She hadn't had to force herself to sit across the table from him. It had been easy.

Manu and Gia and Starla had all been a slower build to where their presence provided more calm than chaos. And Toshiyo still doesn't know what to do with Simca's incessant energy. But the first time she met El, he had been instantly soothing.

Of course, she hadn't thought to do anything about it until about a year ago, when it occurred to her they *could* spend time together outside their random encounters at work. She'd recommended a book to him, he'd invited her to watch a movie. And now Toshiyo isn't sure what to call what they are to each other, and she doesn't care, because it works.

She lets go first.

"Are you doing all right?" he asks.

She's doing amazing, now. "Yeah. You?"

"I need a shower." He laughs. "But I'm good. Just a little bruised."

"Thanks for coming home."

"Always." But his smile fades. "I'm not staying here

tonight, though. Sim and I are going to help everyone get settled, then we'll see what Starla needs."

She's disappointed, but she knew that was coming. "I'm not going to have to watch the new Loa Kelsang vid on my own, am I? You know Manu won't go near it after I made him watch the first one."

"Don't you dare watch it without me. I'll get back out here soon. Or you'll be back home. When this blows over."

His smile is easy, but she's having trouble matching his optimism. There's no way to know when that will happen. And now Simca's calling his name from the other side of the hangar. His smile softens. "See you soon, Toshiyo."

She stays out of the fray as the *Coldfire* is loaded back up. As the chaos subsides, she finally spots Gia talking to a couple of the younger girls. Dust grays her black twists of hair, her arm is in a filthy sling, and her temple is smudged with dirt, but her eyes are bright.

Finally Starla and Gia help guide the *Coldfire* out into the night. Toshiyo lets out a breath when the bay doors are shut and locked behind them, leaving just a small pile of gear where a few minutes ago there was a swarm of activity.

"Hey, G," Toshiyo calls. She walks over to help with the gear. "Are you staying here tonight? Or heading back home? We have plenty of extra room."

Gia shares a long look with Starla. "I'll stay here tonight. We've got some things we need to talk about."

"Let me carry that." Toshiyo reaches for a bag Gia has been trying to catch with her good hand, but Gia waves her off.

"I can get it, I just need to — " She fumbles at the

strap to her sling, then turns to Toshiyo. "Can you help me with this?"

"Of course. What happened to your arm?" She works at the knot carefully, trying not to jostle Gia's injury.

"It's a long story." Gia tosses the sling on a crate, then shrugs out of her coat. Her sleeve is shredded and stiff with dried blood; Toshiyo's stomach does an uneasy flip, but Gia doesn't seem bothered by it. "But the short version is nothing." Gia pushes back her sleeve to reveal smooth dark skin. Not a scratch, not a scar. Nothing to explain where all the blood on her sleeve came from. "I need a shower, some coffee, and everything you can tell me about that alien venom."

Toshiyo's eyes widen.

"We haven't told anybody," Starla signs. Toshiyo can see the faint flicker of her lens in her pupil; she must be connected to the local network again, because she apparently understood what Gia said out loud. Toshiyo taps her own eye in question and Starla nods.

"You haven't told anybody what?" Toshiyo says.

"She got bit," Starla signs. "By the alien."

"And I feel completely fucking fine," Gia says. "Tosh, what happened to me?"

"The Gift of the Fallen," Toshiyo says. Whispers. Not thirty minutes ago, Lucky had escaped his cage and attacked her in her office. And she knows he didn't mean it, but she can't shake the vision of those triple rows of razor-sharp teeth, the bat-like face she normally finds so friendly. What if he'd done more than knock her over?

"It bit you and you lived," Toshiyo says quietly. "So now you're . . ."

"I'm what? Immortal? Please don't tell me I'm immortal."

Toshiyo shakes her head. "I don't know."

"Tevi's going to be pissed," Starla signs, and Gia groans.

"Don't remind me," she says. And she reaches down to pick up her pack, slinging it easily over her shoulder. "Shower first, then let's figure out what kind of mutant I am."

5

________

## JAANTZEN

Jaantzen opens his eyes to an empty bed and voices down the hall — his lieutenant and his lieutenant's husband. He doesn't hear Phaera. His stomach drops. He dresses quickly, steeling himself to find that she's left before he can properly apologize for stepping over the line last night. He'd been so caught up in his own fears that the rational part of his brain — the part that had been yelling for him to stop talking, he was moving too fast — had been drowned out.

It's been little more than a week since the first and only time she shared his bed, maybe two weeks since she asked him for a date, and he's been exiled in the desert for most of that time.

They've moved fast. He can't shake the feeling they've known each other their entire lives, but is that in his own head? He has no real idea what she thinks, and he confessed love.

She has every right to disappear on him.

Phaera's laugh catches him just below the ribcage as

he opens the bedroom door. He takes cautious steps, sure it can't be true.

But she's still here, sitting with Oriol and Manu at the dining table, dressed in drawstring house trousers and a slouchy sweater, her hair pulled out of her face in a short ponytail. The bruise on her cheek already looks better thanks to the doctor's treatment last night, even though she's not wearing makeup. Her throat is encircled in bandages, and the parts of her right hand not covered by the splint are livid purple and red.

Aside from her injuries, she looks . . . rested. Happy. He's never seen her like this, relaxed and casual — even during the one night she spent at his penthouse she'd kept her mask from slipping entirely. She laughs again at something Manu says, and there's no trace of the usual poise and polish she wears like armor.

He can't get over how stunning she is.

Her smile warms when she sees Jaantzen, and something unknots in his chest.

What the hell has he gotten himself into?

Oriol nods a curt greeting at Jaantzen and Manu pushes himself easily to his feet. He's looking good this morning, too, none of the stiffness of injury that's plagued him for the past few weeks. Maybe this last week of enforced inactivity has given him a chance to heal.

Manu crosses to the doorway of the tiny kitchen. "Coffee, boss?"

"Thank you." Jaantzen accepts the mug Manu brings back. Phaera's still watching him with an expression he can't quite read, but it's not the uneasiness he was anticipating. "Can you give us a minute?"

There's nowhere really to go besides the kitchen, but the two men disappear inside. The clinking of dishes,

Manu's laugh, Oriol's low murmur. Jaantzen finally sits across from Phaera, cupping the coffee in his palms.

"I'm sorry for breaking down last night," she says, before he can form his own apology.

He blinks at her. "No, I'm sorry. I was presumptuous."

"Stop it," she says. "This week has been an emotional roller coaster. I let Tierren get in my head, with the cards, and the things she said to me on the roof. Then to have Oriol, and Hiro, and Vanessa — and Cavy — being so kind. I wasn't prepared to hear that from you, it was too much." A smile tugs at her cheek. "I don't know your middle name."

He's caught unaware by the sudden topic change. "I don't have one."

She tilts her head.

"They gave me the name Willem at the orphanage, so I gave myself a surname when I got out. But I didn't think to pick a middle name." By the time he'd learned middle names were common, it felt like a useless affectation to adopt — and he'd been right. In nearly five decades, Phaera's the first person to ask.

"Oh." That uncertain mixture of surprise and sadness in her expression, it occurs to him that she didn't know about his past. "Your parents," she says delicately. "They died?"

Jaantzen shrugs. "Probably. But, no, they gave me up. Poverty, most likely. Or youth." Or they'd seen something in him that scared them — something Tae would have eventually seen. That Phaera will someday see.

Phaera's fingers twine through his. "I was trying to say I love you, too, Jaantzen." Phaera tugs him towards her.

"And I want to kiss you, but it hurts to move. Give a girl a hand?"

He laughs and stands, closing the space between them. Her lips are soft and warm, she tastes like coffee and smells like cardamom and citrus and honey and sweat, and her jaw, her cheek are smooth under his fingertips. They finally break the kiss and she leans her forehead against his.

"The boys wanted to brief you," she murmurs; he's almost managed to forget Manu and Oriol in the other room. "But afterwards I think we should send them out for a bit and enjoy the morning."

"I agree."

Her cheek presses into the palm of his hand, the fingers of her good left hand tighten around his, let go. Jaantzen straightens from the awkward stoop and settles back in his own chair.

She frowns at him. "What's wrong with your leg?"

"It's nothing." That look; he's not getting away with dismissing it. "It's my knee, it's bothered me for years. It's a routine surgery, Gia tells me."

"But who has the time?" Phaera gives him a rueful smile. "Especially right now?"

"Especially right now. Manu?" he calls.

Manu and Oriol come back out of the kitchen, but only Manu sits at the table. Oriol crosses to the picture window, the view of the casino drag hazy in the morning light with Bulari's dusty skyline beyond. Since his nod of greeting, Oriol hasn't met Jaantzen's gaze. Anger at himself for the breach of security that allowed Phaera to be attacked, probably. Well-earned, but this awkwardness isn't going to be productive. Jaantzen will deal with that before they go.

"Phaera's apartment was clear," Manu says, lounging back in his chair, long scarred fingers tracing the handle of his coffee cup. "No sign that anyone but Phaera had ever accessed the security feeds, and of course I wouldn't know if anything was missing. But there was a takeout container on the counter that looked fresh."

Phaera's gone pale; Manu's expression turns grim. "Oriol said you'd been staying at the Table. So I take it you didn't order in at your apartment yesterday?"

"No."

"Then you were smart to stay at your office," says Manu. "Your instincts were right."

"Though Tierren got through the Table's security, too," Phaera says. Oriol doesn't turn from the window, but his shoulders tighten.

Manu leans forward. "Phaera, this woman was exceptional at what she did. Since we've got her biosign now, and some of the tech that was on her body, we've been able to trace her." He glances at Jaantzen, makes Starla's cousin's namesign. Mona is one of the best identity forgers in the system, and damned good at untangling the forgeries others make.

"Tierren was from Corusca," Manu continues. "Originally tapped by the Alliance to be a special agent, though she was tagged psychologically unfit and placed on a watch list instead. She eventually disappeared off the Alliance's radar, leaving behind one dead watcher and another on trial for the murder under very suspicious circumstances.

"As far as we can tell, she's bounced around the system from job to job for the past two decades. There are one or two high-profile assassinations we think she might have been involved with. And then she answered a job

Leone put on the boards three weeks ago, and found out she'd bit off more than she could chew.

"This woman has taken down NMLF generals in the mountains of New Manila," Manu says; now he's looking past Jaantzen and Phaera to Oriol's ramrod-straight back. "At least one Arquellian senator. We think she was behind the dissolution of the Chakmani Cartel in Durga's Belt and the hit on the Yadzira family capo last year. She gets what she wants. Or at least she did until last night."

"I can't thank you enough, Sina," Phaera says.

Oriol turns and gives her a tight smile, but doesn't answer.

"How much was the job?" Jaantzen asks, and Manu names a sum that makes Phaera laugh in disbelief.

"I could retire very comfortably on that," Manu says contemplatively.

"Remind me to up your pay." Jaantzen folds his hands, considering. Offering rates like that, it's no wonder Leone was able to secure a headhunter like Victoria Tier-ren. She would have already paid a deposit, so how much does she have left in her coffers? And will she put the job back up on the boards when she learns that her woman is dead?

"Who even has that much money?" Phaera asks. "And then just throws it away on . . ."

"I've become a very expensive problem for Leone, apparently. But three weeks ago?"

"The night we . . ." Manu rolls a wrist: *You know.*

"The night we rescued Coeur." He finishes Manu's sentence for Phaera's benefit, hating his lieutenant's reflexive false-casual smile. "The Alliance had a plan to get back what Coeur stole. But Leone made her own, too. I became a threat to a bigger payday."

"From the Alliance."

"Exactly. But the Alliance failed to get it back, and now so has Leone," Jaantzen says. "What will the cost of that failure be?"

"To her or to us?" Phaera asks.

Manu's comm chimes, and the corner of his mouth tugs into a smile, a real one. "It's happening," he says, and flicks the file he just received onto the tasteful screen embedded into the far side of the room. The windows dim automatically.

The first of the newsfeeds have picked up the story. As Phaera leans forward with interest, Jaantzen realizes she hadn't actually read the draft — or even heard the theory beyond what he'd told the entire group last night. When he'd finally been in a position to speak with her alone, that had been the furthest thing from his mind.

"Good morning," the anchor says. "A shocking story from north of the Jupari Desert. For nearly a century, Arquelle — and then the Alliance — have been granted a concession in northern New Sarjun. They've tightly controlled access. Until one reporter managed to pull back the curtain and reveal what, exactly, the Alliance is doing on New Sarjunian soil — and how they were able to get away with it."

The vid cuts to Kumail Anh, looking slightly gaunter than when Jaantzen last saw him, but cleaned up and ready to speak his piece. Phaera lets out a gasp of surprise.

"You know him?" Jaantzen asks.

"Of course — I mean, no, not personally." Phaera looks impressed. "You got *Kumail Anh* to take this story? I've been following his work for years."

"Letizia got him, not me."

"Oh now you're just showing off," Phaera says with a

sly smile. "You got Letizia Diamante to handle the press."

"I think Starla did that," Jaantzen says, but Phaera shushes him; Kumail's beginning to frame the story.

"For centuries, settlers on New Sarjun have tried to tame the desert, living a razor's-edge existence sustained by greenhouses and international trade. When I heard rumors the Indiran Alliance had managed to develop a terraforming technology to grow food in even the harshest conditions, I had to see it for myself. And find out why — and how — they were keeping their discovery a secret."

Kumail's current version of the story focuses on how the Alliance and New Sarjunian officials have profited off prison labor, along with how the trade agreement would allow the Alliance to sell food secretly grown in their Redrock concession to New Sarjunians at profit margins that would devastate the local agricultural industry.

The piece includes interviews with an expert on trade policy, a farming collective from down south in Alusina, a prison reform activist, a historian with perspective on the Redrock concession, and the wife and children of a man allegedly sent to Redrock after his public disturbance charge was somehow distorted into terrorism.

And it includes a glimpse into the terraforming facilities themselves. It's fascinating and terrifying all at once to watch Kumail put the pieces together. After what feels like an eternity of painstaking research and wild theories and fantastical conversations involving only Toshiyo and Manu and Starla, it's surreal to hear Kumail's calm voice-over while Toshiyo's satellite images and Starla's night-vision footage scroll by.

He's left the escaped convicts and the alien technology out. For now, at least. He's promised to work with Jaantzen's rules on when to release sensitive information in exchange for access to stories no one else could ever touch — and as long as Jaantzen doesn't try to control the direction of the story. But Jaantzen can see the subtle questions he's weaving in about the origins of the terraforming technology. Questions the man must be champing at the bit to answer in his next report.

Kumail ends the segment with a query about how long this has been going on in the Alliance concession, and who in New Sarjun's government knew about the terraforming, the prison labor scheme, or both. And the promise that he will get to the heart of the story so the New Sarjunian people can hear the truth they are owed.

Jaantzen knows Kumail is still hard at work getting the evidence that will actually tie Leone to this. The story will make a splash as it is, but until they can attach Leone's name to it for sure, it won't touch her personally.

There's always something else.

The vid cuts back to the anchor, who gives the camera a grim look. "The story is still unfolding, but it's becoming increasingly clear it will be troubling news for proponents of the Alliance trade agreement currently being debated in parliament," he says. "And a document that surfaced today brings up an even more troubling question. Have New Sarjunian officials been taking bribes from Alliance-based companies in order to get the agreement passed? Our next guest explains."

It's a short interview between the anchor and a reporter who's been covering the agreement for the past month, and is clearly excited that someone is finally interested in hearing about it. They don't release the names of any of the alleged bribe-takers, but they do name some of the companies involved in paying out bribes, and announce that the full list will be posted for their viewers.

Jaantzen's comm is chiming with incoming messages. Aiax and Lhasa Demosga. Letizia Diamante. One from — that's interesting. Youssef Tabari.

Tabari is an old fair-weather friend who's now the trade commissioner, which means he must be having a heart attack at seeing this agreement fall through at the last minute after the months of negotiations. He's been attending Leone's dinner parties for years, but he and Jaantzen go back farther than that. They've never been close — Jaantzen doesn't trust him enough. And he's been under the impression that Tabari's in Leone's pocket.

If Tabari's calling Jaantzen now, that suspicion is confirmed. Otherwise he'd have no reason to suspect Jaantzen of financing Kumail Ahn's trip to Redrock, or being behind the release of the list of bribes.

But is he calling Jaantzen on Leone's behalf? Or because he's always been a rat, and now he can see the ship he's on is sinking?

Jaantzen turns off his notifications.

The anchor moves on to a segment on the upcoming city council races and Manu turns down the volume.

"If Leone's Alliance partners didn't already know she failed to solve their Jaantzen problem, they do now." Jaantzen steeples fingers over his lips, thinking.

"You must be glad Starla's home," Phaera says.

She just means glad in general, he realizes; it hits him again how far from his world she is. She has no idea who Starla's parents are, that his goddaughter was once held at Redrock Prison as an OIC terrorist, that he helped break her out. If he told her Starla was a Dusai, Phaera probably wouldn't blink — even if she did recognize the name, it must be so far from reality for her. She probably heard stories about the infamous Dusai pirates when she was younger and wrote them off as fiction.

He's going to experience this moment again and again, he realizes. And probably in reverse, when some fact she considers integral about the world surprises him.

There's so much they haven't talked about. He's doesn't know if she has siblings, he realizes. Cousins. *Children.* Wouldn't he know if she had children?

"Turn it up." Phaera's voice cuts into his thoughts. Because now Calanthe Yang is on the screen, speaking to a mic swarm on the steps of the courthouse, in vicious eye makeup and fierce mourning red that hugs her belly. Manu turns the volume back up to catch the tail end of the voiceover. ". . . paperwork was filed today on behalf of an Alliance agent seeking amnesty after she claims she was ordered to attack a New Sarjunian civilian here in Bulari. Was it related to the Alliance terraforming allegations or the bribery? Details are being kept under wraps, but stay tuned to our feed for every update."

Now it's Manu's comm that's chiming. He smiles grimly. "Our friendly Alliance liaison," he says. "I don't think he's too happy about the news."

"Do you think it's safe to set up a meeting with him?" Jaantzen would have liked to meet Alliance Deputy Chief of Mission Marquez ó Lauris in person, though he suspects the cordial window for that has now passed. He'd agreed to keep the Alliance agent from filing for amnesty in exchange for ó Lauris keeping the Alliance diplomatic mission in check and not letting them murder any more of Jaantzen's people. That, of course, had been before Jaantzen knew how deep the Alliance conspiracy on New Sarjun went.

Manu shakes his head. "I'm going to guess that's a no.

I'll get in touch with him." He lowers the volume again as the segment shifts. "We've dulled Leone's teeth by killing Tierren. You should keep moving. I'll set up another safe-house for tonight."

"So no going home just yet?" Phaera asks.

Manu shakes his head again. "Not until we know what else Leone has planned for you. You should keep a low profile at work, too. You both need to stay out of the public eye for a bit."

"How do we use this?" Phaera asks, gesturing at herself. "What happened to me."

Jaantzen's jaw clenches — We don't, we keep you out of it — but he lets that knee-jerk response go. Her instinct is right.

"We fire up the rumor mill," says Manu. He glances at Jaantzen, notes his disapproval, moves on. "Eventually the doctor's report will need to come out. As will the footage of Tierren attacking you." Phaera tenses, but nods. "And the evidence we have linking her to Leone. Do you trust Vanessa and Hiro to run the reopening of the Devil's Table tonight without you?"

Phaera nods slowly. "But if I'm not there, people will talk."

"Exactly. Have your staff give the official story that you're ill, but find someone low-ranking — a security guard you trust, maybe — who can let it slip that there was an assassination attempt. Tomorrow, if you're feeling up for it, let yourself be seen out in public with your injuries but don't grant any interviews. Yet."

"I feed the rumor mill, and by the time I go public with what actually happened, everyone will be screaming to know the truth." Phaera smiles; Jaantzen hates this. "I like it."

"For now, we all sit tight and watch the bomb we dropped work through the system," says Manu. He stands. "And prepare as much as possible for Leone's next attack."

"I'll get your bags for you, ma'am." It's the first thing Oriol's said. The ex-Alliance special agent shoulders a pair of bags that are sitting by the front door, heads back to the bedroom. Phaera gives Jaantzen's hand a squeeze, then follows.

Manu's friendly smile turns dark as soon as Phaera's out of the room. "We'll take Leone down, boss," he says.

"Did you watch the footage?" Jaantzen asks. That grim look on Manu's face is a yes. "Should I?"

"No." Manu glances over his shoulder at the bedroom. "She wouldn't want you to. It was fucking relentless, but she just wouldn't stop."

"Tierren?"

Manu's lips quirk to the side. "Phaera." The smile fades. "It wasn't just the fight, though. That bitch gets in your head. She knows what you're thinking and cuts until it feels real."

"What did Tierren say to her?"

Another glance back at the bedroom. Manu lowers his voice. "She told her that her people resented her success and they'd think she deserved her fate. And that you were just using her and she was an idiot to think it meant anything more."

"The things she said to me on the roof, I let her get in my head," Phaera had said. Phaera's reaction last night suddenly makes more sense. And Jaantzen is suddenly cognizant of the fact that such an intimate emotional reveal should have come from Phaera, not his lieutenant.

"You probably should have told me to ask her myself."

"If I thought you'd actually do it, I would've."

"She knows what you're thinking and cuts until it feels real," Manu had said. Phaera isn't the only one whose ear Tierren's been pouring poison into. She'd been murmuring dark things to Manu when Jaantzen found them together in that alley, her words as deadly as the syringe pressed to his neck.

"What did Tierren tell you?" Jaantzen asks.

His lieutenant's jaw clenches, and for a moment Jaantzen doesn't think he'll answer.

"That you and Coeur had planned the embassy bombing together," Manu finally says. "And the reason you didn't come see me in the hospital afterward was you were disappointed I'd lived."

"I hope you know — "

"I know, boss. Hey." Manu tilts his head, considering. "Believe Phaera when she tells you what she wants."

"Meaning?"

"You." Manu claps him on the shoulder. "And probably world domination. You need anything else, just call. I'll be close."

Jaantzen forces himself to relax; there are footsteps coming from the bedroom. Oriol's. The other man nods tightly at Jaantzen, then walks past him to the door.

"Oriol."

The man turns slowly.

"Phaera's hiring you back officially as her bodyguard?"

"Yessir."

"Good. There's no one I'd rather have at her side."

Another tight nod, but Oriol seems to have relaxed slightly. "Thank you, sir."

"But I want two people on her at all times."

"I've got a gal," Oriol says. "Mel. She's already been taking shifts with me from a distance. She'll clean up all right to do personal detail."

"Thank you."

"All right," Manu says into the awkward silence that follows. "We'll be in touch."

The door closes behind them and Jaantzen locks the mechanical security bolts from the inside. It should make him feel safe, but instead he feels trapped. This is a necessary next step, waiting to see what the fallout is from the news that just dropped, but he's getting tired of waiting. Of the daily uncertainty, of being away from home.

That last thought catches him off guard. He thinks of Cobalt Tower as home, doesn't he? But he's not pining for the cold, empty penthouse he left behind. He's remembering fondly the last night he spent there. Calanthe, Leti, and Phaera were there to plan a war, but it had felt like a meal shared with friends. Something about the way Phaera had programmed the lights — no, something about Phaera's very presence — had transformed the entire apartment.

The shower starts running in the other room, and he sits once more at the kitchen table to begin sorting his thoughts. Messages are still pouring in, but nothing is urgent yet. He's engrossed in a search for where the news has spread when he hears footsteps behind him, feels her fingertips on his shoulder, her breath on his jaw as she presses a kiss to the side of his neck.

"I was going to take a shower, but I need some help," Phaera murmurs in his ear; in the reflection from a glass cabinet he catches a glimpse of bare hip that makes his blood catch fire. "Do you have a minute?"

6

———

STARLA

S tarla can't get over how *good* coffee is. How delicious fried eggs are. How amazing it feels to be clean.

Nothing like being trapped in the desert with a bunch of escaped convicts and makeshift plumbing to make you appreciate a hot shower — even one as janky as the deathtrap's.

Every muscle in her body aches, but in the good way that means a job over and done. For now, at least. Leone's still a threat and Felipe Zacharia has joined the fray, but Starla brought her crew back home safely and they have some time to prepare.

And to figure out what exactly is going on with Gia since she got mauled by that alien.

"How quickly do you heal?" Toshiyo is asking her. She's got a jittery energy Starla notices sometimes, which means Toshiyo is using something other than sleep to keep herself running this morning. Gia, on the other hand, seems completely calm about the fact that her alien injuries have been mysteriously healed.

Though she seems less calm about Lucky perching on

the kitchen table. Starla's a bit more wary of the little guy this morning, too. He's still his cheerful, playful self, but now that Starla's seen — and fought — a full-grown version of him, it's hard to think of Lucky as safe.

He catches Starla watching him and grins, maw stretched wide, teeth bared.

"We don't have enough data to know how fast I heal yet," Gia says. "My arm was shredded, but healed overnight. Is that my new baseline? Or was that injury special because it was filled with alien spit?"

"Venom," Toshiyo says automatically. She touches her neck, below her ear. "They have venom sacs, here. The main teeth are for shredding and capturing, but they have a pair of venom teeth behind — "

"Tosh, I'm already having nightmares, thank you," Gia cuts in. "I experienced the shredding and capturing and venom injection."

"Right." Toshiyo clears her throat and goes back to her tablet. "We may not have data on you, but we have the Alliance's data on their own test subjects. And we also know the Dawn got a supply of venom and made their own supersoldiers out of it in Bulari. The woman who fought with Bennion Zacharia? Oriol injured her when they fought on the *Dorothy Queen* casino, thought she was dead. And then when she showed up again at Julieta Yang's warehouse she only had a scar. That was . . . three days later?"

"She had a scar. But my arm is totally healed. Overnight."

"Because it was the injection site?" Starla asks. Toshiyo repeats the question aloud when Gia looks confused.

"Old scars are still there," Gia says. "But I got a

couple of other scrapes that night and they're all completely healed. And I'm not even sore. I feel like I'm twenty again."

"We can guess all we want," Starla signs. "But we need to experiment."

Gia's lips thin, and there's a split second before she moves when Starla can tell what she's about to do. And maybe Starla doesn't entirely think Gia's serious or maybe she's slow. Either way, Starla has barely moved by the time Gia grabs the paring knife beside the sink and slashes across the inside of her arm.

Toshiyo is shouting, some gibberish Starla's lens doesn't transcribe. Dark red blood wells out of the wound and pours down Gia's forearm, dripping into the sink. Toshiyo snatches up a towel, but Starla blocks her before she can shove it at Gia.

"If she's going to science, let her science," Starla signs. She probably would've done the same thing, though she never would've cut so deep. Maybe Gia misjudged, maybe she doesn't care. Maybe she has more faith in her healing powers than Starla does.

With a chaotic flap of wings, Lucky launches himself from the kitchen table to the counter, which he's far too big for these days. Starla catches a glass before it tumbles to the floor.

"It's all right, buddy," Toshiyo tells him; he's snapping his teeth in agitation at Gia's injury. Out of concern? Or maybe he recognizes a bit of his own kind in her blood now.

For a long moment, three women and an alien wordlessly watch blood spatter the sink.

"You should bandage it," Toshiyo finally says, the

words scrawling across the bottom of Starla's lens. "It's not slowing."

Gia doesn't answer. The cut is deep, but it's not life-threatening. Stitches and sealant will stop the bloodflow. Or? Gia grabs the towel from Toshiyo and daubs at the cut, and when the blood's sponged away, it doesn't well back as quickly.

"I think it's working," she says.

"What does it feel like?" Starla asks.

Gia frowns, considering. "Itchy," she says finally. She daubs at the wound again; even less blood wells up this time. "But it actually doesn't hurt. Shouldn't it hurt?"

Toshiyo shakes her head, the horror in her expression shifting to wonder. "The Alliance reports say their subjects experienced reduced pain."

"And the two Dawn supersoldiers I've come across didn't seem to feel pain," Starla signs. "They kept fighting even with wounds that should've knocked them down."

"They can still be killed," Toshiyo says with a bitterness that surprises Starla. "A lethal wound might not heal fast enough to stop the blood loss. But they won't feel it, it won't slow them down."

"I don't think I want to lose my ability to feel pain." Gia's got the paring knife in her hand again, but this time she presses the tip into the center of her palm. Hard enough a bead of blood appears. "Nothing."

"Stop it," Starla signs. Beside her, Lucky shudders.

"Agreed," says Toshiyo.

Gia gives them both a dark look. "We don't know anything about the long-term effects. Does this last forever? A few years? Does it accelerate other problems we don't know anything about?"

"One experiment was on a patient with advanced

skin cancer," Toshiyo says. "Injecting him with the venom made the cancer worse."

"I'm not surprised," says Gia. "It's accelerating cell growth. Who knows what complications that could end up causing."

"I don't think — " Toshiyo cuts off, glancing at the door to the kitchen. Gia does the same. "Door chime," Toshiyo signs to Starla. They haven't been expecting visitors, so they haven't bothered to rig the chime up to the lights. Toshiyo calls up the security feed on her tablet and her face goes ashen. "It's Tevi."

Starla's learned that when her lens refuses to translate around Gia, it's probably because the woman's swearing up a colorful storm. And the fact that her husband has traveled all the way across the Maraka Valley to find her rather than waiting for her to come home can't be a good thing.

"Clean up and get Lucky out of here," Starla signs. "I'll get the door."

She hurries down the hall and takes the stairs two at a time, leg muscles screaming from the exertion of the last few days. She palms the lock that slides open the hatch leading into the outer shack, then the lock on the shack's front door. The shack is always warmer than the cool underground bunkers, but a blast of heat still hits her when she opens the door. It *is* afternoon, she's lost track of the time.

Tevi Sharaf is standing back from the door, squinting in the sun. A faint sheen of sweat glistens on his golden-brown brow, his silver hair is in damp curls. Starla beckons him into the shade and makes Gia's namesign, points down the stairs. "She's fine," she tells him. Either he doesn't understand or he's too stressed to care, because the combination of fear, worry, and frustration on his face doesn't change.

"I saw the news," he says. "Is your lens working? Okay. I saw the news. Tell me you didn't take my wife up to Redrock to break into a top-secret Alliance facility. She told me you were escorting a reporter to the prison and that was it."

Right.

The news.

Tevi's not here just because Gia's later coming home than he expected. In all their worry about Gia's new powers, it hadn't occurred to any of them that Tevi might end up hearing about this secondhand.

Starla takes a deep breath, then pulls out her comm. YES. WE BROKE INTO A TOP-SECRET ALLIANCE FACILITY, she types. BUT SHE'S ALL RIGHT. COME DOWNSTAIRS AND WE'LL TALK.

For a moment he looks angry enough to walk back out the door, but finally Tevi heads towards the stairs. Starla locks the front door and follows him. When they reach the bottom, she motions him down the hall and indicates the kitchen.

Gia's still standing at the sink, which is now spotless. But for the blood-soaked towel, she could be doing dishes.

The fury on Tevi's face melts as soon as he sees her. He wraps his arms around her, leans his forehead against hers, their lips move as they murmur to each other. Starla exchanges a glance with Toshiyo and grabs her coffee mug, heading for a refill to give them some privacy.

"You're injured?"

The words appear on Starla's screen and she turns back. Tevi's noticed Gia's arm, but his concern turns to puzzlement. The cut on her arm is now an angry red scar with a center still barely oozing blood. Like a fresh cut in the center of a week-old injury.

As they watch, the last seam of the wound knits itself back together.

Tevi lets Gia's fingers drop out of his. "What the hell is going on?"

Gia glances at Starla.

"Tell him everything," Starla signs.

"Everything?"

Starla nods tiredly.

And Gia starts more or less at the beginning, leaving out nothing but Thala Coeur. Given that Blackheart's the one who sent Gia to Redrock originally, she's probably a sore subject. But Gia tells Tevi about the mysterious case that came into Jaantzen's possession, which contained a new life form. A creature whose venom apparently super-charges human cells for rapid growth, enabling incredibly fast healing and dulling pain.

"Two nights ago, we broke into the Alliance research site where it had been discovered. There was another one — a bigger one — and I got bit."

She holds up the arm that had originally been mangled. "It healed overnight."

Tevi glances down at the cut on her other arm; it's now a fading scar. "How long ago did you do that?"

"About five minutes before you arrived," Gia says.

"You said it dulled pain. Does it dull all sensation?" Tevi asks. He strokes a hand down her cheek, and when Gia closes her eyes and leans into his touch, Starla doesn't even recognize her. She looks peaceful. Happy. Completely unlike the woman who taught her to fight, who taught her to shoot, who told her it was up to Starla to protect Jaantzen and Manu and the rest of them when Gia left.

Gia's eyes flutter back open, and for a split second Starla sees something in them she's never seen from Gia before. Fear.

"It just happened," Gia says. She sits back; Tevi's hand drifts down to rest on her thigh. "We're still figuring out what all the effects are."

The gentle expression Tevi's watching Gia with darkens when he turns back to Starla. "What was so important to Jaantzen that he put you all in danger?"

"Important to me," Starla corrects, then pulls out her comm because he can't understand her. NOT JAANTZEN, IMPORTANT TO ME. BECAUSE WE HAVE ONE OF THESE ALIENS AND WE NEED TO FIGURE OUT WHAT TO DO WITH IT.

Tevi's eyes go wide. "You have?"

She sets down her coffee and heads for the door, thumbing Tevi after her. He's in this deep, now. Might as well see if he can be helpful.

Lucky is back in his cage, which they've spent part of the morning making sure is secure for real. With what happened to Gia, Starla's not taking any chances letting Lucky wander around unsupervised.

She pushes open the door to Lucky's room and then stands back to let Tevi come in. The cheerfully terrifying little alien is secure behind a forcefield that leaves a faint shimmer in the air, as well as a ballistic-grade mesh panel meant for fast barricading. It rolls up into a fairly light-weight bolt of fabric, but when it's stretched taut over an opening and locked into place, it's nearly impossible to slash or blast through.

Lucky's been trying, though, sharp claws leaving faint

snags in the supposedly unsnaggable fabric. Is he angry that they locked him in here again?

Toshiyo has rigged up a media player for him with simple buttons to page through a collection of vids and music and books, all with subtitles and USL interpreters. Right now a hologram Ayisha Amadule is belting her latest pop number from the player, the sequins on her hijab throwing off brilliant holographic sparks, an interpreter AI signing beside her.

"He's been playing this one on repeat," Toshiyo signs to Starla.

"Of course he has," Starla signs back. "Ayisha's a goddess."

Lucky tilts his head at Tevi when they enter, then lifts his vicious, needle-sharp claws and signs "Good morning."

Tevi's staring. "Did it just . . . ?"

"This is Tevi," Starla signs back. "He's a friend."

Lucky spells Tevi's name and ducks his head happily, baring his triple row of teeth in a grin. Tevi flinches.

"This is Lucky," Toshiyo is telling Tevi. "He's friendly, but we've made him comfortable and treated him well. Unlike the Alliance."

"Theirs was in rough shape," Gia says. "And it was a whole hell of a lot bigger. Maybe they get more cantankerous the older they get."

"We don't know that," Toshiyo says, giving Lucky a worried look.

"We don't know anything," Gia points out.

"We know he likes radishes and fish," says Toshiyo. "And he doesn't like my music."

Starla lifts her chin to Tevi. WE COULD USE MORE

*EYES ON THE DATA WE GOT FROM THE ALLIANCE. LEARN ABOUT LUCKY. FIND CLUES TO HELP GIA.*

Tevi may know nearly everything there is to know about the human body, but eventually they'll need to get a real expert involved — though no one's really an expert on this. Except maybe the Alliance scientists back at Redrock. Starla wonders where their loyalties lie — did they sign up to help with the alien because they love the Alliance? How many are simply serving out an indenture? Who could they turn to their side?

Lucky deserves better than being bumbled around by a motley crew of mostly ex-criminals, but at least he's not being eviscerated for science like his cousin at the Alliance facility. While there may be people better suited to being the first contact for an alien creature, there are also worse fates than spending your days dining on raw fish and dancing to pop music.

Tevi finally tears his gaze away from the creature. "You can't keep this secret forever," he says finally.

*OF COURSE NOT. BUT RIGHT NOW IT'S TOO DANGEROUS TO LET IT GET OUT.*

"I'll do what I can to help." Tevi seems overwhelmed. Starla can relate.

Toshiyo turns to Lucky. "Tevi is going to help us learn about you," she signs.

Lucky gnashes his teeth daintily, then lifts a clawed hand to Tevi. "Lucky," he signs. "Friend."

"Nice to meet you," Tevi signs, fingers rusty, expression saying he can't believe what he's doing.

Lucky glances at Toshiyo, then runs his claws down the ballistic mesh, tilting his head in question. He wants let out; Starla wonders how long he'll be happy not getting what he wants.

"Later, buddy," Toshiyo says and signs. "We'll be right back."

Starla tries to decide if Lucky's upset, but he just gives a little shrug of his leathery wings and hops back from the barricade, returning his attention to the holo-gram of Ayisha Amadule. His head bobs in time with the beat thrumming faintly through Starla's chest.

Back in the hallway, she considers her options. Toshiyo is frowning back at the door, probably worried about Lucky, though there's something sharp in her since the *Coldfire* returned that Starla can't quite put a finger on. Gia looks like she's trying to reassure Tevi, who seems to have short-circuited. Maybe they all need a project to get their minds off their worries. She lifts her chin to Toshiyo. "The data on aliens we got from the Alliance? Show it to them. I'll join you in a few."

It's time to fill Jaantzen in on Gia.

7

------

## PHAERA

Phaera has spent most of the day either sleeping or on calls with V and Hiro to sort things out for the opening of the Devil's Table tonight. The Table is in capable hands — Vanessa could run an event like this in her sleep, and the security is tighter than ever after last night's breach. Hiro's been working with both Oriol and a team from Admant to secure the building not only from the usual kinds of attacks but also the imaginative sorts of things an ex-Alliance agent might think to do. Like scaling a building everyone else thought unscalable.

Before, security at the Devil's Table was impressive. Now it's probably the safest building on the planet.

She wakes from another nap aching and starving and drags herself out of the bedroom. Stops to splash water on her face. A touch of mascara, a few dabs of concealer to pull her complexion back from death's door. When she finally feels up to facing conversation again, she heads out to the kitchen to find Jaantzen signing with Starla via a hologram call. Jaw clenched, brow furrowed. Not a good sign.

She helps herself to leftover takeout, then settles across the table from him when he finishes up the call. "Is everything all right?" she asks.

"I just learned one of my people was injured." He rubs a hand over the back of his neck. "On the mission with Starla."

"I thought you said everyone got home safely."

"Starla wanted to assess the severity of the . . . injury before briefing me."

So not Starla, then. Phaera doesn't think she's met any other of Jaantzen's people who might have been on that mission. "Are they all right?"

His lips press together, but he doesn't answer.

"What happened? Or you can't tell me."

"No," he says slowly.

Phaera tries to ignore the stab of frustration. She reminds herself she isn't owed an explanation, but her throbbing hand, the ring of fire around her neck? She's fucking owed something, isn't she? "It's fine." She stands. She's probably reacting irrationally, but she's had a long week and her nerves are scraped raw. Anyway, she needs to pack if they're going to move to the next safehouse soon. "I understand."

Jaantzen catches her good hand. "I meant no, it's not that," he says softly. "I'm not sure where to start, and I apologize for not articulating that well. I was unsettled by the news."

Phaera lets him pull her back down into the chair, anger fading. She waits.

Jaantzen rubs his jaw as he decides how to say it. "There's an additional . . . element to the story about the Alliance terraforming operation in Redrock which hasn't been released yet. They didn't invent the technology they're using, they discovered it." He clears his throat. "We believe the technology is of nonhuman origin."

Phaera blinks. She didn't hear him correctly.

"Aliens?" She laughs; he nods seriously. "You're kidding." He's obviously not, she's not sure Willem Jaantzen knows how to kid. "How do you know?"

"I told you Coeur stole an item from the Alliance, which the Alliance attacked Cobalt Tower to steal back? It contained a sample." He holds up a hand before she can ask him to clarify. "I'm sorry, I'm not being deliberately imprecise, I just don't know how to say this." He takes a deep breath. "There was an alien embryo in the case, which has since grown into an . . . alien toddler."

Laughter is a wild thing caught in her chest, a fluttering in her heart that could be amusement, could be panic. The idea of aliens existing is absurd enough, but that's not what shocks her. For the last few weeks, as she and Jaantzen have calmly discussed what to do about Acheta, about Leone? Every time they've had dinner or drinks, every time she flirted with him, this morning when they — through all of this, Jaantzen has known there is alien life in the universe, and he hasn't said a word?

Who the hell is this man? She would have let the cat out of the bag in minutes if their roles had been reversed.

"I couldn't say anything earlier." His tone is apologetic. He must be mistaking her stunned silence for anger that he once again had left her out. "No one knew except for my immediate crew. Coeur doesn't even know what she stole." His expression becomes pained. "Although the Redrock prisoners who escaped apparently know the Alliance is using alien technology, and at least two of them have seen the alien the Alliance has in custody in person. So we expect those rumors will be spreading fast."

And he's probably planned for them, analytical mind moving through the possibilities to find the optimum outcome and timing. As he surely did before he decided to tell her the truth. She can't decide if she finds that quality endearing or maddening.

"It's out at the Maraka Valley property?" Her mind is moving too slowly, it takes a moment for what he just said to catch up with her. "The *Alliance* have an alien?"

"At least the one. There could be others. And it — " He sighs. "There's a chance the Dawn liberated it when their prophet escaped from Redrock. It could be anywhere."

Gods. She's not ready to process that. Let's focus on basics. "What's it like?"

Jaantzen frowns, thinking. "Imagine crossing a bat with a cobra, but it's shaped more like a pigeon. And then give it the mouth of a shark. Not completely accurate, but it gives you a sense. Ah, and it has wings."

Her mind's eye is flashing her spectacularly fantastical images, each stranger and more terrifying than the last. "You said toddler," she says, and holds a hand about the height of Calanthe's youngest. "So, this big?"

"Slightly bigger. For now. The alien the Alliance had in custody was closer to three meters."

The latest terrifying image in Phaera's mind balloons from something the size of a friendly Manilan snow hound to a slavering beast that fills the whole hotel room. She shivers, folding her arms over her stomach.

"Can you communicate with it?"

"Starla and Toshiyo have been teaching it USL. We've been studying it when we have time," Jaantzen says, and Phaera barks out a laugh — when have any of them had time? "But the one thing we do know is that its venom" — Phaera's mental image shifts again, giving the creature blood-red fangs inspired by Coeur's own enameled eyetooth — "reacts potently when injected into a human. It either kills us, or somehow spurs cellular regeneration to improve healing powers and reflexes. Gia was bit by the Alliance's alien while in the research facility, and it seems to have produced the second effect."

In her shock at learning about the alien, Phaera had almost forgotten the start of this conversation: One of his people had been injured.

"Dr. Áte?" Phaera blinks at him. The brusque surgeon who treated her mother out in the medical school compound in the desert? The woman had obviously been friendly enough with Jaantzen to help him out when he needed it, but she hadn't seemed like the sort of person who would infiltrate a secret Alliance facility for him.

"She was imprisoned at Redrock for some time," Jaantzen says in explanation. "She knew the area, and she's one of my oldest, most trusted colleagues."

"Is she all right?"

"It's too early to tell. But we think so." He scrubs his hand over the back of his neck once more, leans back in his chair. "Toshiyo calls the creature Lucky."

"Toshiyo?" Her mind casts back for any mention of the name.

"My — she handles our operations."

"Oh." Phaera doesn't think she can absorb any more information right now.

"And apparently Lucky is very into your friend Ayisha's music."

"Oh?" Now the vicious, slavering creature in Phaera's

mind's eye is dancing. She shakes her head to clear the absurd vision away. "I should pack," she says. It sounds like the most sensible thing to do. "If we keep talking about this I'm going to lose what little sanity I have left after this week."

Jaantzen gives her a rueful smile. "I know the feeling," he says. "I'll help you."

There's not much to do; they hadn't brought much with them. Jaantzen gathers her discarded clothing without offering, bringing it to her so she doesn't have to move around much. She's refolding her slouchy old sweatshirt for the third time, trying to get the lines right, when she realizes how futile it is. She's just going to shove it into the overnight bag.

"Cavy called an emergency Casino District Business Association meeting for tomorrow," she says. There's a safe, normal topic. "I plan to go."

Jaantzen's hands still, he doesn't argue.

"Leone will be wondering what happened last night, though she'll assume I'm still alive since the Table's still reopening tonight. Tomorrow's my chance to make sure we have the whole Casino District at our backs, and to give reporters a chance to ask questions about what happened to me. If I push them right, someone's bound to sniff the trail back to Leone."

"See how you're feeling."

She fights down a stab of irritation. "I plan to feel fine."

"I'm sure you will." He gives her a faint smile, though she can tell he doesn't like the idea. "Here. Is this everything?"

She takes the black and white floral scarf from him;

their hands don't touch but she shivers at the way the silk snags on his calloused fingertips as it slides through them. Or she's shivering from the memory of last night, the memory of why she wore this scarf to last night's meeting in the first place.

Or it's something else.

She frowns down at the scarf, trying to place what's off. She brings it to her face, inhaling. It smells like her, and, as always, like the Table: cardamom, orange — but there's something else. Something strange. She'd thought so last night, too, but there'd been so much else going on she hadn't interrogated the feeling.

Tendrils of horror begin to unspool from her gut.

"What's wrong?" Jaantzen asks.

"This scarf," Phaera says. She drops it on the bed, wiping her hands down her thighs. "Vanessa said I left it in the host stand, but I didn't. I haven't worn it in months, so I assumed . . . but it was definitely in my closet last time I looked. I know it was." She tamps down the rising panic — it's over, that nightmare is over. "Tierren brought it to the Table."

The takeout container left in her apartment, the scarf with another woman's scent on it — what else of hers had Tierren touched? How else had she left her subtle mark on Phaera's life? Did she lie in her bed? Try on her clothes? Paw through her belongings? How many more times is Phaera going to find something out of place and wonder if Tierren was there?

She doesn't realize how cold she is until Jaantzen's arms close around her and she lets herself breathe once more.

"She's gone," he murmurs.

Phaera takes a deep breath. "I know." Being here in his arms is calming, but she's going to break down again if she stays. She frees herself from the embrace and snatches the scarf from the bed, then drops it in the trash and washes her hands. It had blood on it, anyway.

Tierren is dead, and Phaera isn't going anywhere.

It's dusk by the time they're ready to leave, and Phaera takes one last look out the window of their suite in the Aterciopelado. At the far end of the drag, the Devil's Table stands in sharp contrast to the glitz around it. The sand-scoured metal facade is lit tonight by spotlights around the base, which throw up cones of light that cast the rough texture in sharp relief. A pair of torches burn blood red on either side of the door, their two-meter flames a come-hither beacon in the night.

And people are coming.

She's been getting messages from Vanessa — it's busier than ever tonight. No one important is arriving via the street entrance; they'll all go through the valet. But still there are crowds gathered at the north end of the drag, people trying to catch a glimpse of the politicians, celebrities, business barons who are going for the reopening.

Phaera should be there.

Not being there feels like giving up, hiding, even though she knows this is a necessary step. And she's exhausted, muscles she didn't even know she had are aching, even breathing hurts. She's incredibly grateful she won't have to put on a good face and pretend everything's fine.

"It's time to go." Jaantzen smooths a hand down her arm; she leans into the touch. "Are you all right?"

The Devil's Table is back in business. Leone couldn't

quench that flame, and she couldn't kill Phaera. They both may take some time to get back to 100 percent, but they're on their way. And she'll be ready for whatever Leone throws her way next.

Phaera smiles.

"I'm perfect."

## 8

## JAANTZEN

He's not offering Phaera much after the opulence of the Aterciopelado, but they'll be protected here. Jaantzen sets their bags on the bed and turns to survey the safehouse — there's not much to take in. The bed is tucked into one corner, the kitchen table and chairs fold up into the wall next to the kitchenette. Cramped but clean, windowless. And bright — Jaantzen dims the lights and the furrow between Phaera's brows smooths in relief.

"Reminds me of my first apartment." Phaera's laugh sounds artificially bright, but more like exhaustion than disappointment with tonight's lodgings. "Just without the ants."

The safehouse is a studio apartment near the university, in an anonymous tower designed for temporary worker housing: People move in and out frequently enough that no one has noticed one of the studios stays empty for years between uses. The security has been enhanced, of course, dampening systems added to all the walls to keep anyone from eavesdropping on the conversations inside.

The sound of a wailing baby vanishes when Phaera shuts the door behind her. Along with the security concerns, the dampening will make for a more restful sleep than anyone else in this crowded building will get.

"How many of these nooks and crannies do you own?" Phaera asks.

"A few." Even before all these recent troubles began, with Coeur and Acheta and Leone, he'd been keeping up his network of safehouses. Old habits die hard. "And if they become compromised, Manu has people he trusts we could turn to. We could sleep in a different bed every night for a month and not exhaust safe places to stay."

Phaera winces. "My neck's killing me even thinking about it."

"You'll be back in your own home soon." If he's still fighting Leone a month from now, he's lost. Maybe Manu's planning for that situation already, but their time in the desert had Manu pacing like a caged lion, and Jaantzen may have hidden it better but he hated it just as much. Both of them are Bulari creatures. Starla might easily find a new life somewhere else, and Toshiyo seems to be comfortable anywhere she has network access and a drift of cast-off electronics to tinker with. But Jaantzen will die before he lets anyone run him out of his city for good. And he suspects Manu will, too.

"When you said the word *safehouse* I imagined a cot in a warehouse out in Jet Park," Phaera says. She folds down the dining set, then sinks onto one of the two chairs, propping her head in her good hand.

"We could find an abandoned warehouse for tomorrow night," Jaantzen jokes, and is rewarded with her faint smile. He lets the faucet run until it stops sputtering, then fills a glass for them both. "If you miss the ants. Where was your first apartment?"

"Just outside the Tamarind. I was working at a cafe on the parkway and thought living near the Tamarind was so posh! But the apartment was completely rundown. And the owner was a creep, only renting out to young girls. He was always knocking on the door to make sure nothing was broken." She takes a long drink of the water Jaantzen hands her. "Plenty was broken, but we all shared notes and told the new girls not to let him in." She laughs. "Ah, first apartments."

"My first real apartment was a room at an extended-stay hotel in Jet Park," Jaantzen says. She hasn't asked, but he's been noticing a pattern since he told her about the orphanage this morning. She acts genuinely curious about his past, but hesitant to probe, as though worried she'll hit a painful memory. His earlier years may have been unorthodox, but they're not riddled with the landmines she seems to be expecting. A few deaths still gleam sharp and dangerous — Tae's, of course, and Paz, his childhood friend he talked into leaving the orphanage, who got killed their first night out on the streets. But he keeps surprising himself by telling stories he hasn't thought of in years.

He could spend more days like this, he decides. More days with her.

"Living in a hotel was a poor financial decision," he says. "I'd just left the crew I was working for after a big score, but I didn't have an income and the hotel was way more than I would've paid to lease a room somewhere. I was almost out of cash by the time I started working for Julieta." He opens cupboards until he finds the minifridge. "I suppose I didn't think much about the future back then."

"Believe me, I didn't think I was going to live to be this age, either," Phaera says. "And I was waiting tables, not whatever it was you were doing."

"For Julieta? Guarding shipments, mostly." And delivering pointed messages when payments were late or suppliers shorted shipments, but he doesn't need Phaera thinking of him as Julieta's enforcer.

"Is that where you lived with Tae?"

Long seconds pass before he realizes he's still holding open the door to the minifridge, not registering what's inside. He calmly pulls out the lone package on the shelf, tells himself to shut the fridge door.

"Seventeenth Street, out by Carama Town," he hears himself say. "A townhouse." One he doesn't want to talk about, and he casts about for a change of topic. "You never married?" He straightens, realizing what he asked. "I'm sorry, I don't mean to pry."

"No, I didn't." Phaera pulls herself to her feet and takes the package gently from his hand, unwraps the contents. "It's been hard to find someone who can keep up with me. Or who doesn't mind that I'm ambitious." She gives him a smile. "And I give you blanket permission to pry. Where's Jade's?"

He doesn't understand what she's asking until she points to the logo on the takeout package. He relaxes slightly, back on firm ground. "It's a cafe downtown," he says. "Ten marks says this is Jade's finest chicken with black bean sauce — I'm not sure Manu knows other takeout options exist. I hope you like garlic."

"Love it."

He finds a pair of plates in the cupboard, a pair of

glasses, and opens the bottle of wine Manu left on the counter. Pours it into the tumblers and hands one to Phaera. She takes it in her good hand and clinks it with his.

"Takeout? Wine in a tumbler? This studio? I feel like I'm twenty again," Phaera says with a sip. "In spirit, anyway. Every bone in my body aches."

"Should we call the doctor?" He's managed not to say anything for hours, but she left him the opening.

Phaera shakes her head. "Nothing is any more wrong than it was this morning. I'm just tired. It'd be nice to sleep in my own bed again."

Jaantzen smiles tightly. "Soon."

Her comm chimes as they're eating, and she brushes fingertips over her gold cuff to read the messages. "Vanessa," she says. "She says a couple of gossip rags showed up sniffing for dirt. Third-string reporters picking over my bones." Phaera flicks a link onto her comm and lays it in front of her, reading through the feed Vanessa sent. "If I'd been thinking more clearly I would've found a way to spin this. But here, they're talking about shoddy paperwork and corruption. 'The Gem of Bulari's Casino District Loses Its Shine.' And these are just the ones from tonight. Can't wait to see what they pull together tomorrow." She sighs. "V says she's been fielding calls all night to talk with me."

"Anyone worth giving an interview to?"

"We need someone who's smart enough to see beyond what I'll be able to tell them," Phaera says. "And I can't just grant an interview. If we want people chasing the story, I can't be easily caught."

"They'll look for you at your home. At the Lorelei."

"Of course. But who's getting creative about it?

Who'll be willing to do the real research? I'll put out some feelers to friends to let me know if any reporters come sniffing around."

Jaantzen scans through the feeds himself for news on the Devil's Table as she types out messages. One reporter, who seems like he has a historic axe to grind, questions if Phaera was too ashamed to show her face at such a lackluster event. But other than the one, the rest of the reviews offer positive takes on the Devil's Table's reopening — if calling Phaera's absence into question.

She's barely touched her wine but at least she's polished off her meal. He doesn't know when she began losing weight, while he was out in the desert, but the sharpness of her cheeks and collarbones has become noticeable.

He reaches for her plate. "It's fine," he says when she stands to help him clean up. "I've got it." She sinks onto the bed with a sigh, curling on top of the blankets. Jaantzen dims the lights even more, then sets the dishes in the sink and wipes down the table, folds it back against the wall.

"Are you still planning on calling Leone tonight?" Phaera asks.

He nods slowly. Leone'll have been stewing all day, with no report from Tierren, wondering what happened last night at the Devil's Table. Wondering if Phaera is dead. If Jaantzen is back in town. Which of her "loyal" friends showed up to conspire against her. And she'll be dealing with the fallout of today's news reports, which will certainly have angered her Alliance friends.

The preparation may have felt like it took ages, but overnight he's wiped out her base of support.

He wants to hear that desperation in her voice, to use

it to gauge his next move — but Phaera's lying on the bed, less than a meter away, broken and bruised, and it'll take everything in his control to keep his calm during this call.

"Do you want to listen?" he asks, hoping the answer is no. "I can go — "

"Absolutely." The set of her jaw is fierce.

Jaantzen sends through the request.

It's a long time before Leone answers, and when she does, she sounds annoyed. Across the room, Phaera closes her eyes. In the dim light, the magenta in her hair is dark, feathering over the pillow. A strand slices across her cheek.

"Hello, Geum-ja," Jaantzen says. Geum-ja, not Madame Justice; being hunted by her has made their relationship feel strangely intimate. She's brought herself down to his level with this fight. Or perhaps elevated him to hers. "I hope I didn't wake you."

"Willem," Leone purrs. "I've been trying to get through to you for days."

"I got one of your messages." His heart is beating slow, steady. "The one you tried to send through Phaera."

A sharp breath on the other end of the line. "Is she all right? What happened?"

Leone must have guessed by the fact that the Devil's Table reopened as planned that Phaera wasn't dead, but she can't know how badly she was injured. Did she scour her network for news? Or did she simply shrug and go about her day?

"She'll live," Jaantzen says. "Despite your woman's best efforts."

"I would never hurt Phaera, you know that," Leone says. With anyone else the note of worry might sound sincere. "Please tell her. That fucking mercenary went off script. I asked her to scare some sense into the girl; she was never supposed to lay a finger on her."

A muscle jumps in Phaera's cheek.

"Your biggest mistake has always been outsourcing your dirty work," Jaantzen says. "It leaves witnesses." Let her think Tierren is still alive and might talk. "You're finished, Geum-ja."

"Am I? This city still needs me. You still need me. Let's talk about how we move past this so we can both prosper."

Phaera's eyes flash open, her gaze locking on his. He has to force himself to relax, to match his breathing to the gentle rise and fall of Phaera's shoulder. Move past ordering Phaera killed? Past murdering Julieta? The pure gall it takes to suggest it is astonishing. But Chief Justice Geum-ja Leone didn't get this far without incredible audacity.

She's made one mistake, though. She assumed Willem Jaantzen was disposable. That Phaera D was disposable.

"I assume you've seen the news today," he says. "As have your Arquellian friends. How did they take it?"

"I'm very impressed," she says smoothly. "I underestimated your thoroughness, and I underestimated how much support you had. We can obviously both land some heavy blows, but I'm not sure beating each other to death is the best thing for this city."

Leone's phrasing is deliberate, and making this call in front of Phaera was a mistake. Fury churns in the pit of his stomach and for a moment all he can see is what Leone meant him to find, Phaera bloodied and lifeless and hanging on the roof of her own building. He blinks and the image is gone, and the real Phaera shifts, and a strand of hair falls across the blinding white bandage on her throat.

"She's desperate," she murmurs.

And allowing her to goad him shifts the power balance back in Leone's favor. Jaantzen calms his heartbeat once more.

"The news that came out today can't be undone," he says. "And I'm sure you're scrambling to reassure your Alliance handlers you can take care of it. But this was only a taste."

"What else do you have?" Leone's voice is a low growl.

"Keep an eye on the news feeds."

A pause. Then, "What's your price, Willem."

Another bit of deliberate phrasing, that subtle emphasis on the word *price*. Jaantzen ignores it. "I want my name cleared, and Manu's. Wipe the warrants, give me proof, and we'll talk about what comes next." The words taste like poison and he forces himself not to look away from Phaera. He waits, each slow heartbeat throbbing in his temple.

"It'll be done." Leone sighs deeply; ice clinks in her glass. "This misunderstanding between us has been bad for Bulari."

"Misunderstanding."

"Come, Willem. You and I both understand something others don't: flexibility. People think their strength is in their rigidity, but take skyscrapers. Bridges. Politicians. A chief justice of the Supreme Court if you will. All will be destroyed in a violent wind or the aftershocks of an earthquake or the chaos of a political scandal unless they know where to give."

"Then you can see the balance of influence has shifted," Jaantzen says. "I can offer *you* a seat at the table."

"You have influence, but if it's power you want, the path still flows through me." Before, he would have thought it an ultimatum, but something has changed about her tone. It's an invitation. "Anyone you want an introduction to, I can make it. You know I have only ever wanted what was best for Phaera, Willem."

Jaantzen forces his jaw to unclench. "Then if I were you, I'd be thinking about what her life is worth to me."

He reaches for his comm, but her voice stops him.

"Zacharia," she says. He doesn't answer. "Willem, are you still there? I can give you Zacharia."

Jaantzen cuts the connection, heart hammering.

Phaera curses and rolls onto her back, splinted hand cradled on her chest. Her eyes are wide, staring at the ceiling. "That fucking bitch."

"'The mercenary went off script.'"

Phaera laughs bitterly. "Tierren made it pretty clear killing me was part of Leone's plan to get to you," she says. "She was thrilled she'd finally been given permission." When she looks back at him, the anger in her face softens. "I'm all right, Jaantzen."

"I know."

"You look like you're about to tear someone apart."

A chill seeps through his gut; this is exactly the side of him he doesn't want her to see. The side that's willing to commit whatever violence is necessary to protect his people. To protect her.

"I am," he says finally. No point in denying it. "If she'd killed you — "

"She didn't. And she won't touch me now. She's desperate, and she sees that she's got to make a deal with you if she wants to maintain even a scrap of her former power." Phaera squeezes the bridge of her nose between the fingers of her good hand. "Plus, she probably still thinks I'll come to my senses and ditch you."

Especially after I almost got you killed, Jaantzen wants to say. He doesn't. They've already had that argument.

"How's your headache?" he asks instead.

Phaera's eyes close as though she's thinking over the question. "Worse? I'm exhausted."

Jaantzen clears his throat. "Let Cavy handle the meeting tomorrow."

She drops the hand from her brow and rolls her head to look at him. "I thought I told you to cut out the machismo bullshit." Her tone is lighthearted, but there's warning in her gaze.

Jaantzen bites back the stab of irritation. He wants to say he's trying to keep her safe, and she . . . is not a woman who will let herself be managed. "I thought you were tired enough I could slip it by you," he says with a faint smile.

"Not a chance." Her expression softens. "I need to be at that meeting."

"And I worry about you being so exposed. Even if you're right about Leone, it's still dangerous for you."

"What does it look like if I go into hiding, Jaantzen? I haven't done anything wrong, but the gossip rags will declare me guilty by sundown tomorrow if I don't show my face. Believe me. I've danced with them on more than one occasion."

And Jaantzen has not. Or if they've ever run anything about him, he hasn't cared. In this game, she knows the rules better than he does.

Doesn't mean he has to like it.

"Oriol stays with you at all times," he says.

"Of course."

"And his backup. I want two people on you." He holds up a hand before she can respond. "Every meeting. In public or private. Phaera, I want them staying with you in your apartment."

He expects her to snap at him once more, but she nods. "I'll make up the guest bed," she says quietly. "Jaantzen. Don't think I'm not taking this seriously. I've never been so terrified in my life. I don't know this world, I only half know what I'm getting into, and I need your help to make sure I'm taking the proper precautions. But I'm not going to sit this out."

He takes a deep breath. "Understood." And he means it. She may not be from his world, but she's proven time and again she's perfectly capable of handling herself in it. She needs his support, not his protection.

"Thank you." She shifts closer to the wall with a wince of pain, making room. "Come to bed."

The bed is less uncomfortable than he expected, though he's not paying it much attention with Phaera's back pressed against his chest, the scent of her hair on the pillow.

"I never thought I'd hear Leone apologize," Phaera says after a time. "For anything, let alone for this."

"Was that an apology? Or is she pulling us deeper into her trap?"

"I think she was being sincere," Phaera says softly. "She knows she underestimated you, and making nice with you is the best way to keep her own power."

"And she thinks I'll look past what she did to you."

"She would take power over loyalty any day, and she

assumes you will, too. She told me as much. She was trying to get into my head at the time, but I think she actually believes you'll drop me as soon as I'm no longer useful."

"She's wrong."

"I know."

After a long time, her breathing becomes soft and even, and he wonders if she's fallen asleep until she finally smooths a hand over his grip on her shoulder. "I'm not going anywhere."

He hadn't realized how tightly he'd been holding her; he lets his hand relax. "I'm sorry."

She begins to softly snore a few minutes later, but it's a long time before Willem Jaantzen is calm enough to sleep.

9

———————

## TOSHIYO

Toshiyo Ravi, who has yet to keep a houseplant alive, is going to help feed a planet.

And she's going to use this burbling vat of weird alien algae to do it. She spent the day figuring out how to replicate the sample Starla brought back from the Alliance research facility, and now she's got the vat set up in one corner of the deathtrap's kitchen. It's an unnatural deep green, glimmering with emerald swirls, like the vivid jungle greens you see in vids — though she's always assumed those are enhanced. There's no way plants get this green, even on Indira.

She'll have to ask Oriol.

This verdant, earthy brew is the key to unlocking the terraforming plans she's been studying. The Alliance discovered the algae in the crashed alien spaceship, along with a variety of chemicals designed to mutate it in the right way to adapt to whatever planet the ship landed on. Need soil with richer nutrients and better water retention? Got it. Better drainage? We can do that too. No soil at all because you landed in a swamp or a vast wasteland of scoured rock? Just grow food in algae mats that float in the water or cling to the rock surface.

The system is designed to be adaptable and easy to implement, since the ship appeared to be driven by autopilot with a crew of dormant embryo clones like the one in the other room that's currently the size of Toshiyo's fist. Landing triggers a clone to begin hatching, and then the ship nourishes the hatchling and runs a series of training programs to teach it how to operate the terraforming equipment. Feed soil samples in here, the ship adjusts the base algae, then instructs the hatchling how to use it.

The Alliance observations suggest that when the planet is considered habitable, the ship is set to automatically hatch more clones and alert the homeworld.

But is there a whole swarm of Lucky's cousins on their way? Probably not, says the Alliance report. The Alliance had to do so much by trial and error because the ship had been too damaged during the crash landing to begin the initial process — the Alliance triggered that accidentally instead when they began messing with the ship. Hence the giant alien clone that bit Gia.

It's too early to see if the algae sample she seeded outside is affecting the soil like the research says it should, but she's tentatively hopeful. After all this time and all this struggle — all her sleepless nights trying to deliver on what Jaantzen has promised the Demosgas — it would be awfully nice to just add the secret alien ingredient and watch everything start working.

Though, as in all things, it's the prep work that makes things go smoothly when the secret ingredient arrives. All her study of the documentation they *did* have meant she knew what to do with the algae sample when Starla brought it home. When Jaantzen and the Demosgas are ready to start talking business for real, everything will be ready.

She hopes.

She turns away from the vat and pours herself another cup of coffee. No one's touched the pot since she was last in the kitchen, which probably means Starla's asleep and it's too late to be drinking coffee — she doesn't bother checking the time.

She's managed to get the terraforming process ironed out today. Now if only she could come up with a way to program the algae to sneak into Leone's house and suffocate her in her sleep, or attack Felipe Zacharia and his band of murdering cultists. Get it to release some sort of poisonous gas, maybe, then seed it around the edges of whatever safehouse Zacharia landed at until it seeps into the walls and smothers all the residents in a cloud of gas so they die writhing, like the workers at Blacklode mine had.

And then they wouldn't be able to kill anyone else.

Toshiyo checks over her work on the algae, makes sure her little makeshift biochemical laboratory in the kitchen is all secured, then fires off a status report to the boss and tentatively checks "Deliver the miracle of terraforming" off her mental to-do list.

That leaves only a handful of other impossible problems on her plate tonight.

Fix Gia. Understand aliens. Destroy the Dawn.

Gia and Tevi are back at the Andel Medical School poring over the Alliance research themselves, so maybe they'll make some progress on the first two problems. She can tackle the third.

Toshiyo tops off her coffee, heads back to her desk, shoos Starla's cat Pepper off her chair, and pulls up a new search.

An idea has been brewing in her mind ever since Starla told her Felipe Zacharia had escaped. The Dawn weren't the only mysterious group interested in the alien serum, were they? Oriol had told her about the two women he met — Sister Kalia and Sister Zahra — who he thought belonged to a splinter group of the Dawn.

Allies? Or yet another threat to Toshiyo's family?

Oriol and Manu had come across Sister Zahra most recently; she'd been in the Dawn's laboratory in that old smelter in Carama Town. She'd been a prisoner of the Bulari remnant of the Dawn, but helping them successfully replicate the alien venom. She told Oriol she didn't trust the Dawn in Bulari, and that she'd sent the successful formula to Felipe Zacharia himself.

She's dead now though, and Toshiyo has no idea how to track down her past. But the other woman, Sister Kalia, had hired Oriol for the job on the *Dorothy Queen* by posting a listing on a merc board, which means she left a trail.

Toshiyo does check the time now — not yet midnight — and figures it's not too late to ping Oriol. He gets back to her right away with the exact merc board Kalia used, and she calls up the site.

Toshiyo used to scan the merc boards regularly to keep tabs on who might have a grudge on the boss, though she's fallen out of the habit. If she'd kept it up, she thinks bitterly, she might have caught wind of Leone hiring a headhunter like Tierren and saved some lives.

Every site wipes the listings once they're filled — from the public area, at least. It's not much of a challenge for Toshiyo to sift through the back end of the site and find the old listing and the profile information of the woman who'd posted *WANTED, SECURITY FOR A SHORT TRIP TO THE DOROTHY QUEEN. EXCELLENT PAY.*

Kalia White.

She's dead now, too. Killed on the *Dorothy Queen* by Bennion Zacharia after she tried to steal the terraforming plans some Alliance scientist was trying to sell to Aiax Demosga. Which Oriol eventually brought home to Jaantzen instead. The same plans Toshiyo has been studying for weeks.

Kalia may be dead, but her profile is still active. Whoever's using it has been hiring other mercenaries since the job on the *Dorothy Queen*, all off-planet. Two bodyguards for a trip to Corusca, a small crew for a run out into Durga's Belt, and a headhunter for some business in Arquelle.

Toshiyo feeds Kalia's scant profile information into an AI and sets it to scour the usual haunts, but after nearly an hour the search results are still zero.

That's hard to do.

Puzzled, Toshiyo tries a different tactic. Starla's been digging into the Dawn holy texts and has pulled out passages that have to do with the Fallen or the Gift of the Fallen — Zacharia's name for the aliens and their venom. Toshiyo feeds those passages into a search.

She's about to call it a night when one of her searches hits the jackpot. A few choice quotes from Felipe Zacharia's ravings, originally posted in a thread on a secured messaging platform. Toshiyo's search never would have penetrated that platform, but someone had copied out the thread and sent it on as an unsecured message her searches were able to read.

Toshiyo scans through the thread, her excitement growing. In it, people calling themselves Sister and Brother So-and-So are arguing about exactly what allows someone to survive the ordeal of being injected with alien venom. Or, the Trial of the Fallen, as they like to call it. It's instantly clear this group isn't the Dawn — they have a pretty low opinion of those "backwards, bloodthirsty zealots."

No, these folks call themselves the White Star.

Toshiyo smiles. And here's the login page to their secure messaging platform.

Perfect.

Toshiyo slips a bitter tab under her tongue and head-phones over her ears to sharpen her flagging attention, hacks into the secure platform in minutes.

She scans conversation threads, frowning.

There, mentions of Sister Kalia, Sister Zahra, both gone on to their reward. Oriol had thought they were from a splinter group who'd broken away from the Dawn, but to Toshiyo it sounds like they'd already known about the aliens before they discovered Felipe Zacharia's writings and decided to adopt them.

But while they like Zacharia, they really don't agree with what his followers are doing in Bulari. A misguided flock, led astray by Zacharia's brother and by the "priest" who took over from him. A guy named — ha! Toshiyo checks "Find out who succeeded Bennion Zacharia" off her mental to-do list.

Thomas Deté.

She opens a new search for the priest's name and sends out her crawlers, then dives back into the threads.

Could these White Star folks be allies?

After all, they seem intent on stopping the Dawn from carrying out their plan to poison everyone. But they're awfully happy about Felipe Zacharia escaping from prison. Lots of "Our teacher is free, he has come home. He will clean up the divided house his brother built and lead all the Dawn to enlightenment."

Seriously?

Toshiyo's read Zacharia's texts, same as the White Star, and she thinks he comes off as deranged. Megalomaniacal. He claims only he can save the world, only he knows the truth — and this group is eating it up with a spoon. Wild.

Her crawlers have brought back some information on the priest Thomas Deté, but nothing that points to his current location. She'll dive deeper later. For now, she writes up a quick note to the boss and Manu letting them know about White Star and Deté in case it helps. She can keep looking, but Manu might be able to send out some feelers through his physical network of contacts.

She's still buzzed, but the threads on the message board are starting to get repetitive. Maybe she can track down some of these people outside the board?

She picks a few of the most fervent users and feeds their profile information into a search. Soon she's managed to track down a handful of matching profiles in the greater network — including one that seems to be based in Bulari. On the White Star board they call themselves GraySeeker, and they're one of the more rational voices of the bunch.

Another half-dozen social profiles in the wider network match GraySeeker's signature, and running those profiles through a program to match for writing style and common phrases makes her confident she's found the right person.

One of the profiles is on a public conspiracy theory message board where GraySeeker is a regular commenter. Toshiyo skims through a handful of posts to get a feel for which ones are GraySeeker comment bait, then crafts her message carefully.

SORRY IF THIS ISN'T THE RIGHT PLACE TO POST, BUT I DON'T KNOW WHERE ELSE TO GO. MY PARENTS WON'T LET ME COME HOME AND I CAN'T TRUST ANYONE I USED TO KNOW. IT'S A LONG STORY AND YOU'LL PROBABLY ALL THINK I'M CRAZY. BUT I WAS IN THIS . . . I THINK YOU WOULD CALL IT A CULT. I DON'T KNOW. THEY BELIEVED IN ALL SORTS OF CRAZY THINGS, LIKE ALIENS, BUT REALLY IT WAS JUST A FRONT TO MAKE DRUGS. I DON'T KNOW, IT ALL MADE SENSE AT FIRST, BUT NOW I FEEL SO STUPID.

OBVIOUSLY THIS IS A THROWAWAY ACCOUNT. BUT I NEED TO GET THIS OFF MY CHEST. I CAN'T TALK TO ANYONE ABOUT IT HERE, I'M AFRAID THEY'LL TAKE ME BACK OUT TO THE DESERT. BUT SOMEHOW I THOUGHT YOU ALL WOULD UNDERSTAND.

She pushes Post, then sits back and cracks her ring fingers.

Is that the right amount of detail to pique GraySeeker's interest and make them think the poster is a refugee from the Dawn? GraySeeker has leapt at the chance to talk about the Dawn on this board in the past. If Toshiyo can strike up a conversation with them, maybe it will help her get more insight into where Felipe Zacharia and his band of murderers ended up.

And if she pushes herself hard enough, maybe she'll

be able to find them before they can kill any more inno-cent people.

She's gone too far tonight, though. She's crashing as both the tab and the coffee start to wear off, so she shuts down her desk and slips across the hall to the conference room, where she throws a familiar vid on the holopro-jector to distract her thoughts as she falls asleep.

## 10

# PHAERA

"Ayisha's is one of the few places on the drag I haven't actually worked," says Phaera, continuing the meandering monologue she's been at since the cab dropped her and her bodyguards off in front of Ayisha's Palace. The warning look Oriol gives her says he knows it's nervous chatter, but she ignores him. Even though they're not alone today.

This morning he showed up at the safehouse with backup, an imposing woman with broad shoulders, short dark hair slicked back out of her eyes, and biceps bulging against her suit jacket. Mel Nehrusitha is even stonier than Oriol, and maybe Jaantzen would be showing a new bodyguard an unbothered mask, but that's not Phaera's style.

Besides. Oriol knows her well enough by now — knows how she acts in front of her people. He wouldn't have brought on someone who needed to be impressed by some bullshit false front from their new employer.

And that's a good thing, because Phaera D is nervous as hell.

She takes a moment, tells herself she's stopping to admire the view from the second floor of Ayisha's. They're standing on the invitation-only promenade overlooking the dance floor and the stage; it's popular with elites who want to enjoy the big-name acts Ayisha brings in without having to rub elbows with the sweaty dancers below. The view's showpiece is the Teardrop Bar, suspended over the center of the dance floor and veiled with layered strands of crystal beads that scatter brilliant rainbow sparks across the scene below. Crystal strands curtain the balcony Phaera's standing on, too, like she's suspended in a glass of champagne.

Ayisha called her this morning to say she didn't need to come to the meeting, which means Cavy told her something of what happened night before last at the Devil's Table. But Phaera's not staying away. Cavy's assembled the Casino District Business Association to talk about the list of Alliance companies paying bribes to make the trade agreement go through — including Silver Dice, the Arquellian casino chain Phaera already edged out of town once. Phaera needs to remind her colleagues she led them in this fight before.

Leone won't physically touch her again, and in Phaera's mind, this fight has already moved beyond Leone. Sure, she can still make their lives miserable. But right now they need to stay ahead of the greater fallout coming from the trade agreement they've shattered. To unify New Sarjun against hostile takeover.

And Phaera will be damned if she misses a chance to make herself an integral part of this historic fight.

She spent an hour in front of a mirror this morning trying to correct the effects of several exhausting, stressful weeks and minimize the bruise on her cheekbone. But she can't do anything about the mottled discoloration on her hand, partly obscured by the brace. Or her throat — she still hasn't dared peel back the bandage, but violent black bruising peeks beyond the edges.

She'll just have to bring scarves back into fashion. She's started trends before.

"Phaera."

Oriol touches her arm and she suddenly realizes how fast she's breathing. She stops and straightens, takes a deep breath to slow her pulse.

"I'm all right," she says.

Mel Nehrusitha glances at her, then goes back to scanning the room. Oriol studies Phaera, gaze sweeping head to toe: navy-blue dress flaring out at the hips, silk moiré scarf in shimmering cream. Finally he nods.

"Eyelash," he says, touching his right cheek. Phaera brushes fingertips over her own. "Looks like you're ready for battle, ma'am."

Phaera straightens her shoulders. The last time she saw most other members of the business association, she was knocking down their doors to get them to stand at her side while Levi Acheta terrorized the Casino District. Since then, Leone's done her best to drag Phaera's name through the mud; whether she's been avoiding them or they've been avoiding her is difficult to say. Still, she fought for years to earn their respect, to get them to stop thinking of her as a bartender or dealer on their payroll and instead as their peer. Years of work that are threatening to crumble, but this, at least, is a fight she knows she can handle.

She pushes open the door to the conference room before she has any more time for second thoughts.

The room falls silent for two heartbeats.

"Phaera!" Ayisha hurries to embraces her in a rustle of fabric and bangles, the gold threads edging her silk hijab scratchy against Phaera's cheek. Ayisha's hugs can crush bone, but today she holds Phaera gingerly. Concern flashes in her dark eyes as she lets Phaera go, but she doesn't make a fuss. She's a show woman, too. "We're waiting on a few more."

A few chairs still stand empty around the table, and Wiljo Cavenaugh pats the one next to him with a gnarled brown hand when she catches his eye.

There are other immediately friendly faces: Dal Jaxon and his counterpart in the service workers union, M.J. Gutierrez. Phaera gives them a wave with her good hand and lets herself breathe out. Ayisha's exuberant greeting, Cavy saving her a seat at his side, the easy friendliness from Jaxon and Gutierrez; her closest allies here are still visibly standing with her. She makes her way around the table to Cavy, greeting the other usual suspects who have already arrived — casino and nightclub owners, trade organization representatives — and noting who seems pleased to see her and who's listening to the rumors Leone's been spreading about her.

It's a mixed bag. Janvier Ibn Rushd, Cavy's business partner at the Aterciopelado, and Angeliq Shaw, owner of the Horus, both greet her delicately — neither had the backbone to stand against Acheta. Herran Tarri, owner of the casino next door to the Lorelei, ignores her greeting to continue his conversation with the owner of a string of boutiques, who waves awkwardly at Phaera while pretending to listen. The owner of a local restaurant chain pointedly turns away when Phaera calls her name, but they've clashed for years, since Phaera worked for the service workers union. Luz Orveto of Orveto's Thousands wavers with indecision before finally returning her greeting with a sharp nod.

The stragglers arrive while Phaera is making the rounds. She sits down, and Cavy raises his hands to get things started; gold rings flash on every finger. Today he's wearing a burnt-orange suit over a teal silk shirt, twin silver braids framing his face. Phaera sinks into the chair beside him, grateful to have the attention finally off her.

"Thank you all for coming on such short notice," Cavy says. "I assume by now you've all seen the news that certain officials in our government have taken kickbacks from Alliance corporations in exchange for letting through a trade agreement stacked against New Sarjunian businesses."

Murmurs of assent hum around the room. Even if someone had missed the media blitz from yesterday morning, the entire city is buzzing with energy today. Protesters are gathering in front of the Alliance embassy, Phaera's cab took the long way here to avoid them.

"I forwarded you all a list of companies allegedly giving kickbacks," Cavy says; he pulls the list up on the conference table now. "And you may have noticed a familiar name."

"Silver Dice," says Angeliq Shaw with disgust. She may not have stood up against Acheta, but she'd been one of Phaera's most reliable allies in the fight to keep Silver Dice out of Bulari. And the battle-ready look she shoots Phaera now says she's ready to wade into the fray again.

"Silver Dice," agrees Cavy. "Key players within our government have chosen to elevate foreign competitors over our own endeavors, and we must keep them accountable. I have drafted an open letter to Prime Minister Nikolas de Grazal from the Casino District Business

Association calling for an immediate cessation of trade agreement talks. All of you have received a copy. I'm open to feedback and recommendations, but my goal is to end this meeting with every one of your signatures on this document."

Silence falls as everyone leans in to read the document that appears in front of them on the conference table. Phaera read drafts as Cavy worked on it yesterday, but she skims it once more anyway. And clenches her jaw at the predictable grumble coming from the other end of the table: Herran Tarri, grousing to the boutique owner beside him.

"Do you have something you'd like to add, Herran?" Cavy finally asks.

Tarri straightens. "I do. It's an excellent letter. But some of us are a little concerned it won't be taken seriously if we allow anyone to sign it." He's not looking at Phaera when he says it, but the boutique owner darts a glance her way — and she's not the only one.

"Point taken," Angeliq says acidly. "Maybe you shouldn't, then."

A few of the others laugh. Spots of color burn in Tarri's cheeks, and as much as Phaera appreciates Angeliq's tacit support, antagonizing Herran Tarri won't do them any good.

"I'm concerned about particular members of our association dragging down our image," Tarri says to Cavy. "In particular, Ms. Harris's lack of business experience is a problem."

"I wouldn't call bootstrapping one successful casino well enough to buy a second one a lack of business experience," Phaera says drily.

"You're certainly good at flashing around your money."

"Herran!" Ayisha gives him an arch look.

"I'm happy to open my books at any time," says Phaera.

"So we can see how you're laundering your boyfriend's shard money?"

A clamor goes up around the table, but Tarri's booming voice remains the loudest. "Why else do you think Acheta shot up the Lorelei? Why do you think the Devil's Table got shut down?"

"Enough!" Ayisha's soprano cuts through the din, her voice trained to reach all the way to the back of the noisiest club. "Herran, hon, be careful about throwing around accusations."

"You don't think it's the truth?" Tarri lifts his chin and looks around the room. "Phaera Harris may have pluck, but she's brought down the quality of our industry since she got airs and thought a waitress could open a casino. You can all agree business is down."

"Oh, is business down, Herran?" Phaera can't raise her voice above a hoarse whisper right now, but the way Tarri's glare deepens, he heard her anyway. "Maybe people are getting bored of your cage fights and looking for something a little more entertaining."

He'd ignored her when she opened the Devil's Table — it was at the far end of the drag and didn't share a clientele with the sort of person who spent their money at his casino. But when she'd opened the Lorelei right next door, Tarri had become her most vocal opponent. She knows she's drawn away business, but that's how the game is played. He could have changed things up, brought in better entertainment, listened to the market, remodeled his dingy, out-of-date cavern. But, no. He'd chosen to fixate on driving Phaera out instead.

Before today she'd been able to laugh it off. But between the attacks against her by Acheta and then Leone and the false accusations against Jaantzen, he's gaining support Phaera can't afford to ignore.

"Do you have a motion to make, Herran?" Cavy says. "Because this is not the forum for slinging baseless accusations."

"I do." Tarri stands, taking the time to tug his sleeves into place. The room goes silent, all eyes on him. "I motion that Phaera Harris be formally removed from the association for illegal misconduct, and because her underworld associations threaten the safety of the rest of the drag."

"Acheta came after all of us," Phaera snaps. "He fixated on me because I refused to pay the protection fee he wanted — unlike some people in this room. Paying money to a criminal organization for protection? That's illegal misconduct."

She notes the averted eyes around her. Herran Tarri wasn't alone in picking the easy road of paying the bribe over fighting back. Angeliq and Ibn Rushd had done it. Even Cavy and Ayisha had wanted to go that route.

"I have fought time and again for our neighborhood," Phaera says, cursing the hoarseness of her voice. "As a member of this association, and through the service workers union back when I worked in a casino instead of owning one, as Herran is so fond of pointing out. I have defended your businesses from bad laws. From unfair competitors. From a violent criminal organization. And I know I've rubbed some of you the wrong way, but if being pushy and opinionated isn't the number one qualification for sitting at this table, I think we're all in the wrong group."

She gets laughs around the table, and the knot of anxiety in her chest loosens a touch. "And maybe I turned to Willem Jaantzen for help with Acheta when I couldn't find it in this room. And maybe he's got underworld ties. But what does that matter, in this room. For fuck's sake, Herran, everyone knows you contract with that Jet Park crew to collect your debts."

"The Young Emperors," Angeliq says helpfully. Someone else laughs; Phaera doesn't see who.

She leans back in her chair and waves her good hand impatiently for Cavy to go on.

"The motion stands." Cavy's face is a mask of disapproval. "Do we have a second?"

Silence for a long time before someone clears their throat. "I second."

Janvier Ibn Rushd wasn't meeting her gaze before, and now that he is, Phaera can't read his expression. Cavy raises an eyebrow at his business partner, but Phaera's not shocked. While Cavy has always seen the Devil's Table's competition with the Aterciopelado as healthy for them both, Ibn Rushd would love to see the Table shut down for good.

"This is ridiculous," snaps Ayisha, but Cavy holds up a hand.

"Then it's a vote," he says. "I'll abstain unless there's a tie. All in favor of Herran's motion to remove Phaera from the association?"

There are more hands than Phaera would have expected, and worry squeezes her heart with every one that goes up. Tarri, Ibn Rushd, three of the smaller casino owners, the director of the street performers' guild. And of course the owner of the local restaurant chain who'd had a bad relationship with Phaera since she was with the union.

Cavy surveys the group with a frown, waiting for the final hands to tentatively rise.

"All against?" he asks.

Hands rise more enthusiastically. Ayisha, Angeliq, the owner of the boutique chain who's sitting beside Tarri; she raises her hand and ignores his glare. Dal Jaxon and M.J. Gutierrez both raise their hands defiantly in her support. Luz Orveto, who's been respected in this business longer than Phaera's been alive. Another half-dozen hands from the owners of casinos, restaurants, hotels.

Phaera breathes a sigh of relief, doesn't let her mask slip.

"Good," says Cavy impatiently. He nods to her, then gives Tarri an irritated look. "Now that that nonsense is over, I'd like to talk about the real threat to our businesses: Silver Dice."

Minor debate around the language of the agreement follows, but no one's going to argue the need to sign it. Maybe everyone wasn't as fired up as Phaera that Silver Dice needed to be kept off the drag last year, but now they're all furious that New Sarjunian officials are taking bribes from Alliance competitors to local companies. Other industry and neighborhood associations have already released their own scathing demands for the trade agreement talks to be halted, immediately, and the Casino District Business Association needs to follow.

Phaera's ready to crash by the time the last of the logistics are finished. The painkillers she took before the meeting are starting to wear off, the adrenaline from Herran Tarri's attack left her shaky. And she's starving, even though she ate breakfast not too long ago. Her appetite finally returning? Or maybe her healing body is forcing her to find food appealing in order to get the energy it needs.

Or maybe what's been missing is this heady feeling of winning, of being tested and shooting down those who don't believe in her. The last week had been setback after setback, and the anxious waiting had ground her down. But now? She survived Tarri. She survived fucking *Tierren*, and she's not only going to survive Leone, she's going to use this to thrive.

Phaera D is about to have her day in the sun.

Dal Jaxon catches her before she can get to the door "How you holding up, Fay?" he asks quietly. His gaze flickers to the scarf around her throat and she adjusts it self-consciously before she catches herself. She lets her hand fall back to her side. Casual. Comfortable.

She wants to make a joke — I've felt worse — but she hasn't. Physically, mentally, socially, she can't think of a time that compares to what she's going through now. The PR smear campaign Silver Dice threw against her last year had pushed her until she was physically ill. But no one had really believed them — they were outsiders. She'd been their target, but everyone was their enemy.

And they hadn't tried to assassinate her.

"I'm doing better," she says finally. "I'm tired." She'd say more, but M.J. Gutierrez has come over. They reach to shake Phaera's hand, startle when Phaera offers her uninjured left. Gutierrez's eyes harden at the brace and bruising on Phaera's right hand.

"Jaxon said the assholes who are behind this anti-business, anti-union trade agreement tried to shut you down the other night," Gutierrez says. Phaera nods in agreement; it's true. "Let me know how we can help, you know the union's with you."

"Thank you."

"And Wagner at the space terminal workers' union is ready to apply more pressure if letter-writing doesn't work. Also?" Jaxon gives Phaera a conspiratorial look. "Wanted to let you know a reporter's been calling me about you. She's trying to track down why you weren't at the opening last night, and she got wind it was an anti-union intimidation thing. I may have let her know you'd be at this meeting."

"Thanks, Jaxon."

"Any time."

"Walk me out? It wouldn't hurt right now for me to be seen with a representative of the workers instead of with the bosses."

The spindly man grins. "Feel like I'm being used, Fay."

Phaera smiles back. "You know the game as well as I do." She looks at Gutierrez. "Are you coming?"

Gutierrez shakes their head. "I need to lodge a formal complaint with Cavy about Herran's bullshit claim that 'used to be a waitress' is grounds for disenfranchisement from the business association."

Phaera escapes with a brief hug from Ayisha and a promise to catch up, then makes her way out of the Palace with Jaxon at her side, Oriol and Mel trailing behind. They cut through Ayisha's dance floor, where early revelers and devotees of the opening band are starting to congregate. In the ambient pre-show music, the shivering crystal strands draped around the Teardrop Bar chime faintly. Rotating lights spark and shimmer in the beads.

Someday Phaera's going to be able to come and enjoy

a show here again without feeling like there's a target on her back.

"You need a ride somewhere, Fay?" Jaxon asks once they're outside. He reaches for the door of the first spinner at the union stand, but before Phaera can answer, someone's yelling her name.

"Phaera? Ms. Phaera?"

She ignores the voice, the clatter of heels on tile as someone runs towards her.

"She's unavailable for comment," says Oriol behind her.

Phaera glances over her shoulder. He's blocking a young woman, a drone at her shoulder, branded for her feed and pulsing red to indicate it's recording. Phaera recognizes the feed — it's one of the gossip rags, one that's had a particular grudge against her over the years. Odd that a RaYa reporter would be the one to do the work of digging for her connection with Jaxon; their feed is better known for lazy hatchet jobs.

"Ms. Phaera!" the reporter calls. "Last night at the Table, they said you missed the opening because you were sick. But my source says you were injured in an assassination attempt the night before. Is that true?"

Oriol is between her and the reporter, a wall of muscle. The girl tries to get around him and his hand closes gently but firmly around her arm, holding her away from Phaera.

"She's not available — "

"Who's your source?" Phaera turns around and the girl — and her drone — get a good look at the bruise on her cheek, the mottled black bruising beneath her slipping scarf. The girl's eyes widen, a touch of shock, but mostly delight. The knowledge that her bet paid off.

"I can't reveal my source," she says, serious once more. "But is it true someone tried to assassinate you because of your association with Willem Jaantzen?"

Right to the trap questions. Which are the perfect place to lay her own bait.

"I do have a comment," Phaera says, and the drone edges forward. Oriol's grip on the girl's arm doesn't loosen. He glares at the drone like he's about to crush it in his bare fist.

Phaera lifts her chin, gaze boring into the reporter's own. "I'm from Bulari, born and raised. I love my city, I've always fought for it, and it will take more than a black eye and broken hand to get me to back down and let outside corporations make this city their playground."

"What does this have to do with the trade agreement?" the reporter calls after her, but now Jaxon's shutting the door to the cab.

"Don't you read the news, love?" Phaera can't make out the rest of Jaxon's response as he shields her from the reporter's view. But by the way he's gesturing, he's about to give her a hell of a quote himself. The drone banks up for an aerial as Oriol and Mel both get in and the driver peels away from the curb.

Mel's mouth is set in a serious line, but Oriol's laughing. "You made her week."

"I made her career," Phaera says. "All the other gossip rags have been calling me all day trying to find out why I wasn't at the reopening last night, but none of them asked about the attempt on my life." She likes the phrasing, it's clinical. Unemotional. "She tracked down Jaxon and scored."

Which hopefully means she's the sort of reporter you can throw a line to and might dig into it rather than splicing it into a fluff piece. Phaera is curious to see what kind of context the girl will manage to find about Phaera's "fight for Bulari" by the time the story airs.

"Where to, Ms. Phaera?" asks the driver.

Phaera sinks back into the seat. She knows Leone was sincere in her apology to Jaantzen last night, which means Phaera isn't in danger. And Tierren is dead. She's not going to take the risk of staying in her unsecured apartment, but she can at least run by and pack up a few things.

She gives her address.

"Home."

## 11

## JAANTZEN

The sign on the front door says Closed. Jaantzen walks in anyway, Manu a step behind him.

It's one of those stores unique to the Fingers that sells a bit of everything. Groceries, battery packs, water filters, toiletries — everything bought on closeout and sold cheap until it's gone. This month they must've gotten a great deal on novelty-print dust masks, because they're stacked up in front of the register at a good discount next to a display of saint medallions. It smells like fresh-brewed coffee, cinnamon, earthy barbecue.

The man behind the register straightens when he recognizes Jaantzen, then points wordlessly to the back.

They're inside the boundaries of Altamira, far enough that the BPD doesn't bother patrolling. Not even to get their hands on Bulari's current number one most wanted, Thala Coeur. There was talk of a blockade earlier this week, before the fierce public backlash forced Mayor Hu to issue an apology. Now the neighborhood is humming with fresh signs of uprising, from grassroots anti-police graffiti everywhere to a more organized campaign of holographic signs in windows proclaiming Keep Altamira Free. The police wouldn't have stood a chance blockading Altamira, even before the protests at the Alliance embassy called for all hands on deck there.

Though Blackheart is definitely still on their minds.

Just this morning he saw an interview with the chief of police skirting delicately around the Coeur problem. "We know where she is, we're keeping tabs on her," he'd said — like anyone believes that. There have been public calls for her to turn herself in, but not in the Fingers. Because along with the anti-police graffiti are tags Jaantzen has never seen before, though he knows what they mean. Everyone must know. Some are secret and small, some emblazoned across buildings. Some are carefully cut stencils with paint dripping down like blood, some hastily drawn marker sketches.

All are new: a black heart stabbed through with a dagger.

If that graffiti were only being found in Coeur's home territory, it would be one thing. But Manu's said he's seen the tags in Carama Town. They're all over Jet City. And Jaantzen saw one scrawled on a utility box downtown. The police are going to have more than a riot on their hands if they try to do anything about Blackheart. And not just in the neighborhoods under Coeur's direct control.

Jaantzen pushes through the store's back door to find a tiny plaza formed by a few apartment buildings butting up against each other. Colorful sheets are strung between the buildings to provide shade from the sun. Planters full of bright, healthy flowers and trellises covered in trailing vines add a touch of coolness to the air. The day is already hot, but the tiny plaza is cool. Hidden fans stir the breeze.

Even the rush of traffic is a distant hum, and an ornate cage with songbirds sits in one corner, their songs providing a melodic air.

Thala Coeur is lounging at a corner table with a good view of the entrance, Aden Damyati at her side. The plaza is otherwise empty but for a pair of her soldiers sitting a good distance away. Jaantzen gives them a respectful nod. They return it.

She's looking better. The burn scars on her cheeks are losing their angry redness, she's gained some weight, and though her bones are still pronounced, they're no longer jutting through her skin. Her hands are still encased in therapeutic gloves; a silver-headed cane leans against the table beside her.

She lifts a hand in greeting when she sees Jaantzen, but doesn't offer it to him. Jaantzen shakes Damyati's.

There are four chairs at the table, but Manu doesn't join them, he settles on a crate over Coeur's shoulder with an eye on Jaantzen, an eye on Damyati, an eye on Coeur's soldiers across the courtyard. Someone who hadn't watched him fidgeting in the spinner on the way here might not notice the tension in his jaw now, even as he lounges back against the wall. Coeur greets Manu, then ignores him. Damyati shifts to keep him in view.

"You want a gin?" Coeur asks as Jaantzen sits. "They make their own."

"Coffee. Thank you."

Coeur lifts her chin and a child who can't be more than six comes running over to the table. "Four coffees and some of your mama's lumpia," she says, and the kid scampers back into the store. "Best lumpia you'll find off Indira," Coeur tells Jaantzen.

"I'm sure. Thank you for taking in the Redrock prisoners."

"I should be thanking you. A good handful used to work for me."

"Then I suppose they've debriefed you."

It's the main reason he asked for this meeting. Before they made the decision to send the prisoners on to Coeur, Starla told him some knew about the alien technology. Jaantzen assumed rumors would get to Coeur, fast. And the way she laughs at his question? He assumed correctly.

"They've got some crazy stories, Willem." She tilts her head, piercing him with eyes as sharp as obsidian blades. "About what the Alliance is really doing up there. Don't suppose you know anything about that?"

"I do. Thanks to you."

Coeur raises an expectant eyebrow.

"The cases you stole from the Alliance. Only one was destroyed when I killed Bennion Zacharia."

Coeur leans forward, voice low and dangerous though there's still a smile on her lips. "And what. The fuck. Was in the other case."

Describing it is impossible, as Jaantzen found with Phaera this morning. Instead, he pulls out his comm and passes it across the table, open to a picture of Lucky. Jaantzen's grown to recognize the creature's wings-spread, teeth-bared pose as glee that Toshiyo is bringing him another fish, but to the unfamiliar it's horrifying.

Coeur's eyes go wide. Damyati leans in and lets out a stream of unholy obscenities.

"It's grown by two to three times since we discovered it in the case," says Jaantzen. "We believe the cases are some sort of incubation device."

Suddenly Coeur looks up, lays her gloved hand flat

over Jaantzen's comm to hide the image. The kid's back with four tiny coffee cups and a tray of greasy fried rolls piled around a creamy orange sauce, then off to the store once more.

Coeur waits three heartbeats after the kid leaves before she lifts her hand to take one last look at the image of Lucky. She slides Jaantzen's comm back across the table and reaches for a piece of lumpia. "Careful of the sauce," she says. "It packs a punch." She leans back in her chair, chewing thoughtfully.

"The Alliance knows they exist," says Jaantzen. "We know. And now you know."

"Aiax and Lhasa?"

"I haven't shared this with them yet." He takes a sip of his coffee; it's thick, and rich with cinnamon and cayenne. The secret's getting out sooner rather than later, and the key to getting ahead of this with Coeur is to play to her pride. Honor her role in all this by coming here first. She'll respect the need to keep something secret, but she won't appreciate being the last one in the dark.

It seems to be working, Coeur shakes her head and laughs. "You have an honest-to-god alien and you've managed to keep it a secret for weeks. And managed to keep the Alliance from killing you. People underestimate you."

"You've learned that lesson the hard way," Jaantzen says mildly. "Several times."

She shrugs a bony shoulder. "What's your plan for it?"

If he knew, it would put another ten years back on his life. But he's not here for Coeur's advice.

"We got the last piece of the puzzle we need to go ahead with the food production business with the Demosgas," he says, and her lips quirk to the side at the deflection. "If all goes well, we'll be ready to hire the first wave of your people by next week. Lhasa's got concrete numbers and the positions we'll need filled. I'd like to get the four of us together in one place soon to talk this over."

"Maybe once there's not a price on your head."

"Or yours, Thala. I'm taking care of Leone, and the trade agreement. But it's going to be harder if this city erupts like a powder keg."

"People in this town like to riot," she says. "Only way to make your voice heard sometimes." She gives him an amused look. "I didn't instigate anything, if that's what you're implying. People were already mad before they found out the government has been selling their kin to Alliance prison camps."

"So we let the city burn?"

"Not everybody can get together with their business buddies in a penthouse and sign petitions," she says. "They still deserve to be heard."

"And you know how poorly that message is received when things get too far out of hand."

"Sounds like a problem for the mayor." When Jaantzen doesn't answer, Coeur drops the teasing smile and lifts her chin to Damyati. "Spread the word things need to calm the fuck down." Damyati pulls out his comm and begins typing.

Good. That will ease the pressure somewhat, allow him to keep the conversation focused on what Leone and her Alliance friends did, rather than on the public response.

He takes another sip of his coffee. "There's another problem I could use your help with."

"Is there?" Razors are hidden under the slow drawl of

those words. Jaantzen tenses. "Do you have another request, Willem? It feel good, telling everyone Blackheart's your errand girl?"

She drums her fingers and Manu shifts, ready for whatever she's about to pull. Damyati does, too, and if these two start shooting, the soldiers across the way will. The wildness in Coeur's eye says she doesn't much care which way things fall.

"Did you call us here planning to get into a shootout?" Jaantzen's pulse is a slow pound in his ears. "Or are you picking fights out of habit?"

Two long breaths, and a smile tugs at the corner of her mouth. But her people don't stand down.

"Thala."

Coeur laughs and reaches for another piece of lumpia, leans back in her chair. "Relax, Juric," she says without looking back at Manu. "I'm just messing with you."

She's not, though. Jaantzen may have defused the situation, but she got her message across. The offer of jobs and involvement in this plan with the Demosgas might have whet her appetite, but she's not on Jaantzen's payroll. He needs to be more mindful how he frames things with her.

"I need your advice," he says. "About the Dawn."

"We wiped them out."

Acheta had wiped them out; Coeur put a knife in what was left of the organization in Bulari while she was cleaning up the Dry Creek crew. But Jaantzen isn't going to quibble facts.

"Felipe Zacharia escaped from Redrock with some of his followers. We have reason to believe he came back to Bulari."

Coeur keeps her expression uninterested, but her broken hands have gone still. The Dawn — and Felipe Zacharia's brother — are the reason proud Blackheart will never box again. That she can't walk without a cane.

That her sister's gone and buried.

"You know where he is?" she asks; she could be asking about the weather but for the glimmer of hate in her eye.

"We're looking. If you know anything that would help, I'd appreciate it."

A long, cool look before she judges him to be telling the truth and turns to Damyati.

"Zacharia's brother rallied more than we eventually took out," Damyati says; they're the first words he's spoken since they greeted each other. "We found more than one cell already abandoned. We figured most of his followers were just around for the free drugs, but some could have had real devotion. They could be waiting for him."

"Are they organized?"

"There's a priest we couldn't find."

Coeur snorts derisively, and Damyati shrugs. "A 'priest,'" he amends. "Ran with Dry Creek before Bennion Zacharia converted a bunch of them to his cause. Thomas Deté."

The name Toshiyo sent Jaantzen late last night; good to know Coeur's information matches. "Have you seen him lately?"

"Haven't looked," Damyati says. "We can keep an eye out."

"I'd appreciate any information you can share."

Coeur crosses one arm over the other, taps a finger thoughtfully against her lips. "You going after Zacharia, I want in on the game," she says. "You'll need an army if you want to take him out."

Jaantzen nods like it hasn't occurred to him. Like he doesn't know how spread thin he is right now. Like he didn't plan to come to the one woman he believes can provide both the firepower and the mutual hatred of an enemy to help him take out the Dawn for good.

"You want your revenge?" Jaantzen asks her.

"Course." But there's something more hidden underneath that smile. She knows about the serum the Dawn were using to make supersoldiers. Bennion Zacharia had originally offered it to Acheta in exchange for his help, and Coeur would probably love nothing more than to get her hands on it. "And you're going to want yours. Felipe Zacharia met with Leone last night." Coeur laughs at the surprise on Jaantzen's face, drags another piece of lumpia through the sauce.

"Then she really is scrambling for table scraps," he says.

"Maybe she's found god," Coeur says. She chews thoughtfully. "Or at least someone who hates you as much as she does."

"Perhaps."

Last night, Leone had tossed Zacharia's name out like a lure. Did she actually intend to hand him over to Jaantzen? Or was it the other way round? In the end it doesn't matter, he supposes. Leone's still a dead woman walking after what she did to Phaera.

Jaantzen finishes his coffee and sets the tiny cup back on the table next to Manu's untouched one. "I'll let you know details as soon as I have them," he says as he stands. "About a meeting with the Demosgas, and any plans for the Dawn."

Damyati stands to shake Jaantzen's hand, exchanges a wary nod with Manu. Coeur takes her cane in hand but doesn't rise. Jaantzen gives her a nod of respect, then turns to go.

"You're not going to tell me to stay away from Phaera?"

Coeur's voice carries the faintest mocking lilt. Jaantzen turns slowly, studying her. That hint of a jaguar's smile, it could be a threat. Or it could be she's testing him; either way, he's not interested in playing her games.

"Phaera D's affairs are her own," he says.

Coeur's smile twitches wider, showing a flash of red eyetooth. "I'll keep that in mind, though she's more tightly wound than I usually go for. I can see why you like her."

Manu tenses beside him and Coeur's gaze flickers to his lieutenant for the first time. Is it Jaantzen's imagination? Or does her expression soften at whatever she sees in Manu's face?

"She doing all right?" Coeur asks. Jaantzen doesn't think he's ever heard her try for gentle before.

"Thank you for the coffee, Thala." And he turns and walks out the door, the place between his shoulder blades itching at having his back to Blackheart.

Manu doesn't relax when they're out of the store, doesn't relax even when he's driving them away in his sleek black Taosa Scorpion. "Message from Leti came in while you were talking, boss," Manu says. His tone is light but his knuckles are tight on the controls, and there's only one thing Jaantzen could say to make this all right: Coeur is no longer useful, go ahead and put a bullet in her head.

It's not true.

She's far too useful, and getting more so by the day.

She's no less feral, though. That comment about Phaera, he can't decide if it was meant as a warning, if she was probing for information about their relationship, or if she's simply allergic to ending a perfectly civil conversation on an amicable note. Had to have one last barb for the road.

One day, though, she'll cross a real line. And if the universe is just, Jaantzen will be the one who'll get to put her down for it.

Jaantzen pulls up Leti's note while Manu drives. She's been slowly leaking news related to the Alliance operative's amnesty plea, right on schedule. And the first outlets are starting to run the clip of the Alliance agent with Levi Acheta, attacking Cobalt Tower.

Jaantzen plays the segment.

It's a short clip. The vid from the stairwell where the Alliance woman's face is clearly visible as she shoots two of his security team point-blank — they both have their hands up, weapons on the ground. Jaantzen's seen this before, but it's hard to remain calm.

His people are dead.

The reporter is identifying the victims as security guards in the employ of local businessman Willem Jaantzen, owner of Cobalt Tower and Admant Security. Jaantzen waits for the inevitable "but"; it doesn't come. Instead of delving into rumors of Jaantzen's past or repeating Leone's recent lies linking him to the bombing of the Alliance embassy, the reporter pivots to a guest expert on foreign policy who explains the legal ramifications of the allegations and speculates about the fallout between New Sarjun and the Alliance. The final vote on the trade agreement has already been pushed back, but there are rumblings now it may be off the table altogether.

The vid cuts back to the scene outside the Alliance embassy this morning, where the gathered protesters are still chanting angrily.

Jaantzen's comm pings with another incoming message. Trade Commissioner Youssef Tabari again.

Tabari hadn't come up rough, but he'd run on the outside of some of the same crews Jaantzen had, years ago. Only Tabari somehow got himself a university degree and a series of increasingly valuable positions within New Sarjun's government — which he's been more than willing to use to get ahead, as evidenced by his longtime presence at Leone's dinner parties.

The trade agreement is Tabari's darling. And the fact that he's pinged Jaantzen twice now means he's tight enough with Leone to know Jaantzen had something to do with its downward spiral, though that doesn't mean he's calling on her behalf. Tabari's entire path to success has been a result of careful decisions about who to throw his fortune in with. If he sees Leone's ship going down, he might be calling to change sides.

The message is four words: WE NEED TO TALK.

"What is it, boss?"

"Tabari's been trying to reach me. He wants to talk."

"He working for Leone?" Manu's relaxing, a puzzle to chew on to take his mind off Coeur, perhaps.

"Hard to tell. But either way, I'd like to see what he has to say."

"I'll set something up. Tonight?"

"Perfect." That will give him time to evaluate his old friend's current ties. The trick to a good working relationship with Tabari is having a clear understanding of what he hopes to gain, and who's currently paying him off.

*Happy to talk. If you have something to share in return on our mutual friend.*

Tabari's affirmative message comes back almost immediately and Jaantzen leans back in his seat. After so long sitting around doing nothing but planning, everything is finally coming together.

He lets himself smile.

12

________

## TOSHIYO

Toshiyo's "Poor me I just left a cult" post on the conspiracy theory forum got dozens of comments.

Some don't believe her. Some offer empty comfort. Some share bloodcurdling stories of their own — Toshiyo shudders; if they're true, they're horrible. But as she scrolls to the end of the replies her heart sinks. Nothing from the user called GraySeeker.

Why not? Their profile on the message board says they've been active today, and this should have been the perfect post to attract their attention. So why . . .

Ah. There.

In the corner of her desk, a pulsing icon of the forum's direct messages, and Toshiyo has a connection request.

Toshiyo opens the message, the corner of her mouth curling up in a smile.

*I THINK I KNOW THE CULT YOU'RE TALKING ABOUT, AND IF SO, I'M GLAD YOU GOT OUT. MY DAUGHTER JOINED THEM. I NEVER GOT HER BACK. IF WE'RE TALKING ABOUT THE SAME PEOPLE, YOU COULD STILL BE IN DANGER. THIS PLATFORM ISN'T SECURE. DELETE YOUR*

*POST BEFORE THEY FIND IT, AND MESSAGE ME AT THE FOLLOWING ADDRESS.*

*I KNOW YOU PROBABLY DON'T THINK YOU CAN TRUST ANYONE RIGHT NOW. BUT THEY KILLED MY DAUGHTER AND I'M TRYING TO STOP OTHER MOTHERS FROM HAVING TO GO THROUGH THE SAME THING I DID. IF YOU CAN GIVE ME ANY INFORMATION IT WILL HELP.*

Amazing.

Toshiyo's managed to make contact with a woman in Bulari who not only might have inside information about the Dawn but also is affiliated with White Star, the strange group Sister Kalia and Sister Zahra belonged to.

A conversation with her could help Toshiyo locate where Felipe Zacharia landed with his band of criminals. It could help her figure out what he's planning to do — and stop him before any more lives are lost.

Toshiyo downloads GraySeeker's message and all the replies to her original post — there might be some clues hidden in there — then deletes the post and burns her account.

How secure is this new address GraySeeker gave her? Toshiyo feeds it into an AI and sets it on a general network scavenger hunt, then runs it through her own reverse-seek program. Nothing.

Interesting. For as easy as it was to find GraySeeker's other profiles on the network, Toshiyo hasn't actually been able to trace anything back to a real person. Even with this new bit of information. Somebody's doing a better job than most of not being found.

Of course, tracing identities isn't Toshiyo's specialty. She dumps everything she knows about GraySeeker into a new message and sends it to Starla's cousin, Mona. Mona can be notoriously slow to respond, but she's always reliable. If she can't find GraySeeker's true identity, no one can.

Toshiyo cracks her ring fingers and opens up a new message to GraySeeker.

*I'M THE ONE WHO LEFT THE CULT. I DELETED MY POST. ARE YOU TALKING ABOUT THE DAWN?*

She stares at the screen, but the immediate response she's hoping for doesn't arrive. She drums her fingernails on her desk, trying to figure out what to do next.

Toshiyo's 90 percent certain she remembered to eat breakfast, but her stomach is growling again and it's been — oh. It's been a while since she got up from her desk. She stands and stretches, then heads for the kitchen. Starla's not in her room or in the kitchen, which means she's probably up in the hangar tinkering with that moto they discovered in the previous owner's piles of junk.

She's been out there a lot since she got home, always moving with an antsy energy Toshiyo's taken to mean Starla's looking forward to heading back to Bulari as much as the rest of them have been. The deathtrap was a nice respite from being actively hunted, but the network connection is slow. It's harder to order parts. It's cramped.

And lunch options are limited.

Toshiyo pops a Celebration! flavor InstaMeal in the rehydrator and sniffs at the coffee dregs in the pot. She's trying to decide if she wants coffee badly enough to make a new batch when her comm chimes with an incoming call from Manu.

"Hey, Tosh, you busy?"

"Making lunch. What's up?"

He's outside, sounds like. Traffic and voices. "I looked into that Thomas Deté you were asking about. Turns out he used to be a mid-level guy in the Dry Creek crew before he started working with Bennion Zacharia. I guess a bunch of folks in Dry Creek actually believed that Dawn bullshit."

"It makes sense," Toshiyo says slowly. "Dry Creek crew always had a big shard manufacturing operation, didn't they? And that's what the Dawn needed to mass-produce the serum."

"That's it. Deté went underground. Coeur's people say they never found him — my guess is they didn't look too hard once he was out of her territory. But the grapevine says Deté took followers with him and kept manufacturing shard and trying to perfect the serum."

"Like the operation you and Oriol cleaned out of the old smelter in Carama Town."

"Exactly."

"Any idea where he's hiding?"

"No. But he probably didn't go too far out of the city."

"Do you think Felipe Zacharia ended up with him?"

"It's a good bet. Hold on." In the background, someone calls out an order number. The rustle of paper; Manu calls a thank-you and starts walking. Behind Toshiyo, the rehydrator dings to let her know her Insta-Meal is ready. "I'll keep trying to track him down. How are you doing?"

"Got a lead, someone from that Sister Kalia cult of Oriol's who might know something."

"Yeah?"

"A woman — she's here in Bulari. I'm going to see if I can talk to her."

"Good. Keep me in the loop."

"Sure thing. Enjoy lunch."

"You too."

She'll try. Toshiyo peels back the film on the Insta-

Meal, covers it with glugs of hot sauce, then freezes with fork midair at the familiar, gravelly, pigeon-like coo behind her. She whirls to see Lucky. He's standing outside the door, like he's waiting for her to invite him in.

"You startled me, buddy," Toshiyo says and signs, but her mind is racing. He's out again, even though she and Starla looked at every part of his new cage to make sure he would be secure. Did Starla let him out? She hopes so.

Lucky seems chagrined. "Sorry," he signs.

"It's fine. Come in."

He advances with his little shuffling hop, though it lacks the exuberance he used to have. He's aware he scared her — still scares her. Toshiyo wonders if it took him this long to figure out how to get past the new defenses she and Starla installed, or if he stayed in his room all morning as a courtesy. Or maybe he's been out for hours and is giving her space.

He holds up his clawed fingers, leathery wings rustling, and makes the sign for friend.

"Yes, friend," Toshiyo signs back, pointing at herself, at him.

Lucky makes a face, scowling. She got it wrong, he was trying to tell her something else.

"What is it?"

Lucky tilts his head as though listening, then shuffles in a slow circle. He stops, facing the wall to Toshiyo's left, and lifts a hand, pointing somewhere near the ceiling. "Friend," he signs again. "Far."

She's pretty sure she didn't teach him the sign for far, which means Starla's idea of having the AI USL interpreter on while vids are playing must be working. She files that away to tell Gia and Tevi.

"What kind of friend?" She makes Jaantzen's namesign and Lucky makes another face. She tries Gia's, he shakes his head. She'd try Manu's, but Lucky still doesn't like Manu, despite all her attempts to get him to see that Manu isn't a threat to her.

Lucky signs his own name, then points again. "Far friend."

The hairs on the back of Toshiyo's neck rise. "A friend like you?"

A vigorous nod. He's taken to mimicking human gestures and body language to get his point across; Toshiyo wonders how he'd signal assent or dissent if he'd been raised by his own kind instead.

"Like the . . . baby?" Toshiyo doesn't know how to sign embryo, but she gestures down the hall at where Lucky's little cousin is slowly growing into a new problem.

Lucky signs no, then spreads his wings expansively, craning his neck back like he's looking up at something much bigger than he is. The gesture tips over a precariously placed water glass; Lucky doesn't notice, and Toshiyo is too unnerved to care when the glass shatters against the kitchen floor.

He means an alien who's much, much bigger.

The other clone? The one that bit Gia?

"Here?" she clarifies. Starla had suspected the Dawn brought the big alien with them, and this could confirm it. Unless Lucky has only recently developed this ability to sense others of his kind — and that ability extends halfway around the planet.

Lucky nods. "We go," Lucky signs. He takes a couple of hopping steps back towards the door, then turns to make sure she's following him. When she doesn't, his expression darkens. "Friend hurt."

"How do you know your friend is out there?"

He gives her a puzzled look. "You know friends you? Same."

Toshiyo shakes her head. "I know where my friends are because we call each other. And we have trackers. Come here."

She pulls her tablet over and opens up a map as Lucky launches himself into the air and lands on the chair beside her. He's almost too big for it these days.

Toshiyo zooms out on the map, toggles on the tracking layer. "See, this is how I know where my friends are," she signs. Jaantzen's dot is at a safehouse outside the downtown core. Manu's dot is in the streets near his apartment building. Starla's is here at the deathtrap. Toshiyo could request others turn on tracking — or override them and turn it on remotely if she needed it — but she doesn't regularly keep an eye on anyone but these three.

"Where is your friend?" she asks.

Lucky shakes his head impatiently at the map, then points back at the wall. "Far."

Fascinating. He must have some sort of psychic link with others of his species. Some way of knowing where they are — or even communicating with them?

"Can you talk to your friend?"

Lucky looks at her like she's crazy; either he doesn't know, or he doesn't understand the question.

"Okay. I need to talk to Starla."

Lucky's grimace bares razor teeth. "Now." The force with which he signs it would seem violent in any hands; mix in the claws and strangely jointed fingers and it's downright terrifying. Toshiyo flinches back. Lucky's wings droop and his glaring eyes soften.

"Sorry," he signs.

"It's okay," Toshiyo signs back, but her heart is pounding. "C'mon."

Starla's indeed in the hangar, tinkering on the old moto she'd been thrilled to find in the junk pile. They hadn't let Lucky out into the hangar yet, but Toshiyo's starting to think it doesn't matter. Obviously if he wanted to escape, he'd already be gone, and there's no level of security they could set up to stop him.

Toshiyo leads Lucky in a wide arc to put them both in Starla's field of vision; Starla jerks her chin at them but goes back to her work, tightening down the bolts on the engine block. When she's done she sits back on her heels and shoves her safety glasses up on her forehead, leaving a smudge of grease on her pale cheekbone.

"Almost there," she signs, then gives the moto a loving look. She's polished up the chrome and cleaned the dust off the cherry-red paint job; the al-Jurjani Trespass logo is scrawled in gleaming silver on the side.

"Is that even street-legal?" Toshiyo asks. Light glimmers in Starla's iris as the words transcribe.

Starla grins. "If they can catch me," she signs. "These GS3s are legendary."

"Legendarily dangerous is what you told me."

"If you don't know what you're doing." Starla glances at Lucky, who's increasingly annoyed at the banter. "What's going on?"

"Lucky . . ." As Toshiyo's puzzling through how to say it in her mind, Lucky bares his teeth.

"Friend," he signs to Starla. He shuffles to the right and points. "Go now."

"I guess he senses another alien? A big one, the original, maybe? You thought the Dawn might have brought it with them."

Starla's gone still. "Maybe," she signs. She turns to Lucky. "Here? Or near Bulari?"

He shakes his head in confusion, points again at the wall.

"We need to try to find it," signs Toshiyo. "It could lead us to the Dawn." And then they could pour fuel over the encampment and set the whole thing ablaze.

But Starla's shaking her head. "And then what do we do with it?" she signs.

"Does it matter?" Toshiyo asks. "We can figure it out on the way. But if Lucky can lead us to Zacharia, we need to go. Now."

For a moment she thinks Starla is going to shut her down, but then the younger woman nods and stands, wiping her greasy hands on a rag. "Let me get cleaned up and call Jaantzen," she signs. "Then we go."

## 13

## MANU

There's a different sort of energy downtown today. The protests at the Alliance embassy are far enough away to be out of sight, but they've left the whole city tinged with an electric buzz of wary excitement. More people than usual are braving the midday heat of downtown Bulari's streets, streaming through to join the protests or watch the show. The business lunch regulars are trying to ignore them.

But everyone's on edge — not just Manu. Office workers aren't lingering in cafes, and building security guards are looking more alive than usual, though that's done nothing to deter the pint-sized pickpocket Manu's been watching work the plaza. The kid's gonna make a haul today with all the police concentrated down at the embassy; Manu gives her a warning glare when he catches her sizing him up, and she melts away into the crowd.

He rolls his neck and keeps walking, takeout container in hand.

Jaantzen's spending the afternoon making calls from a

safehouse and Manu wants to head home. Kick off his shoes, relax on the balcony with a beer and a view of Oriol working through his routine in the corner of the living room. With how frequently they've seen each other in the weeks since Oriol's been home, his husband might as well be on another eight-month security contract on a rock-hauler in Durga's Belt.

Husband. Now there's a word Manu thought Oriol would be allergic to forever.

Manu hadn't really thought it'd make a difference himself, not after a couple of decades together, but since that day in the hospital there's been a shift. So subtle, so foundational, that Manu can't quite put his finger on it — but it's there. And he hasn't even had a chance to appreciate it.

The constant running, the constant adrenaline, it's getting to him. He'd hoped they'd left those days behind, but the past has a way of catching up with you. And at least he knows how to play this game. He'll live through Leone; and goddammit, he'll live through Coeur.

Again.

At least the constant aches and pains of the last few weeks are gone, burned away by whatever he got a lungful of in that secret science lab inside the smelter. Bumps and bruises he's gotten since hurt just as bad, but the persistent ache in his ribs, the bruises, the cut on his arm, the tightness in his lungs — gone. He feels fantastic.

He probably needs to have a talk with Gia and Toshiyo about that at some point, but after weeks of setbacks, he's not going to say no to this one positive.

Besides, there's always something more pressing, isn't there?

For example, that pair of suits too-casually sauntering

after him as soon as he walked out of Jade's; either they're not trying to hide the fact they're following him or they're not too practiced at tailing people. Another pair are waiting near the door to his apartment, but he wasn't heading there anyway. He was on his way to the streetcar stop; now he takes a left onto a pedestrian side street, shaded with arching bamboo awnings and packed with the business lunch crowd.

The first two guys pick up the pace as he slips through the crowd and into the lobby of an office building that acts as a thoroughfare between this street and the next. A public cafe takes up most of the main floor, with tables alongside a manufactured stream complete with brilliant yellow and blue fish playing in the current.

Another pair of suits are waiting for him at the far end of the lobby, they straighten as soon as he walks in. This was hardly the most intuitive route he could've taken, and Manu's having a hard time imagining they randomly picked the right place to head him off.

So.

How many of these guys are there? And who the hell are they?

They've all got the same clean-cut vibe: mass-produced haircuts and off-the-rack suits with shoulder holsters underneath. They're not BPD, they're not New Sarjun military, and they're not a street crew. And they move too much like well-trained fighters to be overzealous missionaries bent on making sure Manu's heard the good word. That leaves government secret service, and he'd bet New Sarjun doesn't have the resources to send this many guys after one low-value target.

Only one person out there who's been blowing up Manu's comm with messages and has a squad of government goons at his fingertips, but talking to Alliance Deputy Chief of Mission Marquez ó Lauris wasn't on Manu's agenda today.

He makes a beeline for the escalator to the mezzanine, where he knows there's an open-air terrace he can leap from if he needs to; before he reaches it, a fourth pair of suits step squarely into his path. One opens her palm to show a police-grade shock-baton. It's not extended, but a flick of the wrist and it can send arcs of pain through its target.

The other four have closed in around his back.

Manu isn't surprised at the Arquellian drawl that comes out when one of the suits finally opens his mouth.

"Mr. Juric. Deputy Chief of Mission ó Lauris would like to speak with you."

"I'm a little busy right now."

Manu glances over his shoulder. The others are approaching slowly, no outward displays of weapons, though he can see at least three of the suits behind him also have shock-batons in their fists.

"You can walk out of here or we'll carry you," says the first soldier. "Doesn't matter to me either way."

Manu breathes out a frustrated curse, but he's not going to make them use the batons. He'd have a tough enough time taking one trained Alliance operative in close combat, let alone six. "Fine," he says. "I'll go."

One of the soldiers grabs the takeout bag from his hand and drops it on a nearby table, then pats him down. Takes his pistols, his comm, the knife in his dress boot. Another soldier starts to snap cuffs around his wrists, but Manu swats her away. "I'm coming peaceful," he says.

The soldiers on either side of him flick out their

shock-batons. Electric energy sizzles blue along each shaft.

"Orders," says the soldier with the cuffs drily.

Orders.

Orders to give Manu a clear message from ó Lauris: Answer my calls or I'll drag you to see me publicly in cuffs.

It's a risky move, to be honest, the way this city is poised to explode. If they were closer to the protests, or somewhere in the Fingers, all Manu would have to do is yell he's being harassed by Alliance agents and the crowd would turn ugly. But standing in the middle of a corporate plaza, they're only getting curious side-eye from office workers who're otherwise minding their own business. These Alliance agents could simply be security guards if you don't know what you're looking for.

The one person giving them much attention is the pint-sized pickpocket from before. She catches Manu's eye and jerks her chin at his newly abandoned takeout, he gives her a *Help yourself* wink. She snatches it up, melts away once more.

Who says kids these days have no manners?

The soldier grabs Manu's arms roughly and secures the cuffs, then shoves him towards a spinner parked in the street. They don't go to the embassy, but instead to the western edge of town, where sand drifts over the maglev tracks and the wide streets are lined with hulking two-story buildings scoured gray by the wind. RKE has a warehouse out here, but Manu doubts ó Lauris is in the market for a deal on an industrial stove. They stop in front of a rusted security gate; broken glass bottles top the surrounding concrete fence. Two of the Alliance soldiers climb out of the spinner to wrestle the gate open and they drive inside.

Manu keeps his breathing low and even, tries to remind himself this is ó Lauris, not some underworld boss. Not Coeur. This is the Alliance, and as pissed as ó Lauris is going to be, Jaantzen still holds too many of the cards for Manu to be in real danger.

The inside of the warehouse is stuffy with old dust and broken air recyclers; one of the soldiers behind Manu sneezes as they enter. Manu blinks as his eyes adjust to the light.

The warehouse is empty but for Deputy Chief of Mission ó Lauris, sitting on a chair, reading a book, while a pair of soldiers stand at attention behind him. He glances up with mild interest as Manu's captors wrestle him into a waiting metal chair, though Manu's hardly resisting. He holds onto anger to keep that little panicked voice inside his head from screaming he's trapped.

This is a power display.

Ó Lauris isn't going to hurt him.

"Your father mentioned you frequent that restaurant," ó Lauris says by way of greeting. He lays the book open in his lap, drumming coppery fingers on his knee like he's annoyed at being interrupted. Well, makes two of them. "Jade's. How is the food?"

"Killer. The black bean sauce is incredible," says Manu. So ó Lauris tracked down his dad. "You gotta appreciate heat, though."

"I've grown fond of New Sarjunians' predilection for spice." Ó Lauris blinks, light playing on the lens in his eye, reading a brief, or Manu's vitals, maybe. Who knows. "Your father is all right, by the way, no need to worry. We just talked."

"I don't give a shit if he's all right," says Manu.

One white eyebrow lifts, but ó Lauris doesn't comment. "You've been ignoring my requests to meet."

"I've had a lot on my plate."

"Something more important than provoking war with the entire Alliance? Then, Mr. Juric, I don't envy your job."

"Keeps my mind occupied." Manu lifts his wrists. "Is this going to be a conversation or an interrogation?"

"I'm no longer certain I can trust you."

Manu leans back in his chair. "Interrogation it is," he says. "I'll warn you I'm tough to crack, but if you've got some time to kill, you can let your guys do their worst."

Ó Lauris may be royally pissed, but he's the kind of man who takes his anger out on you in paperwork and bureaucracy, not blood. Still, despite how casual Manu's trying to sound, his stomach is churning, his fight-or-flight response trying to kick into high gear. The cuffs on his wrists, the big guy standing over his shoulder, the way his voice echoes in the warehouse, the cold, calculating stare ó Lauris turns on him are flashing him back to a very different place. One he'll die before going to again.

Spending the morning with Coeur was terrible for his mental health.

Ó Lauris studies him a long moment, then finally nods to one of the soldiers beside Manu. She hits a button and the cuffs click open. Manu tosses them to the floor and rolls his neck, giving the middle finger to the part of his brain that's still trying to hijack him into panic mode.

"And if it's all right, I need to call my partner," Manu says. "Explain why I didn't show up with lunch before he burns the city down trying to find me. Pretty sure you don't want him showing up at your office."

Ó Lauris frowns, but nods again to the soldier, who hands Manu his comm. He types out a quick message to Oriol, presses Send. Ignores the outstretched hand of the soldier trying to take it back and slips it into his pocket.

"I apologize for the public display," ó Lauris says; he doesn't sound sincere in the slightest.

"I understand. All Arquellians are assholes."

"Yet, your Mr. Sina?"

"He's all right. He's gone feral."

"I'd like to meet him," ó Lauris says. "I've been reading up on his very decorated career in the Alliance special ops."

Manu wonders if that's a threat, figures it's best to assume yes. And he doesn't want to keep talking about Oriol with the people who left all those emotional land-mines Manu's spent years discovering and defusing.

"You brought me here to talk," he says shortly. "So let's talk."

"Explain to me why your employer didn't uphold his part of our bargain."

"Do you know what your colleagues are really doing up at Redrock?" Manu's guess is no; ó Lauris may be in charge of the embassy, of maintaining the Alliance's diplomatic mission on New Sarjun, but his colleagues in Redrock and in the Alliance special operations teams obviously haven't been keeping him abreast of their activities to date. He didn't know about Coeur stealing the cases from the Alliance. He didn't know about the plan to attack Cobalt Tower and get those cases back.

And judging by his careful expression, ó Lauris doesn't trust the story he's been fed about what's happening at Redrock, either.

Ó Lauris, like Manu, deals in information. The fact that his colleagues are keeping him in the dark must be maddening. And as angry as Manu is at this little power play, he can still show ó Lauris how valuable Jaantzen can be to him.

"Go on," ó Lauris says.

"They found wreckage." Manu studies the older man, curious to see which of these next bits of information will be a surprise. "Wreckage of an alien ship that apparently came here with the mission of terraforming the planet, because that's where they found the technology they've been using to grow food. They also found alien embryos in the ship, and they've allowed at least one to grow to term so they can experiment on it."

The various twitches of surprise and shock on the faces in Manu's field of vision are extremely satisfying.

Alliance special ops soldiers are good, but they're not that good — and neither is ó Lauris. He definitely hadn't gotten the "aliens are real" office memo yet. If he trusts his colleagues in the slightest, he might think Manu is bull-shitting him.

He does not.

Ó Lauris closes his book. "Everyone out."

One of the soldiers over Manu's shoulder clears his throat. "Sir. He's disarmed, but — "

"Out. Now."

They sit in silence while the soldiers file reluctantly out of the warehouse. Ó Lauris may have had Manu dragged here in cuffs, but if he's afraid of retaliation it doesn't show. He knows Manu's not going to touch him. Manu's goal is deescalation, and decking the Alliance's second-highest-ranking diplomatic official in the jaw isn't how you deescalate.

Ó Lauris waits to speak until the echoes of the shutting warehouse door have faded.

"Is all that true?"

"I can show you proof."

"I'll get my own. But you didn't answer my question, Mr. Juric. Why didn't your employer hold up his end of our bargain?"

"It's not personal, man. But this is bigger than you and Jaantzen now. Your government has been hiding alien technology you discovered on our planet, disappearing New Sarjunian citizens, and bribing our leaders to push through a trade agreement that would be economically devastating to our planet."

Ó Lauris waves a hand. "As you noted, your leadership is complicit. I've been on New Sarjun a long time, and let me assure you, corruption is business as usual. I wouldn't be so dismissive of the system that allowed you — and your employer — to thrive. If we were in Arquelle — "

"We're not in Arquelle, are we?" Manu leans forward, elbows on knees. "That's the fucking point. Your back-alley operations on our planet are over. The covert missions, strong-arming government officials, attacking private citizens? You've finally messed with the wrong people."

Ó Lauris is silent a moment. "Who else knows?"

"Just us. For now. But the cat's clawing its way outta the bag, man. Pretty soon the whole system's going to know what's been going on. If I were you, I'd stop worrying about intimidating a Bulari businessman and start trying to figure out how you're going to save the Alliance's diplomatic mission."

Ó Lauris blinks three times and the ever-present

glimmer in his eye disappears as his lens switches off. "Listen to me, Mr. Juric. I *am* the diplomatic mission. Ambassadors come and go, but I run the embassy. The fire of public opinion raining down on our ambassador right now? It won't hit me. That trade agreement? Whether it goes through or not doesn't affect my day-to-day. The rioting? Maybe I won't be able to go in to my office for a few months. But I'm not going anywhere.

"I have lived in nearly every Alliance country, and I've lived on New Sarjun longer than in my own home-land. But my home — all of our home — isn't one planet or moon or asteroid. It's this system. We might've been the only ark to make it. We might be the last of our species. *That* is what keeps me up at night. Not squabbles over who got a bigger slice of cake."

He leans forward, jaw set. "I don't care about your ambitions, and I don't care about the Alliance's games. But I do care that people are going to die in the streets in front of my embassy if these protests continue, and the way your employer released this information is making it extremely difficult for me to stop that from happening."

Ó Lauris's words echo out into silence, and neither of them move.

That was not the kind of ultimatum Manu expected to receive, and it's slowly starting to dawn on him that he's miscalculated. Ó Lauris isn't just another Alliance tool, he's playing his own game. One which very much aligns with Jaantzen's.

"I don't know your world," Manu finally says. "So I'm not sure who your squeaky wheel is that's trying to over-turn this cart. But in our world, it's Chief Justice Geum-ja Leone. When she's gone, the man can hold together peace with the rest of the underworld players."

"I'm well aware of who the culprits are on my side," says ó Lauris. "And I will take care of them. We need to share our cards, Mr. Juric."

"Agreed." Information is the primary currency they both use to do their jobs, and they're both holding different pieces of the same puzzle. Let that information flow, and things might get a whole hell of a lot easier from here on out. Manu clears his throat. "I'll go first. The Alliance agent was sent to attack Cobalt Tower because there was an alien embryo in the case Coeur stole from you all."

Ó Lauris's eyes close briefly, as though the revelation is a physical blow. Manu knows the feeling.

"Is it safe?" ó Lauris finally asks. Manu nods. Ó Lauris swears under his breath. "Our ambassador and your prime minister are meeting this afternoon; Prime Minister de Grazal plans to address the matter of the trade agreement officially tomorrow night. I have no reason to believe either knew about the kickbacks, or the prisoners sold to Redrock Prison. The warden and our special operations chief of station have been working directly with Chief Justice Leone and a handful of other officials in your government on that project."

"Trade Commissioner Youssef Tabari?"

Ó Lauris blinks his lens back on; light plays in his iris as he searches his notes. "No. Why."

"The man's meeting with him later, so it's good to know what side he's been playing for. Do you have proof Leone is working with the Alliance?"

"I'll send it to you, along with my notes on Commissioner Tabari." Ó Lauris types something into his cuff, and a heartbeat later Manu's comm chimes with an incoming message. "What else do I need to know?"

Manu cracks his neck, thinking. Oh, right.

"Coeur agreed to help calm tensions in the streets, but I'm not sure exactly how she plans to do it. Just, you oughta know."

Ó Lauris arches an eyebrow. "What a strange time we live in." He sighs and stands. "I'm off to get some of my colleagues court-martialed. Let me know if I can be of any more assistance."

Manu stands as well, shakes his hand. "Likewise."

"And again, I apologize for the public display." Ó Lauris does sound sorry this time. He frowns at Manu, one last thing apparently bothering him. "What, ah, does it look like?"

Manu gives him a faint smile; ó Lauris doesn't need to spell out what he means by "it." Only one thing in this system gives people that particular brain-glitched expression he's getting so familiar with. Manu pulls out his comm, opens a photo of Lucky, and holds it out to the other man.

Ó Lauris stares a long time. "My word," he finally says, then shakes his head like he hopes that will help this new reality go away. "As I said. I do not envy you your job, Mr. Juric."

"Back atcha." Manu holds the warehouse door for him, blinking as his eyes adjust to the bright sunlight. "I'd like my guns back," he says to the soldier who took it.

"I don't believe these weapons are registered," the soldier says drily.

"And I don't believe you have any fucking jurisdiction on this planet." But he leaves the heat out of it; there's no point in riling up a pawn, especially now that he and ó Lauris are working on a level beyond any of this posturing.

"Please return Mr. Juric's property." Ó Lauris's voice cuts through the staring match and the soldier follows orders reluctantly, making a show of draining the charges and dumping the bullets. Ó Lauris gives Manu a respectful nod before disappearing inside the waiting spinner — there are two parked in the warehouse yard, but no one offers Manu a ride and he sure as hell wouldn't take it anyway.

He props a shoulder against the doorframe and watches them go, then pulls out his comm and dials Jaantzen.

## 14

## PHAERA

The first sign of trouble is the traffic, backed up throughout Bulari's downtown core. Phaera leans around Oriol to see out the window of the union cab; he's watchful, but not tense. In the front seat of the cab, Mel Nehrusitha is impassive.

The streets are filled with people, all streaming towards the Alliance embassy. Some are already yelling angry chants, some look like they're in it for the adventure.

The cab driver shouts at a knot of teens to get out of the way and gets a rude gesture in return. "I'm going to try another way," she tells Phaera. She's a small woman, an unruly twist of flame-red hair piled on top of her head. "Been getting worse all morning."

Phaera glances at Oriol, even though he hasn't said it yet: Maybe heading to her apartment isn't the wisest thing to do right now. But Phaera's exhausted, and all she wants is a nap in her own bed and to pack a few of her own things before heading back out into the unknown. The longing for home has been gnawing at her all morning.

Her neighborhood isn't anywhere near the embassy, but it seems the protests are spreading. Or the party surrounding the protests, at least. A bass riff thumps from a makeshift soundstage in one intersection, where food vendors have set up a brisk trade out of coolers and carts.

"I guess Bulari gets a day off," Phaera says.

"The city does like a good riot," Oriol answers.

Mel cracks a smile. "Been years since we had a proper one." Is it Phaera's imagination or does she sound almost wistful?

The cab driver scowls as she maneuvers through a group of jaywalkers. "Some of us still have to work."

Phaera doesn't see who started it, only that suddenly two of the pedestrians surrounding the cab are brawling, a circle widening around them as fists fly. The cab rocks violently as one man throws the other up against Phaera's door.

The cab driver lays on her horn and lurches through the rest of the crowd, sending pedestrians scrambling until they're in the clear once more. There's a smear of blood on Phaera's window.

"Sorry, Ms. Phaera," the driver says once they're flowing again. "Seems like they've shut down the core, I can't get to your address. Anywhere else you want to go?"

She wants to go home.

If Leone was sincere last night — and Phaera knows she was — then Phaera's safe. Leone didn't get this far without knowing how to pivot, and she has to understand how badly she underestimated Jaantzen's support. She knows she can't isolate Jaantzen anymore, so she's going to attempt to ingratiate herself with him. She's making a new mistake, of course, in underestimating how much Jaantzen cares about Phaera. But that's a different story.

For now, Leone will at least be respectful of the relationship if it means she can get Jaantzen on her side.

Besides. Tierren's dead. And there are probably a few gossip reporters staking out her front door who are spinning lurid stories about why she disappeared. Better to be seen by them before they start coming up with theories about why she's so ashamed to go out in public.

"It's a few blocks," Phaera says, and the taxi driver turns to her in surprise, because it's not, it's over a kilometer still. And normally Phaera would enjoy the walk — it's her city, it's her neighborhood — but in her current state it'll be a stretch. Way less of a stretch than not going home, though.

Oriol takes a resigned breath. "Ma'am, I don't think — "

"It's fine, Sina." Phaera swipes marks to tip the driver, then opens her door. Oriol and Mel are out faster than she is, and she doesn't miss the look that passes between them: *Is she always like this? Yes, she is.*

Oriol and Mel flank her as she walks through streets both familiar and not, streets she's walked every day. Protesters are nothing new; Oriol was right, the city likes to take to the streets when upset. But today there's a wild energy, that chaotic knife's edge of festivity and violence normally reserved for certain holidays hijacked by young drunks or certain party streets, like Market Street in the Tamarind, where the police work extra shifts to stand on every corner and babysit the Indiran tourists who think Bulari is a city you can come trash without repercussion. Phaera's worked more than her fair share of those nights, and called her fair share of police to cart away Indirans who thought as little of Bulari service workers as of their city.

The key is to walk fast with a purpose, gaze straight ahead, don't make eye contact, polite nods when you do, cross the street when you see more than two men together. But Phaera can't walk as fast as she wants to right now, and even the impressive amount of muscle trailing behind her isn't much reassurance. Her skin prickles when she can't get around a knot of young men lounging against the wall and a spinner that's obviously not theirs. She doles out polite nods and runs the gauntlet, unable to step onto the traffic-clogged street. They ignore her. She catches snatches of conversation about the big fight last night, plans for after the protest.

Her shoulders don't relax until she's more than half a block away and a glance behind her shows none of them even registered her passing.

"How are you doing?" Oriol asks.

"I'm fine," she snaps. The scrape on her knee screams with every step, her hand throbs, and her headache is back, but she can't point to anything else in particular — she's just exhausted. Adrenaline leaves a sharp taste at the back of her mouth, but that seems completely normal at this point, she can barely remember what it's like not to have an animal voice in her head telling her to run.

She touches Oriol's arm, pointing to an upcoming alley. "There's a shortcut here."

She starts to turn down the alley, but the shortcut she was hoping for is now a seething mass of people cheering, yelling epithets. Glass shatters somewhere, and she finally remembers there's an Arquellian restaurant down that street. She's eaten there — she applied there, once upon a time. Passable food and decent service, and people are tearing the place to shreds because the owners are from Arquelle.

Phaera starts down the alley, not sure what she can do but needing to stop it somehow. She tries to push past someone and they turn on her, swinging; Mel Nehrusitha jerks her back out of range of the fist.

"Not that way." Mel's hand is on Phaera's arm, steadying her. One look at Mel and the man who'd tried to hit Phaera forgets his quarrel and goes back to jeering at the destruction.

"What are they doing?" Phaera yells, but Mel shakes her head and juts her chin at the exit to the alley, then presses them both into a doorway as a pair of men slung with weapons walk by.

One raises a rifle and fires a short burst into the air. "Leave the Arquellians alone!" he shouts into the surprised silence that follows the screams. "Blackheart's orders. You here to protest, you enjoy the party. You here to fight, Blackheart crew's got your fight right here."

Phaera stares at them. Thala Coeur sent people to keep tabs on the peace, like that's perfectly normal.

"C'mon," Oriol hisses to Phaera.

They leave the alley behind and go the long way, but the crush of people is still thick. Chants from the actual protest echo off the buildings from blocks away. A drunk reveler jostles against Phaera, striking her hand; the pain shoots through her like a knife and she presses back against the wall, vision gone black for a split second. When she opens her eyes, Oriol's yelling at the man who jostled her, his Arquellian drawl more pronounced with anger. The man's teeth flash in a grin.

"We've got ourselves an arkie," the man calls, and faces turn to take in Oriol. With his shaggy bronze hair and sharp suit you don't quite see it at first. But once you hear that drawl? He does match the vid caricature of an

Arquellian member of the Alliance special ops. Phaera pushes forward as the crowd turns on Oriol, but she can't shout over them, her voice is wrecked. He could probably obliterate them, but this many? Somebody grabs her from behind.

"What're you doing with an Arquellian?" someone hisses in her ear. "You never been with a real man?"

"Fuck off," Phaera growls — she's had plenty of experience with this type, but before she can drive her elbow into his groin the man drops. Mel steps over his body and decks a lanky kid who's coming for Oriol with a knife, the sleeves of her suit jacket hiked up to reveal thick black snakes coiled around each of her wrists. She puts a solid hand on the lanky kid's chest, stiff-arming him to a halt, her other hand protectively on Oriol's shoulder.

"He's with me," she snarls at the kid, who sees the tattoos a second later than the rest of the crowd; most have already taken a step back from her.

"But he's — "

Mel raises her voice. "I said he's with me."

And the kid backs away, hands raised. No one else challenges her.

Mel jerks her chin at Phaera and Oriol and tugs her sleeves back into place. "Come on."

The crowds thin as they close in on Phaera's apartment building, and they make it the rest of the way without incident. Phaera doesn't see any reporters staking her place out, which doesn't mean they're not watching; she keeps her head high as she smiles at the security guard, keeps a proud expression on her face until they're safely inside her apartment.

She shuts the door and secures the biolocks, adrenaline shaking her hands. Oriol's directing Mel in a room sweep like he's familiar with the place, and it hits her that he's been here before. Without her, picking through her closet at her request.

And before him, Tierren made herself at home pawing through Phaera's closet, ordering takeout, lounging on her couch. Phaera finds herself frozen in the entryway, scanning the room for signs of anything out of place. Nothing is, but everything feels off somehow. Tarnished. Violated.

She thought she'd be thrilled to be home, but instead she's nauseous.

Oriol comes back first, holstering his weapon and grabbing a tissue to daub at the trickle of blood from a cut by his ear. "It's safe," he tells her.

It's not.

But Phaera forces herself to slip off her shoes and walk in anyway, heading to the kitchen like nothing's wrong. "Water?" she asks. She's having something stronger, but Oriol's never accepted alcohol when she's offered. Either he doesn't drink or he always considers himself on the clock when he's around her. She hands him a glass of water, starts on one for Mel.

"Are you all right?" Oriol asks her.

"I'm fine." Phaera points to her own ear. "You're — "

"I'm fine, it's just a scratch."

"You gotta keep your mouth shut, Sina," Mel says from her seat at the kitchen counter; she drops into a teasing Arquellian drawl. "Situations like these, it ain't smart to advertise."

"You — " Phaera cuts herself off, not sure how to ask. She hands Mel a glass of water and opts for direct. "Zmiya. You were in Zmiya, your tattoos."

Mel shoots a look at Oriol. "Sina normally warns people."

"But why not get them removed?" Phaera has a vague notion that having Zmiya tattoos could get you arrested, especially the way anti-Alliance sentiment is surging again.

Mel grins. "Because I still fucking hate the Alliance, and I don't care who knows it." Her smile fades. "Don't worry, ma'am, I know the drill. I keep them covered when I'm with you. Today was — "

"It was fine." Phaera's brain is too tired to unravel how somebody like Leone or Silver Dice could spin her being photographed with an ex-Zmiya member. And she can still hear the breaking glass and jeering crowd gathered in front of the Arquellian immigrant family's restaurant, she can see the thirst for violence in the eyes of the man who was about to tear into Oriol. "Thank you."

She drains her water, then crosses to the liquor cabinet and pours herself a glass of mezcal. "I'm going to sleep for a bit," she announces. "Then we'll go."

"We'll be right here, ma'am," Oriol says softly, and that does nearly as much as the shot of liquor to calm her nerves.

She pauses in the door to her bedroom, and it's a minute before she realizes what she's looking for. Some glint of gold, another mystix card set out for her to find. Lying on her pillow maybe. She slips a hand into the pocket of her dress, brushing fingertips against the comforting edges of the fortune killers Tierren already sent her, the Mask, the Fallen Tower, the Mirage. But if the mercenary spent any time in Phaera's bedroom, she didn't leave a sign.

Phaera crosses the hall and climbs into the guest bed instead.

———

By the quality of the light, she can tell she slept far longer than she planned to. But it was good sleep, solid, and her mind is more restful even if her body still aches as soon as she shifts. Phaera levers herself stiffly from the bed, wincing as she pulls her dress back over her head, runs a comb through her hair.

Voices drift from the living room, low so as not to wake her. They become clearer as she pads barefoot down the hall.

"You just have to ask her what she wants," Oriol is saying. "Because this isn't working for you."

Phaera stills, curious if they're talking about her, especially after the conversation about Mel and Zmiya. But instead of Mel answering, an unexpected voice cuts in.

"You go back to her place after work every time?" Vanessa Dosantos asks. "Okay. And how often do you stay the night?"

"The last few times," Mel answers.

"But she's been asking you to longer than that," Oriol says. "Hell, she asked you back after the first job we pulled with her."

Vanessa lets out a low whistle. "Girl, it sounds to me like you're already dating."

"I sleep on the couch," Mel protests.

Phaera lets her footsteps be heard and the conversation falls silent. Faces turn to greet her; Oriol, Mel, and V have made themselves comfortable in her living room, a pile of unopened takeout boxes from the local korris place are stacked on the dining table.

"What time is it?" Phaera asks. "You weren't supposed to let me sleep so late."

"You needed the rest, ma'am," Oriol says, getting easily to his feet and crossing to her as though he's going to catch her if she falls. She's about to snap at him, but no, he's heading for the takeout boxes. Though she doesn't miss the clinical, evaluating look he gives her. She gins up a smile and his worried expression softens.

"Are you hungry?" he asks. "We were waiting for you."

"You shouldn't have."

"Food's still hot, Fay, I only showed up a few minutes ago." Vanessa waves her over to the couch, and when Phaera sinks beside her, V drapes an arm around her shoulders, hugging her close. Phaera tucks her feet up underneath her and relaxes against V's side, savoring her warm scent of beeswax and sunflowers. "How are you doing?" Vanessa murmurs.

"Better." Phaera considers. More than better, actually. The sleep helped, but not as much as waking to the lively banter of friends in her living room, the laughter cleansing the ghost of Victoria Tierren that's been lingering in her apartment. She's not letting that bitch take what's hers — but she *is* done with these concerned looks. "I'm fine. What are we talking about?"

Mel's cheeks go pink; Oriol laughs from the kitchen. "A few weeks back I took a job for this woman who needed an extra hand, so I brought in Mel."

"A job doing what?" The words are out of her mouth before she realizes she might not want to know.

Oriol doesn't miss a beat. "Demolitions. Anyway, she and Mel have been working together ever since."

"Now Mel's getting into this girl, but she doesn't know if the feelings are mutual," explains Vanessa. She gives Mel a pointed look. "Even though the feelings are obviously mutual."

Mel holds up her hands in defeat. "Fine. I'll talk to her about it." She accepts a plate of korris from Oriol.

"Good." Oriol sets plates on the coffee table in front of Phaera and Vanessa, then perches on the arm of the couch. "Can I see your hand?"

He eases the brace off to reveal the mottled, livid bruising beneath. He cradles her hand gently in his, then smooths a small scanner over the joint at the base of her pinkie, watching the image appearing on his comm. "You're healing all right," he says, fitting the splint back into place. "It's just time, now. How's your head?"

"Let her eat, cowboy," Vanessa says. "She said she's fine."

Phaera pulls herself upright and reaches for the plate in front of her, suddenly aware of how hungry she is. "My headache's better," she tells Oriol. "How much time do we have before we need to leave?"

His lips thin. "The man called while you were sleeping. He's got some things he needs to take care of tonight, and we think you're safe to stay here if you want."

Phaera stills. Is that what she wants? After days of wishing she could return to her apartment, this isn't the homecoming she'd hoped for. But would she rather spend another night in some anonymous hotel? Some sterile safehouse? On her office couch at the Devil's Table?

"It's my night off, Fay," Vanessa says quietly. "I can stay if you want."

Phaera doesn't miss the look she shares with Oriol. They've talked this over. "Just like old times," Phaera says, and something is set free inside her, filling her with the first sense of peace she's felt in weeks. This is exactly what she needs right now. Food, friends, conversation — to make new memories and chase out the bad. She smiles. "Sounds like a party."

## 15

## JAANTZEN

The past few weeks have hit them all hard, but Ajesh Paiman could've aged a decade.

The last time Jaantzen came to the Oasis, Ajesh had also been waiting for him, beside the dry fountain in the pedestrian plaza outside his restaurant. The day Naali Hinoja had been murdered and Jaantzen had found out Thala Coeur wasn't in fact dead after a blissful handful of hours thinking she was.

Since then, nothing has changed, except for everything. Laundry is still strung between apartment windows. Incense still burns in the twin shrines at the plaza's entrance. The knotted mosaic tilework around the dry fountain is still immaculately swept, the potted fan palms and fire tongue beside the benches an ashy gray from the last dust storm.

Ajesh is smoking on the same bench as before, but there's more silver in his hair and beard, deeper lines carved into his brow, a gauntness to his round cheeks. A spark of fear in his eyes Jaantzen never saw there before.

He crushes his cigarette into a pot of succulents.

Slides his palms down his thighs as he rises to greet Jaantzen. He smiles bravely at Calanthe, who's walking at Jaantzen's right, as though drawing some small assurance from her presence. The look he gives Manu borders on abject terror.

There will be no jovial grins, no warm hugs from Ajesh today. Not after he lied to the police and told them Manu had been the one to kill Naali Hinoja. Tierren may have been holding his daughters prisoner, and Jaantzen isn't going to blame the man for being afraid for his family. But he should have known who to turn to for help.

Jaantzen holds out a hand; it's a long time before Ajesh takes it.

"It's good to see you," Jaantzen says. "How are the girls?"

"They're — " Ajesh swallows hard. "They'll be okay. Thanks to you. I'll never forget it, sir."

"Won't you?"

The last bit of color drains from Ajesh's face.

"If you're in trouble, where do you turn?" Jaantzen asks. "To your friends. Did you really think the police were going to be able to get your girls back?"

"She said she'd kill them if we said anything." His voice is little more than a whisper.

"And you would do anything for your family."

Ajesh nods miserably.

"As would I. I'm sorry I made your family vulnerable to attack, Ajesh. And thank you for telling the truth to the police. I hope you remember who your friends are next time you need help."

The other man straightens, wariness giving way to tentative hope. "I will," he says finally.

"Good." Jaantzen claps him on the shoulder, then

holds out a hand for Ajesh to lead the way. The tension between them won't fade easily, but at least there's hope for repairing the damage Tierren did to a relationship Jaantzen values. "I've been looking forward to your cooking all day," Jaantzen says; it's true. The loss of Ajesh's friendship would also mean the loss of a favorite korris restaurant. "I was disappointed my last meal here got interrupted."

Last time Jaantzen walked through these doors, he'd been greeted by still-warm corpses. Today the restaurant is similarly empty — technically the Oasis hasn't reopened to the public yet — but the man Jaantzen's here to meet is alive and well.

Trade Commissioner Youssef Tabari isn't alone, however. He's joined by a tall woman wearing a sharply tailored suit in pale cream, a maroon hijab framing warm brown skin, her nails and lips painted maroon to match. Her face seems familiar, but Jaantzen doesn't place her. Beside him, Calanthe lets out a curse of surprise.

"Madinia Ulrich," she says under her breath. "The prime minister's chief of staff. Tabari didn't say she was coming?"

"He did not." Now that is interesting. What had started as a conflict between two players in Bulari's underworld has apparently moved into a larger arena. With what intel ó Lauris gave Manu about Tabari, Jaantzen is reasonably certain the man is here to save his own hide rather than to betray Jaantzen to Leone. And he's brought Jaantzen a gift to prove it: a new and potentially powerful connection.

The pair fall silent, turning to face him as he enters. Jaantzen inclines his head in greeting, but he waits until Manu gives him the all clear from the kitchen before he crosses the restaurant and shakes a round of hands. "Thank you all for coming. Ms. Ulrich, it's a pleasure to meet you."

"Likewise," she says; her handshake is strong, she sounds sincere.

Jaantzen turns to Calanthe. "I'm sure you know Calanthe Yang," he says to Ulrich.

"A pleasure," says Ulrich.

Tabari's expression dims. "My condolences, Calanthe," he says quietly. "Your mother was an incredible woman."

Calanthe's face is a mask of professional detachment.

Jaantzen pulls out a chair for Calanthe, then seats himself. Pours them each a glass of water and tops off Tabari's nearly empty glass, letting his mind settle. He's walked into hundreds of dangerous meetings in his lifetime, a half-dozen just in these last few weeks where he wasn't sure he'd walk back out. This feels different.

He's not in danger — certainly not physically. Tabari is fleeing Leone's sinking ship, and Prime Minister Nikolas de Grazal didn't send his chief of staff here in subterfuge to take down some underworld figurehead. No. Ulrich is here because New Sarjun is about to go up in flames and Jaantzen has the information the prime minister needs to keep that from happening.

Somehow, this orphaned street rat has made himself indispensable to the most powerful elected official in New Sarjun.

"The trade agreement with the Alliance is done," says Ulrich without preamble. "That hasn't been made official yet, but it will be soon. Youssef tells me you're the man responsible for unearthing the prison labor scheme, and the terraforming. I wish you'd handled that differently."

"It was information it seemed the public should know."

"Maybe they shouldn't have found out that way."

"Someone in my position doesn't exactly have the ear of top government officials," Jaantzen says. "Nor did I know who I could trust with the information."

Ulrich tilts her head to acknowledge the point. "Well, you've managed to shake out the roaches. That reporter, Kumail Anh. How did he get all that footage?"

"He's a reporter," Calanthe cuts in smoothly. "You'll have to ask him if he's willing to give up his sources."

An arch look. "Are you here in a professional capacity, Ms. Yang?" Ulrich asks.

"Willem is an old family friend."

"And you're representing the Alliance agent who attacked him, is that right?"

"I am."

"It sounds like it would be worth having another go at the trade agreement anyway," Jaantzen says; they're not here to talk about the Alliance agent. "It was my understanding it stood to be very lucrative for many of our elected officials, if not our citizens."

Madinia Ulrich's smile is pained, but she doesn't answer. Her gaze flickers past him; Ajesh and his oldest daughter — still walking with a faint limp — are bringing the first course.

Wine and honeyed tea, trays of herbed flatbreads and sweet and sour condiments. Ajesh doesn't take their order, though he does inquire after preferences and restrictions in his typical charming way, his gaze never quite meeting Jaantzen's. His daughter gives Jaantzen a shy smile.

"You're in for a treat," Jaantzen says when Ajesh walks away. "I've never had a bad meal at the Oasis."

"I'm looking forward to it," Ulrich says. She takes a sharp breath and leans forward, elbows on the table, manicured hands clasped in front of her. "I'll be frank. De Grazal will be running for reelection, and if we don't appear strong in standing up to the Alliance, I guarantee our opponents will milk that for all it's worth. You can see what's happening in the streets right now. People are furious."

"Did you know about the kickbacks?"

Ulrich waves a hand. "There are always kickbacks. But, no. We didn't know to what extent this was going on."

"Making a few public examples will help with the elections," says Tabari, with a tone that says he doesn't anticipate being on the list. "As will renegotiating the trade agreement from scratch with new people at the helm."

"You weren't at the helm, old friend?"

Tabari gives him a flat look. "You know Leone."

Ah, here it is. The name evoked.

Ulrich straightens, barely managing not to glance over her shoulder.

"There's a reason I chose the Oasis for this meeting," Jaantzen tells her. "And it's not just because the food is superb. You can speak freely here."

She smiles tightly as Ajesh returns with a tray of chilled mint soup. Takes a spoonful and mulls it over before finally speaking.

"She's already pressuring the prime minister to push the agreement through or he'll 'lose face with the Alliance.'" Ulrich throws disdainful air quotes round the last phrase. "But she's the reason we won the last election, so de Grazal can't easily go against her."

"And, presumably, she has something on him."

"She has something on everyone," Ulrich says. "That's the problem. We can placate the public by making a few examples and rewriting the agreement, but Leone's role in this can't come out."

"It will come out eventually," says Calanthe.

"And de Grazal will cover for her. He has to."

"Is he willing to burn for her?" Jaantzen asks. Ulrich's lips thin. Jaantzen turns his gaze to Tabari, who shifts uncomfortably. "Youssef, are you? Because I'm not. Compromising secrets are easy to come by. Sometimes they help smooth a thorny path. But Leone uses them to maintain a stranglehold on this city — this country — that isn't healthy. And she's selling us all out to the Alliance."

"Treason." Ulrich drums her fingernails thoughtfully on the table. "Do you have proof?"

Jaantzen and Calanthe have spent the last hour reviewing the files ó Lauris sent to Manu. Meeting dates and times. Photographs, recordings. Leone met with the warden of Redrock Prison and the Alliance special operations chief of station multiple times, but there's no proof they were discussing a prisoner supply chain to Redrock. He remembers Kumail Anh's warning that the public won't care enough about the welfare of prisoners to consider it a treasonous offense, and Jaantzen isn't sure the terraforming operation and the trade agreement will push it into that territory, either.

But when it comes out Leone was assisting the Alliance in covering up the discovery of priceless alien technology on New Sarjunian soil — whether she knew it or not — that would definitely be treason.

Only problem is, Kumail has yet to trace the money path that irrevocably links Leone to any of this.

"We're working on proof," Jaantzen says.

"It would need to be rock-solid," says Ulrich. "Or she'll weasel her way out like she has everything else in her storied career."

She goes quiet again as Ajesh and his daughter come back with the main dishes, far more food than four people could possibly eat. The pair pull a second, smaller table close to fill with the remainder of the food, refill drinks, and retreat once more.

Ulrich spoons chile-roasted cauliflower onto her plate, then passes the dish to Tabari. "I've told you what we want, Mr. Jaantzen. Your turn."

"To go about my business without a target on my back, whether that's a police warrant, an Alliance special agent, or a headhunter's bounty."

Ulrich stills. "Leone hired a headhunter?" She sits back in her chair, studying him. Because while Tabari and Calanthe may play in both worlds, he and Ulrich are both crossing lines this evening. Jaantzen isn't used to the political maneuvering it takes to run a country and negotiate with the Alliance; Madinia Ulrich is probably insulated from the darker ways people get and maintain power in this city.

"She did," Jaantzen says. Across the table, Tabari straightens and mouths Phaera's name; he saw the tabloid speculation about her strange absence from the Devil's Table opening night like everyone else. Jaantzen nods. Tabari swallows hard.

"All right." Ulrich apparently missed the exchange. "Well, I can tell you the prime minister and the Alliance ambassador met today, and they are taking all of this very seriously."

Tabari clears his throat. "And Prime Minister de Grazal and I will be convening a group of Bulari business owners in the next couple of days to get their input on the next draft of the agreement. You should come, Jaantzen." Beside him, Ulrich's professional expression slips in surprise before she pastes it back into place.

"If my presence would be productive." He'll give Tabari and Ulrich the opportunity to hash that one out in private.

"We're also taking an Alliance agent attacking a private citizen very seriously," says Ulrich. She turns to Calanthe. "But it is being treated as a rogue incident."

"You've seen her testimony," Calanthe snaps. "She wasn't rogue."

"It has to be this way, Ms. Yang," Ulrich says with a sigh of frustration. "You know that. And if your client wants her amnesty plea to be accepted by the New Sarjunian government she'll change her testimony to match. Or she can recant altogether and take her chances when we send her back to her handlers. But either way, the Alliance didn't order an attack on a private citizen in a sovereign country, are we clear?"

"I don't care what the public story is," Jaantzen says. "I want your reassurances the Alliance won't attack me again."

"We can't make those reassurances without knowing how you made yourself a target."

"I will tell the prime minister," says Jaantzen. "And him alone."

Ulrich frowns, then pops a fried almond in her mouth and chews thoughtfully, evaluating him. Finally she sits back and pushes up her sleeve, revealing a utilitarian government-issue cuff. "How's tomorrow?" she asks.

"I'll be at a funeral."

Ulrich's gaze flickers to Calanthe with pity, then back to her cuff. "The end of the week, then? I can send you some potential times."

"That works." Provided this situation hasn't completely blown up on them all by the end of the week.

"Good." Ulrich seems about to reach for another almond, but she pushes her plate back. "I'm stuffed. This was incredible."

It's the cue Ajesh and his daughter have been waiting for to begin clearing plates, ask about dessert, insist on pressing take-home containers of pastries into willing hands. Ulrich leaves Jaantzen with a firm handshake and Ajesh with a promise to see him again soon; Tabari lingers briefly out of her earshot.

"It's time for new blood to lead this town," he says quietly. "Let me know what you need."

"Thank you, old friend." Jaantzen gives him a warm smile, but, still. He knows better than to truly trust Tabari.

"That went better than I expected," Calanthe says when they're alone. "I'll be honest, I'm getting so used to setbacks, this was a bit of a shock."

"Don't make jam before the fig tree bears fruit," Jaantzen says, and Calanthe's breath catches. It was one of her mother's sayings. The woman never trusted a deal would come through until it was over, and that level of paranoia kept her business thriving.

"Would you like me to come early tomorrow?" he asks; they're both already thinking about Julieta now, he might as well broach the subject of the funeral.

"Yes, thank you."

"Starla has a security team ready," he says. She'd taken care of that this morning, before she and Toshiyo went off on their quest to find Zacharia. "You focus on your family."

Calanthe nods, then scrapes the tip of one pale pink manicured nail along her lower lash line, collecting the tear there and flicking it away. "I should get back to the office," she says. She winces and puts a hand on her belly. "Settle down, sweetie," she murmurs. "Mama's got too much work to do."

"I'm sorry for my role in that."

She waves a hand. "This is . . ." But her voice catches and she squeezes her eyes shut a moment before swiping at her other lash line. "Goddammit. I want to be working, Willem. It's the only thing that makes sense right now."

"Let's get you back to the office, then. Manu?"

He can hear Manu in the kitchen, his low voice along with a woman's laughter. When Jaantzen walks to the doorway, Mirana Paiman is smiling at whatever Manu said. Mirana's smile doesn't cool when she sees Jaantzen standing in the doorway to her kitchen. Manu has managed to convince Ajesh's wife he has no ill will towards the family, even if Ajesh is still walking on glass.

"Thank you for the meal, and your hospitality," Jaantzen says, and she bows her head.

"My pleasure, Mr. Jaantzen," she says. She reaches for the younger of her daughters, hugs her close. "It's the least we could do after you brought our girls home."

"Always, Mirana," he says. "Remember that."

It's a promise he'll fight like hell to keep.

The lift opens to a hush.

Jaantzen isn't sure what he was expecting — chairs turned over, the contents of cupboards and bookshelves spilled out onto counters and floors — but the penthouse suite of Cobalt Tower looks as it did when he left it.

The penthouse is two stories, a wide sweeping staircase going up to the second level, a kitchen tucked under the stairs and open to the rest of the main floor. A pair of electric-blue couches forming a comfortable seating area, the massive conference table hosting war meetings and dinners alike, a hydroponic garden — a feature he'd added to house all of Julieta's gifts over the years — cutting a swath through the middle of the floor. Floor-to-ceiling windows offer a view over downtown Bulari; the city looks so peaceful from above, but Jaantzen knows the truth. The streets are still filled with protesters, but they haven't turned to riot — in part, strangely, thanks to Coeur's crew.

Still. A lot can change overnight.

He scans the room again, but there's no sign the police turned it upside down searching for whatever evidence against him they could find. Everything's sterile, precise, in its tidy place. Except one thing: a cheerful yellow pot in the middle of his kitchen counter, a single cutting from a jadau plant thriving in the soil.

Grief hits him fresh.

The cutting Julieta Yang gave him the day she told him Coeur had died. He'd forgotten it, unplanted, even before he went out to the desert, not realizing it would be the last cutting she'd ever give him. He'd assumed it had shriveled and died, but someone had found the cutting and potted it. Has been caring for it.

He picks up the note beside the plant and his suspicions are confirmed.

*I found this little guy and kept him happy. Glad you're back. Lo*

Lo é Njeri, Cobalt Tower's . . . well. He's not entirely sure what title she and Manu agreed on, only that she's the reason any of this is still running.

The lights flicker as the doorbell chimes, and security vid appears automatically on the kitchen counter. The miracle woman herself, nervously adjusting her skirt while she waits.

"It's good to see you, Mr. Jaantzen," Lo says as soon as the lift door opens. She doesn't hesitate to take his hand, same as the first time they met in person, and her handshake is firm, her smile warm and open. And somewhat relieved. He realizes somewhat guiltily that he hasn't thought much about how Lo's been managing the pile of responsibilities she inherited. He's been too focused on his own immediate circle and their welfare, and she's seemed unflappable — but being the public face of Willem Jaantzen's business during the past week can't have been easy.

"It's good to see you, too. Come in. And thank you, holding down the fort on your own couldn't have been easy, but you've done an admirable job."

Her cheeks flush at the compliment, but she just gives him a quick nod. Her pixie cut is a fading orange that calls out the freckles in her light brown cheeks. Her pale green blouse and brightly patterned skirt are as relentlessly cheerful as her disposition.

"Is your family safe?"

Lo looks up at him with a frown.

"With all the protests." Lo may not have an Arquellian drawl, but her parents are immigrants. And as Arquelle is the wealthiest and most aggressive of the Alliance's founding members, it's no surprise public anger has been made manifest against those who were born there.

"They're fine," she says. "Staying close to home since the embassy got bombed — and definitely with the protests. But they have good neighbors who are checking on them and making them welcome."

"Where do they live?"

"Carama Town."

It makes sense. A lot of immigrants end up in Carama Town. "Let me know if there's anything we can do to help," Jaantzen says. "Has anyone been bothering you personally?" She may not have the accent, but the Arquellian naming convention — "Lo the daughter of Njeri" — stands out.

"I think most people have been too afraid of you to give me much trouble," Lo says; he notes the words *most* and *much* with a mental reminder to ask Manu to find out who has been bothering Lo and explain to them why they shouldn't. Lo's bright smile dims a bit as she turns to take in the penthouse. "The police left this place wrecked," she says. "I think the cleaners did a good job, but if anything's still wrong, let me know. They were rough with the plants."

He hadn't examined the hydroponic garden closely until now, but there are signs of damage. Broken-off stems, torn leaves, though someone has carefully pruned to try to mask the trauma. He strokes a finger gently over the tip of a variegated leaf, letting the bead of water at its tip transfer to his fingertip, crystalline, magnifying the pattern of his fingerprint below.

"Whoever you hired did a good job repairing the damage," he says to Lo; she relaxes slightly. He turns away, wiping the droplet off on his trousers. "Do you suppose they found anything interesting there? Or were they just having fun?"

"They were having fun." Her expression darkens. "I'm glad you weren't here to see it."

Jaantzen lets the fury roll through him, surprised at it. He hadn't thought he'd care what Leone's police did here. But after losing Julieta? Seeing the damage done to her garden rips that wound open fresh. And, after all, this is his home — not simply another place to stay. Maybe it's felt cold and empty all these years, but that's because he kept others out of it. That night he'd dined with Phaera, Calanthe, and Letizia Diamante, it had felt warm.

He's not about to let Leone chase him out.

"Do you want to go over today's reports?"

Jaantzen shakes himself out of his thoughts. Lo's here for a reason, and an idea is forming in his head. "Yes," he says. "And then I'd like some help with logistics for tomorrow night after the funeral. Will you be free then? I'd like for you to meet the rest of the crew."

It's after dark when he and Lo finish up, and Jaantzen checks the time; Starla and Toshiyo should be home by now. He settles on one of the couches with his comm in hand, a pour of whiskey on the table in front of him, and makes a call.

## 16

## TOSHIYO

Starla's shifting the ORV into park with a heavy clunk as Toshiyo's comm chimes.

It's the boss.

Lucky flaps irritably in the back seat of the ORV, a claw-tipped wing flicking past her cheek. "Calm down," Toshiyo mutters under her breath, not sure if she means it for Lucky, for Jaantzen's insistent chime, or for both. She fumbles for the door handle with one hand, her comm in the other, and Lucky pushes past her with a screech. She manages to catch her comm on the toe of one boot, barely slowing its descent before it hits the cement pad of the hangar floor.

She scoops it up — all good. "What is it?"

"Are you all right?"

"I'm fine," she snaps; her tone startles even her. "It's been a long day," she adds in explanation. Hours and hours in the boneshaking ORV while Lucky zeroed in on the location of his full-grown cousin. They'd tried to stick to the main roads but had cut through plenty of rutted dirt tracks and dry washes, too. She's exhausted and achy from the cramped, stuffy vehicle, and Lucky's in a mood. Understandably so. They found his cousin, and didn't do anything to save them.

"I haven't had a chance to look at what you sent over," Jaantzen says, and she bites back irritation — why had she spent the last two hours fighting bumpy roads to type it on this stupid little screen, then? "But I take it you found the Dawn?"

"We did."

Starla's gone to close up the hangar while Toshiyo takes this call; now she's barring the doors shut against the last wash of inky blue from the fading sunset. And Lucky's — dammit. Toshiyo spins, worried he's decided to do something dangerous in his frustration. Go off on his own, maybe, try to find his way back to the Dawn encampment without them.

But he's crouched by the door to the bunkers, glowering at her.

Angry and disappointed.

Same, buddy.

She missed whatever Jaantzen said. "Sorry," she says. "We just got back, I'm a bit distracted."

"I asked for your take on the Dawn situation. Starla already told me she thinks it's impossible with our current resources."

Impossible? This whole thing has been impossible. Working with Lucky today was maddening — it had taken some heated conversation for Lucky to understand the concept of a map, of roads. That when he pointed due east, sometimes Starla had to zig and zag in order to get there, because ravines and cliffs were in the way.

But eventually they'd made it to their destination: an

abandoned corporate mining claim on the far side of Bulari. A ghost town like so many others in the desert. Rows of prefab houses in cheerful primary colors scoured by the wind and rusted in the occasional rains, now with sand drifting through the open doors, dziva hounds making their dens below the flooring, and scorpions crouching in the corners. The map said Tsau-Kohl, a lithium mine that ran out three decades ago and has been abandoned ever since. Until somebody who wanted to hide a couple of stolen Alliance transports, several dozen escaped Redrock prisoners, and probably an entire alien took up residence.

They'd managed to find a secluded spot on a ridge not too far away to observe, while Lucky vibrated with excitement that they'd finally found his cousin. Only one problem.

"There were maybe a hundred people there?" Toshiyo guesses. On the other end of the line, the boss makes a noncommittal noise. "Well-defended settlement, and it didn't look all that new. I'd guess we found the place that priest Thomas Deté escaped to when Acheta started wiping out the Dawn inside the city."

"And the escaped Dawn prisoners?"

"Hard to tell. We couldn't get close — they picked a good spot with plenty of perimeter visibility. Out of range for beetle drones. We set up some cameras, some trip sensors on the roads out of there."

"So we'll know if anything changes."

"Maybe, boss." Starla shoots her a questioning sign from the door to the bunker, and Toshiyo gives her a thumbs-up, leans wearily against the still-warm hood of the ORV and tilts her head back, staring up at the bright lights of the hangar's ceiling. This is maddening. They were so close. *So close.* And they couldn't do anything to touch the Dawn.

"Was Zacharia there?"

"Couldn't tell. Based on the equipment we could see — and the trash heap in the ravine behind the place — they've got another shard operation running. Two trucks came in while we were watching, they dropped off a lot of empty crates and loaded up some full ones. They drove by close enough I could tag them, so I know where they ended up. Warehouse in Carama Town."

"Thank you."

"Sure. But if we don't do something about the main operation, there are going to be more of those trucks going out, and they may not be headed to the same warehouse. And I'm not there to tag every single one of them manually."

Jaantzen sighs. "We're stretched too thin, Toshiyo," he says. "You said there were a hundred people out there."

"Not all fighters. Some looked like workers."

"Still. You're sure the creature is there?"

"Lucky was certain." She prepares to defend trusting their new telepathic dowsing rod of a friend, but Jaantzen doesn't argue.

"They won't kill it," he says. "It's too valuable."

He can't be serious. "They might not kill it, but they're torturing it. We can't leave it there."

"And we can't spare the people we'd need to take down an operation that big. We wait, and we watch. And once we've dealt with Leone, we can tackle this next problem."

"I don't think we have time, boss. What if we get help? Did you talk to Coeur?"

"I did. She offered assistance, but it's too much of a

risk. Julieta's funeral is tomorrow. The situation with Leone is up in the air. And sending in outsiders means risking the creature falling into the wrong hands."

"It's already in the wrong hands."

"You know what I mean, Toshiyo."

She breathes out a curse. "If that was me? Starla? You wouldn't hesitate to mobilize everything you had to get us back."

"This isn't the same." Jaantzen's voice sounds strained. Or maybe he's surprised she's digging in on this — Toshiyo would be surprised herself if she wasn't so dead tired from the long day.

She never argues with the boss. She presents alternatives. She gives recommendations. And even those rare times when she's disagreed with him completely — like when he tried to assassinate Coeur when she was mayor, knowing it would probably cost him his life — she only offered her opinion, knowing he would make the final decision.

Her job is to provide information. His job is to have the final say.

And he's making the wrong decision.

"It's not the same," she agrees. "But it's not just about rescuing Lucky's cousin. You're not paying enough attention to what the Dawn might be planning."

"I'm paying attention to every other problem in this city." His voice sounds like it's coming through clenched teeth. "I can't be responsible for them all."

Toshiyo bites back an angry response — she's not mad at the boss. She's hungry, she reeks from a day spent riding in an ORV with intermittent air conditioning, and her boots are filled with sand. She needs food, a shower, and an actual night's sleep if she's going have a real chance at convincing Jaantzen.

As she's trying to come up with a way to say this, he speaks again.

"I'm sorry, Toshiyo. Let's talk about this tomorrow when we're both fresh."

"We should at least take care of the trucks I tracked."

There's a long pause. "Keep an eye on the warehouse for now. And the compound. Let me know if anything changes."

If anything changes, it will be too late to stop more people from dying. But Jaantzen's made his decision.

"Good night, boss." Toshiyo thumbs off the comm and pushes herself off the hood of the ORV, her lower back aching. She should get some rest, so she can bring all this to the boss with a solid argument and a plan tomorrow, when she goes into town for yet another funeral.

First it had been Ximena Nayar, Blackheart's sister, whom Toshiyo had started to like. Then the security guards at Cobalt Tower, people Toshiyo knew by voice if not by face, from years of listening to them banter over the tower's internal security channels. Then all the dead indentured workers at Blacklode Corp's mine in Ruby Basin. Toshiyo had tuned in to the memorial, listening to the names read out with breath held for the moment she recognized one. She hadn't. El had sat with her through that.

And tomorrow she'll mourn Julieta, who had always been kind to her.

She's so tired of wondering if the people she loves are going to come home safe.

Something pricks the back of her neck and she whirls to find Lucky watching her from a perch atop a pile of crates. She'd seen him go down to the bunker with Starla and she hadn't heard him return — much less climb all the way up there.

She tamps down the spike of adrenaline and beckons for him to come down. "I'm sorry," she signs. "We'll help your friend, but we need more people." And more information. And a better plan. And for Jaantzen to let them do it. "We'll figure it out tomorrow."

Lucky doesn't respond, just glares at her with his glassy, alien eyes. She's failed him. He came to her for help, and trusted her to make things right. And when they finally found his cousin, she and Starla had simply watched the Dawn for a while and then drove back home.

Footsteps on the stairs: Starla's panicking. Her shoulders slump in relief when she sees Toshiyo with Lucky. "I put him in his room," she signs to Toshiyo. "But when I came back with dinner he was gone."

They can't keep living like this, with an increasingly large and irritable alien wandering through their home at will. Lucky needs to be with people who know what they're doing, who can learn more about him and his kind, who won't hurt him.

Another unsolvable problem.

Starla frowns at whatever she sees on Toshiyo's face. "Are you all right?"

"Tired," Toshiyo signs back. She waves a hand at Lucky. "C'mon, buddy. We all need to sleep."

But even after she gets him settled, says good night to Starla, gets her shower and a snack? Toshiyo is exhausted, but not sleepy. Normally when she feels like this she camps out in the conference room and throws on a horror movie until she can't keep her eyes open anymore. But she still has work to do, so tonight she slumps in front of her desk, palms it on, and checks her messages.

There's a new one. From GraySeeker.

All of Toshiyo's exhaustion drains away.

*I AM TALKING ABOUT THE DAWN. I HAVE DEDICATED MY LIFE TO DESTROYING THEM LIKE THEY DESTROYED MY DAUGHTER. AND IF YOU HAVE ANY INFORMATION ABOUT WHERE THEY'RE HIDING NOW, I WILL MAKE SURE YOU — AND EVERYONE ELSE THEY'VE HURT — ARE SAFE FROM THEM FOREVER. ARE YOU IN BULARI?*

A stab of triumph causes Toshiyo to smile. At least one thing is going right.

*HOW DO I KNOW I CAN TRUST YOU?* she types back.

There's a long delay; Toshiyo cracks her ring fingers.

*I'VE ALREADY DESTROYED A FEW OF THEIR SHARD PLANTS.*

What follows is a link to an article about a destroyed shard operation from back before Coeur regained power and started shutting them down herself. Toshiyo flips through the images of the charred building, fire kindling in her own veins. She's had her own visions of burning the Dawn to the ground since she first started reading about the towns they poisoned in their attempt to replicate the alien venom. And this woman, GraySeeker, is out there doing it.

Except.

GraySeeker seems to be a part of White Star. Which means even if she's working against the Dawn here in Bulari, she probably still believes the stuff Felipe Zacharia wrote.

As Toshiyo is puzzling out her next response, her comm chimes again.

*Can you meet? I promise you'll be safe. I only want to know where else they have facilities.*

*Who do you work for?*

*Myself.*

Even if Toshiyo was currently in town, she wouldn't trust an in-person meeting. She needs to know more about the Dawn, but she can't really ask outright without tipping her hand that the "cult refugee" persona is a ploy. And GraySeeker seems to be as cautious about revealing new information as Toshiyo is — they could go round and round for days unless they find a way to trust each other.

*Other people have contacted me about this, too,* Toshiyo writes. *But I think they really believe what that psycho Zacharia wrote. Do you?*

*I know people who do. I don't. He's a bad man who deserves what's coming to him.*

*He's back,* Toshiyo writes.

*Then I will take him down.*

*It's too much for one person.*

*Trust me.*

"Trust me" doesn't give any insight into whether or not GraySeeker has allies, or is working on her own here. Toshiyo gnaws on the inside of her lip, thinking. She can't make a decision about whether or not to trust this woman over messages, but she can give her a test, and then maybe meet her in person when she's back in Bulari.

She opens up a channel to Jaantzen, and he answers immediately.

"I think I have a way to destroy those trucks without risking any of our people," she says. "I've been trying to get in touch with a local mercenary who's been hunting down the Dawn, destroying their operations. She got back to me."

"You trust her?"

"No. But this doesn't expose us." Three heartbeats; Jaantzen still hasn't said anything. "If this is that same tainted shard, people are going to start dying as soon as it hits the streets."

Finally Jaantzen takes a deep breath. "All right."

"Okay. See you tomorrow, boss."

Toshiyo cuts the connection; her black-lacquered fingernails are already clacking against the keyboard as she types her response to GraySeeker.

*THEY SENT TWO TRUCKS TO A WAREHOUSE IN CARAMA TOWN. THEY'RE FULL OF SHARD, BUT WORSE. THE STUFF THEY'VE BEEN MAKING.*

GraySeeker's response comes immediately: *THE GIFT OF THE FALLEN.*

A chill traces its way down Toshiyo's spine. *MAYBE. I'M SCARED OF WHAT WILL HAPPEN IF IT GETS OUT.*

*I'LL DESTROY IT, PROVE YOU CAN TRUST ME. SEND ME THE ADDRESS.*

Toshiyo's fingers hesitate over the keyboard a heartbeat before she types it out. Hits Send. GraySeeker confirms receipt of the message, and Toshiyo turns off her desk, pulse pounding.

She's either found a powerful ally, or delivered a shipment of tainted shard into the hands of an organization she doesn't know she can trust. But at least something's going to be done about it. Now to wait and see if it pays off.

17

## MANU

The whole town's turned out to honor Julieta Yang.

Politicians. Members of her horticultural clubs. Society matrons who were both friends and customers. Suppliers. Business partners. A retired police chief, who exchanges casual nods with Manu.

Their very expensive spinners fill the large circular driveway, ringed by the Yang family home, the gardens, and the massive greenhouse. A few mourners have wandered off to visit the gardens and greenhouse, whether to admire Julieta's handiwork or talk business in private, but most are paying their respects to the grand dame of the luxury black market in the black-draped living room, then gathering in the shaded central court-yard to share memories and hors d'oeuvres.

Manu's found himself a comfortable seat in the courtyard, across from the entryway and the curtained entrance to the living room, and has been watching mourners come and go for hours. The courtyard is the size of his apartment, shaded by an ancient silver willow, the air cooled by mister drones and fans. Elegant, colorful orchids have been brought from the greenhouse to decorate every surface — living blooms explode around the bases of garden statuary, peek between plates of food, and cascade from the silver willow's branches.

Jaantzen and Phaera have been continuously caught up in conversation, sometimes as a couple, sometimes apart. Manu makes conversation when he needs to, steps in from time to time whenever he catches Calanthe or Alex Yang noticing an empty appetizer tray before the caterers do. Otherwise he's letting himself enjoy a moment of peace and keeping an eye out for trouble.

He doesn't need to. Starla's team is monitoring the driveway, watching the crowds, and politely making sure anyone who's come armed takes advantage of the secure weapons storage while they're here. Probably no one's planning to make a scene; rivals typically put aside their spats at something like this, and anyone who did business with Julieta should be content to do business with her son Liatris. They've been pressing their condolences on him for hours, and he's taking it all with gravitas.

Manu might not recognize everyone in this crowd of politicians and smugglers and society ladies and horticulturalists, but he knows instantly that the two newcomers walking through the entryway don't belong. They wear sharp funeral suits, but they're holding themselves with the sort of casual professionalism that says they're not here to mourn. He straightens, then sees the young woman they're flanking. She's so drawn into herself, so defeated, he barely recognizes her.

Aster Yang.

Julieta's youngest daughter, the one who betrayed her mother to the Dawn and nearly got them all killed. He's wondered where Calanthe and Liatris have been keeping her.

She keeps her head down as she skirts the edge of the courtyard, hands clasped primly in front of her, though Manu can't tell if the heavy bracelets she's wearing are actually cuffs. Her family is ignoring her and he's about to do the same when she glances his way. Her gaze locks with his and her tear-streaked face goes a shade paler.

He gives her a curt nod and she flinches away, slipping into the living room and sinking into a chair near her mother's prone form. She buries her face in her hands, shoulders shaking.

The hairs on the back of his neck prickle with discomfort.

Starla's come back in from one of her rounds on the tail of Aster and her two guards, and now she's watching Aster with an expression he can't quite read. Despite being about the same age, the two never were friends. Even before Aster turned traitor.

Starla turns her back on Aster. Snags a pair of sugar-dusted almond cakes from a catering table and makes a beeline for Manu, settling onto the bench beside him and handing him a cake.

"I can't talk about flowers anymore," she signs with sugar-dusted fingers. "What happened to Toshiyo?"

"She talked Oriol into giving her a ride back downtown hours ago." He pops the tiny cake into his mouth.

"Guess she couldn't talk about flowers anymore either." Starla blinks a notification off her lens and licks sugar off her fingertips, then types a few sentences into her gauntlet and relaxes into the bench. She frowns, and Manu follows her expression. She's watching Jaantzen and Phaera; they've just finished speaking with an

Indiran gem dealer and now Jaantzen's hand drifts to the small of Phaera's back. He leans down to murmur something in her ear, she smiles.

"She's got him wrapped around her finger, huh?" Starla slides him a look. "Oriol, too."

"You don't like her?"

"Only other time I met her, Jaantzen suspected she'd ordered the hit on me."

"She's all right."

"Just all right?"

Manu laughs. "She's good for him. Stop being so nosy."

"Says the king of getting in other people's business."

"I'm gonna get a desk plaque made."

Starla's hands still in mid-retort, her attention drawn past Manu to the entryway. She grins in surprise and springs to her feet.

Another new arrival — Absolon Chevalier, the Arquellian arms dealer, an old friend of Starla's parents and Julieta Yang alike. The man smiles, crosses the courtyard, and throws arms wide for a hug.

"I didn't know you were going to be here," she signs when she steps back from the embrace.

Absolon's expression clouds. "I heard the news Julieta wasn't doing well," he signs. "But I hoped I would be arriving on New Sarjun to wish her the best on her recovery." Absolon is proof you can transpose the Arquellian drawl onto USL; his signs are languid and easy, slight variations showing his foreign roots. He shakes hands with Manu. "Always a pleasure, even in these dark times."

Absolon glances over his shoulder, beckoning forward an attractive young man who's obviously related: the same smooth black skin and refined features, those same dark, copper-flecked eyes that always seem to hold an amusing secret.

"My nephew, Luc," signs Absolon. The young man greets Manu politely, then turns to Starla with a smile that could only be called devastating. His cheek dimples. "Starla, you remember Luc?"

Does she ever remember Luc, her face says, and Manu fights to keep himself from grinning as she wrestles her surprised expression under control.

"It's good to see you again," Luc signs, and Starla returns the greeting coolly, but Manu didn't miss the complicated flicker of shock, lust, and fury that flashed through Starla's eyes.

He cannot *wait* to pry.

"I'm glad you came by," Manu signs. "I know Calanthe and Liatris appreciate it."

"Julieta was an incredible woman." Absolon turns to Starla. "But I also have something I've been meaning to give you in person."

He reaches into his suit pocket and pulls out a soft suede pouch. It seems heavy in his hand, hard edges visible through the suede.

Starla glances around the courtyard, but no one is paying them any attention. She unties the leather thongs and slips a smooth gray tablet into her palm. Her eyes go wide, and she hands it to Manu.

"Where did you find this?" she asks Absolon.

It's surprisingly heavy for how small it is, surprisingly cold for having been in Absolon's pocket during the heat of the day. And it's etched with a now-familiar image: a stylized winged figure, spiraling upwards. Manu slips the tablet back into the pouch before anyone else catches a glimpse. No one's watching them.

"In Durga's Belt," Absolon signs. "The same place your mother found the one she always wore."

"You were with my parents? And Felipe Zacharia?"

"Not for the job itself. I helped them fence some of the haul, and I went back on my own, years later. There wasn't much left, but I did find this."

"I was talking to Mona last week," Luc signs. A muscle jumps in Starla's jaw. "She said you were looking for any info on your mom's necklace, and I remembered Uncle Absolon had this."

"You can track down Mona, but you can't let me know you're coming to Bulari?" Starla gives Luc her shoulder before he can respond. Luc flashes Manu a *You know how it goes* look, but Manu holds up his hands — kid can save his own neck if he's pissed off Starla.

"You said you fenced the goods," Starla signs to Absolon. "Do you know what happened on that job? With Zacharia?"

Absolon shakes his head. "Normally your parents loved to tell tales, but on this they stayed quiet. I just know it ended badly."

"Will you tell me where you found this?"

Absolon's lips thin. "It's in a very dangerous part of Durga's Belt."

"This job? I need to know what happened. It's the reason my parents got killed."

Absolon's fingers flex in thought. "In the end, yes. That should tell you something about how dangerous it is. I will ask you once as a favor: leave it alone."

"I'm already mixed up in it." Starla takes the stone tablet back from Manu and slips it into a pocket. "Besides. If you'd wanted me to leave things alone, you wouldn't have brought this to me."

"A worried old man can hope. And offer advice — but it's not my place to make decisions for you." Absolon types a long list of numbers from memory into the gunmetal-and-onyx cuff on his wrist, then presses Send. Starla blinks, light playing across her iris. "The coordinates," Absolon signs.

"Thank you. And I appreciate the warning."

"No, you don't." Absolon smiles sadly at her. "Not yet, at least. If you decide to pursue this, I'll help in any way I can." He turns with a slight bow to Manu. "I'm going to make the rounds," he signs. "It was a pleasure."

Luc doesn't make a move to follow his uncle, and Starla finally takes an annoyed breath and turns back to him, the arch of her eyebrow saying he has one shot to explain his way out of whatever hot water he's gotten himself into. Luc parries her glare with a devilish smile, that dimple popping back into his cheek, and the tension flying between the two is so electric it could spark a brushfire.

Manu can read a room. "I'm gonna go rescue Gia," he signs to Starla, who barely acknowledges him. "Nice to meet you, Luc."

Manu does a quick scan of the now-crowded courtyard — only a few dozen of Julieta's closest friends and family will remain when the Knives come to bury her at sunset, and the afternoon is peak time for those who don't plan on staying to make their visit.

Jaantzen's sitting at a garden table with Teo Lordeur, shaded by palm fronds. Phaera is helping one of the caterers refill a tray of sandwiches. Liatris and Calanthe are accepting condolences and loyalty assurances from a tall woman Manu doesn't recognize, and Gia and Tevi are chatting with an old woman in boxy black lace. Gia's half paying attention, so Manu catches her eye across the room and jerks his chin at the door. She nods, then smiles at whatever the old woman said. And leans in to excuse herself, murmuring something into Tevi's ear.

Nobody's supposed to be comfortable at a funeral, but Tevi Sharaf looks more uncomfortable than most. He's dressed up: nice suit, shoes shined, fresh haircut, and Manu supposes he goes to enough galas and fundraisers to not be bothered by the wealth and titles present in this crowd. But he knows what kind of business Julieta Yang ran, and he obviously knows he's at a funeral attended by people who live in the same grayscale economy Julieta did. Including, probably, many of the same people who donate to the Andel Medical School.

Tevi shoots Manu a wary look, then shines his smile back on the old woman.

Gia meets him at the door to the entryway. "Who's the eye candy Starla's about to murder?"

"Chevalier's nephew, apparently."

"I'm dying of curiosity." Gia rolls her shoulders, cracks her neck. She's wearing a black silk blouse and loose trousers, soft fabrics that do nothing to hide the hardness of muscle underneath. "What's going on?" Something in the way Gia asks makes it seem like she's hoping for trouble. Manu's going to have to disappoint.

"Walk with me a sec? I got something to talk to you about. C'mon. Let's find someplace quiet."

The house's entryway is cool compared to the courtyard, but when he pushes through the front door into the front yard the midday heat hits him like an open hand.

Julieta's house is on one side of a big circular driveway, her greenhouse is on the other. There's no trace now of the battle that shattered the greenhouse, put scorch marks in the driveway, bullet holes in the center fountain.

There's no trace of that battle in Manu now, either. Which is what he wants to talk to Gia about.

Manu exchanges nods with the Admant guards who are directing spinner traffic, then sets out across the driveway.

The greenhouse is open for mourners to visit, but that's not where Manu's headed. Too many people, too many ears potentially listening in. He leads Gia past it to Julieta's meditation garden of hardy desert plants and hybrids she bred herself. The path is smooth, with acacia and white-barked eucarix arching overhead to provide shade, a sweet nectar scent from the blooms of lavender and thieves' rose and a dozen other plants Manu can't name. It's hot enough no one else is wandering around here.

"How are your superpowers?" he asks once they've walked a moment in the silent hush. "Still going strong?"

She gives him a sidelong look. "Far as I can tell."

"Glad to hear it." Manu takes a slow spin, taking in the garden, making sure they're alone before propping one shoulder against the trunk of a eucarix and shoving his hands in his pockets. "You know how when you were out of town, Oriol and I busted up this secret lab where they were trying to replicate the alien venom you got dosed with?"

She blinks at him. "No."

"It was good times. Sorry you missed it. But I think the *Coldfire* was getting shot down right about then, so I guess you were having some fun of your own."

"Just a little." She clears her throat. "Don't tell Tevi about the ship getting shot down."

Manu laughs, incredulous. "G, he's gonna find out one way or another."

"Well it better fucking not be from you." Her glare could kill. "I don't want to talk about it. What do you want."

He untucks his shirt, hiking it up to reveal the stab wound Tierren left above his hipbone, the one Gia herself had stitched up a bit over a week ago. Now the scar's barely noticeable. Gia's eyes go wide. "I got a good lungful of whatever they were cooking up. Breathed it in. Anything that's happened since then isn't healing faster than usual, but it gave me a clean slate."

"What *is* this shit?"

"I don't know. I've been waiting to talk to you and Tosh about it. What's going on with you?"

She sets her jaw, then finally sinks onto a nearby stone bench. Something's buzzing in the brush around them; a bird calls overhead.

"Toshiyo gave me the research the Alliance had been doing on what the alien venom does to humans. It stimulates rapid cellular regeneration, makes humans more resistant to disease. Stronger. The Alliance was experimenting on prisoners, and as far as I can tell all the test subjects died within a few months. Reading between the lines it's because they got unruly, not because the venom killed them. So there's no data on longevity, or how this progresses beyond a few months."

"So this is all new territory."

Gia nods, lips pressed together. "According to the files Tosh gave me, the aliens don't produce much venom. The Alliance has been trying to replicate it, but it doesn't seem like they have yet."

"But the Dawn has. That's what we found in their creepy science lab."

"That's too bad."

"Understatement of the year."

"I'm kind of overwhelmed," Gia says. She takes a deep breath. "So. The Dawn can make more of me."

"And what are you?"

Gia frowns, considering. "I'm not sure. Far as I can tell, it dulls pain. Dulls all sensation, actually." She doesn't offer details, Manu doesn't press. "The wound where the alien bit me healed overnight without a trace, wounds since then have healed rapidly, but not as completely. Like yours." She jerks his chin at his hip, then unbuttons her sleeve to reveal a faint scar on her forearm. "I did that two days ago."

"You feel all right?"

"Amazing. I'm stronger, better stamina. I beat Tevi's ass on our run this morning." Her grin fades quickly, though. "I guess we're both freaks now. I'll have to get you in the lab."

Manu holds up his hand. "Hey, no. You're still the only freak. Mine was a one-time deal."

"So getting injected with the venom can change you for good, but breathing in the gas just gives you a temporary help? You ought to stock up on that juice."

"I'm gonna hold off and see if it makes you grow wings or glow in the dark first." He holds out a hand and helps Gia off the bench. "Better get back. Tevi's going to think I'm getting you into trouble."

They walk in silence until they're out of the meditation garden, then Gia reaches over to brush ashy dust from the eucarix bark off Manu's shoulder. "All this?" she waves an arm, indicating the funeral, the alien, the Dawn,

Coeur. "This is shitty. But I've seen you more than I have in years. That's been nice."

"Let's not be strangers once this is over."

"I'd like that."

Manu grins at her, a grin that fades as a new spinner pulls into the driveway.

This day's been far too peaceful, and it's about to change.

Chief Justice Geum-ja Leone is here.

## 18

## JAANTZEN

Jaantzen isn't listening in on Admant's security channel, so he doesn't hear the call come in. But Starla's in his field of vision — she's been chatting with a young man who must be some relative of Absolon Chevalier — and when she holds up a hand to cut the man off, it immediately catches Jaantzen's attention.

She blinks the message off her lens and her eyes lock on his from across the courtyard.

"Leone," she signs. "She's here."

The woman he's talking with, an antiquities dealer, glances over her shoulder to see what's caught his attention. "My apologies," he says to her. "There's something I need to take care of. Thank you for coming."

"Keep her outside," Jaantzen signs to Starla. "I'll take care of it."

The gall she has to show her face here. The arrogance. With anyone else, Jaantzen would be surprised, but Geum-ja Leone has already proven she has no shame. He's been half waiting for this moment all afternoon.

Phaera's radiant in a circle of other women, some he

knows, some he doesn't, and he gives them all a friendly smile as he approaches. One part of him is still amazed at the way she leans towards him, even in public, even in front of these women who surely know who he is. The citrus and cardamom of her perfume, the silk strands of her hair brushing his cheek as he bends to whisper in her ear, it's all so incredibly, blissfully normal.

And maybe someday he'll get to appreciate it for more than a heartbeat or two.

"Leone's here," he murmurs. Her back stiffens under his hand. "I'll take care of it."

Fear and resolve are warring in her face, and he can't tell if she wants to come with him. But she takes a sharp breath and nods, forces a smile and goes back to her conversation. Her fingers tangle in his as he turns away.

Calanthe is sitting in the shade near the door to the living room, directly under a mister. Her face is flushed red, one hand pressed against her belly.

"I've got myself a diva," she says when Jaantzen approaches. She winces. "Can't stand for the attention to be somewhere else."

Jaantzen blinks at her, realizing what she's saying. "Are you — "

"I've been having contractions all morning," she says. "But no. It's not quite time for our diva's grand entrance." She grits her teeth and glares down at her belly. "You hear that, baby girl?"

"Do you want me to call someone?"

"Willem, I'm fine," Calanthe snaps. "I've done this once or twice before."

"Let me know if I can help." Jaantzen clears his throat. "And speaking of grand entrances, Leone's here."

The color drains from Calanthe's cheeks. "She wouldn't dare."

"You know she would. I'm taking care of it."

"Take my brother." She waves a hand. "Li!" Across the courtyard, Liatris turns from giving directions to a caterer. "She is not welcome in my mother's house, and I don't care if the entire world has to watch the security guards drag her ass back out."

Jaantzen nods. He explains the situation quickly to Liatris, and the other man follows him through the entryway and out into the driveway.

Leone's spinner is parked in front of the door, the driver arguing with one of Starla's team. The driver stiffens when he sees Jaantzen; doors open and a pair of big men, Leone's bodyguards, get out. They're sizing Jaantzen and Liatris up like they're ready for a brawl.

"Madame Justice, do you have a moment?" Jaantzen says quietly. He knows she can hear him through the driver's open window. At first no one moves, then Leone opens her door, glaring daggers at the bodyguard who tries to stop her. She turns a perfectly calculated smile on Liatris: friendship tinged with grief and compassion.

"Liatris." She takes his hand. "I'm so sorry for your loss. Your mother — "

Liatris pulls his hand back. "You're not welcome here, Madame Justice," he says coldly. "We'd like you to leave."

Her eyebrows shoot up. "I'm here to pay respects to one of my oldest friends."

"I'm sorry," Liatris says firmly. He doesn't sound sorry.

"Where's your sister? Calanthe — "

"Would deliver the same message, but would probably make more of a scene," Liatris says. "Please. Go, or I'll be forced to ask security to escort you out."

Leone turns her incredulous expression to Jaantzen. "Willem, are you hearing this?"

"I respect the wishes of the Yangs," he says. "And so should you. Walk with me, Geum-ja?"

She seems like she wants to argue more, but between Liatris's bulk blocking her path and the Admant security guards standing not-so-discreetly in front of the door to Julieta's home, she changes her mind. Manu had also appeared while they were talking and is now lounging against the hood of a spinner nearby, with Gia beside him. Manu's armed, and so is Jaantzen. He wonders if Gia is — wonders if she needs to be, any more. They still haven't had a chance to talk about what happened to her up at Redrock.

Leone finally takes Jaantzen's proffered elbow with a disappointed scowl at Liatris, then waves her bodyguards back and allows Jaantzen to lead her into the relative privacy of a shaded bench not too far away. Her expression is calm but her pulse is fluttering rapidly in her throat.

Good.

She sits, patting the bench beside her. Jaantzen remains standing, his skin crawling where her hand had been on his arm. Her neck cranes back so she can meet his gaze and he can't help but think how easy it would be. His hands around that frail old throat, or — why touch her again? — simply put a bullet between her eyes. Her bodyguards couldn't stop him, and with Manu here, neither of them would get a shot off at Jaantzen before they were dead themselves. He knows his lieutenant is watching him, ready for whatever move he makes.

Leone is watching him, too, her syrupy smear of a smile saying she can see the calculations going on in his head.

"You wouldn't do it, Willem," she says quietly. "Harming me is a death sentence. Even without all these people around."

He knows. It's the reason he's still playing this game.

"I believe we're at an impasse, then," he says.

"I was hoping you'd see that." She folds her papery hands in her lap. "So stop fantasizing about killing me, and let's talk business. I've already apologized to you."

"For trying to murder the woman I love."

A dismissive laugh. "Such a strong word."

"Murder? Or love."

"Don't be dramatic, Willem, I thought this was purely a business relationship." When he doesn't rise to the bait, she waves a hand. "Yes, well, I explained what happened there."

"Your mercenary went off script."

"I only want the best for Phaera. I wouldn't hurt her."

"Then try to look a bit more remorseful."

Her eyes narrow dangerously. "Believe me or not, but I'm not here to perform for you. I didn't realize how much support you had, but you're underestimating how much of this city I own. If we continue this fight, we risk another civil war. But if we work together?" A slow smile spreads across her face. "Imagine what we could accomplish. And I'm not a young woman. I know I'm mortal. Imagine the empire I could leave you."

It's beginning to dawn on him that she's not here for Julieta at all; there's no way she expected Liatris and Calanthe to let her inside. She's here for him. A public reconciliation, the shining stars of the Bulari underworld gathered here today to witness Geum-ja Leone and Willem Jaantzen making up.

She was willing to risk the humiliation of being turned away for this staged reunion. She's either truly desperate, or she's playing an even longer con.

"Keep talking."

"I know you don't approve of my relationship with the Alliance, but that's because you're not in the room at these meetings, Willem. If you could see how a stronger relationship with the Alliance benefits New Sarjunian businesses, you'd change your mind."

"Enlighten me."

"The trade agreement you managed to dismantle would have reduced food prices for all New Sarjunians. It would have made it easier for our businesspeople to export their wares to Alliance companies. Made it easier for Alliance corporations that are already working in our country to bring in new innovations to serve our people." She holds up a hand. "Yes, Alliance companies would also make a profit. But that's how business *works*. Protectionism stifles growth and opportunity for New Sarjunians. The only people getting hurt are our own."

Tell that to the people of Corusca, New Manila, and a half-dozen other countries whose economies have been ravaged since joining the Arquellian-led Alliance. But Jaantzen isn't here to argue politics, he's here to understand what game Leone is playing so he can beat her at it.

"Perhaps you could accomplish this without also angering New Sarjunian business owners and unions."

"And we'll try. That's what I wanted to talk to you about — you and I both want what's best for this city, and we need to align our vision. They're rewriting the trade agreement. You should be in these meetings. I can get you access." A slow smile tugs at the corner of her mouth. "You think you've tasted power here in Bulari? Try having influence throughout the Durga System."

And she's the path to power, she wants him to know it. Jaantzen pauses like he's actually considering her offer. Following that thread could get him evidence to put a lid on her coffin.

"The prime minister is giving a speech tomorrow night," Leone says. "There's to be a soiree beforehand, it'll be a veritable who's who of Bulari's business community. You should come as my guest."

An invitation which puts him squarely back in her debt. She must see it on his face, because she holds up a hand.

"If we're to work together, I want to introduce you to some people. I'm not expecting anything in return." She sighs when he doesn't answer. "I'm serious, Willem."

"I'm interested," he says finally.

"Then I'll make it happen."

"Zacharia," Jaantzen says. "You know where he is?"

A flicker of something over her face, he can't read what it is. Satisfaction, maybe. That he's taking her bait? Or that she has something valuable to offer? He knows now that when he called Leone the night before last, she was also meeting with Zacharia. But which one of them is she planning on betraying?

"Zacharia came to me, looking for you. He thought I could help."

"And what did he offer you."

"Coeur," she says without missing a beat. Jaantzen keeps the surprise off his face. "He's been stringing her along to make a deal. He has people with her, some of the escaped prisoners you brought back down from

Redrock?" She smiles. "I know about them, too. But don't worry. Your secret is safe with me."

Doubtful; he makes a note to tell Starla. Both that the escapees who chose to remain north of the Jupari Desert are in danger of being exposed, and that some of those she brought back may secretly be working with Zacharia.

"And here's where we can both benefit, Willem. Zacharia is obviously a menace to society. He's a zealot, he can't be reasoned with. And I know you meant well, reinstating Coeur, but you're still watching your back around her, and you should be. She'll stick a knife in it the moment she gets a chance. That's why she's sniffing around this deal Zacharia is trying to make with her."

"I'm well aware."

Leone smiles. "Zacharia hands me Coeur, and I hand you Zacharia. Two birds, one stone. And then we can get this city back on track."

"And how do you propose that?"

"I'll set up a meeting. Get him in place, and you can do the rest."

Meaning he'll act both as the bait and the trap. And in exchange, Leone will get the opportunity to take out Coeur. He agrees with her that Zacharia is a danger to this city, but he's not so sure anymore about Coeur. She's unpredictable. She wants power, but she brings a level of stability, too.

Though Leone's intel about Zacharia and Coeur in conversation is troubling, if it's true. Coeur has wanted the serum from the beginning, and Jaantzen doubts she's forgiven him for keeping the cases she'd stolen from the Alliance. Access to the serum would increase her own power, yes. But it could also heal her. Reknit shattered hands and salve aching bones. There's a very real chance

Zacharia made an offer to Coeur that far outweighs anything Jaantzen ever could.

Or Leone is lying. She knew about the escaped prisoners, she might also know about the serum. After all, the most convincing way to build a lie is always around a kernel of truth.

"Get in touch with Zacharia," Jaantzen says. "Let's come up with a plan. And once that threat is out of the way, we can talk about what comes next."

"And you'll call off your slanderous attacks on me, Willem?"

"I will."

"Thank you." Leone holds out a hand and Jaantzen takes it, helps her to her feet with expression carefully schooled to neutral. Her hand is clammy, cloying in his. Leone's gaze shifts past him, back towards the house. "I came to pay my respects to one of my dearest friends."

"Pay respect to Julieta by honoring her family's request."

Leone finally accepts his arm. "You'll talk to them for me, won't you? I made Calanthe's career, and Liatris won't go far without support from his mother's oldest friends. I want to see them succeed."

"I'll talk to them."

The pavers are uneven beneath his shoes. It would be so easy to pretend to stumble, to twist an ankle and land wrong, shove her just so, her head cracking open against one of the ornate stone planters ringing the driveway.

So easy, and yet without unassailable proof of her wrongdoing, her name would be mourned throughout the nation. And Jaantzen's would most likely be held guilty, no matter if it was ruled an accident. No. When he takes care of this problem for good, it will be clean.

Jaantzen helps her into her spinner and stands in the driveway, watching until the vehicle finally disappears through the gates. He turns their conversation over in his mind, but he can't see the path laid out in front of him yet, there are still too many twists and turns. Zacharia offering Leone a chance to remove Coeur. Leone offering Zacharia to him. And Coeur? It's tricky to tell what she wants.

Jaantzen has promised her a stake in the terraforming business. Stability and jobs for her people — things he thought she would be mature enough now to value. But Zacharia could offer her real power. A serum to turn her fighters into something superhuman, to heal her broken body, to take whatever she wants by force rather than through finicky alliances.

When he made the decision to put her back in power, Jaantzen knew he had bought himself merely a short period of loyalty. Are they already at the end of it?

Boots crunching in gravel: Starla on his right, Manu appearing at his left, leaning a hip against the hood of someone's spinner and sweeping his gaze back to take in the house behind them.

"All good, boss?" he signs.

"Apparently Zacharia promised her Coeur if she gave him me. Leone's proposing a double cross."

"With you as bait and Coeur as collateral damage," Starla signs.

"She claims Zacharia and Coeur have been talking. Is there any way some of the escaped prisoners you brought back could be sympathetic to the Dawn?"

Starla rubs her palms together. "Unlikely," she finally signs. "But not impossible. Henri and Jude both knew Zacharia from before, but they both said they hate him."

"And the way the Dawn escaped . . ."

"Might not have been an accident," Starla finishes. "I'll look into it."

"The Dawn tortured Coeur half to death," Manu signs. "Killed her sister."

"And Zacharia has a serum that might heal her. She doesn't have to like someone to work with them."

Manu sighs. "There a solution gets rid of all three of them?" When Jaantzen doesn't answer, Manu squints at the sun, sinking low towards the horizon. "Knives oughta be here soon."

The afternoon's still boiling hot, but the crowd has begun to thin out as it gets closer to sunset. There's no hard and fast rule about who should stay to witness as the Knives sever the soul's connection with this plane and send it on to the next, but traditionally it's only close family and friends. Other guests will leave before the Knives arrive; superstition says it's bad luck to see them without staying for the ceremony. That it calls Death's attention.

"My team's already starting to sweep people out," Starla signs.

"Thank you." Jaantzen takes a deep breath, preparing himself for the onslaught of goodbyes; after that conversation with Leone, the last thing he wants to do is shake hands and pretend some part of him isn't fundamentally destroyed by the fact that Julieta Yang's body is lying inside this house while Leone walks free.

"Mr. Jaantzen?"

Jaantzen stiffens at the voice of the absolute last person he has the patience for right now, then turns. She's so small, flanked by guards who're watching her like hawks. One has a hand resting discreetly on the electric barb on his belt.

"Yes, Aster?"

She swallows, glances over her shoulder. "I need to talk to you," she says, and the way she flinches back, she expects him to tell her to go to hell. He wants to — and maybe he's about to — when Starla steps past him and wraps her arms around the other woman.

Starla, who never got along with Aster, who rarely shows affection to anyone outside her close-knit group of friends.

Aster seems as stunned by the gesture as Jaantzen is, but the shock wears off fast and she melts, face crumpling as sobs well up from inside, her hands fisted in the back of Starla's suit jacket like she's holding on for dear life.

And maybe she is. Jaantzen wonders if she's had anyone show her real affection since she betrayed her mother — betrayed them all — to the Dawn.

With anyone else, Jaantzen would turn away and give her this private moment of grief. But he still has nightmares of being trapped while Bennion Zacharia aims his pistol at Starla's head, finger tightening on the trigger. Of Ximena Nayar's lifeless, blood-spattered face. Of being trapped in a burning spinner while Thala Coeur screams at him to leave her and save himself.

He doesn't care how much Aster Yang is grieving right now, he's not taking his eyes off her.

She finally pulls herself together and takes a shaky step back, mopping at her face with a handkerchief.

She stares down at Jaantzen's shoes. "I just need a minute," she says.

"A minute," Jaantzen agrees. He leads them back into the entryway, then down the hall to the guest bedroom across from Julieta's room. He motions Aster inside but shakes his head at the guards.

"She's fine with me," he says.

"Mr. Yang said — "

"Believe me," Jaantzen says. "She won't be going anywhere."

"Like I could," Aster says. She touches the side of her neck, where a new red scar pinpoints the location of an implant. "I know what happens if I cross the boundary."

The guards share a look, then finally relent, taking up positions on either side of the door. Jaantzen goes in after, followed by Starla and Manu. Starla sits beside Aster on the bed, but Manu slides his shoulder blades against the wall behind her. She cranes her head nervously to track him.

"I'm sorry," she says to Manu. "That you got hurt. I'm sorry to all of you."

Jaantzen isn't in the mood to listen to any more apologies today, though this one at least feels genuine. "What do you want, Aster?"

"I need to warn you. Ben — Bennion — he was planning something big with that serum he was trying to get from you. To infect people." Her jaw clenches. "They're still planning it. No one else believes me."

Or is willing to talk with her, more likely.

"They've been doing it," Starla signs. "Putting the serum in shard, in the water supply." Jaantzen repeats the words when Aster frowns in incomprehension at Starla.

"Small attempts, yes," Aster agrees. "But they want to infect the whole city, to see who passes the test. It's a small percentage who will, Ben said, maybe as high as twenty percent. But those who remained would be as

God wanted them to be. Saints. That's what he believed, at least," she says bitterly.

"And you? What did you believe?"

"I was stupid to trust him." Her voice shakes, she's on the verge of tears again, but she pulls herself together. "Ben wanted to pass the test. He didn't think he was pure enough, but he thought he deserved to after all the work he'd done. He was trying to find a way, to make sure he would survive. To circumvent God's plan. But he said he'd use it for himself and his brother Felipe." She stares down at her hands. "And me."

She's so frail, so different from the Aster he had known as a child. That Aster was standoffish and distrusting, but maybe she hadn't found the right person to trust, before. Maybe Bennion Zacharia spoke to something imaginative and wishful in her that her practical, blunt, no-nonsense family had shot down. "Head in the clouds," Calanthe has always said, dismissively. Maybe all she needed was for someone to listen to her.

"Did you believe him?" Jaantzen asks.

Aster purses her lips; she's honestly considering the question. "I wanted to," she says finally. "But that would have been foolish, I think."

"Wanting to trust someone isn't foolish," Jaantzen says. "Trusting someone without being sure of them, though, is."

"And you don't trust me."

"I don't know who you are anymore, Aster."

"You never did," she says. But she's smiling sadly, no accusation there. "None of you bothered to. And now . . ."

A tear leaks down her cheek, and she dashes it away with a fierceness which is a perfect copy of her older sister's own.

Jaantzen shifts uncomfortably. Starla rubs small circles on Aster's back.

"Did Bennion Zacharia figure out how to make the transformation certain?"

"It had something to do with the artifacts of the Fallen, he said."

"'The Fallen' is what they call the aliens," Starla signs to him, not bothering to hide it from Aster; she won't understand. "There was a whole virtual museum of alien artifacts, I visited it once. But nothing that looked like a weapon. And I don't know where the physical objects are stored."

Jaantzen nods to her. "Did he succeed?" he asks Aster.

"If he had, he would have taken it. But he was close."

"Why didn't you tell anyone earlier?"

She shrugs. "Coeur took out the rest of the Dawn after Ben was killed, I thought. It didn't seem important anymore. Until the prophet came back." Her eyes are still shining bright with genuine tears. "I thought you should know."

This isn't a negotiation, Jaantzen realizes. She doesn't expect to get anything from him for this information, she's merely trying to make up for her sins.

"Thank you, Aster."

She nods once, sharp, and focuses back on her hands. They sit in silence while Jaantzen tries to think of what to say, then Starla stiffens, light playing over her iris.

"It's time," she signs. "The Knives are here."

Jaantzen nods, then holds out a hand to Aster. "It's time to let your mother go."

The day's oppressive heat has started to cool by the time Julieta Yang is laid in her final resting place, on a hill overlooking the desert beyond her property, beside paths she walked, amid the plants she harvested and propagated, serenaded by the birds she fed. The sun is sinking into the horizon as the Knives lower the coffin, never ceasing in their chanting. Long shadows streak away from the mourners, black on the red earth, and the evening breeze picks up a touch to snatch at veils and hats and jackets, setting the silvery gauze robes of the Knives flickering.

The Knives have formed a loose circle, Julieta's family and the grave at the center. Liatris and his wife Michele are silhouetted against the setting sun. Calanthe's face is pinched with pain even in the shadow of her veil; Alex and the two boys are by her side. She looks up suddenly, frowning — searching for her sister, maybe — and her eyes meet Jaantzen's. She holds out a hand to him, gives an impatient sigh when he doesn't move at first.

Jaantzen squeezes Phaera's hand and lets go; the Knives part to let him through the circle.

"Thank you," Calanthe says, linking her free arm with his. Her oldest son, Julian, leans his shoulder against Jaantzen's thigh.

"Aster," Jaantzen says in response.

Calanthe's jaw sets firm. But after a moment she nods. Liatris beckons to their youngest sister, and she stumbles through the circle and into her brother's arms, sobbing against his shoulder while he strokes her hair.

The sun sets, painting the desert in vivid magenta, rose, violet as the Knives chant Julieta free.

19

———————

## JAANTZEN

I t's well past time for dinner when they return to Cobalt Tower, but the table in the penthouse suite is already set. Lo é Njeri meets Jaantzen at the door to the lift. She's dyed her pixie haircut since he saw her last night, from a burnt orange to a deep ruby red, her lipstick and sensible heels the same cheerful shade, her dress patterned with sunflowers. It's a stark relief from the mourner's black he's been surrounded by all day.

And the shock of realization on her face at his dark suit, Phaera's black lace says it didn't occur to her until now everyone else will be dressed for the funeral. Not that it would matter what she was wearing; Lo could probably manage to make mourner's black relentlessly optimistic.

As in everything, though, Lo recovers her footing quickly. "Welcome back, Mr. Jaantzen," she says. "The caterers just left, you have perfect timing."

"I have no illusions; the perfect timing is yours, Ms. é Njeri." He turns to Phaera. "I'd like you to meet Phaera D, she owns the Lorelei and the Devil's Table."

Lo's wide eyes says she knows exactly who Phaera is and can't believe she's shaking hands with her. "Nice to meet you, ma'am." A flush creeps under the dense spray of freckles on her light brown cheeks.

"Phaera, Lo is our . . ." He trails off, at a loss. If she and Manu have agreed on an official title, he doesn't know what it is.

"Head of Operations?" says Lo. "I manage . . . I guess, everything."

And she does it with a firm hand and level head Jaantzen's grown to rely on completely in the few weeks since she was promoted from her position as Manu's secretary.

"A pleasure," Phaera says. Her attention turns to the penthouse, maybe scanning for damage as he had when he returned home for the first time last night. They haven't had much time to talk about what her experience returning home had been like. Whatever she sees — or doesn't see — seems to steady her, though. She turns her smile back on Lo. "I need a drink," she says cheerfully, heading to the kitchen. "Lo, what can I get you?"

The lift chimes again, and the rest of the crew have arrived. Manu, Oriol, Gia, Tevi, Starla, Toshiyo. He hadn't been certain he'd be able to pry Toshiyo away from Lucky for the day, but the strange creature has taken to El, so even if Jaantzen isn't comfortable bringing it back to Cobalt Tower yet, at least it's in the care of a trustworthy . . . babysitter? Guard?

He ignores the now-familiar anxiety squeezing his heart at the thought of Lucky. They have to figure out what to do with their alien guest, and fast.

Tevi hasn't been to Jaantzen's home before, and he's taking in the penthouse with an unreadable expression.

Jaantzen's been giving the man space all day, appreciating that he and Gia came at all, and not wanting to press his luck. Julieta had donated to the Andel Medical School's foundation originally, and if Tevi was uncomfortable with where the Yang family fortune came from, at least he didn't seem to associate Julieta with violence the way he did Jaantzen. The Yangs mostly keep their hands clean; they can afford to.

"Thank you for coming," Jaantzen says to him. "It means a lot to me. To everyone."

"Of course." Tevi takes a deep breath. "I know I've been a bit standoffish over the years. But Gia is very fond of you, and I hope we can find more occasions like this. That don't involve funerals, or you asking my wife to put herself in mortal danger."

Jaantzen hadn't asked; Gia had insisted. But he merely inclines his head. "I do, as well." Jaantzen holds out a hand to invite him in, Phaera calls Tevi and Gia over to take a glass of wine, and the moment is over.

Dinner is simple: rosemary zaadish, tabbouli bursting with fresh herbs, egg and lemon soup. Between the food, the company, the warm laughter after a day of whispers and mourning, Jaantzen is more relaxed than he's been in ages. Or maybe it's not just the environment; Phaera's refilled his wine glass before he realized he'd finished it. He smiles and clinks glasses with her.

As plates empty, Manu tosses a crumpled-up napkin at Starla to get her attention. "I still haven't heard the whole story of your heroic escapades," Manu signs and says aloud. There's a mischievous quirk to his smile, and from across the table, Gia shoots him a dark look. "And I know for sure Lo and Phaera haven't heard it."

Starla sits straighter, obviously delighted to share;

Manu starts interpreting with a wink at Gia, who flips him a rude gesture when Tevi's not looking. But Starla eventually coaxes Gia into telling her part of the story, too. The *Coldfire* getting shot down. The trek through the desert to find the *Coldfire*'s crew that led to the discovery of a colony of former Redrock prisoners who'd escaped and been hiding in the desert, some for over twenty years. The back-and-forth with the prisoners, then the raid on the Alliance secret facility.

Lo raises a hand. "I'm sorry," she says to Starla. "Did you say the secret facility where the *alien* was being kept?"

"Oh, shit." Manu grins. "Sorry, Lo. I'll catch you up on aliens after this."

"I'm new to learning about aliens, too," Tevi tells Lo.

"We're all new to it," Starla agrees, then launches back into her tale.

Jaantzen hasn't heard the whole story, either, at least not from start to finish. He's glad he's being told now, when everyone's sitting safe and whole around his dining table — Phaera's hand slips onto his thigh at one point, her raised eyebrow asking if he's all right.

He is. "Starla can handle herself," he murmurs in response.

This whole time, Tevi's expression has been slowly shifting from horrified to incredulous to impressed as Starla dishes up a vivid description of what it's like to fight alongside Gia against the Dawn, Alliance marines, and finally Lucky's bigger, more dangerous cousin.

Starla finishes her story with a flourish, and the buzz of conversation rises as people ask questions and add anecdotes.

"So," Lo finally says. "Aliens?"

"Remember that case smuggled in the RKE shipment?" Manu says and signs. "It had an alien in it. That's what the Alliance attacked Cobalt Tower to find. But he's not here now, he's at a safe location."

Starla's pulled out her comm; she pulls up a picture of Lucky and slides it across the table to Lo. Lo's lips part, close again.

"What is it?" she finally asks.

Manu laughs. "Tosh?"

Beside him, Toshiyo gnaws on the inside of her lip. "I'm not a biologist," she finally says. "But, ah, Lucky doesn't seem to be related to us or any known species we brought with us to the Durga System. He's a clone, one of many that were sent to New Sarjun on a ship that seems to be designed to begin terraforming the planet. Probably to make it habitable for others of their species to come later." Toshiyo shrugs. "He likes fish, radishes, Ayisha Amadule, and cheesy comedy vids. He doesn't like rocks with a high quartz concentrate, horror movies, or Manu."

"He doesn't like Manu?" Lo asks. "He *must* be an alien."

Manu points to his upper arm in mock outrage. "He clawed me," he says. "When I was just trying to save Toshiyo's life."

"Anyway." Toshiyo cracks her ring fingers, clearly not wanting the conversation to turn to the night of the attack on Cobalt Tower where she'd nearly died. "I'm not a biologist."

"Then what will you do with it?" Tevi asks.

"The Alliance already knows about it," says Manu. "But it was discovered on New Sarjun. Both governments are going to feel like they have a right to it."

"No government should control it." Tevi gives

Jaantzen a pointed look. "Neither should you. A discovery like this, you need a neutral research institute that isn't getting funding from one government or another. One that's operating with an independent, internationally agreed-on charter. Scientists from throughout the system, dedicated to learning how to understand — and live with — Lucky and . . . any others."

Jaantzen stares at him, the skin on the back of his neck pricking as an idea finally begins to form.

"Something like the Andel School," he says. "Neutral. Independently funded."

Manu's sitting straighter. "Could the institute operate as part of the school?" he asks. "You already have the secure infrastructure, and the experience running a nonprofit."

"No," says Tevi quickly. He glances at Gia. "No?"

"Your New Manilan friend." Gia says it like her mind's racing ten steps ahead. "The one who just stepped down from running the Warren Institute? She'd be a perfect director. And we both have contacts we could tap throughout Indira and Durga's Belt. We'd need a separate facility eventually, but right now we're not using the old lab building for anything. Starla and Tosh can help us build it out for Lucky."

"I've been talking with a professor at the University of Bulari who's already been studying the aliens," signs Starla. "He has a few years on his indenture, but the institute could always buy it out."

"We've done that before with teaching staff," says Tevi, before realizing what he's implied. He curses under his breath.

"And if Lucky was with you," Toshiyo says, "he'd be safe. You wouldn't cut him open and torture him like the

Alliance did to his cousin. Or like the Dawn are doing to the poor thing now." She slides Jaantzen a look.

"We would never do anything to hurt Lucky," Tevi says to her; he turns to Jaantzen. "If we do this — *if* — the institute has to be independent."

"Believe me," Jaantzen says. "I want nothing more in this world than to give up responsibility for that creature."

His shoulders already feel lighter. It will be tricky to pull off, but not impossible. Since the first time Jaantzen saw Lucky's snarling face he's known he couldn't keep him secret forever. But until now he hasn't seen a solution that didn't involve inciting an international war or getting him and everyone he loves killed.

"With the right mix of people and the right press," says Phaera, "you give every country a stake in working together on this. Make it too much of a major issue for either New Sarjun or the Alliance to force control over this."

"We can hire Leti," says Starla. "I'll call her."

"Gia and I will talk about it," Tevi says firmly, hands up to halt the avalanche of planning around the table. But he's mulling it over, the suspicion that clouded his face from the beginning replaced now by intrigue.

"We've got a long drive back home to talk," Gia says.

And that seems to be the cue for everyone to remember how late it's gotten. Chairs push back from the table, plates are gathered, and although Jaantzen insists he doesn't need help, the others carry dishes to the kitchen. Jaantzen accepts a stack from Gia and sets them beside the sink, where Manu's started rinsing them. Tevi and Lo are back at the table, partly gathering glassware, mostly admiring the view out over glittering, night-dark Bulari.

Gia glances at them, then smacks Manu on the arm. "That's for not keeping your mouth shut," she says.

"Hey!" he protests. "I didn't tell Tevi about the *Cold-fire* going down."

"You instigated Starla's story time."

"I got you laid, G. The way Tevi was eyeing you by the end of the story? You'll be thanking me tonight, def."

Jaantzen clears his throat.

"Sorry, boss," Manu says with a grin. "But I'm just saying, you ever taken him out to the shooting range with you?"

"It's not really his thing."

"Show him how well you know your way around a gun and I bet he'd make it his thing."

"You should stay here tonight," Jaantzen says before either of them can say anything else. Manu turns back to the sink, humming to himself. "We have plenty of space."

The way her jaw tightens, though, he knows she won't ask Tevi. "It's fine. We both have to teach tomorrow, so it's either make the drive tonight or get a super early start in the morning. And you know how much I hate an early start."

"The offer's always open."

"And we'll take you up on it." Gia glances back at Tevi, and everything about her face softens. Jaantzen's been catching glimpses of them together all day. He's never had an opportunity to spend time with Tevi before when the man wasn't bristling at being in Jaantzen's presence. But Gia was never this peaceful when she was working for him. She'd taken his money reluctantly at first and been fiercely loyal by the end, but she wasn't meant for the sort of work he needed her to do. Good at it, yes. Willing? Of course.

Tae's death and then the civil war with Coeur had broken something in each of them, but it had broken Gia free. And Tevi'd been there to help her heal. Jaantzen's happy for that, even if it had meant her leaving.

Gia turns back to Jaantzen, and her smile stays soft. "Thank you for tonight," she says. "Are you heading back out to the valley with Toshiyo tomorrow?"

Jaantzen shakes his head. "The prime minister's giving a speech about the trade agreement tomorrow night. I'll need to spend the day preparing."

"Be safe, then," Gia says. "And we'll let you know. About Lucky."

"Take your time. This shouldn't be a hasty decision for any of us."

"Will do, boss."

Lo announces her intention to catch a bus after Gia and Tevi say their goodbyes, and Manu shakes his head.

"We'll give you a ride, Lo," Manu says.

"It's out of the way."

"Not a problem." Manu's smile is easy, but there's a firmness behind it. Lo's become more than his secretary, more than the linchpin holding Jaantzen's entire business operations together. She's becoming crew, which paints a target on her back even more than being an Arquellian on New Sarjun during these volatile times.

Starla and Toshiyo are both staying at Cobalt Tower tonight; Toshiyo is headed back to the Maraka Valley early tomorrow morning in the *Coldfire* to collect Lucky and the important things they've left out there. They head for the lift with Manu and Lo, but Oriol hangs back with Jaantzen. He reaches into an inner pocket of his suit jacket and pulls out a slim volume Jaantzen recognizes immediately, but stares at a long moment before he reaches to take it.

"Manu said you were asking about her books," Oriol says in explanation. "I have the rest. If you want, I can — "

"No." Jaantzen cuts him off. "I don't need them." He turns the book over in his hands. *A River No More.* Collected poems from New Sarjun over the last century. The binding is well-worn and soft, the cover creased, the corners of the pages rounded. Tae had always carried a book of poems around with her, he remembers, battered each one half to death before retiring it in favor of a new obsession.

He flips through the pages, recognizing fragments of the ones she used to read aloud to him. To them all, sometimes, during cheerful dinners like this one.

Oriol's gaze shifts past him; Phaera's waiting over his shoulder, curious.

"Thank you," Jaantzen says, and Oriol nods, makes his way to the lift where Manu and Lo are waiting.

Jaantzen stares down at the battered book. This is the sort of memento he would normally put away in the small box containing other relics of the dead. The titanium Coatlicue statue Coeur left in the bomb that killed his family. His children's handprints, cast in glass. The pocketknife his childhood friend, Paz, had been carrying the night Jaantzen convinced him to leave the orphanage. But that box is back in the Maraka Valley.

And maybe it's gotten too crowded.

He lays the book on the coffee table, next to the sturdy little jadau cutting Julieta had given him. It's already got a new pair of leaves, he notes. And maybe tomorrow he'll read one of the poems over breakfast.

Phaera's glances at the book on the coffee table, a

strange expression on her face. *Her* books, Oriol had said, she has to know what he was referring to.

"Do you want me to stay?" she asks.

He probes at the sore spot in his memories that normally threatens to overwhelm him if breached, but somehow in the last week the ghosts he's always carried with him have dissipated somewhat. He feels — not peace, but quiet, at least.

Phaera's fingers twine around his when he reaches for them, the lace of her dress catches on his hands as he smooths his palm over the curve of her waist. Her lips part against his.

"Please," he murmurs into her hair.

"Always," she answers.

## 20

## TOSHIYO

I t's late, but not in Toshiyo Ravi's world. She doesn't come in contact with a lot of windows during her normal day — not here at Cobalt Tower, not at the death-trap — and her natural rhythm tends towards being a night owl anyway. It's been years since anyone tried to make her come to an in-person meeting, so she does most of her work for the boss's businesses without worrying about when other people are sleeping or awake.

She is scheduled to meet Beto and the *Coldfire* at sunrise to fly back out to the Maraka Valley and collect Lucky, which means she should probably sleep — but she's wired, and if she takes something to help herself get drowsy she'll be all gummy and brain-dead in the morning.

Plus there are some things she wants to check in on.

She switches on the light to her office on Cobalt Tower's fourth floor. She'd arrived this afternoon to find it as she left it. Stacks of salvaged wiring and supplies she might someday need. Half-finished projects waiting for her to have time for them. Her full desk rig set up about halfway into the room, a warren of miscellaneous equipment and gear beyond. Shelves filled with security system prototypes for Admant, weapons projects she's working on with Starla. Robotics. Circuit boards.

Heaven.

She has a cot in the far corner for when she needs naps, a shelf for clothes, and the boss has long since stopped reminding her she has a nice apartment several floors above she could use if she wanted it. She hasn't run out of storage space yet on the fourth floor.

Toshiyo ducks under the low-hanging swag of cables and sits at her desk, tucking up her feet and taking a slow spin on her chair while the desk powers on.

It's nice to be home.

And the speed with which her messages load over the tower's superior network?

It's *really* nice to be home.

You up?

El's response is immediate.

Yep. Hanging out with the little guy.

Got time for a call?

A moment later, El's connection request chimes. His hologram is grainy and shot through with static, but still she grins. He's sitting on the couch in Toshiyo's makeshift meeting room at the deathtrap, Lucky flopped beside him with one clawed foot draped over El's thigh. Starla's two cats are there, too — Mango is tucked under Lucky's wing, Pepper is wedged between El's hip and the arm of the couch and keeping Lucky firmly in the corner of his suspicious gaze.

Lucky straightens when he sees Toshiyo's hologram appear, mouth splitting in a razor-toothed grin.

"You all are quite the menagerie," she says to El, then

raises her hands to greet Lucky. She still hasn't figured out if he can understand their spoken communication, since he only responds when they use USL.

And with relief she remembers the conversation with Tevi tonight. Pretty soon, the poor buddy might have actual scientists trying to understand him.

At least one enormously impossible task will be off her shoulders.

"How was the . . ." El's obviously avoiding saying the word *funeral*. "Today?"

Today was abstract, and strange. Toshiyo liked Julieta Yang, but she hadn't planned on going to the funeral, and she suspects the boss asked her to come into town more for the dinner after than for the social ritual of making sure other people saw her paying respect. Something about being out at the deathtrap made Jaantzen nostalgic. He's been bringing up memories of his and Tae's house on Seventeenth Street, commenting on the dinners they used to have there. Maybe the close confines of the deathtrap made him appreciate having a good space for entertaining. Maybe having Starla home safely made him want to spend more time together with them all. Maybe being with Phaera is making him feel more domestic.

All Toshiyo knows is that Jaantzen seemed actually happy tonight. It was nice.

El's still waiting for an answer.

How was today? It was emotionally messy and uncomfortable, but overall good. At least the family part. The part where the Dawn still have Lucky's cousin in captivity and the boss isn't doing anything about it sticks into her psyche like a metal splinter.

"Today was fine," she says. "What are you watching?"

"I tried to get him to watch some classic Loa Kelsang,

but he wasn't having it," El says. He's signing, too, out of politeness. His long brown fingers move in that easy way he has, not missing a beat even as he uses two languages at once. He's a natural at it; his and Simca's parents are both deaf.

"He gets anxious," Toshiyo signs.

"Yeah, he was a mess," El agrees. "So I put on *Violet Wave*. He's really into it."

"Seriously? Eamon?" Toshiyo is appalled but not surprised; Lucky's already demonstrated a saccharine sense of taste when it comes to his music choices. "Lucky, I can't believe you like Eamon over Kelsang."

"I told him he has no appreciation for art."

Loa Kelsang is a master. Dark color palettes splashed with vivid reds, purples, yellows. Incredible sound design that ratchets up anxiety with delicious precision. The perfectly timed humor defusing the tension, only to have you screaming seconds later. Scare jumps when they're least expected — but never for cheap thrills, Kelsang is far too good for that.

Eamon's vids, on the other hand, are mindless slashers with predictable plots and laughably high body counts of attractive, scantily clad actors.

"You'll learn to appreciate Kelsang when you grow up," Toshiyo says and signs to Lucky, who grimaces.

"How much longer until that happens?" El asks.

"No clue." Another mystery Tevi can hopefully help them with, if he does agree to the idea of the research institute. She'd love to tell El about that, but not in front of Lucky. She doesn't want to set expectations around something that might not work out, and she's also afraid he'll worry they're going to give him up. That he'll end up flayed open on some slab like his cousin.

Maybe her worry shows on her face, or maybe Lucky can read her mind — she wouldn't put it past him at this point. He raises clawed hands. "You find hurt friend?"

"We're working on it," she tells him. And pushes back a rush of frustration. Because even though it should be their top priority, everyone else is more or less ignoring the fact that the Dawn have Lucky's cousin captive, and are torturing him. Lucky's watching her with what Toshiyo imagines to be a mixture of reproach and disappointment. A wave of guilt washes over her. They should have done something, she should have insisted — but the boss gave the order.

If it had been Starla inside that shack instead of some unnamed alien? El? Manu? None of them would have said, Let's wait a few days and see what happens.

"Can you still sense your friend?" she asks Lucky.

He grimaces. "Found friend. Didn't help."

Toshiyo winces at the stab of guilt. "I know," she signs. "I'm sorry. It was wrong."

"We'll get your friend, buddy," El signs, and Lucky slumps back beside him. El's hologram flickers until the connection stabilizes once more. His hands are moving, but Toshiyo didn't catch what he said. "I asked if you were going to bed," he says and signs when she asks him to repeat himself. "You have to be up even earlier than I do."

"I will soon," Toshiyo says, though she's still not tired. "But I'll let you and your menagerie finish the vid. I'll see you in the morning."

"Night, Toshiyo," El says, and with a warm smile, he's gone.

Toshiyo skims through a security checklist on Cobalt Tower and the deathtrap out of habit, then pulls up the feed of the surveillance she left at the Dawn encampment. She gets regular updates, but it doesn't hurt to check manually, too.

Everything is fine, everyone still in place, though there's still no sign Felipe Zacharia has returned. Which means Jaantzen's plan to catch him there isn't working and they should have just called in reinforcements. Coeur, the police, whoever it took to get rid of the Dawn and save Lucky's friend while they had the chance. She pushes away a stab of frustration. Tomorrow, when they get back from the deathtrap, if they still haven't seen a sign of Zacharia she'll insist on making a plan to save the alien.

She checks her messages, not expecting anything to have shown up between now and the last time she checked, before dinner. But something new is blinking.

A message from GraySeeker.

THE TRUCKS YOU SAW WERE FULL OF SHARD. I TOOK CARE OF THEM. MEET ME TONIGHT?

Toshiyo stares at the message a moment, then checks the network. The beetle drones she tagged the trucks with didn't have enough charge to last without sunlight this long, so they blinked off hours ago. But she'd hacked into a nearby street camera with a decent view of the warehouse, and when she pulls it up she can see smoke at the far end of the street. Police spinners parked down the block. When she tunes into their feed she confirms it: structure fire at the right address.

She scans back through all the angles she has on the place. She doesn't see GraySeeker go in before the flames start, but she *definitely* doesn't see two trucks worth of shard being taken out. Whoever she is, whatever her association with White Star, GraySeeker didn't take the shard for herself.

Starla's upstairs, probably asleep by now — she'd had a couple of glasses of wine and she doesn't normally drink. The boss is here, too . . . but he's probably a bit preoccupied, given how Phaera was watching him all night.

Toshiyo cracks her ring fingers and opens a connection to Oriol. He knows the most about this White Star group, and she needs some advice.

It takes him a while to answer, and when he does he's out of breath. "What's wrong?"

"I had a question. You all right?"

"I'm fine," Oriol says. "I was just working out."

But in the background, Manu is laughing. "Dammit, Tosh," he calls.

Oh. Right. "Sorry," Toshiyo says. "I'll make it quick and let you get back to 'working out.' This woman I found on the White Star forums, she wants to meet up tonight. Do you think it's safe?"

"No."

"Sure. But I don't think she's working *with* White Star. She could know where Felipe Zacharia is. Or what these artifacts are that Aster told the boss about. Or literally anything — we need all the info we can get."

"She say where she wants to meet?"

"I was going to tell her Jade's, but if you're busy . . ."

He sighs, and fabric rustles on the other end of the line. "I'll meet you there."

"You don't have to." So far GraySeeker seems to be telling her the truth, and if so, Toshiyo's not in any danger. And showing up with Oriol might scare her off — though Toshiyo would prefer having him there. Her stomach is doing flips at the thought of going to meet this woman on her own, no matter how much she tells herself she wouldn't be in danger.

"If you're going, so am I."

"I'll tell her thirty minutes," Toshiyo says. She cuts the connection and opens up a reply to GraySeeker. The response comes almost immediately.

*I'll be there. Black jacket, red knit cap.*

Toshiyo sends the address and calls a cab before she can rethink her decision.

She's early, but by the time the cab lets her out in front of Jade's there's already a woman sitting in one of the three booths. She's facing Toshiyo — and the window — but she's staring down at her comm, or her hands, or her coffee, and her face is in shadow. Black jacket, red knit hat. It's GraySeeker.

Oriol's not yet downstairs, so she pings him. Stares across the street at GraySeeker; she seems to be alone. And Oriol will be here any minute.

Toshiyo takes a deep breath, a mixture of fear and excitement squeezing her chest and rushing in her ears, so loud she almost doesn't hear the whine of a pistol warming to the hand of its owner as she steps into the street. She starts to turn back a split second before a hand grabs her arm and the barrel of the pistol jams against the base of her skull.

Toshiyo freezes, panic flooding through her — she needs to warn GraySeeker somehow if the Dawn hacked their communications and is coming after them both. But by the time she blinks and looks back at Jade's, the woman who'd been sitting inside is gone.

Either she saw what happened and ran, or this is a trap.

"Don't say a word," the person holding her growls.

Toshiyo's hands are still in her pockets and she's already thumbing open her comm — she's got a call poised to Oriol — but her assailant roughly jerks her hand out. The comm hits the gutter. "Hands where I can see them."

The punch of an engine around a corner, and a spinner screeches up beside them, the rear passenger door swinging up automatically. The woman in the black jacket and red cap is driving.

So, definitely a trap.

"Get in, sister," the woman says. "I've got some questions about your 'poor me I accidentally joined a cult' bullshit."

The massive wall of muscle holding Toshiyo shoves her towards the open door, and Toshiyo braces herself against the spinner, stalling for time — the fact that the woman in the red cap has questions for her probably means they're not going to shoot her and leave her in the middle of the street. So the gun's out of the equation — though the strength disparity between herself and her captor is not. But if she can make enough trouble, Oriol might get here before they manage to wrestle her under control.

"Get *in*," the woman with the red cap hisses.

Toshiyo kicks back, her heel connecting with shinbone and earning her a curse; when she drops her weight she nearly slips through the grip of the person who's holding her. But they're fast as well as big, and a massive forearm tightens around her throat.

"Let her go."

Oriol's voice in the night is eerily calm and deadly serious, and Toshiyo goes still, mind racing as she readies herself to react. She can barely see him out of the corner of her eye, a dark shadow, the glint of streetlight on the barrel of his gun.

"Let her go, or you're dead. I — what the fuck, Mel?"

"Sina?" The strangling pressure around Toshiyo's throat vanishes and the grip on her arm loosens. Toshiyo reacts instantly, shoving herself away from her assailant, away from the spinner, catching herself against the side of a building, heart pounding.

Oriol holsters his weapon and jogs to her side, not caring if he's putting his back to the woman who'd been trying to kidnap Toshiyo. But she's putting her gun away, too.

"You okay, Tosh?"

"Yeah." She does a quick mental inventory, but she's not hurt. Gonna have some bruises where the woman grabbed her, otherwise all good. "I'm fine."

Over Oriol's shoulder, the big woman is staring at her in surprise. "You're Toshiyo? Well, shit." She leans into the still-open door. "Nas," she says to the woman in the red cap. "She works for Jaantzen."

"And what the hell were you two doing?" Oriol drags a hand through his brassy hair, more annoyed than worried. He knows these women. Trusts them enough to turn his back on them, Toshiyo thinks, trying to calm herself back down.

The big woman — Mel, he called her — is laughing. "We thought she worked for the Dawn." She shakes her head at Toshiyo. "Sorry about all that. But your story was obviously bullshit, and the Dawn have been trying to track Nacea down for weeks."

The woman in the red cap — GraySeeker, Nacea — gets out of the driver's side of the spinner and folds her arms on the roof. She doesn't seem convinced. "If she works for Jaantzen, why's she farming out jobs like this?" she asks. "It's a setup."

"I told you the truth," Toshiyo says. "I saw the shipment, but I couldn't do anything about it."

"Jaantzen couldn't do anything about it." Nacea snorts a laugh. "Oriol, you could've hired us the normal way."

"I didn't know. You know I don't — "

"You don't work for Jaantzen." Mel waves a hand. "Well, we've got a conversation to have, and the middle of the street's probably not the best place. Let's go get a drink. Sina, coming with?"

But Oriol's shaking his head. "You good, Tosh? Great. Then you ladies have a lovely evening."

"Need your beauty sleep?" Nacea calls after him; he holds up a rude gesture without looking back.

"I don't think that's what he's got on his mind," Toshiyo says, and Mel laughs — the sort of hearty, friendly laugh that makes your lips turn up almost on their own. Toshiyo eyes the two women, her back still to the wall. She's safe, Oriol definitely wouldn't have abandoned her here if he thought she was in the slightest sliver of danger. She probes at the anxiety pinning her to this spot, trying to decide if it's warning her of real peril or it's residual whiplash from how quickly the situation reversed.

Mel gestures at the door of the spinner. "Sorry again," she says. "C'mon. Nacea's buying."

Toshiyo swallows hard. Pushes herself off the wall and forces herself to walk casually towards the spinner.

"Sounds fun," she says.

The bar Nacea picks is a dingy one on the northern border of downtown Bulari, right before the well-lit business district dissolves into a nighttime no-man's-land of low-rent apartment buildings, cheap office space, and wholesalers. Toshiyo doesn't even see a sign, but Mel pushes right through the rust-pitted metal door.

Toshiyo trusts Oriol, but she's also really relieved to see this is not a murder warehouse.

The room is long and narrow, with a dingy stretch of stools along the bar to the right, a handful of gaming tables stretching into the grimy shadows at the far end. There's a bank of screens along the back of the bar where other bars might display their menus or liquor bottles. It's like a security system, monitoring the outside and back door of the building. Toshiyo watches security feeds all day, but she can't imagine there's enough entertainment on this block for the bar patrons come here for the video.

Though maybe she's wrong. Maybe they get a kick out of watching people get mugged on the street in this part of downtown.

Nacea raises her hand to the bartender, who gives her and Mel a familiar nod, then turns and pulls a couple of lagers out of the fridge. "You playing mystix tonight, Nas?" the bartender asks, cracking the lids and setting the bottles on the bar in front of her.

"Not tonight." Nacea hands Mel one of the lagers and turns to Toshiyo. "What are you drinking?"

Somewhere, under the reek of stale smoke and sweat and beer, Toshiyo can make out the bitter aroma of coffee that's spent too much time on the warmer. It's probably atrocious, but she's already in over her head. She can't afford to let herself get muddy.

But even the bartender gives her a look that says *You're gonna regret it* when she orders a coffee.

"And three sugar vipers," Nacea says. On Toshiyo's other side, Mel swears under her breath.

The bartender lifts the lid off a matte-black canister with an opalescent hologram of snakes on the front, pulls out a trio of writhing neon snakes, handing them to Nacea one at a time. They whip their tails, trying to wrap around the bartender's tongs.

Toshiyo stares at them in horror. "What do you do with those?"

"It's a shot," the bartender says wryly, then heads down to dole out snakes at the other end of the bar — apparently now that someone's called for a sugar viper, the other crusty regulars on the bar stools want in on the fun.

Nacea grins at her. "Sister's never been to a dive bar?" She's holding the three writhing snakes in one fist. "You like sweet or sour?"

Toshiyo glances at Mel; even though the big woman was holding a gun to her head less than ten minutes ago, she feels like the sane one here.

"You want guava, trust me," Mel says, a touch of resignation in her voice.

"Guava it is." Nacea hands Toshiyo the acid-yellow snake, then tosses the vivid orange one to Mel. Toshiyo holds hers carefully, securing it behind the jaw with her forefinger and thumb. The body's about as wide as her pinky, and silky smooth. It tries to wrap its tail around her forearm.

"Cheers," Nacea says, then nips off the head of her glowing blue snake and downs the body in one gulp. She makes a face, then whoops with delight. Mel shares a resigned look with Toshiyo and does the same with hers.

This is just another sort of girls' night, Toshiyo tells herself. Another sort of nonsensical social ritual to bond people together. This is the sort of thing Manu does constantly, she imagines, when he's out hunting down a lead. The sort of thing Starla would do without blinking.

And sugar vipers aren't alive.

She doesn't think they are, anyway.

Toshiyo bites the head off the snake and a burst of too-sweet, too-sour liquid gushes over her tongue; she barely manages not to aspirate the gush of artificial fruit and potent alcohol, choke it down, then she bends over coughing as the sugar viper venom hits her bloodstream with a wave of dizziness. Someone's rubbing kind circles between her shoulder blades with their palm — Mel, she thinks — and when she straightens the colors in the room flicker bright and multilayered, the haloes around them pulsing in time with the music.

Someone shoves a mug of coffee into her hands and leads her to the back, past the gaming tables where people are playing mystix with colorful cards that swirl and dance.

They find an empty table in the gloom and Toshiyo tries to blink away the double vision. The effect of the sugar viper venom's already wearing off, though the sickly-sweet taste still coats her tongue.

"Let's talk, sister," Nacea says. She tugs off her red knit cap, revealing messy blue-green hair pulled up into a bun, the sides of her head shaved.

"You're GraySeeker," Toshiyo says. Nacea's form flickers into doubles for a second, Toshiyo blinks her back whole.

"I am. How'd you find me?"

"I got into the White Star forum. I could tell you lived in Bulari and you didn't seem as fanatical as the rest of them."

"They're as crazy as the Dawn," Nacea says. "But at least they're not brainwashing kids and pouring drugs down their throats."

Even through the residual swimmy buzz of the sugar viper, Toshiyo can see the pain in Nacea's face. "I'm sorry," she says. "About your daughter."

Nacea's lips twitch; she drains half her bottle. "So your boss is planning a move against the Dawn."

"A bunch of them escaped from Redrock, including the prophet," Toshiyo says. Nacea nods impatiently; it's been all over the White Star forum. "We found out where they landed."

"So let's go get them."

"We're working on it. But we need more information. What do you know?"

Nacea leans back, scraping a fingernail through the condensation gathering on her bottle. "After Bennion Zacharia died, almost everything went dark. His priest, Thomas Deté, gathered up the scattered flock and retreated into the desert. Except for that secret laboratory in the smelter we took down with Sina and Juric last week, I haven't been able to find a trace of them. You know what they're planning, right?"

"To infect everyone with their serum."

"'And bring about the new Dawn of humanity,'" Nacea says; Toshiyo recognizes the phrase from reading Felipe Zacharia's writings. Nacea pulls a small bag out of her jacket pocket and tosses it across the table. "This is what was in those trucks you sent me and Mel to destroy."

Toshiyo glances around, palms slick, but no one is watching her study a bag of shard in a seedy bar. "I'd have to run some tests," she finally says. "But it looks like the other serum-tainted shard we've found." She slips the bag into her pocket.

"It's definitely alien venom," Nacea says. Toshiyo blinks at her, and she laughs. "It's aliens, you know that, right? All this Dawn shit is from aliens."

"I knew that," Toshiyo says slowly.

"Good." Nacea downs the rest of her beer and lifts her bottle to the bartender. "Then we don't have to have that conversation."

"Right." Toshiyo takes a deep breath. "We think they're going beyond delivering the serum through shard, though. What do you know about it?"

"They're testing it in the water supply, and I've been hearing rumors they're trying to figure out how to make it airborne," Nacea says. "That's why I've been trying so hard to shut down their shard operations."

"And alien artifacts? Do you know anything about those?"

Nacea's eyebrow shoots up. "I've heard rumors of those, too. But I haven't looked into it."

"Can you? I can lurk on the White Star forum without anyone noticing, but I can't ask questions."

"You got it, sister. And if you need any help with the Dawn in real life, let us know."

Mel lifts her bottle in a toast. "Say the word and me and Nas are there."

Toshiyo should be relieved — they have two more strong allies in this fight. But a chill slips down her spine. She can't help but feel they're already too late.

## 21

## JAANTZEN

It's still dark when his comm blares with an incoming call and Jaantzen tumbles out of troubled dreams, heart racing. Swims through a tangle of unfamiliar sheets before he remembers he's back in Cobalt Tower, in his own bed, and he's not alone.

Phaera calls his name sleepily.

His hand closes on the comm to stop the earsplitting noise. He blinks at the name on the screen until it makes sense.

Major Hector Ngara of the Bulari Police Department.

Jaantzen takes two deep breaths to make sure he's fully awake. Phaera shifts beside him, a gleam of bare shoulder in the dark.

Jaantzen clears his throat. Opens the connection.

"Yes?"

"Mr. Jaantzen, apologies for calling you at this hour." Ngara doesn't sound apologetic. He sounds business-like and tired. He's outdoors: quiet hiss of wind in the background, distant voices calling out orders "There's been an accident."

Phaera rolls to face him, her eyes bright and clear. Jaantzen flicks the call to speaker so she can hear Ngara's voice.

"What happened?" Jaantzen asks.

"It was called in about an hour ago. A Bierat ORV, silver. On Skyline Road." Jaantzen's stomach drops; he knows that road leading out to the Maraka Valley, he knows that vehicle. "ORV's registered to the Andel Medical School. Are you familiar with it?"

Gia and Tevi. Part of his mind is screaming to ask what happened to them, if they're all right. But the other, calmer part sounds a warning. Jaantzen gave Gia and Tevi the initial funding for the school, and Admant has done pro bono work on their security, but it's all been off the books. He's done everything in his power to keep his name unassociated with Gia's — there should be no connection between him and the school.

So why is Ngara calling him?

"I'm familiar," he says carefully. "What happened."

"We're not sure. The vehicle is crashed in a ditch and shot to hell, hard to tell which came first. Blood, but no bodies."

No bodies could mean many things, few of them good. "They walked away from the accident?" That has to be it — Gia could easily have survived with her new abilities, and she would have taken Tevi with her.

"Do you know who was in this vehicle, sir?" Ngara asks.

"What makes you think I would?"

The desert wind picks up behind Ngara, a faint howl. "Because someone left a note. 'Tell Jaantzen it was Z.'" Ngara pauses for that to settle in; Jaantzen's racing mind stills. Beside him, Phaera pushes herself to sit up, half-wrapped in the sheets, good hand covering her mouth in horror.

"Mr. Jaantzen," says Ngara. "Who was in this vehicle?"

"Dr. Giaconda Áte and Dr. Tevi Sharaf," he says. "They run the Andel School. It's a — "

"Training school for physicians, I know it. What's your relationship with them?"

Jaantzen rubs a hand over the back of his neck. The truth — or as close to the truth as he can get — will be the most valuable thing for Gia and Tevi now. "Dr. Áte worked with me in the past and we've remained friends. She was also close with Julieta Yang. I had them over for dinner last night after the funeral."

"I sent an officer up to the school," Ngara says. "The student who answered said they hadn't heard anything from either of them. Do you have any idea where they might be, Mr. Jaantzen? Who might have them?"

Z — it has to be Zacharia. Ngara might be able to help, but Jaantzen's not about to point the BPD in that direction before he can explore it himself.

"I don't."

"No enemies of yours?" When Jaantzen doesn't answer, Ngara makes a small, disappointed noise. It's clear he doesn't believe Jaantzen has no suspects in mind. "We'll do our best to find them," Ngara says shortly. "Let me know if you can be of any help." And he cuts the connection.

"Gods," Phaera murmurs.

Jaantzen dials Gia, gets no answer. Calls Manu, who answers with a voice adrenaline-crisp and freshly awake.

"Someone kidnapped Gia and Tevi," Jaantzen says. "Ngara just called, said they found their ORV crashed on the road out to the Maraka Valley, full of bullet holes, no bodies. Gia left us a note: 'Tell Jaantzen it was Z.'"

He recites the details with dispassionate calm; his initial shock is worn off, and any fear or speculation must be locked away where it won't interfere with the job he needs to do now. Worry never made anyone come home faster.

"Z," says Manu.

"Zacharia," agrees Jaantzen. "Could it be anyone besides the Dawn?"

Manu is silent, Jaantzen knows his mind is running through the same list of enemies his is, sorting them into categories. Capable enough? Motivated enough? Powerful enough?

Brash enough to assume Jaantzen wouldn't find them and burn them to the ground?

"The Dawn," says Manu. He lets out a curse; in the background comes rustling sheets, Oriol's low murmur, Manu's terse response. "We'll be there in thirty. Boss. Tevi knows where Lucky is."

So does Gia, but she's not going to crack. She has experience, training. Jaantzen is sure Tevi wouldn't turn on them, especially if it meant putting other people in danger, but how long can he hold out? Especially if they're threatening his wife? Jaantzen turns to study Phaera, pale arms marred with bruises, gaunt collar-bones, that blinding white bandage around her throat. Gia might be able to stand anything the Dawn might do to get her to talk, but Tevi won't be able to stand watching.

"I'll call Toshiyo."

"Be there in a few." Manu cuts the connection.

Jaantzen slips out of the bed and begins fumbling in

the dark for his clothes; Phaera switches on the bedside lamp.

"Why would the Dawn have taken them?" she asks.

"Hostage exchange. He wants Lucky." Jaantzen hopes that's true — Zacharia would know what was in the cases Coeur stole, and that Jaantzen ended up with them. There's no way Zacharia could know about Gia, is there? They were the most vulnerable of his family, and Zacharia took advantage of the opportunity. He should have insisted they stay here last night.

A hostage exchange means Gia and Tevi will be safe — for now. If Zacharia knows about Gia, though, all bets are off.

Either way, he's not letting Zacharia get his hands on another alien.

Jaantzen pulls on a shirt and opens a channel to Toshiyo.

No answer.

Tries again with the same result — she could be asleep, but that's never stopped her from answering before. If she's asleep, she's probably in her lair on the fourth floor . . . but when he pings her location, he gets a notice she's not in the building, she left in the middle of the night.

Fear coils slowly around his spine.

Does Zacharia have her, too?

He's about to call Manu back when his comm chimes: Toshiyo's number. He sinks back onto the edge of the bed, grim anticipation squeezing his chest. "Yes."

"Hey, boss, sorry."

He drags in a breath of relief at her voice; he'd been preparing himself to hear her captors. Someone's chattering behind her, a muddy din of faraway conversation.

"Are you all right? Where are you?"

"Yeah, I'm fine. At the terminal, I'm meeting the *Coldfire*'s captain in an hour and thought I'd get breakfast here."

Wariness squeezes his chest once more. That doesn't sound like her at all.

"Tell me you're safe."

"Yeah, boss." She switches on her video, spins so he can take everything in; she's telling him the truth. She's alone. She's at the terminal. The clattering beneath her voice is coming from a dumpling cart. Jaantzen relaxes.

"What's going on?"

He tells her what he told Manu and her eyes go wide.

"I'll come right back home."

Jaantzen shakes his head. "I need you to help El bring Lucky back. But be fast, and keep a guard out."

"We will."

"And be careful."

Toshiyo swallows, clears her throat. "Will do. See you soon."

Phaera's gingerly pulling on clothes; the mottled bruising on her ribs flashes in the light, disappears under a sweatshirt.

"This is a nightmare," she says softly.

You have no idea. The words are almost out of his mouth before he stops himself. She does have an idea; she's lived through her own share of nightmares already since she threw in her lot with his, and no doubt she'll be treated to more if she continues to associate with him.

Her thigh is warm against his when she joins him on the edge of the bed, her fingers gently twining in his. "We'll get them back," she says.

They're empty words; she can't know that. But he

tries to accept them in the spirit in which they were offered, even as he desperately wishes she was out of the room so he could turn all his rage towards finding Zacharia. The white-hot focus he needs right now won't burn Manu, it won't burn Starla. They know him, they understand.

But Phaera?

"The timing," she says quietly. "You don't think it has anything to do with the prime minister's speech tonight?"

Gia and Tevi are gone, and Phaera's thinking about a social event. "How could it?" His tone was too sharp and her hand slides out of his.

"I'm just throwing out ideas," she murmurs. "I'll go make some coffee."

He catches her wrist. "We'll find them," he says.

Her kiss is soft and sweet and far too brief for him to forget that Gia and Tevi are in enemy hands and it's his fault.

## 22

## TOSHIYO

After the bumpy two-hour drive from the Maraka Valley deathtrap to Bulari yesterday — and given their pressing timeline — the quick hop in the *Coldfire* is welcome. Though Toshiyo is having trouble believing this thing made it over the Jupari Desert to Redrock and back.

"You don't have to hold on so tight," says the pilot, Benedicto Kulikutan. "She flies better than most ships half her age."

Toshiyo tries to return his carefree smile and forces her hands to unclench from the armrests. They clamp back down of their own accord when the *Coldfire* drops like a boulder, then evens out once more.

"Just turbulence," says Beto. "Almost there."

She can see that. The deathtrap doesn't look any more impressive from the air than it does from the ground: a sturdy, wind-scoured hangar and a one-room shack that could belong to any homesteader or independent miner. The sun's lifted above the horizon behind them, painting the outbuildings, the runway, and the surrounding desert a flat pinkish gray.

Toshiyo feels a stab of fondness for the place as Beto swoops them in for a landing. The deathtrap's been the perfect hideout. Maraka Valley folk tend to keep to themselves and mind their own business, and if any of them noticed the place got sold to a family who have more going on than simple homesteaders would, none of them would breathe a word and get the authorities sniffing around.

"Keep the government outta the Valley" seems to be the one thing Maraka Valley folk agree on.

Beto's flying isn't all that has Toshiyo wired, though, and it's more than turbulence churning her stomach. She and Mel and Nacea were out late enough that Toshiyo just had them drop her off at the terminal, where she'd gotten some food and coffee and popped a couple of tabs to sharpen her mind after the all-nighter.

She'd already been stressed about bringing Lucky back to Cobalt Tower, before she got Jaantzen's call. Gia and Tevi won't spill where Lucky is located, she tells herself, not for a while at least. And she and El will be in and out of here in no time at all. And Starla's back home organizing an assault on Zacharia and Deté's desert compound, which is where Gia and Tevi surely must have been taken.

Maybe this was an accident — Gia and Tevi were easy to grab. Maybe this is a hostage situation, and he won't realize what Gia's become.

But if he does?

Gia could be in trouble.

"Hold on," Beto says as he fires the stabilizing thrusters and guides them through a heart-pounding, chaotic descent into a surprisingly gentle landing. Toshiyo doesn't even feel it when the *Coldfire*'s landing gear touches the ground. Beto's grinning, obviously delighted by the ride.

No wonder Simca likes him.

Beto reaches slim brown fingers into the collar of his lime green and teal paisley lumosilk shirt to touch the gold medallion at his throat.

"Saint Alixhi?" Toshiyo guesses, closing the door on the part of her mind that's worried about what Zacharia might be doing to Gia and Tevi. Leaving it open will only cause her to make mistakes in the now.

"A gift from my grandma when my sis and I left New Manila. Maybe it's superstition, but she's kept me in the air this long." Beto's good-natured smile slips into a frown. "I thought it was going to be in a crate."

She follows his gaze. In front of them, the hangar door is sliding open to reveal El, a pile of crates, and one excited Lucky. He flaps his wings at them.

Toshiyo jams fingers into the buckles of her harness, already sifting through her mental checklist of what she needs to do in the short window they have. So long as El got everything else, coaxing Lucky into a crate is low priority. "He'll be fine," she tells Beto.

"If you say so." He flips a switch to lower the cargo bay ramp, then hits Broadcast. "El, man, it's good to see you."

El holds out a thumbs-up.

Toshiyo hurries down the cargo bay ramp and across the roughly fifty-meter gap Beto left between the *Coldfire* and the hangar, the program she's already rehearsed running in the back of her mind: check El's work, double-check her office, wipe the data, get the hell out of here. Lucky crashes into her leg in a leathery tangle, burying his flat, fanged face against her thigh. She tugs on one of his ears and he grins up at her.

"Hey buddy," she signs.

"I couldn't get Lucky into his transport cage," El says. "But I gathered everything else on the list you sent me."

"The embryo?"

El gestures to the carefully packed pallet beside him. "Got it, and everything from the lab."

"Starla's cats?"

An annoyed yowl comes from the pallet in response.

"I tricked them into their transport cage last night before bed. Should've tried that with Lucky."

Lucky gives El a sly grin. He *is* starting to understand speech, she thinks, and files that into a compartment to deal with later. "It probably wouldn't have worked. The algae?"

"Yep. Set up with a power cell to keep everything bubbling during transport."

Anyone else, she'd double-check. But El always follows her directions precisely without coming up with his own interpretations. He and Oriol are the only two she can trust not to go off script on missions and do something dumb like set off a bunch of hornet tags or go running off to explore an interesting-looking room.

The algae can come with them and she can continue working with it back at Cobalt Tower. But the small plot of land she'd staked out behind the deathtrap? She can't transport that. She'd set it up with automatic watering and telemetric sensors even before they started talking about going back to Cobalt Tower, not trusting herself to remember to keep the crops alive. But she was excited to watch those little bastards grow in person.

"I'm going to run through my office," she says. She

turns to Beto, who's joined them. "I'll be five minutes, which should be enough time for you two to load up."

"Got it," El says.

The hairs on the back of her neck rise, and Toshiyo turns slowly to take in the horizon. Nothing seems out of the ordinary, but then she didn't spend a lot of time out here admiring the scenery. The smudge of cottonwood and willow and eucarix along the river to the south. Plumes of smoke from distant homesteads across the valley, silhouetted against the now-blinding horizon. The racket of morning songbirds.

"What's wrong?" El asks.

Toshiyo shakes her head. Maybe the caffeine and the attention-sharpening tabs are making her paranoid, maybe she's letting worry about Gia and Tevi ghost in on the current job. Or maybe this is that gut instinct the boss is always insisting she pay attention to.

"Keep the channel open, watch for trouble," she says, then turns to Lucky. "We're heading somewhere safe," she signs. "Go with El. I'll be right back."

She hurries down the stairs into the bunkers, still unable to shake the uneasiness that plagued her in the hangar. All her data is backed up remotely and secure, but there are a few things in her office she needs to grab. She tosses them into a backpack, then takes a slow spin to jog her memory on if anything else needs to come with them. She's got everything important. Everything else here is junk. Interesting, but junk nonetheless.

Toshiyo double-checks her backups, types in the code to wipe her desk, the boss's desk, everything out here. Her wipeout program is as thorough as it gets — if she wanted to be any more certain of it she'd set the place on fire. But it's just a precaution. No one's getting in, and even if they did get far enough into the deathtrap to turn on one of these desks, the whole place would likely already be completely ablaze. Between the stairwell kill chutes and the other handful of the original owner's boobytraps she's restored, if anyone gets inside, the deathtrap will live up to its name.

She pokes her head in the kitchen, but El left it pristine of course. Flips the switch in Starla's room, Manu's room, finds them empty. And Jaantzen's — there's a small wooden box sitting on his desk. She hesitates, then slips it into her backpack without opening it.

One last look in Lucky's room and Toshiyo hurries back up to the hangar, pausing to check that the triggers in the top set of stairs are armed.

As she locks the door behind her, she can feel the distant rumble of the *Coldfire*'s engine. El and Beto have packed up the crates, and El is a black silhouette against the bright sun at the hangar's entrance. Toshiyo shields her eyes and squints at the horizon once more, trying to understand what has her so on edge.

"We all good?" he asks.

Toshiyo runs through her checklist once more before answering.

Everything down below is locked up, and the security systems are set. She's less certain about the structural stability of the hangar, so they've moved everything she thought was valuable — and they could carry — down into the bunkers themselves. There are still piles of interesting electronics that could potentially have valuables in them. She can hope they're still here for her when she comes back.

If they get to come back.

"We're good," Toshiyo finally says.

"All right. Then one last thing, for Starla." El winks at her, then heads to the corner and pulls a tarp off a lumpy shape. The moto Starla had been working on, the al-Jurjani Trespass. El grins at it, then throws one leg over. "She said — "

He cuts off at the noise, because Toshiyo's comm is shrieking at them. A new alarm she'd programmed in but never expected to hear.

The deathtrap's perimeter alarm.

Beto's voice sounds in her ear. "You two see this? We've got incoming."

Toshiyo whirls. Dust plumes rise against the brilliant horizon. Strangely even. Unnatural.

Someone's coming.

"What do you see?" she asks.

"Two — no, three vehicles. ORVs. Maybe they're headed somewhere else?"

"That road doesn't go anywhere else," Toshiyo says.

"They're splitting up," Beto tells her, but she can see it, too — now that the vehicles are inside the perimeter sensor they're showing up on her comm. One's still headed towards the house, but the other two have peeled off. One taking the runway, the other aiming to circle around behind the compound. But how far out are they? She curses the tiny screen.

Toshiyo types in the code to shut down the driveway, and a distant rumble rolls through her chest. The ORV that was still on the road blinks off her comm.

"What the hell was that?" Beto asks.

"One's heading towards you on the runway," she says. "We'll be there in a sec."

"Gotcha. I — shit, you've got trouble."

A spray of bullets strafe the ground in front of the hangar. Sparks fly off the hull of the *Coldfire*.

"Both sides," says Beto. "Didn't see where these assholes came from."

Doesn't matter, because they're about to be joined by the two ORVs heading towards them from different directions. A flash bomb detonates near the mouth of the hangar; bullets are singing through the air outside the hangar door. No matter how fast El is, they're running a gauntlet that could rip them apart before they make it even the short distance from the hangar to the *Coldfire*.

"Tosh?" El asks.

Time melts away, ticking slow as her heart rate.

"Keep them out of the *Coldfire*," she says to Beto. "We'll come to you. Anything happens to us, you get out of here with Lucky." She grabs El's outstretched hand and hauls herself onto the back of the Trespass — its sleek body was designed for speed, not passengers. Toshiyo wraps one arm around his waist and grabs her comm with the other. Out at the *Coldfire*, Beto manages to get a couple of shots off before the return volley sends him diving back for cover.

"Hold on!" El revs the motor. "Beto, we're on our way, cover us."

"Wait!" Toshiyo yells over the roar of the engine, and El glances back, quizzical. "Beto, wait. Let them get closer to the hangar."

"They're already too close."

"Wait."

Toshiyo frowns down at her comm, letting the pieces fall into place. She ignores El's tension — he didn't hesitate to follow her order to wait, the result of years of obeying her without question on missions and coming out alive. But his bare brown knuckles are white on the moto's controls.

"Tosh," he murmurs.

"One more second." A round of bullets strafes the wall in front of them and El flinches. Revs the motor once more. Toshiyo has the exterior cameras patched through to her comm, and none of the four figures she sees are at an angle where they could actually hit them. Yet.

Lulled by the silence, they creep forward.

And, there.

Toshiyo thumbs in another code, sets it loose, and a plume of fire erupts in front of the hangar.

One of the original owner's designs: tiny nozzles attached to an underground tank of pressurized liquid fuel, spark caps and plugs on one long bar that springs to the side when the catch is released, ten of them in a haphazard pattern in front of the hangar, all of them sending off plumes of flame nearly three meters high.

"Go!" she yells.

El guns it out of the hangar, skidding to avoid both flame plumes and the three burning figures caught up in them. A pair of rifle shots crack through the air, but they're from Beto in the *Coldfire*'s cargo bay door, taking out the fourth figure, who hadn't been caught in the inferno. Toshiyo squeezes her arm around El's waist, but opens her eyes enough to press Arm on the viper bots she restored and reburied around the compound, and make sure the entire system is shut to lockdown. The hangar door swings back and locks. The kill chutes in the stair-wells glow red on her comm.

The *Coldfire* is in between them and the ORV racing towards them down the runway, and El guns the Trespass up the ramp and skids to a stop a handsbreadth from the cockpit. Beto is already slamming his palm on the button to lift up the cargo bay doors. A bullet ricochets off the wall in front of Toshiyo, but that iron-hot-ice-cold plunge of a bullet tearing into her gut, it doesn't come.

The cargo bay door seals with a hiss. Beto throws himself in the pilot's seat.

"Grab Lucky," El yells, and Toshiyo forces herself back into action, sliding awkwardly off the back of the moto. Lucky won't really *work* with the *Coldfire*'s uncomfortable transport-seat harnesses, so she straps herself in and beckons him to her, clutching his strange bony body to her chest as the *Coldfire* lurches away from the ground.

El's managed to get the moto secured, and he collapses into a transport seat across from Toshiyo. She fumbles for her comm around Lucky's ungainly bulk and thumbs it on to the feed of the hangar's external cameras. The flames have died down, leaving blackened bodies lying in front of the hangar. The ORV that had been charging at them down the runway is also in flames, caught in the *Coldfire*'s thrusters.

Her stomach clenches — but those people are Dawn. *Were* Dawn. And the way they died wasn't much different from what they'd inflicted on others with their poison.

The ship lurches forward and up, and the blast of relief washing through Toshiyo leaves her almost as shaky as the adrenaline. Or maybe it's the inevitable crash from the tabs she took with breakfast. Either way, El's unhurt. She's unhurt. Lucky and Beto are fine, and they're on their way back home.

"All good back there?" Beto's voice crackles over the *Coldfire*'s system.

"We're good," El says. He gives her a smile. "Might

tell Starla the Dawn got the Trespass and keep it for myself, though."

Toshiyo grins back. "I won't say a word."

"What was all that?"

"A few surprises. The Dawn got here so fast. Did they — did Gia . . ."

"Did they break Gia or Tevi?" El shakes his head. "They can't have had them long enough. Even Tevi."

"But we don't know how long they've been prisoners," Toshiyo says. "It could have been all night."

And coming out here meant she lost time in helping Starla plan their rescue. She scoots Lucky off her lap and opens a new message.

On our way with everything, safe. Dawn showed up. We need to get Gia and Tevi out now.

The reply is a long time coming.

Compound is abandoned. The Dawn are gone.

The words hit her below the sternum.

Abandoned? How the hell is the compound abandoned, the Dawn were there last night when she checked in on the security feeds she'd left. And if they abandoned the site, where did they take Gia and Tevi? Beside her, Lucky growls, upset by her distress.

"What's wrong?" El asks. "Toshiyo?"

"They're gone," she whispers.

## 23

## STARLA

The Dawn are gone.

Completely gone, the site abandoned, the surveillance devices Toshiyo left showing nothing but a sand-scoured ghost town with no people, no equipment, no alien. And no Gia and Tevi.

Starla swipes through visual views, heat maps, but there's nothing. The Dawn have completely abandoned their camp overnight, and she's not even sure exactly when, because there's time missing in the surveillance footage. Starla wouldn't have thought the devices they left were even noticeable, but someone found them and messed with them.

She's been exchanging messages with Toshiyo for the last hour, taking advantage of Cobalt Tower's better network to run searches that Toshiyo isn't able to do from her comm while en route. Now she's hacking through a series of government and private satellites with Toshiyo's remote instruction, trying to get a time lapse of the night before to figure out where they might have gone.

She drums her fingers in frustration as she waits for

Toshiyo's code to work on a poorly secured private satellite — one of the Demosga Corporation's, actually, she'll have to tell them how bad their security is if they do end up working together. It finally goes through, and she downloads the data, starts combing through to find the right timeframe.

There.

If she weren't searching for Dawn activity, she wouldn't have any reason to zoom in on this particular part of the desert. But now that she does, she can track vehicles leaving the compound under the cover of night, big transports like the two she and Toshiyo had seen carrying shard a few days back.

Two head towards Bulari, one heads further into the desert, one skirts to the west as though heading out to Ruby Basin.

The two vehicles headed back towards Bulari are now hopelessly lost in the city's traffic. Toshiyo walked her through running a search on similar vehicles in the city's transportation cameras, but she's guessing make and model from grainy satellite footage. And they were out around sunrise, which means every delivery driver in the city was out in a van or truck that could match the vague description.

Starla tracks the one heading towards Ruby Basin through a few different poorly secured satellite feeds before it somehow manages to drive into the margins between two available images. She could spend hours trying to locate it again, but it's probably not important — she can tell it was heading away from the city, away from the Maraka Valley. It's not the van that intercepted Gia and Tevi.

She's pretty sure that's the fourth one. But she hasn't been able to find it anywhere.

Toshiyo's also given her instructions on running Felipe Zacharia and Thomas Deté's faces through her facial recognition software, but it's spitting back nonsense. Or maybe it's not, but Starla can't really tell. She prefers the soldering-wires end of a desk to the data-spewing end.

They should have acted when they knew where the Dawn was, as impossible as the situation was. Yes, they couldn't have done it on their own. Yes, bringing in outside help would mean potentially letting the full-grown alien fall into even more dangerous hands. And yes, it might have made it harder to hunt down Felipe Zacharia if they'd revealed they knew where his lair was while he wasn't there.

But by not doing anything, they lost their chance.

And now Gia and Tevi are gone, and she has no idea where to look for them.

Starla runs her hands through her choppy hair in frustration. It's getting closer to lunchtime, bright midmorning light streaming through the penthouse, the windows dimming automatically. A movement in the corner of her eye catches her attention: Phaera, the coffee pot in her good hand.

"Refill?"

When Starla nods, she pours, a bit awkwardly. She must be right-handed, and her right hand is currently splinted and cradled unconsciously against her ribcage.

Starla thanks her and cranes her head back at the stairs, but her godfather isn't down yet. He'd gone up to make calls about an hour ago. She expects Phaera to head back upstairs again, but she returns from the kitchen with her own cup of black coffee and joins Starla at the conference table.

"Can I help?" she asks. Then, a flash of uncertainty. "Your lens is transcribing me, right? Or should I . . ."

Starla gives her a thumbs-up.

She's not sure what to make of this woman. She'd only met her once before the funeral yesterday, at the Devil's Table, the night she'd consulted with Phaera's staff about their security. And, of course, going into that meeting, Jaantzen had been half convinced Phaera had ordered the recent attack on Starla.

So Starla'd been completely shocked when Manu told her Jaantzen and Phaera had gone from working together to sleeping together, and she still hasn't been able to figure out what Jaantzen sees in her. She hadn't thought a highly polished gossip-column darling would be his type. Though Starla's had no idea who *would* be. She's pretty sure he's had a handful of relationships over the past few years, but they've been brief, discreet, and kept at arm's length. If Manu knew anything, he didn't share those details with Starla, and that's fine by her.

Phaera D, though? Bubbly sound bites and camera-ready smile, everything about her completely calculated to present the exact image she wants you to see? A woman like that seems flashy. High-maintenance. Fake.

Extremely not Jaantzen's type.

But the woman sitting across the table this morning isn't Phaera D. She's wearing a comfy, well-worn gray sweater that's falling off one shoulder, drawstring house trousers, bare feet tucked up crosslegged on the seat beneath her. Her magenta hair is pulled back in a messy ponytail, loose strands tucked behind her ears. She's wearing makeup, but it's minimal, and she hasn't tried to obscure the soft crow's feet around her eyes, the creases around her mouth.

She's not trying to hide the damage Tierren left, either. Yesterday that yellowing bruise on her cheek had been expertly touched up and she'd been wearing a scarf despite the heat. Starla knows most of the details about the attack, but the violent black and purple ring around Phaera's throat, the raw scratches — it's awful. And the worst of it must still be under that bandage.

"Still pretty bad, huh?" Phaera says. She laughs ruefully and cups her good hand around her coffee. "I've had my adventure for a lifetime. I don't know how you do it."

Starla frowns at her. "Do what?" she signs.

"That story you told last night? Charging in to one dangerous situation after another?" Phaera waves a hand over the table. "And here you are getting ready to do it again. And Dr. Áte — " her expression sobers. "What can I do to help?"

The question seems genuine, so Starla beckons her closer. Phaera scoots forward on her chair with a wince.

WE HAD A LOCK ON THE DAWN'S LOCATION BEFORE, Starla types. BUT THEY MOVED LAST NIGHT. WE TRACKED THE VEHICLES, BUT WE'VE LOST THEM.

She zooms out to a bigger map, points *here*, *here*, and *here*.

I'M LOOKING THROUGH THE CITY FEEDS. MANU AND ORIOL ARE ASKING THEIR NETWORKS.

Phaera points to the spot Starla's indicated north of the city where one of the vehicles disappeared. "This one could have ended up in Jet Park. There are still lots of places to hide out there, and no one controls the neighborhood."

Starla shrugs. They could be anywhere, that's the point.

Phaera types something into the golden cuff she's wearing. "What are we telling people to look for?"

Starla hesitates, not sure how much to share. Jaantzen trusts this woman, and he wouldn't risk his family for a fling. But infatuation can go to your head, cloud your judgement.

Although, Oriol obviously adores her, and Starla knows how rare that is. And from the brief time Starla spent with Hiro Matapang and the rest of Phaera's security team setting up systems at the Devil's Table, it's clear her people are devoted to her.

Phaera D's brand is nothing if not charming — but Manu can't be charmed. And he definitely would have put a stop to the relationship if he thought Phaera was dangerous. Starla knows that firsthand.

If Manu trusts her, Starla will.

She calls up images of Felipe Zacharia and Thomas Deté.

*WE'RE SPECIFICALLY LOOKING FOR THEM. ALSO FOR WHITE CARGO VEHICLES, WOULD HAVE SHOWED UP EARLY THIS MORNING. THE DAWN ARE ARMED, DEFINITELY DANGEROUS. AND THEY'D NEED A SPACE BIG ENOUGH TO CONCEAL HOSTAGES. AND A FULL-GROWN ALIEN.*

"I'll make some calls," Phaera says, swiping Zacharia's and Deté's images onto her cuff. She glances towards the stairs, where Jaantzen has finally emerged, and her concerned expression melts into something more. There's pure affection there, simple joy, and a deep, empathetic worry.

And Starla has seen enough of Phaera D's perfectly polished masks to know this is real.

Whatever Starla thinks of her, this woman truly loves her godfather.

Phaera unfolds herself from the chair and goes to meet Jaantzen, and Starla turns back to her work to give them some privacy. Because while she can be happy he's happy, she definitely does not need to watch them paw each other.

A new message from Toshiyo: 20 MIN.

*Finally*. Starla's not doing Gia and Tevi any good combing through satellite footage and spreadsheets like this, but at least she laid the groundwork for Toshiyo to do her magic. She cracks her neck. Time to start readying the troops.

Sure, she has dozens of trained fighters on her payroll through Admant, but they're security guards, not soldiers. She can hire them to guard Julieta Yang's funeral, but there's no one she'd ask to follow her into a fight like this.

She knows Jaantzen used to have soldiers, she remembers safehouses full of them during the civil war with Coeur, remembers trying to stay out from underfoot while learning as much as she could. But he hasn't needed them for a long time. These days, anything needs done, she can handle it with the Anahoys or Manu can get it done with some of Oriol's trusted merc buddies.

Speaking of.

*THE WOMEN YOU AND O WORKED WITH THE OTHER NIGHT? WE NEED THEM.*

Manu's response is quick: *NO PROB.*

Yesterday she wouldn't have hesitated to send her next message. Henri and Jude, the two former Redrock prisoners who went with her to infiltrate the Alliance's secret facility, have already offered to help her hunt down

Felipe Zacharia. They're both good fighters, and they both seem to hate the Dawn.

Or, they *seemed* to.

Ever since Jaantzen told her what Leone said yesterday — that Zacharia claims to be working with some of the escaped prisoners — she can't help but replay the events leading up to the Dawn escaping.

They'd had a plan. Henri would create a distraction and cut the power to the facility so they could break in. But something had gone wrong. There'd been an explosion — an accident, probably the result of an overloaded system, Henri had told her later. And the next thing Starla had known they'd been fighting their way through Alliance marines and escaped Dawn prisoners alike.

What if it wasn't an accident?

Maybe Henri had allowed the Dawn to escape on purpose . . . or maybe Leone's trying to mess with their heads.

A reflection in the conference table startles her out of her thoughts, and she glances up to find her godfather. "Any luck?" he asks, taking the chair Phaera had just left. Phaera's curled up in the corner of one of the electric-blue couches. She must be making the calls she promised, though Starla has no idea who someone like her might know who could help them.

Starla drums her fingers on the table before answering. "Toshiyo will be here in twenty minutes to help look through the data I got for her," she signs. "Working on gathering troops now. What's your gut say about the escaped prisoners?"

"Do you trust them?"

"I want to. They made multiple raids to get produce from the Alliance, they said. If they wanted to free the

Dawn, they could have done it any time. And they both seemed to hate Zacharia."

"Any chance Leone was talking about one of the other prisoners who came home with Jude and Henri?"

"Maybe. I didn't spend as much time with them."

"Can we do this without them?"

"We're stretched thin. Especially if you're going to the prime minister's speech tonight."

Jaantzen shakes his head. "Gia and Tevi are my priority. Leone can wait."

"But — "

"Everything else can wait," he repeats.

Jaantzen frowns into the distance, index finger tapping idly against the conference table as he makes his decision. His shoulders rise, fall.

"Coeur," he fingerspells. "We need her help."

"And if she's working with Zacharia, like Leone said?"

"It's because she wants what he has, not because she wants to be his partner. We offer her another way to get what she wants, while also betraying the man who killed her sister."

"Or Leone's lying."

Jaantzen nods. "Or Leone's lying," he agrees. He swipes open his messages.

Zacharia kidnapped Gia. May need backup when we find out where she is.

He turns back to Starla and lifts his hands, but before he can say anything, a call pulses on the table in front of him.

"We split the haul," Coeur says by way of greeting.

Jaantzen lifts an eyebrow to Starla: *See?*

"We're there for Gia and her husband," Jaantzen says. "And my goddaughter is running the show. As long as you follow her orders I don't care what you loot."

"Listen to the kid, got it. Zacharia's mine."

"Of course, Thala."

"I'll see what I can turn up. How many soldiers do you need?"

"I'll have a better idea soon. How many can you spare?"

It's a delicate way of phrasing it, without seeming like he's probing after Coeur's strength. Jaantzen's conversations with Coeur have all the grace and strategy of a knife fight or a ballet, and it's a game Starla doesn't have the patience for. Good thing Jaantzen's always there to act as a buffer — she'd've stepped on Coeur's toes and started another civil war ten times in the last minute.

"I can spare a couple dozen," Coeur answers. "I'll send Damyati."

"Thank you. I'll be in touch." Jaantzen ends the connection and turns to Starla. "Are you comfortable with that?"

"I'll have to be." She's read up on Damyati, and he seems solid. Even Manu mostly trusts him. And Jaantzen will be there. Oriol. The Anahoys — other people she can trust. Once she knows what they're up against, she and Toshiyo can design this operation so Coeur's people are boxed into tight parameters.

"We'll need Henri and Jude," she signs, and Jaantzen nods, trusting her decision. She's only known the two men for a few days now, but she's known Leone for years. She opens a new message.

MIGHT HAVE SOME TROUBLE BREWING AND I NEED SOME FIGHTERS I CAN TRUST.

Henri's reply is short and sweet:

*JUDE AND I ARE IN TELL ME WHEN AND WHERE.*

The lights dim — someone arriving via the lift. Starla sighs in relief when Toshiyo enters. The other woman is bedraggled, long black hair tangled, a smudge of soot on her chin.

"What happened?" Starla signs.

"I got to ride the Trespass," Toshiyo replies in her rapid, haphazard mix of USL and fingerspelling. She flashes a grin. "And I got to test out some of those booby-traps. You would've loved it." She swipes the feed in front of Starla over to her. "El's getting Lucky settled in. What have you got?"

"Hopefully something you can make sense of," Starla signs. "And some backup. A couple of Oriol's merc buddies, some of the escaped prisoners who helped us at Redrock, and Coeur."

Toshiyo's surprised gaze shifts between Starla and Jaantzen. "Okay," she says slowly, then lifts her hands again. "So now we just need to find them. Assuming . . ." She trails off, not willing to finish the thought. Starla can guess what she's thinking — the thought's run through her head a dozen times since Toshiyo told her the Dawn had shown up at the deathtrap.

Either Zacharia found them on his own, or he got the information out of Gia and Tevi far faster than Starla would have expected. And if that's the case, is it already too late?

"They're alive," Jaantzen signs firmly. The set of his jaw says he'll burn the world down if that's not true. "And we will find them."

# 24

## GIA

This isn't her body. But she could get used to it.

She likes that the knot where her head hit the window has already receded and the graze from a bullet in her upper arm has already healed. It makes her nervous that neither of those injuries hurt as bad as they should — the clinical part of her mind worries there's more possibility of grave injury when the self-protective pain response is removed from the equation.

She appreciates this body's strength, too — she could probably wrench the door off its rusted hinges if she tried. If she wasn't afraid of what they would do to Tevi if she did.

They were split up after the attack, and she doesn't know if they were even brought back to the same place. She can't help him, not yet. She can only hope Jaantzen got the note she left him and, in the meantime, push the part of her mind that's terrified for her husband back into a careful box so she can focus on keeping herself alive.

She doesn't know how much time has passed, just that no amount of yelling has made her captors return since they threw her in this dusty shed, tore her hood off, and locked the door behind them. It's a prefab storage unit, they've got a half-dozen like it out at the school. Supposed to be airtight, but this one's spent enough time out in the elements that the door's warped and some of the welds have cracked, letting in brilliant trickles of light that slowly crawl down the wall.

The light is nice, but the cracks mean the shed's rudimentary climate control is busted; she's boiling, and the whispers of breeze slipping through the cracks are as hot as the air inside the shed.

She's in the city, she thinks, or barely outside of it. Somewhere near the terminal, maybe? The rumble of launches sounds relatively close, and their captors hadn't driven far after attacking them on the road. She's heard voices a few times, footsteps crunching in the gravel yard, but no vehicle traffic.

Wherever she is, no one's worried about someone hearing her shouting.

This body may heal fast and be strong, but it still feels hunger and thirst. Gia locks that away alongside her fear. She's been hungry and thirsty before. She's been trapped before. She's been baking alive before, drenched in sweat and half-delirious from the heat. The difference is now she doesn't feel the physical pain — but the man she loves still does.

She's never before been this strong. Or this vulnerable.

Her captors know who she is — or rather, what she is. They knew it even before the nightmare in the desert, headlights swerving at them and Tevi running into the ditch to avoid a head-on collision. Bullets strafing the side of the ORV as Gia pulled him down, covered him as best she could until rough hands pulled them out. She would have fought back, but she couldn't. Not with Tevi on his knees, a gun to the back of his head.

"Careful with her," the leader had cautioned the others. "She's a saint."

A saint.

Getting her arm mangled by an alien definitely changed her physiology. But the Dawn have a surprise coming if they think it made her a saint.

It seems like afternoon when they finally come for her, the harshness of the light crawling down the wall gone a bit more brilliant. The random pattern of occasional footsteps in gravel changes, more deliberately aimed at her, and Gia sits up, scooting so her back's against the far wall with her hands draped over knees. Nonthreatening. Even if she weren't worried about Tevi, she needs to get the lay of the land before she rushes an unknown number of armed guards.

Someone throws the lock, and the door shrieks on its hinges as it's wrenched open with a wash of slightly cooler air. A trio of figures, and their guns, are silhouetted against the bright light; Gia throws up a hand to protect her eyes. This body's eyes are more sensitive to the light, she's noticed. Better night vision, and her vision overall is now crystal clear, but the bright sun bothers her more than it used to.

"Get up," a man barks.

Gia doesn't move. "Where is my husband?"

"Cooperate," the man says. His pistol whines as he points it straight at her. "Or we kill him. We both know it doesn't matter what we do to you, *saint*."

Gia raises her hands, gets slowly to her feet. The distant, clinical part of her mind notes the persistent snap in her hip is gone, her lower back doesn't ache from sitting on the ground for hours.

They cuff her hands in front of her, shackle her feet, prod her stumbling forward with their weapons. She drinks in her surroundings, filing every detail away to find the thing that will help her get out of this.

A drab adobe building that could be an old school squats at the center of the yard. The yard is surrounded by a high fence of metal sheeting topped with crisscrossed razorwire — there's probably more-advanced security, too, but nothing she can make out. A half-dozen more of the prefab sheds she'd been baking in line the south wall. Two four-door spinners and the utility van she'd been hauled here in are parked haphazardly in the yard.

They march her in the direction of the main building, maneuver her up a ramp, and shove her through a door into a blessedly cool corridor. Trickles of sweat trace the curve of her jaw, her breastbone, her ribs. She breathes deep and her chapped lip splits; by the time she licks the blood clean the crack is gone.

It *is* an old school, maybe a neighborhood collective that ran out of money or students as the local demographics changed, maybe they'd been bought out by Hypatia or one of the other educational corporations and now the kids are being bussed to a bigger school for a better education at a much steeper indenture debt.

Whatever happened to the school was years ago, though. Inspirational posters left on the walls are defaced with obscenities, drifts of trash fill the corners. The doors lining the hall are still on their hinges, all shut, and Gia can't see anything through the frosted glass panes.

Except one — a dark flash of shadow against the glass, a booming thud behind the door, and Gia almost stumbles at what feels like a physical blow of rage and pain and despair.

What the hell?

But the guards haul her forward even as she cranes her neck to get a better look at what's behind the frosted glass.

They shove her into a classroom at the far end of the hall: bright primary colors all faded and grimy, the window covered in a peeling yellow film. A long table in the middle of the room is covered in makeshift laboratory equipment. At first it looks like they're cooking shard — and maybe they are — but this setup is more complicated.

But she doesn't care one bit what they're cooking, because Tevi is here, along with a trio of armed guards of his own.

She freezes, but he calls her name and starts for her — and is immediately shoved back, a fist to his gut. He doubles over, gasping for air.

"Stop it," she yells. "Tevi, I'm fine." *Don't do anything stupid,* she silently pleads.

He's not bound. There's a bruise forming on his temple, but he doesn't look like he spent the hottest hours of the day locked in a sweltering shed. He's been working with them, she realizes, helping them with whatever it is they're trying to do.

That's good. Cooperating is good. Cooperating gets him through this.

She hopes.

"Are you all right?" he asks, and she nods. She knows she must look terrible, skin ashy and salt-streaked, blood-caked, but she's fine.

"Dr. Sharaf was starting to get uncooperative," says a voice behind her. Gia shifts — she's going for no sudden movements, but still every weapon in the room points straight at her. She finds an old man with a wild mane of white hair, deeply furrowed cheeks made leathery by the elements, his piercing ice-blue eyes unnervingly clear.

She's seen that face in briefings. And at the Alliance facility.

Felipe Zacharia.

"He demanded proof you were unhurt. See?" Zacharia says to Tevi. "She's fine. We have no desire to hurt her."

"Because I'm a saint?" Gia asks. "Whatever the fuck that means?"

"Let's talk about this elsewhere," Zacharia says. "We don't want to disturb Dr. Sharaf's work."

"No," Tevi says. "If you touch her — "

A few of the half-dozen guns shift towards him and he freezes.

"It's fine, Tevi," Gia says, as calmly as she can muster. "We're going to talk, right? Just do what they say. We're going to get through this."

She shakes off the guard's touch when he tries to grab her arm, follows Zacharia down the hall and into the next room. She can hear a guard's laugh from the room next door, even after both doors have shut, which means she'll hear it if anything happens to Tevi. She wonders if they planned it — if they'll play them off each other to get Tevi to do what they want him to. To get her to comply with whatever Zacharia wants.

This second room is still set up like a classroom, though the desks are all gone. Instead, chairs are set in a circle, tables lining the walls.

Not a classroom, she realizes.

It's set up like a chapel.

The tables hold strange artifacts — Gia'd guess they were props from one of Toshiyo's horror vids if she hadn't been reading everything she could about aliens in the last few days. A stylized image is painted on the far wall: a winged, tailed figure spiraling upwards. The resemblance to roly-poly Lucky is there, but now that Gia's seen his cousin, tattered wings spread above her, gaunt body almost graceful, she gets where this image came from. A heavy metal eye bolt juts from the throat of the painting.

"Ah, here she is."

Gia turns at the new voice; another man is lounging in the doorway. He's a bit younger than Zacharia, gray streaks at his temples and laugh lines around his dark eyes. Hands that don't know hard work, a body that hasn't been broken from years of toil, skin that hasn't been torched by the Redrock sun. Whoever this guy is, he didn't break out of prison with Zacharia.

"What do you think?" the newcomer asks.

"I think we haven't been introduced."

"Thomas Deté. I've been tending to the souls of the Bulari flock while our leader was away." His voice is a rich baritone, filled with a con man's swagger, not a priest's humility. "It's a pleasure to meet you."

"I thought you might want to see your heritage," Zacharia says. He holds out a hand to the tables. "The holy relics of those who made you."

Is that an invitation? If so, she'll play along. The armed guards who brought her here have stepped back, though they've still got their weapons trained on her. She takes a tentative step towards one of the tables, and when no one tries to stop her, approaches the first relic.

A glass incubation capsule like the one they found Lucky in, though this one's empty. It's nestled on a bed of black velvet, reverently displayed. A few feet away on another bed of fabric — pale blue silk — is a diamond-shaped chunk of glossy black obsidian, carved with the same stylized winged shape as the mural. On the next table, a pair of spheres, both covered in precise rows of hatchmarks and spirals like a code. Or a written language.

Holy shit.

Gia hadn't gotten the best look at the alien ship they'd taken shelter in during the firefight at the Alliance facility because, well, firefight. But the rows of symbols are tugging at her memory. Did she see writing like that there?

She reaches for one of the spheres with bound hands, brushing a fingertip over the marks. And uses the opportunity with her back to the guards to test the strength of her handcuffs. The sharp edge scores her forearms, but metal links give, ever so slightly. She wonders if the shackles on her feet will give if she tests them, too.

"Incredible, isn't it?" Zacharia says behind her, too close; Gia hadn't heard him approach. She turns to face him, settling against the table. "Of course, you saw the Fallen ship yourself. Life-changing, isn't it?"

"I'd like some water."

"Of course." Zacharia motions to one of the guards, who disappears down the hall and comes back a moment later with a metal cup of cool water. Gia forces herself to sip, keeps her hands around the cup.

"What do you want with Tevi?" she asks.

"He's helping me with a little project. He's been cooperative, but I suspect he was starting to worry about you."

"Let him go. I'll help you with whatever you need."

Zacharia laughs. "Of course not. Come. Sit." He sits

in one of the chairs across from her in the circle, but Deté is still watching from the doorway. If she sits across from Zacharia, Deté will be out of her field of vision. She's not sure which man she finds more unnerving, the grandpa with the serial killer eyes or the priest with the con man's smile.

Zacharia's gaze hardens — he's obviously not used to being ignored — and finally Gia steps forward and sits across from him. The chairs are burly, bolted to the floor, and Gia shivers at the cold metal through the back of her sweat-damp shirt. The heavy air conditioning had been a blessing at first, but now she's starting to feel the chill.

"We found your friends' hideout in the Maraka Valley," Zacharia says.

Gia's heart stops. Tevi? What did they do to him to get him to talk? What had they threatened to do to her? Are Toshiyo, Starla, and the others all right? She curses herself, pushes it all back in a box. She knows she didn't keep her reaction off her face.

Zacharia waves a hand like he didn't notice, or doesn't care. "You've moved on from them, Giaconda. You've been made divine. When you were a child you had childish desires, but now it's time to put those behind you and embrace what comes with leaving humanity behind."

He doesn't seem to be waiting for an answer.

"The chaff in you has been burned away," Zacharia continues. "Your pure core remains, but to attain salvation, the surroundings must match the soul. It's time to burn away the chaff in your life, too."

"I like the chaff."

Zacharia tilts his head, thinking. "Of course, there's a chance your husband could also become divine."

"Don't you fucking touch him."

"The Gift of the Fallen will touch everyone, soon." Zacharia sounds like he's giving her the weather report. "It's possible he survives and you can be reunited in the world that dawns after the fire." He studies her. "What did it feel like to go through the fire?"

"It hurt. Why. You thinking of giving it a shot?"

The answer is in that greedy look.

"So that's what Tevi's helping you with? You have your magic potion to transform people into whatever I am, and you want to try it yourself. But you need to make sure it's guaranteed. Afraid no one will listen to you if you're not a monster, too?"

"Do you really think you're monstrous, Giaconda?" Deté asks behind her in that silky smooth voice. Gia doesn't miss the flash of rage on Zacharia's face at being interrupted.

"I'm not human anymore, am I?" Her mind is racing as she tries to understand what Zacharia wants from her. Not to chat about the transformation, and not just as a tool to make sure Tevi stays compliant — otherwise he would have shown Tevi proof of life and then tossed her back out into the shed.

And maybe that's the key. If he needs Tevi so badly, maybe Gia doesn't need to keep factoring that into her calculations. She might be able to risk an attack, because Zacharia won't immediately have Tevi killed. Of course, she's still handcuffed, and she's up against three armed guards and Deté, who carries himself like he can fight. Maybe she's strong enough to tear apart the cuffs, maybe she can recover quickly from a minor injury, but a bullet to the head still kills. Even a "saint."

Zacharia nods to Deté over her shoulder, and the hairs on the back of her neck rise.

"No, you're not human," says Zacharia, as much to Deté as to her. But before she can wonder what that's all about, Zacharia lifts his chin and searing pain crackles over her skin, an electric barb to the back of her neck. She kicks out blindly, barely aware of one of the guards fumbling with the shackles on her feet, but the sizzle of electricity comes again, and the guard gets her feet secured to the bolted-down leg of the chair. A restraint tightens around her torso, cutting into her upper arms.

Her vision clears enough for her to see Deté cross to the table of relics and pick up one of the spheres covered in the alien script. He places it reverently in a metal bowl, then sets the bowl in Gia's lap.

"Which is why I need your blood," Zacharia says, and Deté takes a small silver dagger from his pocket and begins to cut.

Pain flares along the insides of her arm and Gia tries to shove back, but she can't get purchase, she's pinned down by three guards and the restraints.

"I can take the blood from your wrists," Deté says conversationally. "Or from your jugular. It would be a shame to have to destroy a saint, but there will be plenty more in the coming days."

Gia forces herself to calm down, taking shaky, adrenaline-filled breaths. From his chair on the far side of the circle, Zacharia's ice-blue gaze bores through her, emotionless. Deté's knife carves her forearm, blood pours into the bowl, and through the pain Gia can't help but watch in fascination as the metal sphere drinks it up. The alien script comes alive, flickering as though lit from within by embers.

Deté doesn't bother to hide his delight. "It's working," he says to Zacharia.

"What is?" Gia asks through gritted teeth.

"The light," says Deté. "You could join us, you know."

"If she's interested in finding salvation," Zacharia says coolly.

"She might be," Deté counters. "The light will take you if you're willing to renounce the darkness. Spend some time with your choice. Because I will ask you only once more."

Deté reverently lifts the bowl from Gia's lap and carries it back to the table with the rest of the relics. "We have enough," he tells Zacharia.

Zacharia lifts his chin to the guards. "Take her away."

## 25

## PHAERA

She couldn't tell if Jaantzen wanted her to stay, she couldn't tell if he was relieved when she said she needed to check in at the office. But everyone else had fallen into long-assigned roles without any discussion, and it was only a matter of time before Phaera offered to see to lunch. And the minute that happened, she'd have chosen her own role: the girlfriend who makes sure everyone's fed while they do the real work.

The ease with which Jaantzen's penthouse had turned from a pleasant place to entertain into a war room had been startling. The weapons and supply stockpiles, the calls out to mercenaries, the vast amount of information that probably shouldn't have been at Toshiyo's fingertips. She's lying to herself if she pretends Willem Jaantzen's just another successful bootstrapping story with a rough past that's far behind him, but she can't decide if that matters to her.

It *should.*

But she saw the "honest" Bulari business owners and politicians lining up to pledge their loyalty to Liatris Yang at Julieta's funeral. And despite Jaantzen's reluctance to talk about what he actually did for Julieta, she knows smuggling isn't bloodless. She loved Julieta. And has heard plenty of whispered stories about how ruthlessly the woman ran her business, and the role a young enforcer named Willem Jaantzen played.

How ruthlessly is Phaera willing to run her own business?

Of course, she already has an answer. When Levi Acheta started demanding protection payments from the business owners in the Casino District, she could have paid him like the others. Instead, she went to Jaantzen for help. Acheta ended up dead, and her problem went away. She might not have admitted it to herself at the time, but wasn't that the result she'd hoped for?

She didn't go to Jaantzen because she wanted to reach a friendly agreement with Acheta. She went to him for help because she wanted the bastard gone and she knew Jaantzen could make it happen.

Maybe Jaantzen and Acheta would have clashed in the end, but it doesn't change what Phaera fundamentally asked Jaantzen to do.

If Acheta's death sits uneasy on her conscience, though, that fades as her cab pulls up in front of the Lorelei.

The Lorelei's facade has been repaired seamlessly since Acheta's people shot it up, the cascading holograms flowing to create the illusion of walking through the veil of a waterfall into a mystic cavern beyond. There's no sign left of the bodies of her people, her patrons, who bled out on the sidewalk and in the lobby.

Acheta deserved what he got, and Phaera's chin is

high when she walks through those doors, Oriol and Mel at her back.

Whereas the Devil's Table is understated and elegant, the Lorelei embraces the glitter befitting a casino on Bulari's gaudy drag. Dealers in blue-sequined coats, more holographic columns of water, light playing over the ceiling to create the illusion of being submerged. And the crown jewel: a raised stage in the middle of the casino floor, surrounded by a fountain spraying elegant arcs in time to the music. Tonight, like every night, there will be an act on that stage.

A cocktailer spots her first, setting down a tray of empties with a gasp and bounding across the lobby to hug her. Security guards are calling out welcomes, patrons at the gaming tables glancing over their shoulders to find out who their dealers are grinning at. Regulars lifting their glasses to her as she calls back hellos.

"Is it always like this?" Mel murmurs to Oriol as Phaera is swept into a hug by a dealer with an empty table.

"It takes her an hour to leave every night," he says wryly.

Before Phaera can respond, yet another welcome face appears in the crowd. Jae Bakshi, the Lorelei's head of security. The older woman grins at Phaera and clasps her good hand.

"Good to have you back, ma'am," she says. "Sina. And . . ."

"Mel Nehrusitha, meet Jae Bakshi. My head of security."

"A pleasure," says Jae as they walk. "Swept your office like you asked. Got rid of that bug the BPD put under your desk, but didn't find anything else. And the team from Admant has been here all morning upgrading our systems. Should be done by end of day, they said."

"Thank you."

"Course. A couple of reporters have been by, but we've been telling them to get lost."

"If any show up while I'm here, pass me their names first."

"I'm sure they will. Word's going to travel fast the boss is back."

"Thank you." Phaera palms open the door to her office. "I'll let you all know if I need anything."

It's a dismissal to Oriol and Mel, too, and she half expects him to argue that he should stay at her side, but he merely insists on a quick security sweep, then lets her be.

And she's finally alone for the first time in what seems like ages.

She leaves the floor-to-ceiling window overlooking the casino floor set to clear — she finds the activity on the floor soothing — and sinks into the chair behind her desk to begin the quiet triage: opens a scratch note to jot down all the swirling thoughts in her head, then sorts quickly through her inbox, deleting mercilessly and trying to keep the numb worry threatening to overwhelm her at bay.

Yesterday, she'd been hopeful. Leone's teeth had been filed down and Phaera'd been starting to feel safe again — until a blow she couldn't have anticipated knocked the foundations out of that safety.

A few reporters have managed to impress her secretary enough to loop Phaera in on the requests. There's a note from Letizia Diamante, running by a draft of an exposé of Silver Dice. A long video message from her mother catching her up on the news from Alusina and asking how the opening went. Phaera's parents are probably safe to come home — Leone won't touch them again — but she wonders briefly if she can get them to stay away long enough for the bruises and scrapes on her neck to fade. She doesn't want to have to tell them what happened.

And, finally, a note from Cavy. Subject: *I HOPE YOU'RE FREE TONIGHT.*

Her pulse picks up as she swipes the message open. The prime minister's speech about the trade agreement — the soiree with Bulari's business elite. Jaantzen had been planning to go as Leone's guest, but he won't now, not with his people in danger. And there's no way in hell Phaera would have stepped up to take his place. But Cavy must have secured an invitation as head of the Casino District Business Association.

Her suspicions are confirmed as she scans the note. Cavy's been invited, and he wants her to attend with him.

She hesitates over a response. Jaantzen will be back at Cobalt Tower if his people are still in danger, and she should be there for him. Shouldn't she? But she's not certain what that even means. Sit awkwardly around and listen to orders being given, offer reassurances she barely believes?

No. She can help in the way she knows how. Pushing their play across the finish line while Jaantzen is caught up in other business.

She opens up a response to Cavy.

*I'D BE DELIGHTED.*

Her twinge of annoyance when yet another new message crops up as soon as she's cleared his drains away when she sees the sender.

It's the reporter from RaYa, the girl who waited for Phaera after the business association meeting. Analie

Cruz. She's pinged Phaera a few times since, but Phaera hasn't responded.

This subject line, though?

*I KNOW WHO TRIED TO HAVE YOU KILLED*

Phaera frowns at the message. Even if Cruz did find out Leone tried to kill her, what's she going to do with that information? RaYa will never print the story — they don't have the kind of money it takes to protect themselves from the inevitable libel suit, they're more in the market for stories about cheating celebrity spouses and new restaurant trends. And all of RaYa's reporters are indentured, so Cruz can't publish it elsewhere.

So what's her play?

Phaera opens up a channel; Cruz sounds surprised when she answers.

"Who?" Phaera asks.

"Oh!" Cruz clears her throat. "I'll tell you in person."

"You're making a dangerous accusation," Phaera says. "You have proof?"

"I do."

Phaera takes a sharp breath. If this woman truly has found proof Leone tried to have her killed, some actual link between Leone and all of this, it could change everything.

"I'll meet you at the Coast in an hour," she says, closing the connection and opening a new one to Letizia Diamante.

---

Phaera has known the name Kumail Anh for most of her life. She's traveled vicariously through him to the farthest reaches of the Durga System, explored complicated international conflicts, and gained sympathy for notorious figures, all through his lyrical, unbiased, immersive story-telling.

And now he's waiting for her in the lobby of Lucky's Palladium Coast. He stands with a broad smile as she enters. Thick black hair and beard kissed with silver, warm brown skin creased by the elements — she imagines he can charm his way into most any story with those dashing good looks.

"Ah, another temporary one-hander," he says. He reaches to shake her good hand with his own; his left arm's in a sling, fractured when the *Coldfire* was shot down. "Though I'm sorry to hear what happened. Leti filled me in."

"Likewise," Phaera says, gesturing at his sling.

He shrugs. "First time I've broken a bone on assignment, actually. I can put it on my résumé now."

Phaera tamps down her urge to gush — she'd love to spend the time they have talking about her favorite moments in his work, but that's not why they're here. "Mr. Anh," she starts.

"Kumail, please."

She inclines her head. "Kumail. Thank you for coming on such short notice."

"If this person has the proof she says she does, the trip will be more than worth it."

If Cruz has the evidence she says she does, Phaera will be able to breathe a bit more easily tonight. She gestures him to enter. "Shall we?"

Phaera waves at the bartender, who calls out her name with a smile as they head past the garishly fringed bar to one of the comfy, well-worn booths in the back. The gilt-and-cut-glass chandeliers are decades out of date, the food barely passable, but Phaera loves the Coast. All those nights spent drinking at that bar with her co-workers after a long shift, laughing at each other's horror stories, swapping gossip with industry workers from other casinos. This place holds decades of good memories.

Analie Cruz is here already, ensconced in one of the private booths; the young reporter's focus is so entirely on Phaera, it takes her a moment to recognize Kumail Anh at Phaera's side. But when she does, her jaw drops. She recovers quickly, introducing herself to them both, giving Oriol and Mel a long look when they settle at a nearby table.

Phaera sits gingerly in the booth and studies Cruz. She looks exactly like a RaYa reporter. Light brown skin and thick, curly hair almost the same shade, scraped back into a ponytail on top of her head. Bright red lipstick, bright red star earrings, bright red manicure, glitter eyeliner on thick.

Cruz reaches into her jacket pocket and pulls out a recording cube; it glows an even green when she taps the button. "Do you mind if I record this?"

"You may not."

The girl's red lips part in surprise; her hand pauses above the already-recording cube. "How about audio? For my notes?"

"This isn't an interview," Phaera says. "We're getting to know each other. Afterwards, if I like what I hear, maybe we can talk about an exclusive."

Cruz's gaze flickers to Kumail. "And he's here because . . ."

"I'm curious how good you are at research," Kumail says with a faint smile.

Cruz taps the cube again and it fades to red. She

leaves it on the table in what Phaera assumes is a good-faith gesture she hasn't restarted the recording in secret.

"Impress me," Phaera says. "What do you know?"

Cruz glances at Kumail again, but if she's nervous at being put on the spot in front of a legend in her field, she doesn't show it. Phaera's not surprised. She's done her research on the girl since last they met, and Analie Cruz doesn't seem to have any fear about asking blunt questions of big-name celebrities and politicians. An indenture at RaYa would help anyone develop pretty thick skin.

Whatever calculation's been going through her head, Cruz apparently has decided showing her cards will net her an even bigger story.

She puts her elbows on the table, leaning forward with voice low, even though no one's near them to hear and Lucky's Palladium Coast is famous for its regular bug sweeps.

"I was supposed to cover the reopening of the Devil's Table," she says. "My editor wanted me to keep track of who showed up. One of those 'You Won't Believe Who's Still Taking Their Chances at the Devil's Table' sorts of things."

"I'm sure," Phaera says wryly. "I've read some of your other very flattering work about me."

Cruz's shrug sets her star earrings swaying. "I write what sells."

"And traffic bonuses take time off the indenture, right?" Kumail offers.

"Absolutely. Nobody cares what ran the week before, anyway. It's ancient history. Look." Cruz holds up her hands. "I'm sorry, okay? This is the game."

She's right. And Phaera's not going to win this argument.

"So I was at the Devil's Table that night," Cruz continues. "But the bigger story was that you weren't. I started nosing around, and a source told me somebody'd tried to kill you the night before. I heard you'd be at the business association meeting — I can't reveal my sources," she says before Phaera even asks. It's fine, Phaera knows who the sources are. Hiro and Vanessa had both primed a few of the staff they trust with snippets of the real story in case a reporter came asking, and Dal Jaxon was the one who'd told Cruz she could find Phaera at the business association meeting.

"You wouldn't talk to me last time, but your friend Dal did after you left. He wouldn't say anything about you, he kept deflecting to the trade agreement — which, let's face it, RaYa isn't going to let me publish anything about that. No one cares." She waves a hand at Kumail. "No offense. I mean none of *our* audience cares."

"Why not let it go, then?" Phaera asks.

Cruz's eyes go wide. "Somebody tried to *kill* you, and nobody's talking about it? I wanted that story. Anyway, I figured if it had something to do with the trade agreement, the answer was there. Obviously I couldn't work on this at the office, my editor would have murdered me if he'd caught me reading legal documents and bank statements all day instead of gossip boards. But I struck gold. There are a bunch of people in our government who got kick-backs from the Alliance on the trade agreement thing, but only one of them used that money to hire a headhunter. A headhunter who disappeared from the city the night you were allegedly attacked." Cruz's gaze drops to Phaera's throat. "It's not alleged though, huh? Nobody wears scarves anymore."

A shiver brushes Phaera's spine. "And who hired that headhunter?"

For the first time since they sat down, Analie Cruz seems nervous. She glances over her shoulder, then drops her voice to a whisper.

"Chief Justice Leone." When neither Phaera nor Kumail react, Cruz sits back with a satisfied look on her face. "This is fucking wild. You have to tell me why."

"RaYa won't publish that story, either," Phaera points out.

"I'll fight with my editor," Cruz says. "I'll break my indenture contract and send it somewhere else, I don't care. There's a crazy amazing story going on, and I'm going to get to the heart of it."

"The penalty for breaking an indenture contract is five more years," Kumail says.

"So I spend the next seven years writing about which pop star is sleeping with which senator. I want this story." Cruz smiles slyly at him. "And I bet you need the proof I found."

Kumail scratches his cheek, then glances at Phaera. "Leti's always looking for new blood," he says. Cruz notes the name, but doesn't appear to recognize it as Letizia Diamante, the notorious PR shark. Kumail turns back to Cruz. "I may have a way for you to get your story published. What would you say to a new contract, with someone who'll make better use of your research skills."

Cruz straightens. "Really? Because I was kidding about spending the next seven years writing about celebrities shagging. I'm so over that."

"Two years left?" Kumail asks; Cruz nods. "I'll see if my friend is interested. Because I think what you've found is the missing piece to an exposé I'm working on."

"Let's talk about that indenture transfer," Cruz says. "And then we talk about byline credit."

Kumail smiles. "We'll see what you've got, first."

Cruz looks back at Phaera. "I still want an exclusive with you. A profile piece — a nice one. Consider it an apology for all the shitty things I wrote about you over the years for RaYa."

Phaera laughs. "We'll talk." Her gold cuff is vibrating gently, and she brushes a finger over it: Hiro Matapang. "Excuse me," she says to the others, pulling herself out of the sagging booth and touching the row of opals in her ear. "Hiro? What is it?"

"One of my little cousins is a runner for the Emperors," Hiro says without preamble. Phaera knows the Jet Park gang he's referencing. "Dumb kid. But he gets all over the neighborhood, and he said last night a group opened up the old first-level school on Chavela Street. They've been coming and going all day. He recognized the guy you're looking for in one of the spinners this afternoon — the old one with the white hair."

Phaera catches her breath. Felipe Zacharia.

"Coming or going?"

"Going."

So Zacharia left, but he might be coming back — and he might have left Gia and Tevi stashed there.

"Send me the address," Phaera says.

"Just did. And I've got my little cousin watching the place, do something useful for once in his life. Let me know what else you need."

"Thank you, Hiro."

She opens a channel to Jaantzen.

## 26

## JAANTZEN

The sun's setting over the city skyline, clouds trailing bloody red scratches high above the skyscrapers as though left by the same giant hand that clawed the five Finger ravines into the bluffs west of Bulari. From Jaantzen's penthouse the view is calm, but the news is reporting that the protests in the streets below are bigger than ever, to coincide with the speech Prime Minister Nikolas de Grazal will give in a few hours. De Grazal will be safe inside the capitol building, addressing the politicians and business owners and Alliance delegates who can make or break the rest of his term — his words will be broadcast to the rest of the city, the voters who will decide if he gets a second one.

Jaantzen wonders who de Grazal fears most tonight.

Toshiyo verified new activity at the address Phaera gave them, an old school less than a dozen blocks from the spinner dealership he'd bought with the intention of turning it into a brewery. She thinks there are a dozen soldiers at most, and found evidence of a convoy's arrival early in the morning, coming from the direction of the road to the Maraka Valley. Heat signatures show at least one prisoner being held in the storage units in the yard, and activity in some of the classrooms inside. Hiro Matapang's cousin swears he recognized Gia as one of the people in the yard.

Was it too easy to find them? Always best to assume this sort of thing is a trap.

Starla's already out at the someday brewery, a convenient rendezvous point. Manu and Toshiyo are down on the fourth floor, finalizing the last few things before they all head out to meet Starla. Jaantzen's running through his final checklist in the penthouse, the tactical vest under his suit jacket a reassurance, the pistol slung under his arm a comforting weight.

It pricks at the back of his mind that Felipe Zacharia didn't try to contact him at all today. Jaantzen had thought this was meant to be a hostage exchange, but that requires an overture on the part of the kidnapper. If Zacharia had hoped to trade Gia and Tevi for Lucky, why hasn't he said so?

Unless he kidnapped Gia and Tevi for some other reason.

Either way, Jaantzen is bringing them home tonight.

He checks the time on the comm he's been holding in his hand the past few minutes, trying to decide if he should make the call or if it will be a distraction to them both. It'll only be a moment, he finally tells himself. She doesn't have to pick up if she's busy.

Phaera's breathless when she answers. "Is everything all right?"

"Yes, I'm just . . ." He's just what? She probably thinks he's calling to convince her to stay home tonight. He's not — there's no reason to assume she'd be safer in her own apartment than at the capitol building surrounded by the New Sarjun State Guard, and he knows what this means to her.

It's going to sound ridiculous when he says it. But he can tell her the truth.

"I wanted to hear your voice," Jaantzen says.

"Willem Jaantzen just called to talk?" She sounds like she's smiling, and he can't pinpoint the moment when that quiet laugh became such a necessity, but it rolls through him, soothing. "It's nice to hear your voice, too."

"I also wanted to tell you we verified Hiro's intel," he says. "I'm about to go meet with Starla."

"Oh." Phaera takes a sharp breath. "Is — are they there?"

"We believe so."

"What can I do?"

Jaantzen turns back to the red-slashed sunset. "You're doing it. Continue gathering allies, and we'll see this thing with Leone through to the end. Are you still at home?"

"I'm getting ready. I can't — gods."

"What?"

Phaera sighs. "I can't figure out what to wear. That sounds so petty, I'm sorry."

"We're both gearing up for a battle, though yours has a more complicated dress code. I'm sorry for taking Oriol away. Did he find you someone — "

"You know I can't walk into the Capitol with armed guards, Jaantzen."

He rubs the back of his neck.

"I can practically hear you biting your tongue to keep from saying you don't like it," Phaera says. "Which I appreciate."

He lets himself smile. "The sentiment? Or me biting my tongue."

"Both."

"Be careful."

"You too. Though you don't have to worry about me. At worst I'll get sat between Lhasa and Youssef and have to spend dinner learning about triticale futures and trying not to stab either of them with the butter knife out of sheer boredom. I wish you could be there."

"Mingling with politicians? I prefer my battles with a little more action." Leone's dinners had been enough for him, and at least there he didn't have to wear a mask — everyone knew him, knew who he was. He doesn't have the patience for the kinds of social circles Phaera has to run in for her businesses to thrive.

She laughs. "I'm sorry to say I foresee more of this thing in our future, Jaantzen."

Our future.

He lets the phrase hang in the air, crystalline and fragile, afraid if he touches it, it will break.

"I owe you," he says, a safer subject. "We all do."

"You owe Hiro, I'm just the messenger." Phaera breathes deep. "Let me know. Anything at all I can do to help, I want to."

"I will. Stay safe, and . . ."

"And?"

He clears his throat. "I love you."

Her quiet laugh sweeps through him again. "I love you, too. I'll see you tonight, Jaantzen."

The silence where her voice had been echoes in his ears. He can't see the Capitol from here, but keeping a thing in view never kept it safer. Phaera will be in her world tonight; he'll be in his. And once this is all over . . .

Jaantzen finally identifies the unfamiliar feeling settled beneath his breastbone. Anticipation — but not of the job itself. Of what happens after. He has someone he's looking forward to coming home to.

He could get used to this.

He makes one last sweep, then heads down to meet Manu and Toshiyo on the fourth floor, where they're poring over a map in the conference room, footage from Toshiyo's own drones and borrowed security footage in a tidy array on the wall.

Lucky is perched on the far end of the conference table, watching Manu suspiciously, though the creature bares fangs in what Toshiyo has assured him is a friendly greeting when Jaantzen enters. Jaantzen signs hello, but can't quite bring himself to turn his back on Lucky.

"El and Beto finished loading the rest of the gear," Toshiyo says by way of greeting. Normally she'd stay here, with better equipment and away from the action, but if they find the other alien, they'll need to pacify it. And since Toshiyo knows the most about the creatures, it will be good to have her close.

It's another uncomfortable variable in an already nerve-racking situation — but Toshiyo's led them through operations with much less sophisticated setups than the portable desk and screens Starla already took out to the brewery. All she needs is a tablet and audio feed and she can work miracles as far as Jaantzen is concerned.

"Good," he says. "Are you ready to go?"

"Yeah." Toshiyo sits back in her chair, lips pressed into a thin line. "But I've got something that's probably bad news."

Jaantzen glances at Manu; by the set of his lieutenant's jaw, he knows the news and finds it worrisome.

"Probably?"

"You know the virtual museum of alien artifacts Starla found?"

"Starla mentioned it when I was speaking with Aster." If either Starla or Toshiyo had told him about it before, it's not ringing a bell — though to be fair, he's spent most of the last few weeks focused on Coeur and Acheta and Leone, and trying to ignore the fact that aliens exist.

"Yeah, Starla told me Aster brought the artifacts up," Toshiyo says. "So I asked Nacea — my new contact with White Star — to look into it. She just sent me what she found. Long story short, there were a bunch of alien artifacts collected in a virtual museum out in Durga's Belt. The original curator was friends with some of the founders of White Star, all alien conspiracy theorist types. But when the White Star folks started reading Zacharia's writings, they took them in a weird religious direction."

"Short version, Tosh," Manu breaks in.

"Sorry," she says. "About five years ago, the guy who ran the museum was murdered by the Dawn. They got control of the virtual museum, but no one was quite sure what happened to the physical artifacts." Toshiyo cracks her ring fingers. "Turns out Zacharia has them. Here, in Bulari."

Jaantzen frowns at her, not understanding the urgency. "And?"

"I don't think it was opportunity alone that made Zacharia target Gia and Tevi." She gnaws her lip. Across the table, Lucky trills, watching her intently in what could be sympathy. "Aster said the artifacts had something to do with making the venom foolproof. Nacea says in order to do that, the artifacts need to be activated with blood. But not just any blood. Blood that's already been transformed by the venom. A saint's blood — or what they call a saint."

"Gia's blood."

Toshiyo nods.

"Doesn't Zacharia have his own — " He cuts himself short from saying the word *mutants*; he's talking about Gia now, not the nameless army of hard-to-kill Dawn soldiers they'd come across.

"We killed a lot of them," Manu points out. "Maybe all, it's hard to know."

"One of the Dawn prisoners at Redrock must have seen Gia get bit," says Toshiyo. "So when they saw her again, alive, they figured out what happened to her."

The puzzle pieces in his mind dance to rearrange themselves. Before, they'd been operating on the assumption that Gia and Tevi were bargaining chips, which meant Zacharia had reason to treat them well. But if Zacharia didn't take them as hostages to exchange for Lucky? If Gia is valuable to him on her own — if her *blood* is valuable, that could be the reason Zacharia's expected summons never came.

"None of that changes the operation," he says. "Send this on to Starla, and let's get there as fast as we can."

Toshiyo swipes away the map, types in a code with black-lacquered nails, and the feeds disappear from the wall.

"I owe you an apology," Jaantzen says, and she looks up, startled. "If I had listened to you and taken care of the Dawn when we first found them, none of this would have happened."

She squeezes his elbow, then hands him an earpiece.

"We've got them now. Starla pinged me — they're still waiting on Coeur's crew, but the rest have arrived."

"Let her know we're on our . . ."

Jaantzen trails off as his comm chimes. Geum-ja Leone.

He hadn't quite agreed he'd attend the prime minister's speech tonight with her, but he hasn't told her no, either. He still can't discount the chance she might be working with Zacharia, and a direct refusal earlier in the day might have tipped her — and Zacharia — off that he was planning something.

He swipes the call onto Toshiyo's conference table, audio only. He doesn't need her to see them all prepped for battle.

"Apologies I wasn't in touch earlier," he says.

"It's fine, Willem." There's something in her tone, some secret glee she's dying to share with him. Jaantzen's blood chills. "Turn on the news."

Jaantzen goes still; Toshiyo is already pulling up the feeds.

He doesn't have to ask which news story she's talking about, because only one is dominating every channel right now: an explosion, deep in Altamira. A historic colonial-era church was bombed in what is thought to be ongoing violence between the Dry Creek crew and the notorious crime boss, Blackheart.

Coeur's stronghold is in flames.

Manu's cursing under his breath. Toshiyo covers her mouth with her hands.

Jaantzen turns down the volume as the reporter speculates on rumors the church was actually Blackheart's seat of operations, watching numbly as emergency response crews pull bodies from the rubble, as swarms of drones pour fire-suppressant foam into what remains of the blaze.

"You attacked Thala," Jaantzen says finally.

"Zacharia delivered on his part of our bargain," she says. "He gave me Coeur. Now he wants a meeting with you in return. It's our chance, Willem. Are you ready?"

"Is she dead?"

"I assure you she is."

Jaantzen can't count the number of times he's wished Coeur dead. Dreamed of it. Planned for it. But like this? With this timing?

"Do you know what you've done, Geum-ja? The Fingers will go up in flames." People were already on the brink of riot because of the trade agreement, and Coeur's pacification efforts were the only thing keeping them back from the edge. People listened to her because she'd always been vocally anti-Alliance; it got her elected — and her election is probably the main reason New Sarjun veered from the path of joining the Alliance all those years ago.

No one is going to believe the story Dry Creek did it.

No. People will speculate that this assassination is a government conspiracy, an Alliance plot, and the entire city will be burned to ash by tomorrow morning.

Manu is already typing furious messages on his comm.

"I saved us both," Leone says. "She was plotting with Zacharia against you, and she would have turned on me next. You and I both know who should have the power in this city. Coeur was unstable, a threat to us all while she was alive. And Zacharia is a madman who thinks he's ushering in some new era of humanity. But you and I? We represent the best of our country. My political circle and contacts. Your contacts in the business community and the underworld. We need each other. Together we can steer this city in the right direction."

"Zacharia said she planned to attack me. Did he say how?"

"She was going to try to lure you out under the premise of working together on something," Leone says airily. "Probably to attack me."

Jaantzen shares a look with Manu. It could easily be true; Coeur wanted the serum Zacharia had, whether to create invincible supersoldiers of her own or to try to heal her broken body. If Zacharia had told her he had a foolproof version of it, she might have done anything to get her shattered hands on it. After all, that's the exact motivation Jaantzen had been hoping would keep her loyal to his side in attacking Zacharia tonight.

If she's dead, her crew will assume he had something to do with it. And his goddaughter is waiting for Aden Damyati to arrive with a dozen of Coeur's soldiers at this very moment. He makes Starla's namesign and Toshiyo nods, swiping open their message channel.

"Then it sounds like you did me a favor," he says carefully. Leone makes a satisfied sound on the other end of the line. "What's your plan to meet Zacharia?"

"You're coming to the prime minister's speech, aren't you?" She doesn't wait for an answer. "I've told him to meet us there."

"At the capitol building?"

"We'll meet there, then leave out the back. I'll have my driver take us somewhere your people can get to him."

Jaantzen lifts his hands to Manu. "Can you work with this?" he signs. His lieutenant scrubs a hand over his jaw, nods.

"That's not much time to come up with a plan," Jaantzen says.

"It's the timing we have, Willem. I have faith in you."

"You may have faith in me, but I've yet to rebuild mine in you," Jaantzen says. "I'll meet you tonight, but it will be on my terms. My driver. My choice of location. And the minute things seem off, you're on your own to deal with Zacharia."

"I understand," Leone says. "I'll see you soon." She cuts the connection.

Manu lets out a violent curse; Lucky hisses back at him across the room. "I can't believe I'm saying this, but I hope Leone's lying about killing that bitch."

"This is bad." Toshiyo stares down at the news feed as though expecting to find Bulari in flames already. They're still broadcasting from the site of the explosion. Coeur's headquarters, the colonial-era church now twisted metal, the facade blackened by flames. Toshiyo zooms in on one of the bodies in the street, but it's burned beyond recognition.

"Did you get through to Starla?" Jaantzen asks Toshiyo; she shakes her head. "Get her out of there."

"I'll try for Oriol," Manu says.

"Then change of plans. Toshiyo, you and El meet Starla at the backup rendezvous. I have to go meet Leone. Manu —"

"I'm going with you, Starla's gonna be fine. She . . ." He straightens as the connection goes through to Oriol. He explains the situation, then swears. "Let me know," he says to Oriol. He slips his comm back in his pocket and turns to Jaantzen. "Damyati just showed up."

## 27

## STARLA

The stop-work orders have gone down, but Jaantzen hasn't yet restarted construction on the someday-to-be brewery in Jet Park. Most of the preliminary work had been demolitions and cleanup, knocking down the wall past the service counter to make room for the kitchen, hauling out a decade or more's accumulation of junk electronics and trash.

Tonight she and her little crew are standing around a workbench in the middle of the floor, staring down at the portable desk Starla unrolled there, and she feels dwarfed by the building around them. Three stories of windows allow a muddy light through the stasis wrapping, a pair of twin staircases sweep up to the second-level balcony, and the full glass floor of the third level looms above. Last time Starla'd been here, with Jaantzen, she hadn't seen the potential in the abandoned rubble. Tonight, given the work of the cleanup crew, she can almost imagine the place buzzing with the energy of diners, waiters, bartenders, the slight hint of engine oil in the air replaced by the pungent aroma of boiling hops and scents from the kitchen.

If Jet Park ever gets cleaned up.

And if they make it through this next adventure.

Starla doesn't risk turning on the lights. This time of night, the overhead lights will set those big floor-to-ceiling windows glowing like a beacon. Maybe that's exactly what you want when you're planning a popular dinner spot, but Starla's plotting a covert operation. She doesn't need anyone wondering who's hanging out in the old spinner dealership and coming over to investigate. Police, the Dawn, some local gang thinks this is their territory, nobody.

Along with Oriol and Simca, she's got a pair of Oriol's merc buddies. Mel Nehrusitha is the muscle, burly and armed to the teeth; Nacea Kálas is the thief, petite and lithe, dressed in body-skimming black, her tool belt brimming with gadgets, an expensive night-vision kit pushed up on her forehead. Jaantzen, Manu, El, and Toshiyo are on their way with Benedicto Kulikutan, the pilot of the *Coldfire*, ready to drive the getaway van they've tricked out to contain Lucky's full-grown cousin.

Henri and Jude will round out the rest of the people she knows she can trust. And when Damyati shows up with his dozen or so fighters, she'll have the people she needs to hopefully outnumber the Dawn.

She'll just make sure she's watching her back.

The proximity chime buzzes her gauntlet, and Starla calls up the external security feed on her lens.

Henri is at the loading dock door, a trio of spinners are parked in the lot behind him.

"Coeur's crew is here," she signs. "Oriol, Simca, with me."

Henri greets Starla with a hug when she opens the loading dock door, the scar bisecting his lips pulling his grin into a sneer. "It's good to see you, girl," he says. "An honor to fight alongside Lasadi Cazinho's daughter again."

"It's good to see you, too," she signs. "Sorry I didn't get a chance to check how you were settling in before this."

He shakes his head. "You've been in the middle of trouble of your own. There'll be time to swap stories in the canteen later."

Starla claps his arm with a smile, attention shifting past him to the rest of Coeur's crew. Jude's pulling gear out of one of the spinners, he raises an arm in greeting to Starla. Even in the moonlight, Starla can tell both of the escaped convicts are healthier since she last saw them heading home on the *Coldfire*. They've cleaned themselves up, gotten proper haircuts; they're wearing clothes that haven't been patched for years or been made out of the furs of whatever monstrous beasts they'd been able to hunt up in the deserts around Redrock Prison.

Others are climbing out of their spinners, but Starla recognizes only Aden Damyati. He's standing at the back door to one of the spinners, directing whoever's inside.

Henri's talking again, but an alert blips onto her lens, obscuring the transcription. Toshiyo's trying to call her.

*1 sec*, Starla types, and asks Henri to repeat himself.

"We had a bit of a setback," he tells her as she walks with him to meet Damyati. "Some of Blackheart's soldiers who were supposed to join us got diverted."

"Diverted?"

"There was an attack," Henri says grimly.

Toshiyo is calling her again, and she blinks the notification off, uneasiness churning in her gut. Henri's trying to tell her something important, she realizes, and Toshiyo wouldn't call twice unless something serious was going on.

She turns to ask Henri what happened, but Simca taps her arm. Starla hadn't noticed when Oriol stepped away to take a call of his own, but now he's coming back. His expression is as completely untroubled as always, but he signs: "Problem."

She catches that flicker of a glance over her shoulder to Henri, the way Oriol's subtly prepared himself to fight. Simca's noticed it, too. She's gone loose and casual, shifting her weight even as she's still ready to interpret for Starla.

"Give me a second," Starla signs to Henri, then steps back towards the loading dock to confer with Oriol.

He leans in; she can still see his lips but no one else behind them can. "Is your lens transcribing when I speak this quietly?" She nods. "That was Manu. There was an explosion in Altamira less than an hour ago. Coeur's stronghold. Leone claims it was her, she says Coeur is dead, and that she was planning on betraying us to Zacharia."

Starla blinks at him in shock.

"There's more. She told Jaantzen to meet her at the Capitol and she'll give him Zacharia. He and Manu aren't joining us. We can't trust any of these people."

She already didn't trust Damyati. But Henri and Jude? She's talked this through with Jaantzen, and her instinct remains the same. If they were working with the Dawn, they could have freed the rest at any time, and their hatred of Zacharia seems real. They hadn't been part of Coeur's crew before they were imprisoned at

Redrock, but it's possible they're working with her now. Hell, Jaantzen is working with her now.

But are they here to betray Starla?

She can't believe her mother's old friend would.

She turns back to Henri, ignoring Damyati for now but keeping him in view. "The attack: What happened?"

"A remote strike on the old church Blackheart uses as her headquarters," Henri says.

His scarred lips don't move again, but another line appears on her lens. "We lost the building." She turns to Damyati, who was apparently the one who'd spoken. "And we had to leave some of the soldiers we promised you behind to help with the cleanup and defend the neighborhood. But I brought about a dozen with. They're ready to hit the target on your mark."

"Lost the building," Damyati'd said; he didn't mention Blackheart, and he's not talking like a man who just inherited the most powerful crew in the city minutes ago.

Starla lifts her hands. "Coeur. They're saying — "

Before she can finish, one gloved hand grips the top of the open spinner door behind Damyati. A silver-tipped cane pushes into the gravel.

Thala Coeur pulls herself to her feet.

She's dressed in all black, a cap pulled over her scarred, shorn scalp, a pistol slung in a holster under her left arm. Starla wonders if she can even draw it, let alone shoot. Coeur grins, and in the dim light of the parking lot the enamel replacing her missing eyetooth gleams blood red.

"They're saying what about me, girl?"

Starla's heart slams in her chest, and she knows — she *knows* — the other woman can taste her fear. Damyati alone, she could handle. But Blackheart herself is standing in front of her now, all jaguar's smile and predator's gaze, and neither Jaantzen nor Manu are here to tell her how to deal with this woman.

Oriol's messaging with Jaantzen and Manu on a chain that includes her, the messages flickering in and out of her vision, tangling with a transcription that must be Jude and Henri talking a few steps away. Starla blinks her lens off to get rid of the distractions, signals that to Simca, then squares her shoulders to Coeur.

"They're saying you're dead," she signs. Coeur's dark eyes flash to Simca as she interprets, then back.

"Good," Coeur says. "It's helpful, being dead." Her smile holds secret amusement, and Starla can't figure out why she isn't angrier that her stronghold was destroyed, her people are dead in the street. Either Leone was right and Coeur is still planning on betraying them to Zacharia, or Coeur outsmarted Leone and still wants revenge on the Dawn.

And Starla gets to pick which lying, murderous bitch to trust.

"It's good to see they're wrong." Starla glances at Oriol, but his expression's gone back to zen. "Let's go talk over the plan," she says to Coeur and Damyati. "Have your crew get ready to head out."

She's never been one for mind games. Jaantzen and Manu can mess around with intrigue all they want, but that's not Starla's style, she's not going to guess and second-guess Coeur's motives, not when she can ask her outright and be done with it. But if she's going to force a confrontation, she's definitely not going to do it out in the open, where Coeur may have snipers and — depending on where Henri's and Jude's loyalties lie — she and Oriol and Simca would be vastly outnumbered.

Neither Coeur nor Damyati object, which should ease her mind a touch. But still the skin between her shoulder blades itches as she walks back into the brewery with Thala Coeur at her side.

Starla waves for Simca to do introductions with Oriol's merc buddies, though neither of them need to be told who the ferocious woman with the rust-red skin and million-mark smile is. Nacea's obviously skittish; Mel is untroubled as a cloud in the summer sky.

Coeur cranes her neck to take in the space with appreciation; Starla blinks her lens back on. "Arquellian tourists love rebuilt shit like this." Coeur's words crawl along the bottom of Starla's vision. "A posh restaurant goes a long way to pricing out the current residents, too; Jaantzen oughta be proud." She turns her sly smile on Starla. "What's the plan?"

Starla ignores the jab, and the question. Coeur seems relaxed, not the body language Starla would expect from someone who's planning on betraying them — but then, Blackheart has a lot of practice. She can probably stab someone in the back without her heart rate going up a beat.

"We'll get to the plan in a minute," Starla signs. "But first? What the hell are you doing here? I was expecting Damyati."

Damyati shifts, ready to defend his boss if need be, but if Starla's direct question bothers Coeur, she doesn't show it.

"I came to find out if your godfather was in on the plan to have me killed."

The tension in the room ratchets up another notch as

Oriol steps forward, in front of Starla; Mel rests her hand on the rifle slung at her side. Starla signals them to stand down. They're not helping.

"He didn't have anything to do with it," she signs.

"Obviously," Coeur drawls. "You were waiting here right where you told us you'd be. Your godfather doesn't throw strangers under the bus, let alone you." It's either grudging respect or scorn Coeur's infused into those words, Starla can't quite tell by her expression. "You and I don't have any bad blood. So let's keep this relationship on a good footing."

"I should have met my godmother," Starla signs. Coeur's mocking smile fades. "I should have had a stepbrother and stepsister. With every step Manu took I thought about killing you. So, yeah. You and I have some bad blood."

Coeur's gone completely still, appearing ill at ease for the first time since she stepped out of the spinner. Damyati's hand creeps closer to his gun, not that he'd get a chance to draw before any one of Starla's people took him out. But Coeur stops him with a small, sharp shake of her head.

"Tell me why I should trust you," Starla signs.

"Bennion Zacharia killed my sister," Coeur says. She holds up her glove-encased hand. "Those Dawn assholes broke every bone in my hands, and Felipe Zacharia and Leone blew up my home, so I'm a little pissed."

"But you escaped."

"I heard a rumor on the wind," she says. "They're gonna find some bodies in the rubble, but every one of them's a traitor. My own people are all safe."

"Leone said you're working with Zacharia."

"Zacharia never got in touch to make me an offer, not

that I would've taken it. But you believe Leone over me, you're welcome to put a bullet in my head right now."

Starla shares a long look with Oriol. Jaantzen is trusting Coeur, but she's betrayed him before. Starla's instinct is to trust her — but she doesn't know her as well as Jaantzen does. As Manu and Oriol do.

She can't tell what Oriol's thinking, she never can, but she wonders how long he's dreamed of killing Coeur. If he imagines it every time he sees Manu's scars. He sometimes gets philosophical when they're training, quoting scripture or poetry about how giving yourself over to hate allows your enemy to win the final battle. Has he managed to meditate his way into forgiving Coeur? Given the tensions between him and Jaantzen since Coeur came back into the picture, Starla suspects he hasn't.

But she knows she can still trust his judgement.

Oriol's shoulders rise and fall in breath.

"I believe her," he signs finally.

Starla lets her hand drop from her pistol, senses more than sees the tensions easing in the room around her.

"I'm not going to bullshit you," she signs to Coeur. "And I'm not going to guess what you mean. So if you've got a problem, something to say to me, say it."

"My kinda girl."

"Clean slate, then."

When Coeur nods, the knot in Starla's chest unravels. She takes her first full breath in minutes. "Let the others know she's here," she signs to Oriol.

A minute later, a message from Toshiyo pops up on Starla's lens. ON OUR WAY, I'M PLUGGED IN. GO AHEAD AND START BRIEFING.

Starla waves a hand over the portable desk to wake it back up, then beckons everyone forward to study the map.

Coeur gives her a faint smile, but there's nothing of her usual insincerity in it. If Starla had to guess she'd say the emotion is respect.

"The building outlined in red is where the Dawn are keeping the prisoners," Starla signs. "As far as we can tell there are about a dozen soldiers. They have two hostages, maybe more. Heat map indicates someone may be held in this storage container. Number one goal is to get them out alive, so we need to make sure they're secure before we attack." She points at Nacea. "Oriol says you can get us in?"

Nacea nods. "I've got some ideas."

"Good. Initial team is Nacea, Simca, El, and me. El and I will check out the building itself, Nacea and Simca head for the storage container. Meanwhile, the assault teams will be standing by for my mark. Damyati's team is Coeur's soldiers, Oriol's is Mel, Henri, and Jude." She lifts her chin to Coeur. "I wasn't planning on you."

Coeur drums her fingers on the head of her cane. "I'll stay out of your way. You just let me know when you need someone to kill Zacharia." Her enamel eyetooth shines red when she grins. "Or ask pointed questions about where he went."

"When the hostages are secure, it's go time for Oriol's and Damyati's teams — Toshiyo will direct you, so listen to her. Goal is to take as many prisoners as possible, and either capture Zacharia or learn his whereabouts." She fixes Damyati with a look. "Follow Toshiyo's orders," she signs. "She'll keep you alive."

He nods. She needs him to listen to Toshiyo's direction, because hopefully by then they'll know where the alien is and she can use Coeur's crew to mop up any Dawn soldiers while Oriol's team recovers the creature —

hopefully without Coeur's crew seeing it. Probably a pipe dream, but Starla's going to try her damnedest to make it happen.

She takes a deep breath as one of the docking bay doors opens and a van docks itself; Beto Kulikutan's in the driver's seat, El and Toshiyo will be inside.

"We're all here," she signs. "Let's do this."

28

———

GIA

The screams that started an hour ago have finally stopped.

Gia shivers, back pressed against the cooling metal of the storage container.

She doesn't think it was Tevi, but it's impossible to be sure — the kind of pain that poor soul had been experiencing transforms the voice, takes all recognition of humanity out of it.

But was it torture? Whatever was happening finished before the person could scream themselves hoarse, and it was followed by excited voices. Footsteps crunching in the gravel, someone running, someone else barking orders. A spinner's engine revving. The rusty scrape of the front gates.

And silence.

Are they gone?

They hadn't bothered binding the wounds on her arms, but the cuts Deté made didn't heal like her other injuries, and that extra energy buzzing around her muscles had disappeared after he was done with her.

Something about the alien artifact that drank in her blood? Something about the silver knife he'd used?

Gia tried to staunch the bleeding with strips of her overshirt, wrapping it as tightly as she could with cuffed wrists, tying knots with her teeth. She hasn't checked the cuts for a while, but she can tell they *are* finally healing.

They left her some water when they threw her back in the shed and she's been sipping it carefully, staving off the dizziness of heat and blood loss. The air cooled when the sun sank and the light dimmed in the cracks, and while the shed's still stifling, at least it's not boiling hot anymore.

Bulari never gets quite as cold at night as the desert itself does, but they're on the outskirts of the city, more exposed to the elements, less heat trapped by the tall buildings. If they're planning to leave her out here tonight, she's got nothing to keep her warm but blood-stiff scraps of the shirt she tore up. She considers yelling, but it didn't bring anyone before.

The cold could be a problem if they don't come back.

She waits for them to come back.

Nothing.

The silence bothers her — did they get what they wanted out of Tevi? Had he helped Zacharia make a fail-proof version of his serum? Gia'd tell the old man being a mutant isn't all it's cracked up to be, but she doubts he'd listen. He's just interested in the benefits. Gia's scientist's brain can't help but worry at the side effects she's sure she'll find out about soon.

She doesn't have to unwrap her arms to know when the bleeding finally stops, she can feel the itching under the bandages as flesh reknits at a too-rapid rate. If she concentrates, she can make out that buzzy energy in her muscles once more. Pain drains out of her aching bones.

Gia takes another sip of the water, tests her handcuffs.

Metal gives.

Barely.

She's not sure if she's happy or disappointed to know whatever Deté did to her, it's not permanent.

She hauls herself carefully to her feet, leaning against the wall until the dizziness passes. Leaves the cuffs in place for now and goes to inspect the door. The hinges are on the outside, but she could probably tear out the handle. Use it as a lever to force the rusted-out seam. Or maybe with enough force she could break the lock. A good run at the door, maybe, using her shoulder as a battering ram.

She's testing the handle when voices sound in the distance, coming closer. Footsteps in gravel.

Gia slumps back down, against the far wall, letting every bit of the exhaustion she should be feeling show.

The footsteps stop in front of the door, and a moment later it's wrenched open to reveal a pair of guards, and Thomas Deté. The guards' rifles snap up to sight her. The priest notes the bloody makeshift bandages on her arms with a satisfied smile.

"Having a little trouble with your abilities?" he asks.

"What the fuck did you do to me?"

"Another of our little experiments."

"That knife?"

But Deté ignores the question. He turns, waving a hand at the guards. "Bring her," he calls over his shoulder as he walks away. Gia lets them haul her to her feet.

While the evening air is a relief, the air conditioning inside the school is even more of a shock than before. Cool air blows over her bare shoulders, turns the places where her sweat-soaked top clings to her shoulder blades and lower back clammy and cold. Gia shudders.

"I want to see Tevi," she says, loud enough he might be able to hear her if he's still in the building, not so loud it'll make them angry.

No one answers her, and when they pass by the room where he'd been working earlier, the door is shut. She can't make anything out through the frosted glass pane.

When they shove her through the doorway to the strange sanctuary once more, the stench of necrotic flesh and blood hits her before the rest of her senses can catch up with the horror awaiting her. Gia freezes in the doorway, and Deté chuckles at the fear on her face.

The alien that bit her back at Redrock unfurls its wings, shrieking, the rancid gust of its breath brushing her cheeks even from across the room. Rough hands dig into her biceps, push her forward, and in her shock she barely registers that the creature is restrained. The claw-tipped wings have been left free, but heavy chains weight its ankles, and a thick metal collar tethers it to the wall behind it.

The guards drop Gia in the same chair she'd occupied earlier, directly across from the alien, though a good four meters away. That distance is nothing if it pulls free of its bonds, which are burly. Industrial grade fast-clips like the sort she'd use to secure heavy machinery. Easy to use but solid, and hopefully whatever stud the tether is sunk into is also sturdy.

She risks a glance over her shoulder. Some of the artifacts are still displayed on the tables ringing the room, but the two spheres that drank her blood are gone.

"I know you've already met this miracle," Deté says,

reverence in his voice. "You were blessed, truly, to have achieved sainthood directly from a Fallen One."

"You're welcome to try it yourself," Gia says.

Deté shakes his head. "I've already gone through the fire. Surviving that test was an honor, but I'm truly jealous."

Gia shifts her attention from the creature to Deté. This smarmy priest with the con man's smile, he's . . . whatever she is, too?

He notices her surprise and laughs. "There aren't many of us. And your friends have killed most of the original saints."

"If your blood is so special, what'd you need me for?"

"Mine is transformed, but yours is pure, Giaconda. Better for the ritual. Besides. That didn't seem very pleasant." Deté looks pointedly at the blood-soaked bandages on her arms. "Our knife worked its charm, though. How do you feel?"

"Like shit," Gia says. "It's been a rough day."

"Any changes to your energy?"

"Yeah. I'm pissed. Where is my husband?"

"He's fine. As long as you cooperate."

She doesn't like the wording, doesn't like that he's shifted responsibility back on her. Is Tevi done with whatever work was making him useful on his own? Or is he dead already, and they're still trying to use him to make her behave?

"I'll cooperate if I see him."

"Soon."

The secret amusement Deté manages to put into a single word raises the hairs on the back of Gia's neck. She will get through this, and Tevi is alive. She has to believe those two things are true.

She turns her attention back to the alien to break away from Deté's gaze. It has relaxed a bit since they entered the room; it's no longer thrashing, but watching her curiously. She wonders if it remembers biting her. If it can tell there's something different about her blood. If it remembers the fight, and still views her as an aggressor, a threat.

Deté checks the time. "You have a choice, Giaconda, and you need to make it fast. Fight for the side of truth, the future of humanity. Or die with the others. You and I survived the trial, which makes us special. Others won't be so lucky, but all will go through it soon.

"You see, with the activated artifacts, your Dr. Sharaf was able to achieve the impossible — we can now choose which souls will survive with one hundred percent certainty. If you agree to fight on our side, we can provide your husband with a test he'll be sure to pass; if not, he can take his chances with the original Gift of the Fallen." Deté smiles at her. "Your friends, too — if they choose to help rather than hinder. Anyone you want, Giaconda. You and I, we have the power of life and death now."

"Nice sales pitch, but I'm pretty sure only Zacharia has that power," she says, and a shadow flickers over the priest's face. "I know his type. You and I are still pawns."

"Believe what you want, the choice is still the same. Help us and those you love will live, refuse and watch them die, then forfeit your own place among the saints." Deté leans forward, gaze intense as he waits for her reply.

Something's changed since this afternoon — some plan is now in motion. Whereas this afternoon Deté seemed relaxed, now he's antsy, time-pressed. He reeks of anticipation.

Reeks? Gia frowns at the word thrust into her mind.

She sniffs experimentally, but she can't smell anything but the creature and her own sweat.

"Help you with what?" Gia says, pushing aside intrusive thoughts. "If you need me so bad, tell me what I'm getting into."

Deté laughs. "You still think you're going to talk your way out of this. I admire you." He rocks back on his heels. "Bulari will experience the Gift of the Fallen tonight. The high and the low. And you're the one who's enabled it."

Deté is saying something else to her, but she can't make the words out over the intense longing she has to be free. To have the chains on her ankles drop off, the leash cut free, to be able to soar.

She starts — there's no collar around her neck — and suddenly locks eyes with the alien. *We can be free.* Gia's not sure whose thought it is.

She shakes her head to clear it, focusing back on what Deté just said. "Because of the foolproof serum?" It doesn't make sense — even if Zacharia was waiting until he could transform himself before poisoning the city, he still needs a delivery mechanism with a far reach. "It's gonna be hard to get everyone in this town to do shard at once."

"Especially since your friends keep destroying our shard caches," agrees Deté. "But no matter. Not everyone is willing to slip a tab under their tongues — but everyone has to breathe. And the Fallen provided us with both the Gift and the ability to spread it far and wide."

"The artifacts," Gia whispers.

"The plan's already in motion," Deté says. He lifts his chin to one of the guards over her shoulder. "You won't be talking your way out. You have one chance to save your husband."

There's a scuffle behind her, and Gia cranes her neck to watch Tevi being dragged into the room — bound and gagged, but otherwise unharmed. She starts to stand but Deté has that silver knife back out, the tip a handsbreadth from the hollow of her throat.

A memory of sensation — weakness — floods through her like a flashback. Only it's not her memory, because she's never been chained to a table while Deté tests different metals, different formulas in a thousand shallow cuts on her limbs, her wings.

Yellow, alien eyes are watching her over Deté's shoulder.

"A choice," Deté says. "Agree to fight for us, or we see how Dr. Sharaf handles the same test you passed." The soldiers push Tevi closer to the creature, who turns on them with a growl, knife-edged maw snapping shut.

*Don't hurt him don't hurt him please.* Gia prays this link the creature has made with her goes both ways, and maybe it does, because its bony, fearsome head whips back to her and it hisses.

*Don't hurt him,* Gia thinks with all her soul. *I'll help you.*

Can it even understand words? Gia calls up a memory: she and Tevi with Lucky, the little guy playfully catching the radishes Tevi tosses him.

The creature cocks its head at her.

"It seems you've made your choice," Deté is saying. "I've never put down a saint before. We'll harvest your blood first, of course, but it's a pity your soul couldn't be saved." He flips the knife in his hand, the tip ready to stab into her thigh. "First let's make sure your powers haven't come back."

Not a chance, asshole.

Gia wrenches her hands apart and the weakened links of her cuffs give; she lunges and the power of her tackle knocks Deté back. Gia screams for Tevi as the Dawn soldiers shove him towards the alien — but the creature ignores him and swipes at Deté instead.

Deté screeches, caught with the clawed tips of the creature's wings, but the cuts are already healing as he turns to Gia once more.

A shot rings out. She hits the floor, rolling out of reach of the alien and coming into a crouch near the table of relics. She scrambles for a weapon — the chairs are all bolted to the floor — and grabs the glass sphere from the display. Throws it with all her might. It shatters against one of the guards' heads and he crumples to the floor in a heap.

She turns to deal with the other attacker, but a flood of emotion from the alien staggers her with its vividness. It's not a memory this time, but a desire. To tear free and dismember the men who have been tormenting her.

She shakes her head clear, too late. Lightning turns her spine to water, searing pain from an electric barb, followed by a blow that slams her back into the table. It shatters beneath her.

Someone's yelling, but her ears are ringing; she hardly feels the boot connecting with her ribs. She does finally register the broken table, the spindly leg broken to a sharp spike. She wraps her fist around it and jams it through the boot before it can kick at her again, driving it into the floor.

Another flash of sensation — a warning Deté is behind her — and she rolls out of the way. Almost.

Deté's silver knife plunges into the back of her upper arm rather than into her spine, but even then it does its trick. The strength is draining from her once more. Blood sheets down her arm as she pushes herself to her feet and spins to face him, taking stock of the room. Tevi's slumped against the wall at the alien's feet. One of the guards is down, lying in a shattered halo of broken glass. The second is screaming, his foot pinned to the floor. But others are yelling from down the hallway, and she's not sure she can handle Deté, let alone his backup. Deté flips the silver knife to his other hand, bends to pick up one of the guards' pistols.

Guess he's going to harvest her blood through a hole in her chest.

Fuck it.

Gia turns and dives for the alien, and is rewarded with a wave of elation. Her blood-slick fingers fumble at the fast-clip, then it's free.

Gia slumps against the wall beside Tevi — he's alive, but stunned — and air whooshes past her as the alien beats its wings. It whirls on her, a rush of fetid breath, needle-sharp teeth bared.

She shoves herself back against the wall, staring into the alien's bloodshot yellow eyes — intelligent, furious. It definitely recognizes her from the fight, she can sense the memories of that night throbbing through their connection.

It snarls with jaw wide, the ridged, raw horror of its throat ringed by glittering fangs.

"I'm not the enemy," Gia shouts back. She reaches past snapping teeth to grab its shoulders and roll them both out of the way as Deté fires an electric barb; the wires narrowly miss the alien's head.

The alien's weight is crushing, a tangle of wings and limbs and chains. It rears back, but now it's blinking at her in realization that she'd saved them both. Gia holds up her hands in what she hopes is a universal sign for *I am not a threat*. It gnashes its teeth once more, dainty, then whirls on Deté.

Deté fires again. The alien screeches as the barbs dig into its wing, electricity arcing along its fingers, illuminating torn membranes and scars. It rears back and shrieks, whips its wings through the air, pulling the electric barb out of Deté's hands and flinging it to shatter against the wall.

The guard whose foot Gia had pinned to the ground has managed to free himself, but despite the yelling in the hall, apparently no one's brave enough to be backup. The guard stumbles back and raises his gun.

"Don't shoot the Fallen One!" Deté yells.

The alien hisses at him.

Deté slowly reaches into his pocket, pulling out a snub-nosed tranq gun. The alien twitches back, crouching in a posture Gia knows all too well. She's taken it herself. A cornered animal who's about to fight to the death.

Gia pulls herself to her feet, keeping the alien between herself and Deté and the guard for now. They may not be trying to kill it, but she's still fair game.

And the alien *screams*.

Gia drops to her knees, hands over her ears.

Through the fog of pain piercing her eardrums she remembers — or the alien remembers for her — it did this before, at the facility. It's giving them both a chance, if she can keep it together. Gia forces herself to move, charging past the creature to tackle the guard, using momentum and surprise more than strength to smash his head into the wall while he's still clutching his own ears. She lunges and grabs the silver knife Deté dropped when the alien screamed, then whirls to find him lifting his arm once more to shoot the creature.

Gia throws the knife. It buries itself between Deté's shoulder blades and he rears back, the tranq gun falling from his hand. With a roar of anger, the alien sweeps a wing, claws slashing through Deté's throat.

Deté crumples to the ground.

So does the alien.

Deté'd managed to get the tranq shot out before he died, and the poisoned dart is quivering in the alien's heaving chest. It thrashes weakly, but lets Gia approach. Kneel. She yanks out the dart.

"You're going to be all right," she tells it.

The alien hisses softly at her, eyes fluttering closed.

*You're going to be all right,* Gia thinks, trying to project the feeling into the alien's flutter of panic. Not words, but emotions, sensations. She tries to project safety, healing, compassion.

The alien twitches and goes still.

Its panic washes out of her mind.

Tevi is stumbling towards her, his gag torn free but his hands still bound. He kneels on the other side of the creature's body. "Are you all right?"

"I'm fine." She reaches for him. "Did they — "

"Get back from the creature."

Gia freezes. Tevi's gaze shifts past her to the doorway, his eyes wide with fear.

The command comes again. "Get back."

Gia lowers her hands. Closes her fist around Deté's pistol.

Locks eyes with Tevi.

"I love you," she whispers. "Stay down." And she coils her muscles to fight once more.

## 29

## STARLA

"Gia," Oriol calls. "Get back from the creature."

Slumped bodies, unfurled wings, shattered glass, and Gia's crouched in the middle of it all with her back to them, covered in blood. Fingers closing slowly over the pistol on the floor beside her, gaze locked on Tevi like she's weighing her options — between going quietly and whirling on them and emptying the clip.

Gia's hand tightens on the gun. Starla raises her stun carbine, flips it to the lowest setting. Remembers Gia's newfound powers and tentatively ratchets it back up a few notches.

"Gia. Tevi. Get back." Oriol takes a step towards her, his gun trained half on her, half on the motionless alien behind her. "It's Oriol. Starla's here. You're safe."

She seems to hear him this time; her spine straightens and she spares a glance over her shoulder, battle fury draining out of her face when she sees Oriol. Her fingers flinch away from the gun, her hands rise in surrender, shoulders shaking with ragged breaths.

Relief floods through Starla.

Gia's safe. Tevi's safe. The alien — it looks unconscious, collared, its ankles hobbled together. One claw-tipped, bluish-gray wing is flung wide, the other pinned awkwardly beneath its bulk. Its chest rises and falls ever so slightly.

While Starla and her crew had been fighting their way in, Gia had apparently been fighting her way out. The three men in this room lie unconscious or dead — the one with his throat torn out is definitely dead. And definitely Thomas Deté; Starla recognizes him from the profile images. She's pretty sure Tevi doesn't have secret claws, which means the alien is probably responsible for Deté's throat.

Fighting with Gia? Or merely fighting against its captor? Either way, they need to get this thing contained before it wakes up.

Starla lets her own weapon drop, signing "All clear" to El and the rest of the team outside the doorway. "Tell Toshiyo and Beto they're on, then help them," she signs to El. She points to Henri, Jude, and Mel. "Finish sweeping the rest of the rooms."

She's not sure what they'll find — after all, this room contains everything they're here for. Gia and Tevi, the alien, and a bonus: what look like relics from the virtual museum, on elaborate display across tabletops around the room. And there are more crates under those tables that, with any luck, could contain the rest of the missing relics.

First things first.

Oriol slings his rifle over his back and crouches beside Gia, sliding the pistol she was going for well out of her reach. "I've got you, G," he says. "Tevi, man. You all right?"

"I'm fine," Tevi says. His hands are bound and he's

disheveled, but otherwise he seems unharmed. "She's injured."

Oriol nods, helping Gia her feet and pulling her into a fierce hug, murmuring something too low for Starla's lens to catch. Starla flips out her knife and kneels beside Tevi, slicing through his bonds. She tries to help him stand, but he shakes off her touch, bending over the alien instead like he's feeling for a pulse.

Starla catches his arm. "It's dangerous," she signs, and his USL may be worse than Gia's, but surely he can guess at why she's trying to pull him back.

He shakes his head. "It was helping us," he says. "Is your lens . . . ? Good. It was helping us. Gia was talking to it somehow."

He glances up at his wife — Oriol's sat her down in one of the chairs that are, creepily, bolted to the floor, and she's leaning forward with elbows on knees, drawing in shaky, shallow breaths. The handcuffs on her wrists are broken apart, but her forearms are wrapped in bloody rags and blood is streaming from the knife wound in her shoulder. Why isn't she healing like she should?

Starla catches her eye. "Talking to it?" Starla asks her.

"I could feel it somehow. It — it was in my head. Like feelings and emotions. It remembered me, from when we fought it last time. But I managed to convince it I was here to help." Oriol's trying to unwrap the filthy rags around her forearms but Gia waves him away. "Those are fine. My shoulder's not healing." He nods and moves behind her, frowning at the wound there. "Is it going to be okay?"

"I think it's stable," Tevi says. "It's in bad shape, though."

"We'll get it somewhere safe," Starla signs, and right

on cue, Toshiyo appears in the doorway, eyes widening in shock as she takes in the scene. And El's behind her, thankfully, because this conversation is getting more complicated than anyone else in this room can handle in USL.

Starla snaps for Toshiyo's attention. "It's alive," she signs; Toshiyo nods in relief. "Tranquilized, we don't know how long that will last, or how it'll feel about us when it wakes up."

"Beto's got the van ready," Toshiyo half signs, half fingerspells as she kneels carefully across from Tevi, a wary eye on that razor-sharp maw. She hands him one end of a stabilizing strap. "Help me get this under its shoulders. What knocked the poor buddy out?"

"This," Tevi says, fumbling around on the floor beside him. He hands her a tranq dart; it's half-empty. "Gia yanked it out, but it must have still got a pretty strong dose."

"Are there more of those? We might need it." Toshiyo pats the alien's sternum. "Sorry ahead of time, big guy."

Starla stands and nudges Deté's body with her boot. "See if he's got any more tranquilizers on him, and a key to that collar. Get the alien prepped for transport. I'll — " She cuts off at the horrified expression on Toshiyo's face and spins to the door to see what new threat they're facing.

It's Blackheart.

Lounging in the doorway, gloved hands resting on her cane. She's studying the scene with secret amusement.

"Well, shit," Coeur says. She pushes herself off her lean with a wince and strolls past Starla to examine the creature. "That's a goddamn alien. Glad you're all right, Giaconda."

"What's she doing here?" Gia growls.

"Helping," answers Starla. "We couldn't have done this without her crew."

Coeur gives Gia a sly smile. "You saved my life recently, figured I could return the favor." The smile sharpens when she turns to Starla. "Didn't know we were rescuing an interstellar visitor, too."

"You didn't need to know."

"If that thing had taken out one of my people by surprise, we'd be having a different conversation," Coeur says. She drums her fingers on the head of her cane. "But fine. Say I didn't need to know. You and I aren't playing games, right? You know I'm here for Zacharia's serum. My folks have been searching, can't seem to find it."

"I haven't come across it." She lifts an eyebrow at El, who shakes his head.

"How about you, Giaconda?"

"You can fuck off."

Coeur turns her smile on Tevi. "What do *you* know, Giaconda's man?"

Tevi looks to Starla, she waves an impatient hand: "Tell us." Jaantzen promised Coeur she could loot the place, knowing full well it might mean she got her hands on the serum. That's the least of their worries right now — and Starla needs to know about it, too.

"He wanted to be sure he could survive it," Tevi finally says. "But to make that version, he needed to get these alien artifacts to work."

"Using my blood," Gia says, and Tevi goes pale.

"I know, he told me," Tevi says. He swallows. "It was successful. He took the serum, and he lived."

The corner of Coeur's mouth turns up sharply. "Where is it now?"

Tevi glances at Starla. "With him," he says finally. "He took it, and those artifacts — I don't know where he went."

Starla frowns at him. "Why take the artifacts?" She sweeps an arm around the room, indicating the rest of the priceless alien relics on the tables. "He needed them to make the serum a success, but he left all this other stuff with Deté."

"Deté." Gia curses, sitting up straight. "He said. 'Bulari will experience the Gift of the Fallen tonight, the high and the low.' Said I was the one who allowed it to happen — I think he was talking about the artifacts." She squeezes her eyes closed a minute as though trying to remember. "Not everyone is willing to slip a shard tab under their tongue, he said. But everyone has to breathe." Her eyes snap back open. "The artifacts, they must aerosolize the venom so it can spread faster."

"Spread faster in a crowd?" Toshiyo asks, and Starla knows where she's going. If Zacharia wanted a good concentration of people to infect with his plague, he couldn't ask for a better opportunity than the city's politicians and elite businesspeople all gathered at the capitol building to watch the prime minister's speech. And crowds of the city's lowest citizens gathered in the streets outside, protesting.

"The high and the low," Starla signs. "The prime minister's speech. How many does he have?"

"Two."

Oh, good. Only two alien weapons, activated by transformed blood, designed to spread a mostly-fatal poison.

"I have people down there," Coeur says. "What do I tell them to look for?"

"Spheres," Gia says; she holds out her hands to indicate something the size of a child's helmet. "Black, with strange words written on them, glowing red."

"And if he sets them off?"

"Contain the spread," signs Starla. As far as she knows, there's no antidote once a person becomes infected. "Be aware some of the people who get infected might become aggressively violent. You might have no choice but to shoot — "

Coeur's gaze shifts past her, and Starla doesn't catch the order she barks, but she understands the intent and throws herself out of the way as the other woman draws with lightning speed, firing just over where Starla's shoulder had been. Coeur drops the pistol almost as soon as she fires it, doubling over onto one knee with her hands cradled against her chest, swearing up a vicious storm.

A Dawn soldier with a knife in his hand is lying in the doorway behind Starla, blood leaking from the bullet hole through his eye.

Starla signs for El and Oriol to stand down — they have their own weapons drawn on Coeur — and crouches beside the other woman, a steadying hand on her shoulder. She can't even imagine what it cost her to expose how weak she truly is in front of former enemies.

"You all right?" Starla asks. The response she gets is another colorful curse. Starla scoops up the other woman's weapon and cane, then helps her stand. She holds out the pistol; Coeur takes it gingerly, settles it back in her shoulder holster with shaking hands.

"Thank you," Starla signs, and Coeur nods, jaw clenched with pain. "Let's go get the asshole who did this to you."

Starla turns to Toshiyo. "Tell Jaantzen about the

weapons, then finish up here — El, help her and Tevi with the alien, and be sure to get these relics. Anything else looks interesting, take it. Oriol, Simca, and I will get to the Capitol."

"I'll take my people down there, too," Coeur says. "See what we can do about evacuating those crowds."

And finding Zacharia's foolproof serum, probably — but Starla couldn't care less right now. Coeur finds it, more power to her.

"Wait." Gia pushes herself to her feet and shoves Deté's body over with her boot. A silver knife gleams between his shoulder blades; Gia yanks it out with shaking hands and wipes it clean on his shirt. She offers it hilt first to Starla. "Not sure how this works," she says, "but it counteracts whatever it is I've got. If you end up fighting Zacharia, you'll need it."

Counteract. That explains the bloody bandages on her arms, the unhealing knife wound in her shoulder. Starla slips it into a pouch and gives her a solemn nod.

"I'll see you back home," she signs. "Let's go."

Phaera hadn't anticipated the gauntlet of reporters waiting outside the capitol building, not for a policy speech about a trade agreement gone wrong. But the few short meters from the curb to the ramp in front of the Capitol are lined with state guards, reporters shouting questions, and camera drones edging over the invisible line to get closer to the attendees.

She's suddenly grateful she spent so much time worrying about what to wear.

"I didn't realize this would be the social event of the year," Phaera jokes to Cavy.

"Nothing like an Alliance conspiracy and a few days of protest to turn a failed trade agreement sexy," he says with a wry smile, gesturing her to lead the way.

He's elegant as always in a plum three-piece suit, gems on every knuckle. She'd finally gone for a classic from her favorite designer, Meherzad. A sleeveless, floor-length halter in slate blue that drapes low in the back but fastens high around her neck. It barely manages to cover the bruising, and now that she's finally braved a peek under the bandage, she's planning to contact the designer to order some custom styles. Covering her neck will need to be more than a short-term fashion fix.

She ditched the brace on her hand because the swelling's gone down and Oriol isn't around to tell her she still needs it, but the mottled bruising is horrendous. So tonight she's going retro, with over-the-elbow gloves in dove-gray silk, her gold cuff her sole adornment. Her magenta hair is loose, the black tips brushing her shoulders.

Camera-ready, and ignoring the reporters — though at least tonight an equal number of the shouted questions are about the Casino District Business Association's stance on the trade agreement as about the Devil's Table reopening and her absence. Phaera spares a glance at the press mob for Analie Cruz but doesn't see her. Either this isn't her beat, or Kumail Anh already got her indenture transferred over to work with Letizia.

Phaera's been inside the Capitol once before, as a child on a school trip, and it's as gorgeous as she remembers.

Like the courthouse next door, the capitol building was originally designed to make a visual statement that upstart New Sarjun was operating on the same level as more-established Indiran countries. Of the two buildings, the Capitol is warmer and much more welcoming. The two-story columns of the facade frame a vast entryway showcasing local sandstone and blocks of backlit rose salt, a tribute to all the miners who died in those early days to transport the highly sought-after mineral back to Indira for rich Arquellians.

Normally the entryway is open to the public, but tonight it's been cordoned off; still, the chanting of the crowds outside echoes off the high walls. A smiling host scans their irises against an invitation list, then directs them down a massive, curved hallway to the Founder's Room.

The Founder's Room is steeped in bygone elegance. Tall gilded doors open onto the mezzanine of a vast circular room; the mezzanine sweeps gently down to meet the main floor, which tonight is set with several hundred chairs in semicircles facing the stage. The stage and podium are draped in red and gold, the patriotic colors a clear sign Prime Minister de Grazal is here to speak to New Sarjun, not on behalf of the Alliance.

Tiers of glittering chandeliers cast sparkling light over well-heeled guests, most of whom are enjoying the trays of hors d'oeuvres and drinks stationed throughout the mezzanine. Rose salt columns — common around Bulari, breathtakingly priceless when shipped back to Indira — ring the perimeter of the room, lit gently from within to create a subtle glow. And between the pillars, massive portraits of the city's founders peer out over the room.

"Very impressive," Phaera says.

Cavy chuckles beside her. "They think they can buy us with appetizers."

"Hopefully there will be a little more substance to tonight than snacks and small talk."

"I haven't done a good enough job disillusioning you about politics."

She knows he's joking, but still she gives him a sidelong look. "This time isn't different?"

Cavy sobers. "I trust people's actions, not their words. Goes doubly true for politicians. We'll see what comes out of this."

"Fair enough."

They're later arriving than Phaera would've liked — the speech is due to start in twenty minutes and the room is already full. She recognizes a number of the attendees, whether from meeting them in person or watching the news. Representatives from all Bulari's major industries and heads of the larger unions are here. Politicians whose photos and résumés she spent the evening studying, though not as many as she would have expected. Maybe they're planning to show up right before the speech, in time to make an appearance but not to get cornered by Bulari's frustrated business community. Trade Commissioner Youssef Tabari looks like he regrets showing up early; Phaera spots him at the center of a knot of irritated business leaders.

Geum-ja Leone isn't here.

Phaera hadn't realized how much tension she was holding in her body, expecting to see Leone. She forces herself to breathe, her shoulders to relax.

"Something to drink?"

A server is proffering a tray of colorful glasses, and Phaera half listens until he lists off citrus-and-rosemary sparkling water. That glass of Alusinian cinsuat would be a welcome salve, but now more than ever she needs her mind clear.

She sneaks a peek at her cuff, still no word from Jaantzen. She has to believe his team has been successful tonight, that they've rescued Gia and Tevi and everyone is safe. That this is routine for them.

"Is everything all right?" Cavy murmurs.

Phaera switches on her smile. "Fine."

"Good. There's someone you should meet."

He holds up a gem-studded hand to greet a tall brown-skinned woman in a green silk jumpsuit, and

Phaera holds in her surprise as she realizes who it is they're walking towards. Elena Hu, Bulari's mayor. Close-shorn black hair, vivid green eyes made even brighter by the gold on her lash line, the sheen of gold glossing her lips. Her smile creases a faint scar below her right eye that must get corrected by the cameras, because Phaera's never noticed it before.

"I'd like to introduce Phaera D," Cavy says after he and Mayor Hu exchange an affectionate greeting. "She's become my right hand on the Casino District Business Association and has been spearheading the plan I told you about to form an association with the greater North Bulari neighborhoods."

"A pleasure meeting you." For a brief, terrifying moment Phaera thinks she's going to have to shake hands — she hadn't considered that when she left the brace at home — but Hu only smiles. "Cavy's told me a bit about your plan."

"You agreed to entertain the argument tonight," says Cavy. "So I'll leave you in Phaera's capable hands and make my way to the snack trays."

He winks at Phaera, nods at Hu, and turns to stroll away.

"You're not retired yet, old man," Hu calls after him. "And you won't get out of talking through the rezoning of Mendiola Avenue with me that easily."

"I'll make an appointment," Cavy calls back.

And he leaves Phaera on her own.

Something's missing, and it takes a few heartbeats for Phaera to realize it's her fear.

Every step in her career over the past decade has been taken in the face of fear, and she's become good at pushing past it, at ignoring the skeptical voice whispering that she doesn't belong here, she's reaching too far. But maybe she's distracted by worry for Jaantzen. Maybe she's pushed past fear so many times recently she's become numb to it. Maybe it's the fact she fought Tierren and lived.

Whatever it is, that fear is gone.

Hu turns to her with a smile, giving no sign she believes Phaera's out of her league — because she's not. Phaera belongs in this room, she can feel it in her bones.

"Cavy's told me about your idea," Hu says. "But enlighten me. There's already a Jet Park association. You're planning to join together with them?"

"Jet Park and the Casino District are both dealing with similar issues of crime and development," Phaera says, and it feels so, so normal to be chatting neighborhood politics with the mayor of Bulari. "But they're not the only neighborhoods in the north. Ignoring the space terminal and the more residential neighborhoods of Dry Creek and Altamira is shortsighted. I want to make sure their voices are at the table."

Hu's golden lips purse in surprise. "Dry Creek and Altamira . . . don't exactly have traditional business associations."

"Then we work with what they have."

"Blackheart," Hu says, but there's curiosity in her tone, not dismissal. "You're saying you'll work with Blackheart."

"I'm saying we'll take a frank look at who actually powers our economy in northern Bulari and how we can collaborate to make that part of the city thrive."

"Then let me know how I can help." Hu tilts her head, studying Phaera. "Although I wonder if you're putting your efforts in the wrong place."

Phaera hides annoyance behind a practiced polite smile; she's had this conversation before. "North Bulari is an important part of this city's economy."

"That's not what I meant." Hu's laugh is warm and husky. "I like your vision, but I wonder if you'll be able to accomplish it this way. There are a few seats on the city council open this year that could use a candidate with business experience and strong roots in the community."

Phaera blinks at her in surprise. "That's an interesting prospect," she finally says.

Hu smiles. "Think about it. I'd like to work with more councillors who have a real vision." She holds out a hand and Phaera flinches but takes it, steeling herself for the grinding pain in the recently dislocated joint.

The mayor moves on, and Phaera grips the balcony overlooking the rows of chairs below, focusing on calming her shaky breaths until the pain recedes. Gods, she should have brought some stronger painkillers.

She finds herself searching for Cavy, to thank him for the introduction, but he's already halfway around the room talking to a pair of men she doesn't recognize. Not waiting around for her gratitude, of course — he and Leone have both helped her make connections, but he never expects anything in return. He wants the generation coming up behind him to succeed. He doesn't need to stamp his name on it.

Even before all this business started with her and Jaantzen, Leone had been growing more cloying. Their occasional lunch meetings turned from invigorating to overbearing, Phaera beginning to realize Leone's advice was never optional, her requests were never at Phaera's discretion.

She hadn't realized how long she'd been walking on

glass with that relationship. How much Leone had been throttling the oxygen out of her enthusiasm for her future.

And it's almost as though she's developed a sixth sense after years of managing Leone's ego. The hairs on the back of her neck rise even before she hears the voice.

"Phaera, it's so good to see you."

Phaera straightens her shoulders, schooling her expression into perfect politeness before turning to greet Geum-ja Leone. The chief justice is wearing a boxy, beaded dress which appears understatedly expensive. A ruby-and-gold bracelet — the one Jaantzen gave her, Phaera realizes with a twinge. Ruby chandelier earrings catch the light. Leone takes Phaera's hands and pulls her in for a kiss; Phaera tugs her injured right hand free with a wince.

"They're all watching," Leone says quietly, and Phaera forces herself to go through the motions of the greeting.

"You look well," Leone says.

"You sound disappointed."

"Long gloves are an interesting choice. But of course I don't follow the fashion trends like you do."

"Did you come here to admire what your mercenary did to me?" She should be keeping her voice down. No one's close, but they could still be easily overheard. Phaera doesn't care.

"Be careful, sweetheart," Leone says, warning flashing in her eyes though her smile doesn't change. "If you want to start up the gossip mill, I can feed it plenty of rumors. Everyone knows you've made your bed with a dangerous man."

"What do you want?" Because she's obviously not here to smooth things over.

"To tell you how lovely you are." Leone squeezes her elbow as the light changes subtly, a soft chime signaling it's time for everyone to take their seats. "No hard feelings, Phaera. Not if I'm going to be working with Willem."

Leone adjusts the bracelet at her wrist almost unconsciously. Anger spikes through Phaera, even though she knows Leone's toying with her. And on the tail of that anger, the realization that Leone knows she just scored a point in an old and stupidly effective game: Your man chose me over you.

Stay calm. Don't let her win. "Perhaps we can have lunch again soon," Phaera says — and at the flicker of disappointment on the other woman's face, she understands her real goal tonight. Leone's trying to provoke her. Into cursing her out, maybe slapping her, something to get her thrown out of this event, or at least to turn heads. Because Leone's not going to be content cutting ties with her protégé. No. Phaera has refused to fall back into line, and Leone is going to tear her career to shreds — even while cozying up to Jaantzen.

Phaera trusts that Jaantzen's plans don't include Leone as an ally. She does. She's just not sure she has the stamina to play his game.

"I'd like lunch," Leone says. "Give my regards to your mother."

She gives Phaera a poisonously sweet smile and turns to find her seat, and Phaera can't keep the fury off her face. She pushes back from the mezzanine's gilded railing, whirling away from the rows of filling seats and pretending to admire one of the paintings of the founders that rings the room while she gets herself back under control.

She is not going to let Leone win.

She hadn't been prepared for the jabs, she realizes, in part because she expected at least a shadow of the attempt Leone is making to fix things with Jaantzen. Leone truly is desperate enough to work with Jaantzen, Phaera knows that. She'd been foolish to expect that agreement to extend to her, too — Leone might apologize to Jaantzen for hurting Phaera; she'll never apologize to Phaera herself.

Leone may not touch her again. She may not send such blatant messages as shutting down the Devil's Table or poisoning Phaera's mother. But she'll cut her a thousand times more with that bright, matronly smile, leaving wounds Phaera can't even share with others for risk of sounding petty.

If Jaantzen waits much longer to finish this, she'll bleed dry. After tonight, she tells herself. After tonight, you'll never have to see Leone again.

She finds herself staring blankly at the portrait of Anjali Lumaban, her mind racing.

The city founder stares back at her with the sort of stern, practical expression that says she might have dressed up for this portrait but she's more comfortable in work clothes. Thick black braid and dark eyes, work-scarred hands and sun-rough skin. One of the first of the early homesteaders on New Sarjun to hit it rich, scratch her empire out of sand, and wrestle the other homesteaders in the region into working together to build what would eventually become Bulari. A woman you did not cross, according to the legends and history books.

It had taken enormous strength to birth this unruly city. Phaera can make it through a polite conversation with Geum-ja Leone.

Someone touches her arm and she catches herself before she cries out. Keep it together, Fay. You've got this.

She leaves Anjali Lumaban with one last nod, a deep breath to drink in the founder's legendary strength, and turns.

To find Lhasa Demosga.

Tall and stick thin and draped in gray, Lhasa's an ascetic's dream of deprivation and sour humor, especially against her brother Aiax's bombastic personality. Phaera had been surprised Lhasa joined their little anti-Leone cabal. Lhasa had consistently gone out of her way to make Phaera unwelcome at Leone's dinner parties — and she's the last person Phaera wants to see now.

"What do you want?" Phaera's tone isn't as cheerful as it should be; she shouldn't be here if she can't keep her smile on, she tells herself. She needs to keep her smile on.

Lhasa glances over her shoulder. "I wanted to make sure you were all right. I saw Leone corner you."

Phaera searches for the trap, but there's real concern in Lhasa's eyes. And a healthy dose of anger.

Is Lhasa Demosga . . . here to comfort her?

Lhasa and Aiax both have always rubbed her the wrong way, even before she met them in person. Jaantzen's known them for decades and trusts them enough to bring them into a business deal — and into his inner circle for the battle against Leone. Does Lhasa respect Phaera now because of her proximity to Jaantzen? Or is it because she got a firsthand view of what Tierren did to her that night?

"I'm all right," Phaera finds herself saying. "She wanted to rub in the fact that I'm here wearing gloves and a high-collared gown."

"Wanted to make sure you know she still holds the leash." The venom in Lhasa's voice surprises her.

"And gloat that Jaantzen's still trying to make peace with her, even after . . ." She can't say it aloud. She knows it's a ruse, but she still can't.

Lhasa's severe expression softens. "You know he's not," she murmurs. "Aiax, some of the others — they thought she was a pain, but it wasn't until she shut down the Devil's Table that they realized what she's capable of. But Willem, he's always known how dangerous she is."

Lhasa's trying to tell her something important; she seems ready to break from the stiffness in her spine, the tension in her jaw. "What do you mean?" Phaera asks.

Spots of color appear on Lhasa's hollow cheeks. "I was almost grateful when you started showing up and someone else had her attention," she says. "Well, spiteful at first, but eventually grateful."

The lights are dimming again, the chime insisting everyone take their seats.

"I'm sorry," Lhasa murmurs. "I knew she had her claws in you, but you were handling it, I thought. And I was happy to get away — but you have to believe me. If I'd known she'd hired someone to kill you I would have said something. She'd completely shut me out by then."

Phaera stares at her in shock. These last few years she's felt increasingly stifled by Leone and unable to articulate it to anyone; until she decided to trust Jaantzen, she wouldn't have considered anyone at Leone's dinner parties an ally. If she'd tried to bring up any of Leone's comments or behaviors, she would have sounded ungrateful at best and hysterical at worst.

This entire time she's been letting Leone gaslight her,

there *was* someone who understood exactly what she was going through.

Lhasa Demosga.

Phaera wants to laugh at the absurdity of it.

Lhasa takes a deep breath. "Everyone else needed to see your bruises, but Willem believed me the first time I told him Leone was dangerous. Aiax, Youssef, even Mizal always said I was overreacting — but Willem acted on the information I gave him about the prisoners being sent to Redrock."

"That came from you?"

Lhasa nods. An attendant is coming to gently explain what the incessantly dimming lights and chimes mean, her politest service industry expression covering up annoyance Phaera knows well.

"I'll see you two after the speech," Lhasa says.

Phaera blinks at her, confused. "Us two?"

"Willem. He was just here." Lhasa turns, frowning around the room. "All right, thank you," she says to an attendant. She squeezes Phaera's elbow and slips away.

Phaera scans the room as she allows the attendant to guide her pointedly to her seat beside Cavy. Around her people are applauding; she didn't catch what for but she mimes applause anyway, every jostle making her injured hand throb.

Jaantzen is here? She scans the room, doesn't find him. She glances over her shoulder — she didn't watch where Leone went, but the room's not that big. There, a section with the other four justices on the Supreme Court. And a missing chair.

A chill touches the back of Phaera's neck. Why did Jaantzen change his plans to be here and not tell her? And where has Leone gone?

## 31

## JAANTZEN

Meet her at the far door to the Founder's Room, Leone had said, but she's not there when Jaantzen rounds the curve of the hallway. Now, he either waits outside for her while the state guard at the door wonders why he's loitering, or he slips in and hopes his presence doesn't start turning heads. Both Leone and Madinia Ulrich, the prime minister's chief of staff, have assured him he has nothing to fear from New Sarjun's government or the police department; that didn't stop his pulse from picking up when the host scanned him in against the guest list — and it didn't stop the host's smile from flickering a little too bright.

Leone's put in a lot of effort recently to make Jaantzen infamous.

Still. The main stream of people are entering through the door nearest the lobby, which means most of the attention is focused there, and Leone might be waiting for him inside. Only two heads turn when Jaantzen slips through: an old man, and a woman in a silver suit jacket grazing the nearby hors d'oeuvres trays.

Jaantzen doesn't know them, and they don't seem to recognize him. Still his shoulders tighten as he finds an unobtrusive spot to stand and scans the room.

Leone's not here.

IN THE FOUNDER'S ROOM, WAITING FOR L, he messages to Manu, copying Toshiyo though she won't answer. Starla and her crew — Coeur mercifully alive and with them — left for the school building moments ago. Toshiyo will be tied up managing that operation.

"Who's the woman talking to Mayor Hu?"

The question comes from the old man at the hors d'oeuvres tray. He's not asking Jaantzen, but still Jaantzen turns out of curiosity. Mayor Elena Hu is easy to find in the crowd. She's tall, with shorn black hair and muscular brown shoulders bared in a vivid green jumpsuit.

A smile tugs at his lips when he sees who she's talking to.

Phaera's stunning tonight, and it's not just the way her dress skims her body. He's watched her work a room before, each connection another gleam on her polish, each conversation another spark in her flame, and tonight she must be in her element. She's radiant, and apparently he's not the only one noticing.

"Phaera D," the woman in silver answers. She sounds intrigued. "She owns the Devil's Table, and I think she runs the Casino District Business Association."

"Is that so?" The old man spears a roast date from his plate and pops it into his mouth, chewing thoughtfully.

"Do you do business in North Bulari?" Jaantzen asks; the couple turn to him. Now that he's invited their full attention, he can tell the woman is struggling to place him. He keeps his smile pleasant.

"I do," the man says. "Turei Construction."

"Then she's someone you should know," Jaantzen says. "She's putting together a greater business association for North Bulari neighborhoods."

The man's forehead wrinkles in surprise as he chews on another date. "Very bold, if she can pull it off."

"If anyone can, it's her," Jaantzen says. "She has the charisma to bring people together, and more than enough willpower to make sure things actually get done."

"I'm intrigued," the man says. "I'll have to introduce myself."

Jaantzen inclines his head and the pair excuse themselves to head back into the crowd. Phaera's familiar, crystalline laugh reaches him across the room, and when he turns to watch her once more, Phaera and Mayor Hu are talking like old friends.

She hasn't noticed him, and though she's a mere dozen meters away, she might as well be on a different world entirely. Someday, he might be able to walk up to her in a room like this without destroying the work she's doing to make her own name; today is not that day.

Jaantzen slips back into the hall. Better to risk the guards' suspicions than Phaera's reputation.

*At the far door,* he messages to Leone.

Her reply is almost immediate: *I'll meet you at the washrooms.*

They're back along the curved hallway; Jaantzen passed them on the way to this entrance. He exchanges cordial nods with the state guard at the far entrance, then finds a plaque near the washrooms to pretend to be interested in. He's on his fourth reading of the feuds of Bulari's warring city planners — he has to navigate the crooked warren of streets the bastards left behind — when he finally hears a familiar scuff of footsteps approaching.

Leone seems pleased with herself, but her smile turns business-like when she spots him, so whatever has delighted her probably doesn't have anything to do with him.

He pings Manu to let him know he's made contact, then lets Leone pull him down into a fond greeting, kisses on both cheeks. He straightens with her powdery perfume in his nostrils. Marking him, he can't help but think.

The show's for her alone, though — the state guards stationed at the Founder's Room doors aren't paying either of them any mind, and the last-minute bustle near the washrooms has died down. The prime minister's speech is due to begin any minute.

"Thank you for coming," Leone says, clawing her fingers over his arm as they walk; he forces himself not to shake off her touch. Her glittering beaded dress shivers melodically as they follow the curving hall past the far door to the Founder's Room, and rubies flash on her wrist. Fascinating. She's wearing the ruby bracelet he brought her the night their relationship fell apart. Meant as a token of their supposed partnership, maybe? A symbol she's not afraid of him? Pure hubris? Impossible to tell.

His comm vibrates in his pocket and he steals a look — it's an update from Toshiyo.

*Teams 1 & 2 are in.*

"If you have something more important going on, this can wait," Leone says sharply.

"Not at all." Jaantzen slips his comm back into his pocket, that electric buzz of anticipation running over his skin. Starla has gone into the school building to rescue Gia and Tevi. She can handle this, she has good people at her back, he tells himself. Gia and Tevi will be all right.

The best thing he can do for them right now is trust they've got it under control, and take care of Zacharia on his end.

"I'm glad you could meet on such short notice," Leone says.

"A strange place for it."

"The seat of power." Her smile turns sly.

The place where laws are made and politicians peacock for the camera, she means. The government of New Sarjun hasn't much affected him beyond the occasional annoying tariff or the paperwork he files for his businesses. He knows where the real decisions about this city get made, and it's not in any well-lit, public seat of power.

They're made in secret, like this. A hundred, a thousand, petty interests throughout the city all vying in a battle of egos to see who can force their agenda on the rest. Layers of influence, one nesting inside the other. Do your ambitions contain a single street or neighborhood? A city or state? The entire Durga System? Jaantzen's aspirations have never been that grand, but Leone apparently got bored with the massive influence she already had in New Sarjun; by working with the Alliance she's flying even higher. Maybe even too close to the sun.

"Besides," Leone continues airily. "I had to make an appearance. He's waiting for us in my office."

"Did he seem to have any reservations?"

"None." Leone presses her palm to the panel beside an unmarked door, and it opens to reveal a lift. She smiles at him. "It sounds like you're quite the prize to him."

Maybe. Jaantzen did kill his brother, but Felipe Zacharia has seemed single-minded about his mission to bring about the Dawn's end of days. More likely Zacharia wants Lucky and the rest of the alien technology Jaantzen has, and a chance to kill Jaantzen sweetens the deal.

The lift opens in an unassuming basement, the low ceilings and drab walls a stark contrast to the vaulted passageways and luxurious detail on the main floor they just left.

"There's a passage on this level between the capitol building and the courthouse," Leone says. Her sensible heels send echoes down the hallway ahead of them. She releases his arm, but the skin on his forearm still crawls with her touch. "All these protesters overhead," Leone says, raising her gaze to the ceiling, and by extension, to the plaza above. "Here because of you."

"I'm sure they would have reacted to the news the same, regardless of who broke it to them."

She shoots him a sidelong look. "The damage is done, either way. For the best, I think. We can do a better job of making sure the interests of our city are represented in this second attempt. You and I are going to have fun working together."

"Is that what de Grazal is telling everyone upstairs?" Jaantzen asks. "That he's very sorry the Alliance kick-backs weren't spread around farther, and he'll do better on this second corruption?"

"Don't be sarcastic, Willem. You know how this all works."

"Of course I do. And you know what I mean. Will de Grazal be any trouble?"

Leone laughs. "He's in my pocket, don't worry."

Exactly what Madinia Ulrich had said when she met with him and Youssef Tabari over dinner two nights ago. Prime Minister de Grazal couldn't make a move to stand up against the Alliance because of the dirt Leone had on him.

Soon. A few more moves in this game and Jaantzen can stop with this facade and free them all from Leone once and for all.

"You and I have so much to gain," Leone is saying. "With my political connections and your spheres of influence, I think this partnership will be fruitful. Especially now that I've removed one of the thorns in the side of our city."

"I was managing Coeur."

Leone stops, heels clicking one final rap in the hallway. "You were not," she says sharply, then catches her tone, softening it to placate him. "Surely you can handle the little warlords in the Fingers much better than she was doing."

He doesn't know what kind of business she thinks he runs, but he's in no place to command the obedience of dozens of warring crews. That was the point of Coeur. To tamp down the upstarts and keep the smaller crews organized in the vast and complicated system she'd run even in exile through her lieutenants. Cut off the head of that system, and it dissolves into chaos — it had happened once already when Coeur "died" the first time.

But he doesn't need to argue; it doesn't matter. Coeur's alive, and while the rest of the city's problems are still on his shoulders, at least he doesn't have to worry about war in the Fingers.

What does matter is whether or not Leone is about to betray him.

Her rebuke is heartening, actually. If she was simply trying to sweet-talk him into meeting with Zacharia, she'd've kept her sugary mask. Losing her temper about

Coeur suggests she's truly trying to make an alliance work, and is fighting an internal battle to give up some of her control.

Good.

"Now's not the time to argue about Coeur," Jaantzen says. "We have another thorn to pull."

She smiles smugly, then turns to lead the way once more.

"The garage entrance," Leone says after a moment, palming open an unassuming door. She pulls it wide, and one of the shadows across the garage detaches itself and strolls towards them. Manu nods respectfully in greeting, hands Jaantzen a shoulder holster and pistol, and Leone palms open another lift.

"Geum-ja, you don't need to be at this meeting," Jaantzen says when the doors close behind them. He slips on the holster, shrugs his jacket back into place. "It could get dangerous."

"Felipe asked me here as a negotiator," Leone says. "An impartial judge. I thought you'd be grateful."

Ah, yes. The main reason she inserts herself into relationships and transactions where she doesn't belong: the gratitude, groveling, and boost to her own ego. They're as much reward as the opportunities to twist situations into the shapes she likes best.

"I appreciate your help," Jaantzen says. "But the situation is graver than Zacharia led you to believe. Did he tell you what he wants to negotiate?"

She shoots him an imperious look as the lift door opens to an empty hall. "You both have something the other wants," she says. "That's all."

"He has hostages, Geum-ja. He kidnapped people who are dear to me." He's scrutinizing her face; Leone's scandalized, and a touch disgusted at the idea. Another clue affirming she isn't going to betray him, and Jaantzen relaxes. If she was in on Zacharia's plan, she'd have had time to practice a more human surprise response of horror and worry.

"And what do you have of his?" she asks.

Jaantzen's certainly not going to be the one to explain aliens to Geum-ja Leone — if Zacharia wants to bring up Lucky in front of her, he can do the honors.

"We'll find out."

Jaantzen's never been inside the courthouse before, and it's exactly as oppressive as he would have expected. Sturdy stone-and-cement post-colonial architecture dressed up afterward with marble tiles and columns as a nod to the grand state buildings of Arquelle and New Manila. By day these halls must be bustling; right now they're filled with shadows and the clattering echo of their own footsteps in the eerie silence.

Leone palms a door where her name flourishes gold, it opens into a waiting room that reminds him of her home: red velvet and gold — New Sarjun's patriotic colors, but with a styling that would be perfectly at home in the mansion of an old money Arquellian aristocrat.

"Lovely," he says, since she seems to be waiting for a response. "Where's Zacharia."

"In my office. I left him with four of my personal guards." She crosses the grand waiting room to open an ornate door, then steps aside for Jaantzen and Manu to enter first.

Her office is designed to impress: oversized portraits of past chief justices in gilded frames, dark red velvet curtains brushing the floor, an imposing real-wood desk commanding the center of the room, plush cream carpeting.

It's empty.

An acrid, metallic tang sours the air.

Manu pushes past him into the room; Jaantzen draws his gun and turns back to survey the waiting room. There are no places to hide, and no sign of where Zacharia might have gone.

"Clear," Manu calls. "Think I found the guards."

Manu's standing on the other side of Leone's desk, mouth set in a grim line at whatever's on the floor. Leone gets there before Jaantzen and gasps in horror, her dark eyes wide, one hand pressed over her mouth.

Bodies are piled behind her desk. Four guards, all of them stripped of their uniforms.

"He was alone," Leone says. "How could he have taken them on his own?"

"Could anyone else have gotten in?"

She shakes her head. "He could let someone in now, but he wouldn't have been able to while under guard."

"So now Zacharia is loose in the building, with the uniforms of four dead guards." Creeping dread fills his gut. "He never intended to meet with us."

Leone palms on her desk's screen, giving the bodies of the dead guards a wide berth and a look of distaste. "Then what did he want? He didn't get into my desk, and nothing seems to be missing from the room."

"I doubt he was here to steal your antiques, Geum-ja," Jaantzen says shortly.

His comm buzzes again: Toshiyo.

*TURN ON YOUR EARPIECE.*

Jaantzen holds up a finger to Leone when she's about to say something; she glares at him but he ignores her.

"Go ahead, Toshiyo." Across the room, Manu straightens with a finger to his ear; he's listening, too.

"Everyone's safe," Toshiyo says, and one of the hundred stress knots in Jaantzen's shoulders eases. "We got Gia and Tevi, and secured the creature."

But that's not why she needs to talk; she knows where he is right now. Who he's supposed to be meeting. She would have simply pinged him with the good news if that was all she had to say. She draws in a breath and pauses, waiting for his sign.

"I can talk freely," he says. "What is it?"

"Those artifacts that required blood in order to make the foolproof serum? They can also aerosolize the serum when detonated. Like a chemical weapon, to spread it as far and fast as possible in a crowd. Zacharia has two of them, so I hope you have Zacharia."

"He's gone."

Toshiyo curses. "He told Gia he was going to burn Bulari, high and low. We think he means the protests and the prime minister's speech. Starla and Coeur are on their way to try to evacuate the plaza."

Jaantzen lifts his chin to Manu. "Ó Lauris," he signs, but Manu's already got his comm out.

"Thanks for picking up, man," Manu says as he steps away to make the call. "We're about to have a huge problem on your embassy's doorstep."

"Manu alerted ó Lauris."

"Good. The speech?"

"We're on our way there."

Toshiyo takes a sharp breath. "Be advised Zacharia may have taken the serum."

Jaantzen turns back to the pile of guard bodies with a

chill. That explains how an old man could have defeated them all.

"Thank you."

"Good luck, boss. I'll be in touch."

"What was all that?" Leone asks.

"He's in the Founder's Room," he tells Leone. "Is there a back way in?"

She nods. "I can show you."

He pushes a connection through to Phaera, but she doesn't answer. He tries again. Nothing.

GET EVERYONE OUT OF THERE, he writes. ZACHARIA HAS A BOMB.

## 32

## PHAERA

Something's going wrong, and Phaera can't put her finger on quite what.

The prime minister's been speaking for nearly twenty minutes, reassurances to the business community, promises to get to the bottom of the kickbacks, acknowledgement of people's calls for rewriting the trade agreement. He's hit a good blend of empathy, anger, and understanding, the right touches to appease his three main audiences: politicians, business owners, and New Sarjunian voters. And a pointed message for his fourth audience, the Alliance: You have overstepped our goodwill here.

She has no idea if de Grazal had anything to do with the initial scandal. Maybe it was mostly Leone and her inner circle selling pieces of New Sarjun's economy to Alliance companies, but it wasn't completely behind de Grazal's back — Leone has dirt on him, Jaantzen told her. It's the reason he'd let the Alliance get such a hold in the first place.

Whatever Jaantzen said to de Grazal's assistant the

other day must have given him enough spine to stand up to the Alliance tonight. Whether he follows up on his tough words with action is a completely different matter.

No, it's not de Grazal's speech that's going wrong.

The state guards closed the doors when the speech began, which seemed normal at the time, but something about their stance has shifted in the past few minutes. It's a bit more aggressive — protective, maybe? She's trying to remember how many had carbines slung over their backs during the pre-speech mingling. Is de Grazal's speech having the wrong effect on the crowds outside? Maybe the tone of the protest on the steps of the Capitol has turned ugly.

Phaera's not the only one noticing the change of atmosphere. The spaces in between bouts of applause are starting to fill with whispers. De Grazal blinks as the light of a message glimmers in his right eye, briefly replacing the pale blue web of his speech. But after a slightly longer than usual pause, he continues, more determined than before.

Phaera leans in to Cavy, who's frowning at de Grazal with brows drawn together. She's about to ask what he thinks is going on when he stiffens. Phaera catches her breath, a murmur runs through the crowd; they all heard it.

Gunfire.

De Grazal lifts a hand and clears his throat. "I'm being told the protesters outside are becoming restless," he says. "We're very safe inside the Capitol should anything happen. Be assured everything is under control."

He straightens his shoulders, obviously ready to continue despite the distraction and uneasiness of his audience. "As I was saying, New Sarjunian independence is my utmost priority, and that includes economic inde-pendence. However, we must balance independence with the reality that all nations in the Durga System exist as part of an interconnected — "

A burst of gunfire comes again, this time it's not muffled and distant. In the hallway?

Screams echo through the Founder's Room, and de Grazal waves a hand to cut his microphone, turning away from the podium to have a heated discussion with someone out of sight, one finger touching his ear.

"Stay calm," he says when he waves the microphone back on. "It's being — "

Another burst of gunfire cuts him off. It's coming from the main entrance to the Founder's Room, and Phaera is on her feet before it's over, pulling Cavy with her to the second entrance, the one they're closest to.

A pair of state guards block the door. For a brief moment she's relieved that they don't seem nervous, but they also don't look like they're trying to help. A voice in the back of her mind whispers that something has gone very, very wrong.

"We need to get out of here," Phaera says to one of the guards.

"Orders are you stay here. Safer."

"Whose orders?" She starts for the door, but the guard steps in front of her, whipping his carbine around into both hands and shoving her back. Phaera catches herself against a rose salt column with her good hand, Cavy grips her other arm. When she straightens the guard's carbine is pointing straight at her chest.

The corner of his mouth twitches in a grin, baring a missing tooth. "Get. Back."

These aren't state guards. They're not being protected.

They've been captured.

Phaera backs away carefully and the man's attention moves off her. He sweeps his carbine across the small crowd that had followed her. "Back in your seats," he yells. No one moves. "Back in your seats!"

The crowd pressing up behind Phaera slowly begins to shift, ebbing back towards the rows of seats. Phaera can barely hear the next round of gunfire in the hallway over the nervous, demanding chatter of the crowd.

Phaera jumps when her gold cuff vibrates, then discreetly checks it. Relief washes over her at Jaantzen's name. She reaches to brush a finger over the row of opals in her ear, but the second guard's attention hits her with laser focus and she freezes.

Up on stage, de Grazal is calling for them all to calm down, for the guards to stand down. He still thinks this is about a riot outside the Capitol steps, she realizes. He doesn't know that the state guards have turned — or been infiltrated.

Jaantzen's trying again.

She can't take the call, the impostor state guards are right next to her, and she can't move any faster than the crowd filing back to their seats. A guard prods at Cavy with his carbine. "Get a move, old man," he growls, shoving him hard. Phaera catches Cavy's arm to keep him from falling.

"We're going," she snaps, and the guard with the missing tooth rewards her with a sneer.

Her cuff vibrates once more, a message from Jaantzen this time.

She stumbles into her seat, giving Gap-tooth a wary

look, but he's not watching them anymore. She brushes a finger over her cuff.

Get everyone out of there. Zacharia has a bomb.

Phaera goes cold, heart pounding in her throat. The chaotic noise of the room recedes to a faint static as she tries to process what she just read.

"What is it?" Cavy murmurs, his voice cutting through her shock. She shows him the message on her cuff, then opens a connection to Jaantzen and leans close to Cavy like she's speaking with him.

"Jaantzen," she whispers when he answers.

He's breathing fast, like he's been running. "Phaera? Can you hear me?"

"Yes," she whispers again once the guard's gaze sweeps past her. "Can't leave. The guards are blocking us. What's happening?"

"Zacharia," he says. "Keep this connection open and tell us what you see. Toshiyo is listening in."

Tell them what she sees? Phaera's heart is racing as she tries to scan the room like Oriol would, sorting the important details from the unimportant. But how is she supposed to know what the most important things are? What if she misses something?

"Phaera." Jaantzen's voice is calm. "What do you see."

She takes a sharp breath. "There are . . . ten guards total," she whispers, still leaning in to Cavy. "Two at each door, the rest spaced evenly around the room. Wearing state guard uniforms, but I don't think they are."

"State guard–issued weapons," Cavy murmurs. "Combination carbines, the ones at the door had them switched to live rounds. They'll all have an electric barb and shock-batons, too."

"I heard Cavy," Jaantzen says before she can repeat it. "What else?"

"They're forcing us all to stay in our seats. The prime minister is still on stage, but they're not listening to him."

As she says it, the background drone of de Grazal's voice as he tries to get a handle on the situation abruptly goes silent. He waves an impatient hand, but the microphone is no longer broadcasting. She's vaguely surprised he's still in the room at all. The prime minister should have a security detail, shouldn't he? Bodyguards to rush him away for protection at the first sign of violence?

A pair of men in state guard uniforms, one with three gold slashes on the sleeve, have entered from stage left. Phaera's about fifteen meters from the stage; she can't hear de Grazal over the din. He's actively arguing with the higher-ranked man, though — de Grazal tries to push past him, back into the wings, and the man strikes him across the face with the butt of his carbine. De Grazal hits the stage floor and gasps; screams go up around the room.

"What happened?" Jaantzen asks.

"The head of the guards hit de Grazal," Phaera says. "They won't let him leave the stage."

"I'm almost there," Jaantzen says. "Keep this line open with Toshiyo."

"I will."

"Hey, Phaera, I've got you," a woman says. Toshiyo Ravi, Phaera recognizes her clear, pragmatic voice from dinner last night. "Just keep telling me what's happening."

Phaera glances around, but the guards nearest her don't seem to be paying her any special attention anymore. "The, ah, the guards are dragging the prime minister back to the podium," she murmurs. "I think they want him to read something?"

De Grazal is dazed, bright red blood trickling down the side of his face; his hands are braced against the podium and he's frowning into the middle distance as though reading a message on his lens. When he speaks, even with the microphone back on, it's impossible to hear him over the crowd.

The chief guard steps to the edge of the stage. "Shut up!" he yells, then raises his carbine and fires into the ceiling of the Founder's Room. Phaera throws her arms over her head along with the others, a shield against the hail of plaster and brick.

Toshiyo hisses her name.

"He shot into the ceiling," Phaera whispers. "I'm fine."

None of them are fine. Not if there's a bomb, and not with whatever strange pageantry is happening up on the stage.

At the blast, though, the crowd finally goes silent. The only sound is someone's terrified sobbing and the gritty pitter-patter of the final plaster shards dislodging themselves from the ceiling.

"Read it," the guard orders de Grazal.

"This is insane," de Grazal says in disbelief.

The guard whips out a shock-baton and drives it into de Grazal's side; the prime minister sinks to his knees, screaming.

"They hit him," Phaera says, her voice covered by the gasps of the crowd.

"Yeah, I see it," Toshiyo answers. "I've got eyes in the room now, but keep talking to me. Anything seem off?"

Nothing about this is *right*, so Phaera's not sure how

to tell if something seems off. But she forces herself to turn and scan the room, noting the positions of the guards, the fear on the faces of everyone around them.

"The guards aren't protecting the doors," Phaera says; she has no idea if that's significant.

"You're doing great," Toshiyo answers.

De Grazal has gotten shakily back to his feet and is gripping the podium now; even from this distance Phaera can read the mask of pain on his face.

"What's happening?" Cavy murmurs to her, but Gap-tooth is scanning past them again and she shakes her head. Jaantzen's on his way, that's all he said. She has no idea what it means. If it will help.

"Read it," the chief guard orders de Grazal once more, and de Grazal takes a shaky breath.

"'I'd like to welcome you to the dawn of a new civilization,'" he reads. He glances over his shoulder at the guard, then continues. "'Some of you may choose to embrace change, some of you will cling to the dark night of humanity's current mediocrity. But all of you will experience the flame.'" De Grazal turns and glares at the guard. "What does this even mean?"

"It means you've been chosen," comes a man's voice from stage right, and the room's attention shifts to the old man walking out of the wings, dressed all in white. He's smiling beatifically, his hands folded at his waist — but his peaceful demeanor is ruined by the sharpness of his gaze, the blood spattering the hem of one sleeve.

And by the fact that he's followed by four more men in courthouse guard uniforms, who point their weapons directly at the crowd.

Phaera knows him — knows his face, at least. It's the man Jaantzen's been hunting. Felipe Zacharia, the prophet of the Dawn. She didn't think she could be more afraid, but her mouth goes dry, her spine watery.

"Jaantzen," she hisses; he doesn't answer.

De Grazal is gripping the podium as the man in white approaches, standing his ground though he must desperately want to run. Not that he'd get very far, surrounded by guards.

Not that any of them will get very far.

"Who the hell are you?" de Grazal demands.

The man in white stops a pace away. Phaera could be watching a play, the two men are so completely focused on each other, every soul in the room watching what they'll do next.

"My name is Felipe Zacharia," Zacharia says quietly; the microphone throws his words out into the auditorium. "And I have a gift for you, Prime Minister."

He turns to the guard beside him, who's carrying a padded white pouch. He sets it on the ground, then pulls out a black metal sphere covered in strange markings that writhe red as though lit from within, glowing in his gloved hands. The guard proffers it to de Grazal, who recoils.

"Take it," Zacharia says. And when de Grazal doesn't, one of the guards behind him points his carbine at de Grazal's head. "Take the gift."

De Grazal carefully reaches out his hands. The guard sets it gently in his palms.

At first, nothing happens.

Then de Grazal screams, falling to his knees, flesh searing and smoke rising from his blackening palms. The charring spreads up his arms, preceded by a wave of tiny red blisters; they rise from his collar and up his neck, covering his face as he screams. It goes on forever before he finally gasps and falls silent, slumping back, the sphere rolling from his pain-clawed hand and coming to rest at the edge of the stage in front of the podium.

In the entire auditorium, no one breathes.

"He didn't pass the test," Zacharia finally says to the crowd. "A pity." Phaera expected malice, maybe. Triumph. But Zacharia's voice is merely curious. He steps past de Grazal's body to stand at the podium, hands folded gently in front of him.

"What you just witnessed is the Gift of the Fallen," Zacharia says, his amplified voice echoing in the silent room. "Humans were not the first race to visit the Durga System; we walk in the footsteps of the Fallen. Those who came before did not thrive here, as we did, but they did leave us a gift. One which can transform our broken bodies into . . . something transcendent. Those who are worthy of the Gift of the Fallen experience no pain. No disease. No suffering."

Zacharia stoops to pick up the sphere, holding it in his bare hand. Phaera flinches involuntarily, but nothing happens.

"As we speak, my followers are spreading the Gift of the Fallen throughout the city. When you leave this room, everything you know will be changed. As you saw, not everyone who receives the Gift of the Fallen survives — were I to detonate this sphere, it would spread through the room and show us who is worthy, and who is chaff."

Zacharia pauses, turning slowly with a gaze that seems to take in everyone in the room. "Or? I can give you each a choice."

"What do I do?" hisses Phaera. For a dizzying moment the voice in her ear is silent.

"Stand by," says Toshiyo.

Phaera curses under her breath. Studies the closest

exit. At least four guards stand between her and the exit. And even if she did like her own chances of bolting for escape, it wouldn't do a thing to help everyone else trapped here.

"Join me willingly," Zacharia says, "and I will ensure that you pass the test — as I have. Or you can take your chances like this man here. A handful of you will survive that way, but it's impossible to tell who. Either way, you will go through the fire. Do I have any volunteers?"

No one in the audience moves.

"Very well," Zacharia says. He beckons to his guards around the room, a wide, possessive gesture like he's sweeping chips off a table.

The guards wade into the crowd, grabbing people at random amid shouted threats and more than a few vicious blows. Phaera stiffens as Gap-Tooth stalks by; Cavy lays a hand on her arm as though he'll try to defend her if she's chosen. But the guard ignores her for another target three rows up.

A tall, thin, spindly woman in gray.

Lhasa Demosga.

Phaera's on her feet before she can think.

"Leave her alone," she yells. Gap-tooth turns in surprise, wrenching Lhasa around with him. Lhasa's face is pale with fear.

"You volunteer?" Gap-tooth asks, leering.

"We get a choice, right?" Phaera says. She glares beyond him to Zacharia, who's standing behind the podium, watching her little scene play out with interest. "That's what you said?" she calls. "We get a choice?"

Zacharia inclines his head.

Phaera squares her shoulders.

"Then let her go. I volunteer."

## 33

## STARLA

The al-Jurjani Trespass G3 is a dream to ride. It feels like it has a mind of its own, weaving through traffic and slipping around police blockades with the slightest shift of her weight. Starla gets where the reputation for being twitchy and overaggressive comes from, though. If you weren't confident, you could easily get into trouble. But Starla trusts herself, she trusts the Trespass, and she trusts Toshiyo's instructions flashing on her lens.

She slices through the crowd filling the streets around the government district, clearing a startled wake for Simca to follow behind her.

There are so many people in the streets. The People's Plaza in front of the capitol building was completely packed, Toshiyo told her, and the crowd has spilled out for blocks all around. If the Blackheart crew is making a dent in dispersing the crowd, Starla can't see it.

Toshiyo also said traffic would be clearest from the southeast, but Starla and Simca are a block out and the street is clogged. Starla fights through the crowd, finally making it to the end of the block — and finding the problem. The entire street is blocked off with a pair of white delivery vans jackknifed across the road and abandoned. There's just enough space to squeeze a moto through between them, but no crowd of protesters would be able to get in or out of the plaza from this direction. Starla pings Toshiyo with a snapshot of the mess, then turns to Simca. She's got her helmet folded back and is talking with a group of teens.

"They say city workers parked the vans here about a half hour ago," she signs to Starla. "After the plaza was already full."

Meant to keep people in the plaza. Starla'd already suspected this is where Zacharia plans to set off his weapon; she's sure of it now.

BARRICADES ON ALL EXITS, writes Toshiyo. INFORMING COEUR.

HEADING IN.

"Any of you know how to hotwire a vehicle?" Starla signs to the teens; faces turn to Simca as she interprets. One lanky girl shrugs sheepishly, and Starla jabs a finger at her. "Do it. Get these vans out of here. The people in the plaza are in danger and we need to clear the roads."

And she guns the Trespass towards the vans, knee brushing a bumper as she threads her way through the narrow gap between them.

Most of the crowd in the plaza beyond is clustered on the north end, where the Capitol rises up against a backdrop of gleaming skyscrapers, a stand of sword palms casting jagged shadows against the building's facade from the floodlights below. The courthouse takes up the western block of the plaza, and various administrative buildings line the eastern side. On the south, the National Museum stands proud, energy webs glittering between the arches as a deterrent to thieves who might take advantage of the chaos in the plaza.

The People's Plaza is paved with sandstone and shaded during the day by enormous, delicately woven wings that unfurl from a series of tall poles. At night they fold back in, though it's never dark enough here to make out the stars. And at the heart of the plaza, an abstract statue meant to evoke the perseverance of New Sarjun's original settlers — from the right angle it might be a trio of dancers, blooming from a narrow central base set atop an enormous plinth resembling the wind-scoured bluffs to Bulari's east.

Someone's on top of the plinth.

As Starla watches, two figures secure a rope around the base of the statue and toss down the end, then start hauling up what looks like the sort of shipping crate Absolon Chevalier uses to safely transport volatile weapons.

She pings Toshiyo, and a moment later a message appears on her lens.

*I see it. But you're not close enough. Can't risk it.*

Starla shakes her head and shares a look with Simca; she's on the message chain, too.

What they *can't* risk is the Dawn setting off an alien weapon designed to kill 80 percent of the population in the middle of a crowded protest. She's not about to give up when they're this close, not when she can stop this thing.

Besides. She might have an advantage.

Most moto jackets come with their own helmets, which can fold back inside the collar. The model she and Simca both own is rated for the most severe of New Sarjun's dust storms, meaning the fine sand can't get inside the seals, and in an emergency, the wearer can activate preservation mode and get about ten minutes of oxygen in a closed system. Just enough time to find shelter without suffocating.

Or to dismantle a biological weapon without breathing it in.

*MOTO GEAR RATED FOR DUST STORMS,* Starla types.

Simca gives her a thumbs-up, though worry colors the confidence of her smile.

Starla's expecting Toshiyo to argue, but she gets only a single word in response.

*HURRY.*

The crowd is dense, but Starla guns her motor, flares her lights to bright, and pushes her way through. It's slow going, but she still covers ground more quickly than if she'd tried to force her way through on foot. She growls the Trespass to a stop at the edge of the statue and swings her leg over almost before the engine dies; Simca pulls up behind her, gesticulating wildly at the curious onlookers, probably yelling at them to get back to safety.

She desperately hopes they listen to Simca, because she doesn't trust that she has enough time.

Starla begins to climb, clumsy in her moto jacket and gloves, though she's folded the helmet away — thank the stars the stylized "bluffs" are easier to climb than the real ones. Simca takes another line and quickly surpasses her, of course, graceful even encumbered by gear. Starla keeps concentrating on sticking her holds.

She's vaguely aware of the hubbub below. Two of the street blockages have been removed and people are streaming out of the plaza — in part because there's a fire-fight happening at the intersection at the northwest corner, between the capitol building and the courthouse. Blackheart's version of crowd control?

*THEY'RE ON THE FAR SIDE.*

Toshiyo's message blinks on her lens, blinks away.

*STARLA GOOD STAY LOW. SIMCA STATUE WILL BE IN THE WAY HEAD RIGHT.*

Simca's waiting for her at the top; she shakes out an arm, rolls her shoulder. Lifts an eyebrow: *Now?*

Now.

Starla surges over the top of the plinth between two of the sculpture's flaring limbs, Simca hauling herself easily over the edge next to her, ducking to the right, and circling the statue to find her clear shot. The plinth is wide enough that there's plenty of room to stand, but the abstract limbs of the dancers flaring from the central narrow base make it difficult to maneuver.

Starla ducks under a limb and fires at the closest person, who's whirled to meet her. The bullet tears through his shoulder, but he barely notices. He fires back as she flattens herself against the statue. The second figure stiffens and turns to meet Simca as she comes around the other side.

The top is off the crate. From this angle, Starla can't tell what's inside, but an unearthly red glow emanates from within.

Starla grabs one of the statue's higher limbs and swings around, scrambling onto a blocky perch that's probably supposed to be a breast. She fires again with the advantage of height, but if her second bullet hits her target, he doesn't flinch this time.

He dives for the crate. Now that Starla's got some elevation, she can see a black sphere with glowing red text, nestled inside the crate. The man reaches in with bare hands to twist the halves of the sphere.

Starla almost lunges for him, but — *GEAR ON*, Toshiyo orders. Starla can't get to him before she runs out of time for her moto gear to get into preservation mode, and she can't do a thing to contain the weapon if she's dead. She switches the helmet back on and slams her palm against her sternum, and a second later the faint change in pressure and a yellow oxygen-level bar on her helmet's screen tell her the collar gasket has sealed. She's caught glimpses of Simca's struggle with the other man, she can only hope Simca also got her gear in place in time.

A blinding flash imprints the outline of the man on Starla's retinas before her helmet auto-dims — she frantically gestures it clear again so she can see what's coming at her next. The man had recoiled from the flash, now he's watching in fascination as the eerie red glow inside the crate deepens.

A heavy, dense red smoke boils out, pouring over the sides and swirling into the air, tendrils catching in the breeze and coiling down into the crowd of protesters below. The ones who notice seem curious, until the first few get a lungful and begin to writhe, just like the shard pusher at the Brujería.

The crowd is panicking, now, pushing back, but those closest to the statue don't have anywhere to go.

More and more of them fall thrashing to the ground.

The two men are breathing the smoke and they're fine — which confirms Starla's suspicion they've already gone through that transformation. The bullet wounds the first man took hadn't hurt him.

Starla fumbles at her belt with gloved hands and closes her fist around the silver knife Gia gave her. She drops from her perch, using another one of the statue's limbs to swing herself around and slam herself into the man she'd shot. His mocking grin turns to horror when she yanks the knife out from between his ribs; his inhuman grip on her arm slips and she locks her elbow around the statue's limb, shoving him with all her might. He flails for a grip with blood-slick fingers, then tumbles off the edge.

Simca's losing her fight with the other supersoldier. He breaks her grip and shoves her back along the narrow ledge of the plinth, where a low limb catches her legs and sends her sprawling. She twists midair, scrambling for something to hold onto, one hand barely closing on the edge of the plinth.

The man doesn't see Starla — he rears back when she drives the silver knife into the back of his neck. She yanks it free and pushes herself back from his lunge, then slams a knee into his side. He lands in the plaza below, blood trickling from his mouth.

Simca's already hauling herself back up, so Starla runs for the crate. She watched the Dawn soldier twist the sphere open, so she doesn't think, just reaches through violent red smoke, her heart slamming in her chest, and fumbles for the sphere. Finds a grip. Feels it reseal with a gentle click.

The smoke boiling from the chest is fading to a red haze, and Starla's still alive.

She takes a deep, stunned breath and folds the lid of the hazmat container back. Clamps the seals into place.

Red mist is still trickling through the crowd, but it's thinning. Directly below, dozens of bodies are scattered around the base of the statue, burned black by the alien poison, and there are maybe a dozen more coming through the other side — with the same berserker energy Gia'd had when she'd gotten bit. A woman lunges for a nearby man, snapping his neck before whirling on the person who's trying to pull her off his body.

She rears back to attack — and falls to the ground.

Aden Damyati lowers his pistol, salutes Starla, and jogs over to help another of Coeur's people restrain another snarling protester.

Starla had never thought Blackheart's crew would make her breathe a sigh of relief.

*Leave the crate,* Toshiyo orders. *Boss needs help in the capitol building.*

Damyati catches up with them, stepping around the body of a man he'd just shot mid-lunge. Probably a quicker death than whatever he was about to experience. Starla hits the code to fold back her helmet, drags in a full breath of fresh air.

"State guards have the buildings on lockdown," Damyati says; Simca interprets automatically. "But they're exchanging fire with other state guards — so I'm gonna guess the ones inside the Capitol are fake."

"Bomb's defused," Starla signs. "But he's got another one inside."

"We can take care of things out here," Damyati tells her. A couple of dozen people remain quarantined in the center of the square, but it could have been so much worse. If they'd been allowed to run, if people at the edges of the crowd hadn't known what was happening and stayed put? The crush of people in the plaza would have spread the infection like wildfire if Damyati hadn't been here with Coeur's crew to manage things.

"We need to get in," she signs. "Do the Dawn control the alleys?"

Damyati shakes his head. "We've got the one behind the courthouse, and the west side of the Capitol."

BASEMENT GARAGE ENTRANCE COURTHOUSE, Toshiyo writes. LEONE WILL LET YOU IN.

"Can we get to the courthouse garage entrance?"

"Yeah." Damyati points. "That way. I'll tell them you're coming."

Starla breaks into a run.

## 34

## PHAERA

"What the hell do you think you're doing?" There's an edge of hysteria to Lhasa's voice, pure fear in her eyes. "Sit. Back. Down."

The fake state guard clutching her arm, the one with the gap-toothed leer, looks back and forth between them with interest. He's got a pistol in his free hand, his carbine slung around his back.

The attention of the entire room is a hot breath on the back of her neck, but Phaera's only watching Lhasa and the man who's trying to drag her towards a writhing, screaming death like Prime Minister Nikolas de Grazal just experienced.

"You said you wanted volunteers," Phaera tells Gap-tooth again. "Let her go."

"*Phaera!*" Lhasa hisses. Her face is almost as gray as her dress; her hands are trembling.

"Neither of you are going anywhere," Cavy says from behind her. He grips the back of the chair in front of him and pulls himself to his feet. "If they need blood, let an old man go."

Gap-tooth laughs. "You'll all get your turn," he says. "C'mon."

But something about this little standoff has changed the energy of the room. The veneer of fear that kept everyone in their seats while the guards came through and started pulling out random prisoners is cracking. Some are arguing, voices rising around the room and echoing off the vaulted ceiling as pockets of dissent break out throughout the audience.

These bastards may be armed, but they can't shoot everyone.

Lhasa rounds on Gap-tooth. "I don't know *what* your game is," she says. "But you are dealing with some of the most important people in this city."

"Get your hands off her," someone nearby yells.

Phaera risks a glance at the stage. The guards beside Zacharia are covering him, weapons aimed at the crowd, but he doesn't seem bothered by the outburst. He's placed the strange, glowing sphere on the podium and is stroking it with his bare finger.

The voice in her ear has gone silent — Phaera doesn't know if she's lost the connection with Toshiyo and Jaantzen, and she can't check with all this attention on her. But Jaantzen is on his way, Toshiyo said.

She doesn't know what he can possibly do to help, but charging in to battle terrorists holding hostages is his world. Talking angry patrons down from making bad decisions is hers.

Sure, they don't usually have guns, and they're usually drunk on liquor rather than power, but the principle is probably the same: Keep talking. Keep the focus on her to minimize the danger to other patrons and staff. Be polite yet firm about reminding the asshole that the right choice is to deescalate and get the hell out. Either make them think they decided to leave on their own, or keep them talking until backup arrives.

"Let's be smart about this," Phaera says. She holds out her hands. "You don't want a problem, and like you said, we'll all get our turn. So you're gonna let her go, and let's talk this through like adults. Tell me what you want. What you need from us."

"Not interested in talking, sweetheart."

"Then let me do the talking. Stop me if I'm wrong, but you're here because Zacharia promised you something big, right? An end to suffering. Eternal life."

"You don't know what you're talking about," he sneers.

"I know about the aliens."

Gap-tooth's jaw drops. "How?"

"Did Zacharia tell you he had some precious, mystical secret?" Phaera shakes her head. "He's been lying to you. Keeping you out of touch with the rest of the world so you can't tell he's manipulating you."

Gap-tooth frowns at her, glances at Zacharia. But before he can respond, a scuffle breaks out in the back of the room, a surge of people overtaking the guard there.

Lhasa flinches away from Gap-tooth and he doesn't hesitate to shoot, dropping her to the ground and stepping back with his pistol in hand, wavering back and forth as though to cover everyone in her immediate area. No one rushes him.

Lhasa's fallen to the floor, hands clutched over her stomach like she can stop the red blossom from spreading through the gray fabric of her dress. Phaera kneels beside her, mind racing. Put pressure on it, she thinks; she strips off her gloves, no longer caring about hiding the bruising on her right hand, only hoping the thick material will be absorbent enough. She folds them quickly and slips them under Lhasa's hands. The other woman's eyelids are fluttering in shock.

"Put pressure on it," Phaera tells her, covering Lhasa's bloody hands with her own. "You're going to be all right."

An older woman kneels at Lhasa's other side. "I'm a doctor," she says. "Lhasa, honey, listen to me. We're going to get you through this."

"Volunteer." It takes a moment for Phaera to realize the gap-toothed guard is talking to her, until he grabs her arm, pulling her back to her feet. The hem of her dress is stained with Lhasa's blood.

Phaera cranes her neck to the chaos of the room — a few rounds of gunfire, electric barbs, and the guards have managed to get the crowd contained once more. People are packed back in their rows of chairs, with the guards maintaining control of the perimeter.

And Gap-tooth has backup.

"C'mon, volunteer," he says, and points his pistol at Cavy. "And you, too, old man. You want your shot at immortality?"

Phaera snatches at her skirt to keep it from tangling in her heels as she climbs the stairs, not caring that she has Lhasa's blood on her fingers. Her heart is racing, she doesn't know how much longer she can delay whatever Zacharia is planning. He's left the strange sphere sitting on the podium; it glows ominously at his elbow while he converses with a minister Phaera recognizes by face, though she can't remember his title. The minister's face is ashen, head bobbing as he agrees heartily to whatever Zacharia is asking of him.

De Grazal's body lies where he fell beside the

podium, contorted in pain, his skin charred and still faintly smoking. Phaera's stomach turns in revulsion.

"Phaera."

Phaera almost yelps at the sudden voice in her earpiece.

"Don't say anything," Toshiyo tells her. "I can see you. Nod if you can hear me."

Phaera catches her breath and nods, tries to make it look like she's gathering her resolve.

"Good, okay. Do not touch that sphere. Do not let Zacharia activate it."

She can't help herself from glancing around the room, like Toshiyo will be standing nearby, giving her directions. Gap-tooth glowers at her and she forces herself to stay still.

Don't let Zacharia activate it? How is she supposed to do that?

"It's going to be okay," Toshiyo says in her ear. "Be ready to act at the signal. Stand by."

Be ready to act. But how? To run, to fight? Phaera scans the stage for anything that might help her. The back of the stage is lined with a stand of flags, which look too heavy to pull down. Holoprojectors are built into the floor on either side of the podium, a bank of lighting drones pulse overhead. Zacharia and the minister are wrapping up their conversation, and whatever bargain the minister seems to have made, Zacharia gives him a tight smile.

"You'll be valuable in the new world," Zacharia finally says, reaching to shake his hand. The minister hesitates, then takes Zacharia's hand with fear in his eyes, like he expects it to trigger the painful death they'd all witnessed de Grazal go through.

Nothing happens. Zacharia turns to the guard next to him.

"Put him with the Chosen," he says. "They can all receive the Gift of the Fallen after we're done here."

He turns to the waiting crowd his guards have brought up to the stage, lips frozen in a caricature of a peaceful smile as he studies their faces. He pauses on Phaera.

"Ah, yes," he says. "The woman who volunteered. I had hoped more people would join me willingly, but I suppose fear for a friend's life is reason enough." He beckons her closer to the podium; Gap-tooth is holding Cavy back.

She takes a step forward. Another, until she's less than a meter from Zacharia, from the podium and the strange glowing orb. The sharp, pungent odor of chemical fire and scorched hair fills her nostrils and she gags as she realizes what it is. Nikolas de Grazal.

This close, Zacharia's smile is anything but beatific.

"Now," he says. "What can you offer me."

"I don't know what you're trying to do," Phaera answers. "So it's hard to make an offer."

"You're in this room. You must have resources? Connections? Power? We're entering into a new era. What part do you want to play in it?"

"Keep him talking," Toshiyo says.

"I want you to let these people go," Phaera says. And flinches, because there are more gunshots in the hallway outside, and this time the guards at the doors seem concerned. The real state guards, trying to fight their way in?

Zacharia frowns at the commotion, then turns to one of his guards. "She's nothing. Take her away."

Keep him talking.

"If you're looking for power, I — "

A burst of static lashes through Phaera's earpiece, so loud her hand leaps reflexively to touch the row of opals and turn the volume down before she realizes what she did.

Zacharia's rough, leathery hand closes like a vise on her chin, tilting her head to look at her ear. The ring of fire around her neck blazes and Phaera's heart thrashes against her ribs in blind panic as she expects him to squeeze.

But he digs the earpiece out with rough fingers and releases her. He holds it up to his own ear, then smiles, slow. "Someone's calling for you," he says. "Phaera, I know that name. Turns out you might be useful after all."

He fits the earpiece into his own ear, the row of opals glimmering against his coppery, sun-scarred skin.

"Phaera's here with me," he says. "Tell Jaantzen to call off his people if he wants to see her alive again."

He listens a moment, then shrugs. "She shut off the call," he says curiously. "I guess you're not quite the bargaining chip I was hoping for. It doesn't matter." He waves a hand. "Kill her."

Something explodes at the back of the stage, hollow and booming through her chest, and above them the bank of lighting drones suddenly shifts, their formation shattering as they swoop out of control.

Phaera reacts faster than the guard who's got his hand on her arm. She's not strong, she's not trained, but she's dealt with her share of creepers over the years. Sharp heel with all her weight on it, grinding in between the bones on the top of his foot. Shoulder dropped so the thrust of her elbow has that much more force when she drives it into his groin.

He releases her with a huff, and Phaera scrambles away from him, ducking as a lighting drone swoops at Zacharia.

The room is filling with smoke and her exposed skin stings from tiny shrapnel chips of whatever's still raining down from the ceiling, but even in the chaos she can make out the deadly red orb glowing on top of the podium.

Phaera lunges for it.

## 35

## JAANTZEN

Manu vanishes into the cloud of plaster dust and smoke ahead of him; Jaantzen charges after, ignoring the hail of debris showering the stage. The back entrance Leone had showed them put them stage right, and between the explosion Manu had engineered and Toshiyo taking control of the lighting drones, whatever drama they're crashing has become pure chaos.

"Zacharia's stage left," Toshiyo says in his ear. "Straight ahead from you, maybe ten meters."

"And the weapon?"

"Podium, center stage. Duck!"

Someone lunges at Jaantzen and he ducks, sends the man tumbling into a standing flag with the butt of his gun to his skull. The man goes down, tangled in fabric.

Zacharia's men are all in guard uniforms, their prisoners onstage all in evening wear. A good distinction for now, but Leone assured him help would be on the way soon. And the last thing he needs is to kill a real state guard in friendly fire, then try to convince people that he,

Willem Jaantzen, is one of the good guys when the dust settles.

Ahead of him, one of Toshiyo's lighting drones slams into another fake state guard's gut, sending him wheezing to his knees. Jaantzen snatches the carbine out of the man's hands and cracks him across the bridge of his nose with it before slinging the weapon over his shoulder. He keeps running.

Manu's at the far side of the stage, grappling with one of the Dawn soldiers. But there, on the apron?

Phaera's lunging for the podium, hands stretching for the glowing red sphere.

A guard in the auditorium raises his rifle to stop her, but Jaantzen is a faster draw, and the man falls back with blood pouring from his chest. He was obviously one of the bad ones.

Jaantzen shouts for Phaera to stop, frozen in horror as she reaches for the sphere — but she doesn't touch it. Instead, she snatches up a padded white hazmat pouch from inside the podium, then sweeps the sphere inside. The glowing red light vanishes.

Phaera spins away with it in her hands — then cries out.

Felipe Zacharia grabs her around the waist.

Jaantzen fires, but the old man moves like a snake, whip fast and unpredictable. He wrenches Phaera in front of him, blood staining his white sleeve from the bullet Jaantzen put in him. But if he's taken the serum like they suspect, he won't feel it one bit.

"Boss. Left."

A Dawn soldier is raising his carbine to shoot, Jaantzen fires before the man can take aim. Fires past him at the one who's about to jump Manu from behind — real state guard or Dawn, he's decided to consider anyone trying to kill him and his people the bad ones.

Phaera's scream pulls his attention back.

Zacharia throws her to the ground, tearing the hazmat pouch out of her hands as she falls. She kicks out, hard, but her sharp heel to his knee doesn't slow him. Zacharia sprints for the wings.

Jaantzen runs after him.

Backstage is a mess of towering curtains and holographic columns, all blocking sight lines and providing Zacharia cover. Hazy smoke still drifts through the air from the explosion. Jaantzen finds shelter in a doorway, scanning for any sign of where Zacharia has gone.

"Toshiyo. Where is he?"

"Lost him, stand by."

A pair of lighting drones dive through the hazy gloom, sweeping bright cones of light over stacked crates, cabinets, swags of cables.

"Zacharia," Jaantzen calls. "You and I need to talk."

"Do we?" The man's mocking laugh drifts through the gloom; Jaantzen can't tell which direction it's coming from. "You can't stop the rebirth of humanity any more than you can stop the rising sun."

It sounds like his voice is coming from the other side of the stage, behind that column.

"The slaughter of humanity, you mean?" Jaantzen asks. He pivots out, two steps closer to the column — and dives for cover behind a cabinet as bullets chew the floor where he'd just been standing.

"Shooter in the catwalks," Toshiyo says. "Not Zacharia."

"On it," Manu answers.

Jaantzen tests a look, and another round of bullets

slams into the wall beside his head. He can't hear any sound of Zacharia over the chaos in the auditorium; he slows his heart rate, ignoring the throbbing pain in his knee and trying not to worry about Phaera. She can take care of herself. She'll have gotten herself to safety.

They're going to get through this.

Something crashes to the stage, three meters away.

"You're clear, boss," Manu says.

Jaantzen lunges out from behind the cabinet, running towards the column he's sure Zacharia's standing behind. He skids to a stop, pistol aimed at the man in white.

Zacharia's holding the sphere in his bare hands; the red glow lights up that wicked smile, turns those ice-blue eyes into infernos. Zacharia lifts the sphere so it's in front of his face — in between Jaantzen and a kill shot. Shoot Zacharia anywhere else and it won't kill him. He'll activate the thing anyway.

"You can't stop this," he says.

"Put it down and let's talk," Jaantzen says.

Zacharia starts to laugh. "We'll talk in the new world, Mr. Jaantzen. If you're one of the lucky ones who lives to see it."

Zacharia twists his hands, the two halves of the sphere shrieking as they're forced apart, and a thin trickle of poisonous-looking red smoke begins to trickle out. His shoulders and forearms tense again to wrench it open. He grins.

A shadow lunges behind him.

Starla slashes at Zacharia's shoulder with a flash of silver in her fist, but Zacharia ducks. She seemed to expect it, though, because she pivots seamlessly, driving her knee into his gut and shoving him back. Towards

Simca, who catches him with a roundhouse kick to the jaw.

The sphere tumbles out of his hands, rolling down-stage towards the audience — spewing a coil of smoke as it goes.

"Twist it back," Toshiyo says. "But don't touch it!"

"Twist it back?" Jaantzen growls. He ducks behind the column Zacharia had stepped out from, relief washing over him when he sees the hazmat pouch lying on the ground. He bursts out of the wings, tracing the trail of poisonous red smoke to the edge of the stage. Phaera and Cavy are in its path, but they see it. And they're clearing people out of its way.

Jaantzen takes his first running steps towards them, but something heavy slams into his back. He stumbles, yelling Phaera's name and flinging the hazmat pouch towards her with as much strength as he can muster, then rolls out of the way before another blow comes.

He fires.

A gap-toothed Dawn soldier in a state guard uniform falls back, clutching his throat.

Jaantzen crawls back to his feet, every muscle scream-ing. A faint red haze drifts over the front of the stage, but it doesn't seem like any more smoke is spewing — which he hopes means Phaera has it under control. And Zacharia?

An epic fight is being waged in the wings.

Simca's fighting two Dawn soldiers at once, holding her own though she's flagging. And Starla — Jaantzen finds himself screaming as Zacharia feints and ducks, plunging the knife in his hand up at an angle to miss the lower edge of her armor. He shoves her back against the wall and she slides down, clutching her stomach.

Jaantzen unloads the rest of his magazine into Zacharia's back.

Zacharia whirls on him.

The Dawn prophet's white robes are filthy from the scuffle, blood streaks down from a gash in his forehead that's already healed. He may not be feeling the pain of those bullet holes, but there's no way the rounds Jaantzen buried in his back are healing fast enough. He has to be losing blood. He has to be weakening.

Jaantzen aims between the man's eyes. His pistol whines, empty.

Zacharia grins and lunges, impossibly fast. Ducks Jaantzen's blow and slams the pistol out of his hand, then grabs him around the throat and squeezes, his ice-blue eyes enjoying every minute.

Until they flash wide.

His grip goes slack.

Starla's crouched behind him, silver in her hand — she's too low, she's only managed to bury the dagger into Zacharia's kidney. The man whirls, throwing her back so hard her head cracks against the stage, but he stumbles before he can take another step. He yanks Starla's silver dagger from his side, staring at it in horror.

Zacharia tries to grab onto the edge of a curtain to haul himself to his feet, but his trembling, blood-slick hand slips on the fabric and he falls back to his knees. His strength is gone, Jaantzen realizes. His grace is gone, and now he's simply an old man bleeding out from a handful of bullet holes and a knife to his kidney.

Jaantzen steps past him and picks up his pistol, slotting in a fresh magazine.

Zacharia pivots to face him, panting. "I can make you — "

Jaantzen lowers the gun. A trickle of blood traces the hollow of Zacharia's cheek from where his eye used to be.

The Dawn's prophet slumps to the floor.

Behind him, people are still shouting, but the tenor has changed. There are fewer screams. More barked orders. Someone's yelling his name.

"This is Captain Onye of the New Sarjun State Guard," a voice booms. "Drop your weapons, hands up."

"Boss," Toshiyo is saying — has been saying. "Boss. These guys are real. Drop it, please."

Jaantzen lets the pistol spin on his finger and raises his hands.

## 36

## JAANTZEN

Someone snatches the gun out of his hand and Jaantzen takes deep, even breaths, turning slowly to face the state guards, who have him surrounded. They've got Simca, too, hauling her to her feet and away from Starla's bloody form. He can't tell if his goddaughter is still breathing. Phaera's yelling for him, yelling for them to let him go, but two more guards are holding her back.

He can't see Manu, which means his lieutenant has probably melted into a shadow somewhere, ready to start taking shots if he needs to.

He can't see the hazmat bag with the alien weapon in it, either. Hopefully that melted into the shadows with Manu.

"We're on the same side," Jaantzen says calmly to the man with the captain's stripes, the one whose hybrid carbine is currently set to live rounds and aimed directly at Jaantzen's chest.

The captain scowls at him. "The same side? I know exactly who you are, Mr. Jaantzen. So keep your hands where I can see them."

"I understand." Jaantzen nods to Starla, heart lurching at the blood on her face. "But she needs medical attention. Please."

The captain ignores him, jerks his chin at the two guards beside him. "Cuff him."

"He's with us," says a voice at the edge of the stage, and the state guards straighten. Jaantzen risks a glance over his shoulder to find Leone, regal in her shimmering beads, chin held high. "Tell your people to put their guns away, Captain Onye. These people are all with us."

Captain Onye doesn't move.

"He saved all of our lives," Leone snaps, piercing Onye with a glare that makes the man viscerally flinch. She crosses the line of fire to Jaantzen's side and pats his arm. "Go to Starla," she says, and he tests lowering his hands. Around him, miraculously, weapons go down.

He doesn't thank her, doesn't listen as she continues to give orders — he pushes past the state guards to get to Starla. The guards holding Simca have also let her go, and she drops to her knees and feels for Starla's pulse. Jaantzen smooths Starla's choppy hair back out of her face. A cut on her temple has sheeted her pale cheek in blood, but it's shallow. Her hand flinches in his and her eyelashes flutter, breath coming more quickly.

"Tosh, what are her stats?" Simca asks.

"Pulse is strong, but her blood pressure is dropping," Toshiyo says in his ear. "Tac vest recorded an impact in the lower right side."

"Zacharia stabbed her," Jaantzen says.

"And she definitely has a concussion." Simca fumbles at the buckles on Starla's moto jacket, swearing under her breath — Jaantzen helps her with the last of them and together they peel her jacket open. The lower edge of her shirt is soaked in blood. "We need to get her to help."

But, another miracle. Help is coming to them. A woman in a white jumpsuit with the gold Sulila symbol on her collar is jogging across the stage, a med kit slung over one shoulder. More white jumpsuits are tending to people throughout the room; Leone must have called them when she called in the real state guard.

"Emergency response," the Sulila doctor calls, and Simca moves to let her in.

"She was stabbed here," Jaantzen says. "Tac vest says her blood pressure's dropping."

The doctor nods and tears the straps free, peels up the tactical vest — "Hold this back," she orders Jaantzen — to find the gash in Starla's side. She rummages through her bag for a silver vial and screws it into a spray head, coats the wound in a shimmery silver foam, then covers it with a wad of gauze and directs Jaantzen to ease the tactical vest back over the wound. She straps the vest back into place.

"That will hold until we get her to the hospital," the doctor says. She tears open Starla's shirt collar to access the vest's data port and plugs in a scanner. Blood is splashed over Starla's neck, but when Jaantzen pulls back her collar to see the origin, there's no wound. Not her blood, then.

Starla's eyes flutter open at his touch and her hand flexes in his.

"She also hit her head," he tells the doctor.

She nods and unplugs her scanner, apparently satisfied with the data she got from the vest. "We'll take a look at the hospital. She's stabilizing, she's going to be all right." She glances between him and Starla. "You . . . work with her?"

"She's my daughter."

"We need to take her to the hospital, sir." She waves her arm at someone across the room, and a jumpsuited man with a stretcher tucked under his arm jogs towards them.

Starla blinks at him, her gaze in and out of focus.

"You're going to be all right," Jaantzen signs with his free hand, but her eyes fall closed again, he can't tell if she saw him.

"She'll be okay, boss," Simca says. "I'll stay with her." Her voice has a breathy, sharp edge to it, and Jaantzen finally tears his attention from Starla's prone form long enough to study her. She's holding her own arm pressed to her side.

"You're injured?"

"Janked my shoulder," she says. She flashes the Sulila doctor a smile masking pain. "We can take a look at it when we get to the hospital, I promise."

The medic with the stretcher unrolls it beside Starla and Jaantzen helps them ease her onto it, then stands back as they strap her down. There's a quiet hum as Starla's stretcher lifts into the air. Jaantzen bends to kiss her forehead; he breathes in her familiar spark of engine oil and sweat and vanilla. Her eyelids flutter open again, and he presses "I love you" into her hand. It closes around his, squeezes once.

"I'll meet you at the hospital," he tells Simca. She gives him a fierce smile and turns to follow the medics.

Jaantzen watches them go, finally processing the rest of the scene unfolding in the Founder's Room.

Captain Onye and his team are leaving Jaantzen's

people alone now — they're occupied helping the wounded and sorting the remaining Dawn soldiers from the rest of the crowd, aided by Chief Justice Geum-ja Leone and Mayor Elena Hu. Several of Zacharia's soldiers survived and are now in cuffs. Several bystanders in the crowd were wounded, including two people in the front row of seats who must have gotten a lungful of the weapon's smoke before it was deactivated — they're contorted, skin scorched and jaws still wide with screaming. Just like the corpse by the podium that must be Prime Minister Nikolas de Grazal; his chief of staff, Madinia Ulrich, kneels beside him with tears streaming down her cheeks.

He spots Phaera near a knot of medics surrounding a woman in gray. She's holding the woman's hand as they lift the stretcher; a medic moves to reveal Lhasa Demosga.

There's one body in the room no one is much paying attention to, though. Jaantzen limps a few short steps to where Felipe Zacharia is lying on his back, his remaining eye staring unseeing up at the ceiling. His white robes are soaked in blood.

"Should have been content with your own immortality," Jaantzen murmurs. A shiver traces down his spine as he imagines what could have been if Zacharia had had his way. Imagines opening the doors to this room and finding the place filled with bodies, all blackened and contorted like the ones in the front row. Of finding Phaera here among them.

He turns slowly to take in the room, partly to reassure himself that didn't happen, partly to search for anyone who might overhear him.

"Toshiyo," he says quietly when he's certain no one's around.

"Yeah, boss."

"The weapons?"

"Manu brought me the one from the capitol building. And the other one's secured. In a manner of speaking." She sighs. "Coeur has it."

Unease creeps through his gut. "Connect me?"

A moment later, the connection pops in his ear.

"Thala?"

"That was a wild fucking ride, Willem," Coeur says. A siren wails behind her voice, she sounds like she's still out in the street. "Everything good on your end?"

"Zacharia's dead. I'm sorry I didn't save him for you."

"Eh, it's fine. 'Preciate the thought. How'd you do it?"

"Bullet through the eye."

"That's no fun. Too quick."

"I was trying to stay alive." And he's done discussing the best ways to kill people with Blackheart. "Toshiyo tells me your people secured the first weapon. We have the other. We need to destroy them."

Down in the auditorium, the Sulila team has whisked away Lhasa Demosga, and Phaera has turned back to the stage, searching for him. His heart wrenches at her smile and he returns it involuntarily. Holds up a finger — *I'll be right there.*

Thala Coeur is laughing in his ear. "I know what you're thinking," she says. "You're worried I'm going to get power crazy and keep this thing so you and I can have a dick-measuring contest over who controls the biggest alien virus bomb."

"And are you?"

"Yeah, no. This shit's gotta go. Let's take care of it tonight."

Relief washes through him. "I'll be in touch."

"Hey," Coeur says before he can cut the connection. "I just saw them pull your kid out on a stretcher. She gonna be okay?"

"They tell me she is."

She lets out a breath. "Good."

"You should get out of here. The place is crawling with state guards."

"I can take care of myself, Willem." She sounds amused. "Talk soon."

And the line goes dead.

Jaantzen makes his way to the front of the stage and down the stairs into the auditorium, knee screaming with every step. Each step is worth it, though, when Phaera buries herself in his embrace. He breathes in her scent, smoothing his hand down her back, across the expanse of skin bared by her dress. She shivers in his arms.

"Are you all right?" he murmurs into her hair.

"I wasn't fast enough." Her voice catches and he gently releases her, uncertain what she means. She's staring at the two corpses in the front row.

Jaantzen tucks a strand of hair behind her ear. "If you hadn't been as fast as you were, we'd all be dead."

The corner of her mouth tugs into a smile. "Same with you."

But he can't feel pride for that — he'd let Zacharia lay a trap that had almost gotten Phaera killed again. He'd once again left her exposed and in danger.

"I was too late for the prime minister," Jaantzen says.

"Zacharia killed him, not you." Phaera squeezes his hand.

He traces a hand down Phaera's arm, but before he can say anything, he catches sight of a pair of women heading towards them. Madinia Ulrich, tear tracks drying on her cheeks, and Mayor Elena Hu.

"Mr. Jaantzen," Ulrich says, her voice hoarse. "Let me formally thank you. This could have been — " She glances over her shoulder, where medics are finally removing de Grazal's body. "This evening could have been a far greater tragedy."

"Outside in the plaza, too, I understand," says Mayor Hu. She holds out a hand. "Elena Hu," she says, as though she needs to introduce herself. "It's a pleasure to meet you, Mr. Jaantzen. And I have a lot of questions."

"I would be happy to provide answers," Jaantzen says. "Tomorrow. My goddaughter was injured in the fighting and I need to be with her."

"Of course. Come see me tomorrow." Hu turns to Phaera. "And I can't think of a single city council member who would have thrown themselves on a bomb like that. You and I should also talk."

"I would like that," Phaera says.

Jaantzen lifts an eyebrow at Phaera when the other two women leave them once more alone. "City council?" he asks.

Phaera shakes her head. "She brought it up earlier tonight. Is Starla all right?"

"I think she will be."

"Then we should go to the hospital. Is there anything else you need to do here?"

"I don't think so. Where did Cavy go?"

"With Lhasa. She's . . ." Phaera's lips thin. "They didn't know yet, if she'd be all right. She lost a lot of blood."

"Then let's go." Jaantzen slips his arm around her shoulders and she melts into him. Here, not just in public but among *her* people, in front of potential business and political prospects, the length of her body is pressed against his side, her warmth radiating through him, and when she turns her tired smile up at him the entire world fades away until all he can see is her.

Her arm tightens around his waist. "You can put more weight on me if you need to," she says, and he frowns at her in surprise. "Your knee."

"It's fine."

She laughs, husky, and the sound thrums through his chest. "Liar. I told Gia the other night I have her back about surgery. Now that this is over — "

Geum-ja Leone calls his name from across the room, piercing them both with it like a spear.

## 37

## JAANTZEN

Phaera stiffens beneath his arm, the easiness with which she'd allowed her body to relax against his vanishing. Her open relief, exhaustion, hope — everything in her expression that's honestly *Phaera* disappears behind a perfectly poised mask. Her hand slips from his waist and cool air fills the new space between them.

Leone strolls across the auditorium in a shiver of beads, brow furrowed in a practiced combination of concern and sorrow. "Willem, Phaera, I'm sure you're exhausted, but I'm so glad I caught you."

"Trust me," Jaantzen murmurs in Phaera's ear, and the briefest glitch flickers through Phaera's mask, revealing fury below the surface. She gives him a too-sharp, too-bright smile; he brushes the back of his hand down her arm, but she doesn't respond to his touch.

"Geum-ja!" Phaera turns to the other woman. "Are you all right?"

Leone presses a hand to her sternum, rubies and gold glinting on her wrist, and it suddenly hits him why she wore that bracelet tonight. It wasn't for him. It was to get under Phaera's skin.

"How horrible," Leone says. "Willem, why didn't you tell me what you knew about Zacharia? This weapon he had?"

Ah, yes, already shifting the blame away from herself. "We were still learning what we could," he says. "I'm grateful for your help."

"Oh, of course." Leone turns to Phaera. "Darling, you're so brave, though of course you knew your audience. Were you just speaking with Elena Hu?"

"I did what seemed right." Phaera's good. A month ago, Jaantzen wouldn't have been able to tell how forced her smile is.

"We'll have to have lunch and strategize how to approach Hu after this so you make the best impression," Leone says. "You don't want her to think you're reaching."

Jaantzen smooths his fingers over the small of Phaera's back, willing her to stay calm. Leone is in the palm of their hand — all they have to do is make it through a few more uncomfortable conversations and they can push her out of power cleanly.

"But poor Lhasa," Leone says. "I'll have to go visit her at the hospital tomorrow."

"You should probably let her rest," Phaera's voice is so polite it could shatter, but there's a dangerous edge beneath.

Leone's lips purse at Phaera's tone. "I can see you've had a lot of excitement tonight, my dear," she says, then turns to Jaantzen, the angle of her body subtly cutting Phaera out of the conversation. "What did you do with it?" Leone asks quietly. "The . . . bomb."

Jaantzen takes a sharp breath — does she really think

she can treat Phaera like this? — but Phaera catches his eye, shakes her head ever so slightly, and he bites back what he was about to say. Dammit, if Phaera can keep her calm right now, he owes it to her not to be the one to eviscerate Leone and set them all back.

"You and I will discuss the next steps," Jaantzen says. "But tonight I need to get to Starla. I'll come by tomorrow."

"Good." She pulls him down into an embrace, then turns to Phaera. Phaera's smile as she leans in to kiss Leone's cheek is so perfect it scares him. Leone beams at them both, then brushes a speck of dust off Jaantzen's lapel with a possessive finger. "I'm glad to be working with you," she says to him. "Together, you and I can accomplish so much more for this city than either of us could alone."

"I'm looking forward to it," Jaantzen says. "Good night, Geum-ja."

When he turns away from Leone and offers Phaera his arm, she takes it. Spine straight, heels sharp, head high, and he recognizes this Phaera D from gossip columns and social events, but when he studies her face out of the corner of his eye he can't find a trace of the woman he loves. Neither of them speak as they walk through the curving hall to the Capitol's grand entry, as they exit the building to stand at the top of the stairs and survey the People's Plaza.

Sirens still cut through the air, floodlights in police colors paint the scene as the state guard and BPD clear out the rest of the straggling crowd. He counts almost a dozen charred, contorted bodies around the statue in the center of the plaza, and medics in white Sulila jumpsuits are treating others.

He'd hoped for better, expected worse.

He grips the railing as they descend the stairs to where Manu's got one shoulder propped against a sandstone column, Oriol sitting beyond him on the edge of a retaining wall. The evening has cooled, but Phaera's touch on his arm radiates furious heat.

Manu pushes himself off his lean to greet them, Oriol starts to stand. And Phaera stops on the bottom step, hand pulling free from Jaantzen's arm as he reaches the plaza. He turns back to her with a frown.

"Was I convincing?" she asks.

Jaantzen's pulse slows; there's a trap in those words. With her standing one step up, they're nearly the same height; she lifts her chin in challenge.

"Was. I. Convincing."

"You were perfect."

Anger flares in her eyes. "Good. Because if I have to pretend I'm fine working with the woman who tried to kill me, I want to make sure I'm more convincing than Juric has been about working with Coeur."

Manu scrubs a hand over the back of his neck at that, no comment.

When Jaantzen reaches for her hand, she steps back and laughs — it's thin and brittle with exhaustion. "Just like that, you and Leone are fine." She gives Oriol and Manu each a long look before returning to him. "I don't know how you do it."

"She and I are not fine. Phaera — "

"I admire how easily you can brush off a grudge, I really do. First Coeur, now Leone, but did you think for one goddamn second maybe the rest of us can't just smile at them without reliving what they put us through?

Jaantzen, she tried to kill me. Or do you actually believe her story that Tierren went rogue?"

"I know what Leone did."

"You don't have the faintest idea. She made up with you, but she's going to keep grinding me down until there's nothing left, and you're going to let her do it. Because all that matters is your plan."

"Our plan, Phaera." He tamps down anger, lowers his voice. "Do you want me to walk back into that building and kill her right now?" Her face blanches. "If you ask me to, I will. I know she has to go. But to do this right we need it to be airtight. We need patience. And that means striking a deal, for now."

"I don't have patience," she snaps, but she doesn't sound angry anymore, just tired. "I'm exhausted. I'm overwhelmed, I'm grieving. And now I smell like her fucking cologne. And maybe you all can live day after day being hunted like this, but I can't. And Leone . . ." She glances over her shoulder and Jaantzen looks past her, half expecting Leone to be standing at the top of the stairs, watching them. She's not, but it doesn't quell the churning in his gut.

"Leone isn't going to quit," Phaera says. "She's not going to play fair, and as long as she's in power, I have a target on my back. I understand your plan, but I can't play this game anymore." She cups his cheek with her good hand and leans forward to kiss him. His heart races, like it always does, but this time it's different.

Phaera's kiss is sweet. Unhurried.

Final.

"Good night, Jaantzen," she says. "Go be with your daughter."

He catches her hand as it slides down his arm,

clinging to the one point of contact bridging the vast gulf between them: her fingertips.

"Good night?" he asks quietly. "Or goodbye?"

"Give me a few days," she says. And she squeezes his fingers and walks away. Oriol stands to follow her, giving Jaantzen a solemn nod of respect.

Manu props his shoulder blades back against the sandstone column, shoving his hands in his pockets as Phaera's footsteps echo off the facade in time to Jaantzen's heartbeat; his chest squeezes painfully as they fade around the corner. Jaantzen can't tell by his lieutenant's face how badly he screwed up.

"Was I supposed to follow her?" Jaantzen finally asks.

Manu shakes his head. "Give her space. She knows this is going to take time. It's been a rough night."

"But she's right about Leone. She may think she has a truce with me, but that won't protect anyone else." Cold realization seeps through him as he replays the conversation, feeling every one of Leone's biting comments to Phaera like physical blows. Phaera, the Demosgas, Mizal — even Ulrich and Tabari. Coeur. They're all counting on him pushing Leone out of power without destabilizing the city. The long-game plan will do just that, but he's lying to himself if he thinks he's strong enough to survive a repeat of that conversation.

Jaantzen shakes his head. "I don't think I can do this."

"Boss. Phaera doesn't want you to go to jail and she doesn't want you to bring Leone's head home like a trophy. She trusts you — but she has every right to be angry."

"As do you."

Manu's shoulders rise and fall with a deep, exhausted breath. "I'm not," he says finally. "I was, but I know it wasn't an easy decision for you to make. I gotta admit I've been pleasantly surprised."

"It still could end badly."

"I'd never say Coeur's changed. But she . . . she's been useful. A lotta people would be dead tonight if it wasn't for her."

Jaantzen sighs. "The weapons. We need to meet with her tonight and destroy them both. I'll take care of it, you should head home."

"I got it, boss." Manu straightens and claps Jaantzen's arm. "Tosh and I already came up a plan and I set up a meet with Damyati. I'll drop you off at the hospital."

"You're sure?"

"I'm fine with it. Truly." Manu flashes him a smile. "Still got dibs if we ever gotta take her out."

"She's all yours."

"Good." Manu's smile sobers. "Give Phaera time."

Jaantzen glances back the way she and Oriol walked with some desperate hope she might have turned back — but she's gone. And the coldly smoldering fury he feels for Geum-ja Leone, the certainty they're on the right path to removing her from power for good, isn't enough to fill the aching hole behind his sternum.

## 38

## TOSHIYO

"Has it woken up yet?"

Toshiyo jumps, startled out of the silent world she'd been drifting in, accompanied only by her own thoughts. El's standing in the doorway to one of the larger medical bays on floor twelve, which they've converted to a holding cell for the new alien. Toshiyo's sitting with her legs crossed on the seat beneath her, staring at the desk they set up in the corner. Lucky's absorbed in some sort of spatial geometry game he found in the entertainment deck; his older cousin is curled up on the far side of the room, safely behind a double shield of a forcefield and ballistic mesh.

"I knocked," El says. "Didn't seem like you heard me."

"I was thinking." Toshiyo rolls her neck and shoves away the files cluttering up her desktop. Alliance research notes, Zacharia's writings, White Star forums — she's already read it all, but she still can't figure the whole puzzle out. She's missing the *why*.

*Why* inject human test subjects with alien venom just to see what happened, like the Alliance had? *Why* assume that humans who survived the ordeal were changed for the better just because they healed quickly when you sliced them open? *Why* take that to mean your god wanted you to unleash an alien disease over the entire remaining human population?

And why the *hell* did anyone listen to Zacharia when he said his god was speaking through him?

El tucks a stray strand of blue hair behind his ear. "Thinking about?"

Whew.

Toshiyo takes a deep breath. "You know those guys I killed, back at the deathtrap?"

"The ones who were trying to kill us? Toshiyo, you did the right thing."

Toshiyo's not sure she believes him, entirely. But she waves away his concern — that's not what's bothering her. "The Dawn were monsters, right?"

El settles into the chair across from her, letting her talk. She likes that. He gives her the space to puzzle through things aloud when she needs to, without trying to interject.

"I mean, maybe they weren't monsters, individually," she says. "But they killed a lot of innocent people, and they were going to kill more. If I think of them as monsters, it doesn't bother me that I killed them."

"It's all right if it does bother you," El says quietly.

"I'll tell you if I need to talk about it." And maybe she will, but right now that's not it. Toshiyo studies the alien across the room. "She needs a name."

"She?"

Toshiyo nods. "That's what they said in the Alliance notes. They didn't name her, though — they called her Subject D."

"D. So there were others." A muscle twitches in El's cheek; he gets it. "They did this to others."

"Five, total," Toshiyo says. "She's the only one that survived. It's pretty horrible, how the other ones died. But it's even worse to read it in the scientists' notes, all abstract and clinical. I guess they figured the aliens were monsters, too. Even though they're obviously intelligent."

"We humans have never been too concerned with how intelligent a species is when we needed something to experiment on," El points out.

Toshiyo sighs. "Even the human test subjects — I don't understand how they could be so cruel."

"Maybe they figured the prisoners were monsters."

"But they weren't serial killers or anything." She'd looked up the records of every one of the test subjects she could actually identify a name for. "You know Redrock. Some were murderers like Zacharia, but mostly they were political prisoners. Resistance fighters. Some kid who got caught shoplifting and had his sentence classified as terrorism so Leone and the Alliance could make a few dollars off his free labor."

"I know, Toshiyo."

"I know you know. But I hate it."

When he pulls her up into a hug it doesn't make anything she said less true, but it's warm and strong, and it pushes the teetering mountain of misery in this world back just enough so it doesn't feel like it's about to come crashing down on them all. Toshiyo closes her eyes, letting El's presence work its magic and chase away the white noise.

Finally, she takes a deep breath. "At least we managed to save — holy *shit.*"

She yelps and flinches back in El's grip — she'd

opened her eyes to find the creature crouched at the forcefield a few meters away, golden gaze boring into hers, maw stretched wide.

El whirls, pushing himself in front of her, and Toshiyo stumbles back against the desk, heart pounding. How does something so big move so silently? Lucky's been doing that more and more. Despite his ungainly, roly-poly shape and klutzy wings, he can go into stealth mode when he wants to.

"It's all right," Toshiyo says to El. "The forcefield will hold."

She sketched up the plans days ago, running them by Starla until they were both confident they had a design that would secure something even more powerful — and far more angry — than Lucky. Lucky's sharp claws can snag the ballistic mesh, which they'd tried to use in the deathtrap, but they hadn't tested it with a forcefield. The deathtrap's generators couldn't drum up enough energy to power one.

She'd debated over including the ballistic mesh. Her goal was to build a room that says, *You're safe, you'll be okay here,* and she worried that the visual of the mesh would undermine that. But in the end, she worried more that the alien would run headfirst into the forcefield and be surprised, injured, and angry. If they were going to keep her a prisoner for now, best not to lie about it right off the bat.

Give her plenty of space to roam and a comfortable place to rest. A nest of blankets, bandaged wounds, plenty of fresh water for when she wakes up.

Now to convince Lucky's big cousin they're not actually the enemy.

Lucky's dropped his game, and now he's flapping his

wings with excitement, chirping at a frequency Toshiyo's human ears can barely hear.

She's heard him make that noise before, Toshiyo realizes, but she didn't think of it as communication. She may barely be able to make it out, but the bigger alien's massive ears swivel towards Lucky. She growls at him, but it doesn't seem threatening, more annoyed. She drags one claw-tipped wing along the forcefield, the trailing sparks the same liquid gold as her eyes.

"Hey, Goldie," Toshiyo signs and says. The creature's head wobbles back and forth as she watches Toshiyo warily. "I'm Toshiyo. This is El. We're friends. This is Lucky. A friend." She points back at the alien. "You're a friend."

Lucky grimaces in excitement. "Friend," he signs.

"Goldie?" murmurs El.

Toshiyo shrugs. "She's got nice eyes."

Lucky stares up at Toshiyo and drags his own claws along the same forcefield. "Safe," he signs, glancing at Goldie and then back. "Friend safe let out?"

"In a bit, buddy," Toshiyo signs back, though she suspects it'll be a while before she feels comfortable being in the same room as the huge alien. Or letting Lucky in with her — she doesn't know anything about their species. Do they eat their young? Protect them? Will this new creature even recognize Lucky as one of her own species after spending her entire life chained to a table and experimented on by humans?

Goldie glares at them both and stalks away, shoulder slamming into the forcefield as she turns. A test, maybe. She paces the length of the room, limping, but it quickly becomes clear she doesn't have the energy to do much exploring. Toshiyo has left several comfortable surfaces for her to choose from, but finally Goldie returns to the nest of blankets in the corner, gingerly making herself comfortable in them. She hisses at Toshiyo when she catches her watching, then her expression changes. Toshiyo can't imagine what the alien expressions mean, but she gets the sense Goldie is listening to something only she can hear.

"Any luck with our new friend?"

Toshiyo smiles to find Gia in the doorway, Tevi following behind.

"I thought you weren't going to start without us," Gia says.

"I didn't want to wake you two up."

Tevi's silver curls are still damp from the shower, but there are dark circles under his eyes and his gait is stiff. Gia looks like she's back to her new invincible self, and Toshiyo hopes that's true. Because there's another image she can't shake from yesterday: Gia, bloodied and broken, barely able to stand.

Good riddance to the monsters.

"She still seems pretty weak," El says. "And not too happy to see us. But she and Lucky might be able to communicate."

"She's still in my head, too," Gia says, matter-of-fact. Maybe after the events of the last few weeks, nothing seems abnormal any more. "She doesn't feel threatened, exactly, but she's not happy to be here."

"Sorry, Goldie," Toshiyo says and signs. "We're trying to keep you safe. Are you hungry?"

Goldie stares at her blankly.

Toshiyo mimes eating, then opens the cooler she had sent up from the kitchen and pulls out a container of radishes. Lucky trills in delight and tumble-runs her way, catching the radish she tosses him and shredding it in his terrifying rows of teeth. She pours the rest into a bowl and passes them through the feeding slot she'd set up in the forcefield. Goldie watches her with distrust.

"What were the Alliance feeding her?" El asks.

"A nutritional slurry," Toshiyo says. "Mostly through a tube because she refused to eat otherwise."

"Poor thing."

"Yeah. And who knows what the Dawn were feeding her — she's all skin and bones. I figured I'd start with Lucky's favorite foods, and then we could try other things later to find out her preferences."

Toshiyo pulls out a fillet of raw fish, feeds Lucky a bit first, then pushes the rest through for Goldie. After a long while, hunger and curiosity must get the better of her mistrust, because she uncoils from her nest and stalks over to the food, sniffing it warily before turning on Toshiyo with a high-pitched shriek and gnashing of teeth.

"Let's give her some privacy," says Gia.

They cross to the far side of the room, where Toshiyo gives Lucky another fish of his own — but instead of eating it there, he spears it in his claws and waddle-hops to sit on the floor near Goldie. He nips delicately at the flesh as though reassuring her it's safe, and a moment later, Goldie tears into the food on her own. Lucky gives another series of chirps, almost too high to be audible.

"Goldie, huh?" Gia asks.

"Because of her eyes," El says with a wink at Toshiyo.

"And I don't think we can pronounce whatever she calls herself," Toshiyo says. "But maybe someday she'll be able to tell us what she wants to be called."

"Taking Lucky out to the Andel School to study him was one thing," Tevi says, and Toshiyo cracks her ring fingers, bracing herself for what's inevitably coming next. "But this one? We need to do a lot more thinking about security before we consider it."

Toshiyo straightens, surprised. "You're still considering it at all?"

"If anything, what happened yesterday with the Dawn reinforced to me that this needs to get out of the shadows, and be studied for real. Otherwise the only people who have access to it are those with questionable motives." He waves a hand. "I don't mean you. And I don't even mean Jaantzen."

A voice from the doorway answers him. "I'm glad to hear it."

All heads turn to the boss. Jaantzen's already dressed sharply despite the early hour, despite how late he got back last night. He radiates calm; Toshiyo's pulse picks up.

It's time.

"We were just discussing the needs of a facility for these two," Tevi says. "That is, if you're still behind the idea of an independent, nonpartisan institution."

"You have no idea how grateful I will be to have to walk into my medical bay and not see an alien," Jaantzen says.

Lucky swivels his head to him, then turns back to Goldie and makes Jaantzen's namesign. "Friend," he tells her.

Jaantzen blinks at them, turns back to the humans. "I have some business to attend to this morning," he tells Gia and Tevi. Gia shoots Toshiyo a look — she's got enough history with the boss to recognize something's up by how sharply he's dressed, that deeply calm focus. Toshiyo pretends not to notice. Gia may be helping out with the aliens; that doesn't mean she gets to know all the boss's business these days. "Feel free to make yourselves at home as long as you like. However makes the most sense to study our new friends, whether you come here, we build a facility out there, we'll make it work. Toshiyo?"

She pushes herself to her feet, heartbeat already smoothed back out into logistics mode, and follows him into the hall.

"Everything's ready, boss," she says quietly. "I'll keep a watch on the security in real time to make sure there are no surprises."

"I assumed you'd try to talk me out of this."

Toshiyo shakes her head. "You're doing the right thing." She smiles, then hugs him; it seems to catch him by surprise. "I've got your back. Let me know what else you need, and when your meeting with the mayor is this afternoon. I can come help you explain . . ." Toshiyo turns back to the room behind them, where Lucky has hauled his entertainment deck over to the mesh and is demonstrating the spatial geometry game to Goldie. She seems . . . suspicious yet interested? "All this," Toshiyo finishes.

"Thank you. I have no idea how I'd explain it on my own."

"I've got your back, boss."

She watches him walk down the hallway like she has so many times before and a quiet peace slowly unfurls in her chest.

Everyone's home safe. Gia and El are teasing Tevi behind her while Lucky and Goldie get to know each other. Starla's going to be fine, she's still at the hospital with Simca watching over her. Manu and Oriol — Toshiyo checks her comm for the notification — are in place. And for the first time in what feels like forever, they're not staring down the barrel of yet another problem.

When she turns back, El's watching her with a lifted eyebrow.

"Something I need to check on," she tells them all. "I'll be back in a few."

"Is everything all right?" he signs.

She grins back. "Everything's perfect."

## 39

## JAANTZEN

The last time Jaantzen walked up these broad marble steps to Chief Justice Geum-ja Leone's home, he'd left with a declaration of open war between them. Her vendetta against him nearly cost him his lieutenant. His goddaughter. Gia, Tevi. The Anahoys. It had cost him Julieta.

And maybe in the end it will cost him Phaera.

He'd expected to feel tired this morning — it was well after midnight when the doctors finally finished surgery and told them Starla was going to pull through fine. He'd expected to be apprehensive, expected a sense of turmoil. But this decision has him wide awake and utterly, deathly calm.

Leone greets him at the door with a smile that's lost some of its sheen from the night before. She's dressed already for the day in a rich maroon suit, though her powdery makeup doesn't quite hide the dark thumbprints under her eyes, the pinch of exhaustion in her movements.

She eyes the bottle he offers. "I try not to drink before

work," she says, but her smile widens as she slips it out of the wrappings. "Oh! This vintage is impossible to find."

"I hear it's superb."

"I'm sure we'll have plenty of opportunities to share a glass later."

It doesn't even bother him, now, returning her smile. "I'm looking forward to it."

Leone waves him airily inside, sensible heels clicking in her ornate entryway. "Thank you for coming by, Willem, especially after the late night. I was just finishing breakfast, will you join me?"

"I'd take a cup of coffee."

She apparently takes breakfast in the formal dining room, a lone place setting at the head of her table. A servant brings a second cup and a silver carafe to fill his coffee and refresh hers, then melts back into the kitchen, leaving the carafe behind. Jaantzen already knows this room is safe to talk in — Admant did Leone's security, years ago, and installed the privacy features here. She's wearing the gold and ruby bracelet that's paired to the system, as she had last night.

"Your goddaughter?" Leone asks as she picks up her fork. She swipes away the news feed that was quietly playing in the tabletop. "Is she all right?"

"She'll be fine." Jaantzen traces a finger over the rim of the coffee cup; steam dampens his skin. "They kept her overnight for observation, but they should be releasing her any minute."

"We can make this quick. I want to go in early today and start cleaning up the mess."

"Lhasa's going to be all right, as well. She should be up for visitors today."

The blink of surprise is so quick he might not have

caught it if he'd not been watching. But Leone had forgotten all about Lhasa Demosga, whom she'd played at being so worried about the night before.

"Oh! I'll have to go see her, then."

"I'm sure she'd appreciate that."

Leone spears a piece of fruit. "Last night could have been catastrophic. Bulari is truly blessed that you and your people were there to help. It amazes me, how much influence you've had on this city's history, almost all unrecognized."

"It's how I prefer it."

"Don't be modest, Willem. People know what you did last night, and the news coverage has been incredibly flattering. Haven't you seen it?"

"I haven't." He has had a singular focus this morning.

"Well, I think we let the media play out a few days. I already have a plan for how we spin what comes next."

"Perhaps we can both meet with Letizia Diamante tomorrow and come up with a strategy." The offer is out so easily, it's almost like someone else is speaking the words.

"She won't have a problem working with me, after all that bad press?"

"She'll work where the money is." Jaantzen takes a sip of his coffee, considers Leone a moment. "As for the others?"

Leone sighs and rests her fork on the edge of her plate. "We're not going to have a problem, are we?"

"No." Jaantzen takes a sip of the coffee. "Because you are going to make sure we don't."

Her flicker of uncertainty is viciously satisfying.

"You trust me," Leone says. "Don't you?"

"And I've vouched to the others for you. But Aiax,

Mizal, Calanthe?" Jaantzen shakes his head — *What can I do?* "They need more than reassurances. They want leverage."

"Willem!"

"Listen to me, Geum-ja." He pulls out his comm and swipes a file onto the table in front of her. A draft of the article Kumail Anh and Analie Cruz wrote together, containing every shred of damning evidence linking Leone to the prisoner scandal and the kickbacks from Alliance companies. He sips his coffee slowly while she reads through it, bright spots of color rising in her cheeks. When she's done, she sits back stiffly and folds her hands in front of her on the table, her breakfast forgotten.

"This will go to publication unless you record a confession admitting to everything you've done," Jaantzen says.

"So you can hold that over my head instead?"

"It's the only way I could get the others to agree to work with you," he says. "This is your forfeit, our guarantee. It will be secret, and will not be released unless you break your end of the bargain."

"You can trust me."

"It's not up to me, Geum-ja. There are those who want to throw you out of this town, and I can't stop them without this."

The pad of one thumb is kneading the bony knuckles of her other hand; Leone is too upset to even notice the tell.

"And you'll what?" she asks. "Each have a copy to threaten me with?"

Jaantzen shakes his head. "There will be a single copy, and I'll keep it safe. Record a confession, and Ms. Diamante will pull the story and burn all traces of the evidence they found. I can't stop rumors, but no one will be able to prove a thing against you."

She swallows, knuckles white.

"Do you trust me, Geum-ja?"

Her nostrils flare, but finally she nods. "I trust you."

Jaantzen pulls out a recording cube and sets it on the table between them.

"Start with the prisoners," he says. "Don't forget to mention working with Acheta. And the headhunter you hired to kill Phaera."

He turns the cube on, and after a long moment, Leone begins talking.

His second cup of coffee's empty by the time she finally finishes, and Jaantzen stops the recording, pockets the cube. Leone's jaw is clenched tight, her face bloodless beneath the makeup.

"I know that was hard," he says. "But it's a good first step towards restoring people's trust."

"And are you satisfied?" she says bitterly.

"I am."

Leone types a command in the table, pushes her chair back. "Then I need to go, I'm due at the courthouse. Do you need a ride somewhere? I just called my driver."

"I'm fine. I'll walk you out."

He pings his own driver while she collects her handbag, then holds the door for her, offers his arm. Both of their spinners are waiting at the bottom of the stairs. Jaantzen's heart beats perfectly slow and steady as he opens the door to her spinner.

She pulls him down to kiss his cheek in farewell. "Don't think I won't find something worse on you, Willem," she murmurs in his ear.

He inclines his head, the cloying scent of her perfume clinging to his collar. "I don't doubt it for a moment."

She gives him one last poisonous smile as he helps her inside, and she's already seated before she realizes someone's sitting in the bench seat across from hers. Leone starts to push back out, but Jaantzen's grip is firm.

Thala Coeur grins and taps an electric barb against her thigh, one gloved thumb on the trigger. "Good morning," she drawls.

"You're supposed to be dead." Jaantzen can't see her face, but there's a tremble in Leone's voice.

Coeur's shrug is liquid. "I'm a hard bitch to kill. Gonna find out real soon if you are, too."

Leone twists in Jaantzen's grip. "You wouldn't dare," she snarls at him. "This city will crumble without me."

"It will finally be able to breathe," Jaantzen corrects.

"You and I had a deal."

"Did we?" Jaantzen's going to cherish the moment Leone's righteous indignation drains into fear for the rest of his life. "Did you really think I would shrug off Julieta's death? The headhunter you sent after Phaera and Manu? Did you really think I don't care about the people you've cut through to get to me?"

Before she can answer, Coeur leans forward and slaps a tranq tab on the side of Leone's neck. The older woman stops struggling, her eyes wide with fear, her muscles going slack.

Coeur cracks her neck and dissolves the panel between the back seat and the driver. "Let's get this show on the road," she calls.

Jaantzen releases Leone's arm and she slumps in the seat. "Goodbye, Geum-ja."

Phaera opens the door to her apartment wearing a lounge set in warm cream, a deep blue silk robe splashed with large cream flowers, and a politely distant expression. He wonders if it's what she normally wears on a lazy morning at home, expects not. It's a form of armor, though whether she was expecting him or just fortifying herself for the day after a rough night, he's not sure.

What he does know is that her throat is bare, a banner of red and violet and black rope-burn scabs she's carefully avoided letting him see since the night it happened. She'd had time to cover it before answering the door, and the fact that she didn't is a statement. He forces himself not to look away, the truth she's been hiding from him slowly dawning. It will be years before those scars fade. If they ever do.

He lifts his gaze to meet her defiant one.

"I'm sorry for coming over unannounced," he says. He can't tell if she's happy to see him. She hasn't moved from the doorway — not exactly blocking him, certainly not welcoming him in. "I wanted to take you to breakfast. There's a new restaurant in the Tamarind I think you would love."

"Breakfast?" Phaera laughs in bitter surprise, then shakes her head. "With an entourage of bodyguards and guns and smiles and pretending I'm fine? Jaantzen, I'm too tired for that. But thank you. Maybe in a few days? I still need some time."

She starts to close the door.

"No entourage," he says. "Just us."

She blinks at him.

"It's safe. Leone's gone."

Phaera drags in a breath, lets it out slowly, but she doesn't speak. Her gaze doesn't break.

"Officially, she fled the planet after being tipped off that a damning article was about to be published. She left for Indira early this morning under an assumed name. She'll stay with friends in Arquelle until they report her missing. At some point, a confession she recorded before she left will surface, confirming all the allegations."

"She confessed?"

"To everything. Including what she did to you."

Phaera closes her eyes a moment, hand tightening on the doorframe as though for support. Jaantzen clenches his hands at his sides to keep from reaching for her.

"But she's not headed to Arquelle," Phaera finally says. "The truth, Jaantzen."

"She's dead."

"Did you kill her?"

He could say no and technically not be lying. But she doesn't need him to protect her from the truth. And he can't live with not being honest with her. Not anymore.

"Thala pulled the trigger," he says. "But Leone's dead because I ordered it."

Her gaze falls from his, a muscle jumps in her jaw. "Okay," she says; she doesn't sound okay at all. But she steps back, holding the door for him. "Come in. We don't need to go out, I can make us breakfast."

Jaantzen doesn't move. It's an invitation to continue the conversation — just not somewhere they might be seen together. It tears through him, even though he understands. He doesn't know what kinds of connections she made last night, what kinds of influential people she met. But he does know spending time with him has already been bad for her ambitions. Maybe she's finally coming to realize it herself.

"I understand things have changed," he says quietly. "But if you don't want to be seen in public with me anymore, I need you to tell me."

When she meets his gaze again, there's heat in it. Her good hand slides up his lapel, over his jaw, fingernails on the back of his neck as she pulls him down, her lips so soft and searing on his that he can't remember how to breathe. His entire body is on fire when she finally releases him.

Phaera steps back, tracing the pad of her thumb over her own lower lip; she seems almost as surprised as he is. "It's not that," she says with the faintest hint of a smile. "I'd rather spend some time with you in private first. Come in, Jaantzen."

Her apartment smells like coffee, like her perfume. The entryway and open living space are floored with terra-cotta tile, the curtains are open and flowing in the morning breeze, the view is of the brick building next door. Her furnishings are mismatched; well-loved antiques, trinkets, and mementos fill the shelves and hang on the walls. Where others might have an entertainment screen, she's hung a series of sketches of dancers, midstep.

Her personality is everywhere, an odd notion for a man who's washed his life like a blank slate again and again, stepping through the door of every new abode with nothing but the clothes on his back and a desire for a new beginning. Even now that he has a place he's reasonably sure he'll stay — a place he's lived in for years — he doesn't know how to start making it his own.

Two weeks ago, he would have imagined Phaera D lived in a chic apartment overlooking the drama of the city, something as polished and glamorous as her public persona, like the suite they'd shared at the Aterciopelado the night she was attacked.

But today? He's not at all surprised at how simple and homey Phaera's refuge is. At the carefree way it bares her soul.

He sets his shoes at the end of her neat row in the entryway and follows her in.

Phaera pulls one of a set of mismatched coffee mugs out of a cupboard and pours him a cup, then turns wordlessly to sit on the red leather couch, leaning back against the arm with her feet up on the cushions, knees bent to give him room to sit. Her bare feet are a handsbreadth from his thigh, yet he doesn't know how to touch her again.

She's watching him expectantly.

"You're going to say I should have told you what I was planning," he finally says.

Phaera sips her coffee. "And you're going to say you don't want me thinking of you as the kind of man who could carry out a hit on the chief justice of the Supreme Court." She slides her feet forward until her toes are wedged under his thigh, and heat sparks electric from that point of contact. He lets his hand fall to rest on her calf, sliding under the loose silk of her house trousers.

"But you are," Phaera says.

"Does it bother you?"

She considers it a moment. "I wanted you to. So it makes me a hypocrite that it bothers me."

"Or it makes you human."

She looks away.

Silence stretches on between them, but it's comfortable, so Jaantzen lets it linger. For the first time he notices the music playing in the background; instrumental and sweet, it twines with the sounds of distant traffic through Phaera's open window, and something about the combination wraps around him, soothing. He lets himself relax, muscles he didn't even know he had releasing against the well-worn cushions of the couch. He could stay here forever, and he's suddenly desperate to know what it would be like to live like this. Peaceful. With her.

"That feels really good," she says after a moment.

He doesn't realize at first what she's talking about; he'd barely noticed when his fingers found a knot in her calf muscle and started working it. Jaantzen laughs and sets his coffee down — he certainly doesn't need any more caffeine today — then extracts her foot from beneath his leg and sets it in his lap, working methodically through the small muscles. She closes her eyes, smile tranquil.

After all this.

After the danger he's put her in. The risks he's asked of her. The glimpses he's given her of who he really is. Even after what he just told her, she trusts him.

He will never jeopardize that again.

"You have a tattoo," he says, tracing the soaring bird on her heel.

And she laughs, surprised. "You're the first person in years who's noticed," she says. "It's not a part of me many people see."

His fingers still. "You've shown me quite a few of those," he says. "I'm sorry I haven't been as open."

"I can tell you're trying." Her kind smile fades. "Jaantzen. I don't care how much you think I won't like what you're planning. If I'm your partner, you can't throw me out in the dark."

"I know."

She sighs and sits back up, pulling her feet underneath her. "What happened to the long game? Was that ever your plan, or was it just a line?"

He shifts to face her. "I didn't lie to you, Phaera. But last night I realized you were right. Leone wouldn't have quit, and I couldn't stand there one more time watching her cut you to pieces while I smiled and pretended not to notice."

She sets her coffee down, watching him seriously.

"Every minute I spent pretending to work with her put the people I love in danger, put this city in danger. You made me see that. So I talked to Manu and Toshiyo. I talked to Thala. And I made sure it was clean."

"You're sure it was . . . clean."

"The only people who know the truth are my people, you, and Thala. And I can't imagine anyone else caring to examine the cover story too deeply."

"Then I'm done talking about it," Phaera says. She catches his hand and pulls him to her end of the couch, sliding under him until their limbs are tangled and the length of their bodies pressed together. Her lips brush his jaw, her breath hot on his ear. "And I'm ready for whatever comes next."

The main thread of the Bulari Saga has come to a close, but there's so much more I want to explore in this world.

So many questions.

Will Manu and Oriol finally take that vacation? How will the Durga System react when everyone finally learns about Lucky and his cousins? Will Starla ever find out what happened with her parents and Felipe Zacharia, or visit the place in Durga's Belt where her mother got that necklace?

And what the hell happened between her and Luc Chevalier?

For an answer to that last question — and a hint of adventures to come — get the bonus Bulari Saga epilogue here:

WWW.JESSIEKWAK.COM/BULARI-EPILOGUE

There's more to come in the Durga System universe, including a series of space-pirates-meet-Indiana-Jones adventure novels following the exploits of a certain notorious couple: Raj and Lasadi Dusai.

Head to JESSIEKWAK.COM and sign up for my newsletter to be the first to hear when I release their story (The Nanshe Chronicles), or join me on Patreon for sneak peeks and behind-the-scenes looks at these stories as they come to life.

Until next time,
Jessie

# BONUS BULARI SAGA STORIES!

Get access to a growing library of Bulari Saga novellas, short stories, maps, artwork, and VIP content — when you join the Crew.

*WWW.JESSIEKWAK.COM/CREW*

# ABOUT JESSIE KWAK

Jessie Kwak has always lived in imaginary lands, from Arrakis and Ankh-Morpork to Earthsea, Tatooine, and now Portland, Oregon. As a writer, she sends readers on their own journeys to immersive worlds filled with fascinating characters, gunfights, explosions, and dinner parties.

When she's not raving about her latest favorite sci-fi series to her friends, she can be found sewing, mountain biking, or out exploring new worlds both at home and abroad.

*Connect with me:*
www.jessiekwak.com
jessie@jessiekwak.com

# DID YOU LIKE THE BOOK?

As a reader, I rely on book recommendations to help me pick what to read next.

As a writer, book recommendations are the most powerful way for me to get the word out to new readers.

If you liked this book, please leave a review on the platform of your choice — or tell a friend! It's the easiest way to help authors you enjoy keep producing great work.

Cheers!

Jessie

**The Bulari Saga**

1. Double Edged

2. Crossfire

3. Pressure Point

4. Heat Death

5. Kill Shot

---

**Bulari Saga prequel novellas (Standalone)**

• Starfall

• Negative Return

• Deviant Flux

---

**Ramos Sisters Thrillers**

1. From Earth and Bone

2. With Salt and Ash

---

**Nonfiction**

• From Chaos to Creativity: Building a Productivity System for Artists and Writers

# Humor

- Business as Usual: Corporate Notes from the Zombie Apocalypse

Starla Dusai is fifteen, deaf — and being held as an enemy combatant by the Indiran Alliance. Willem Jaantzen is a notorious crime lord about to end a fearsome vendetta — and most probably his life. When he learns his goddaughter has been captured by the Alliance, will he be able to save her? And her, him?

Manu Juric's quick wit and knack for creating unexpected explosions has taken him a long way in the hitman business.

At least, until he signs on to a job that might just be out of his league: taking out one of Bulari's most notorious underworld figures, Willem Jaantzen.

When Starla receives a tip that her beloved cousin Mona is alive and well on an astroid station out in Durga's Belt, she drops everything to find her.

But saving her might just mean giving up the new family she's come to love. If it doesn't get them both killed first.

---

Find bonus stories and more:

www.jessiekwak.com/durga-system